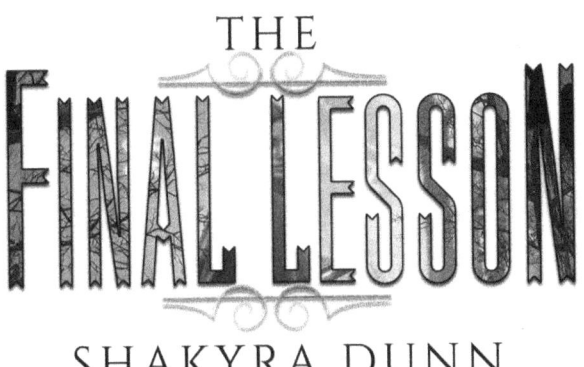

THE FINAL LESSON

SHAKYRA DUNN

A LITTLE LORE

Throughout the story, there are phrases that the main character Leilana uses, known as Minsura (Mihn-soo-ruh), a dead language. Before you dive in, I offer to you a handy-dandy translation guide!

A= An (Pronounced "ahn")

B= Bie (Pronounced "be")

C= Ca (Pronounced "kaa")

D= Di (Pronounced "die")

E= En (Pronounced "ehn")

F= Fe (Pronounced "fee")

G= Go (Pronounced "goh")

H= Hie (Pronounced "hey")

I= Ie (Pronounced "ee/eh," depending on the nature of the word)

J= Ju (Pronounced "jew")

K= Kir (Pronounced "keer")

L= Lien (Pronounced "lane")

M= Mal (Pronounced "mall")

N= Ne (Pronounced "nay")

O= On (Pronounced "on")

P= Pe (Pronounced "peh")

Q= Qin (Pronounced "kin")

R= Re (Pronounced "ray")

S= So (Pronounced "soh")

T= Te (Pronounced "the")

U= Un (Pronounced "uhn")

V= Ver (Pronounced "veer")
W= Wein (Pronounced "wayne")
X= Xun (Pronounced "soon")
Y= Ye (Pronounced "yay")
Z= Zel (Pronounced "zell")

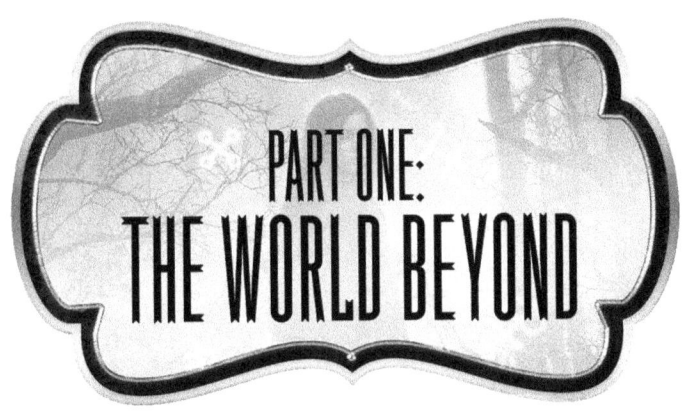

PART ONE:
THE WORLD BEYOND

ONE

The cinders crackled over the singed wood, rising through midnight's earthy air. Gusts of wind drifted through the dry oak trees, the shades of early winter teeming from the branches in the form of cracked leaves. The stars were absent from the sky, yet a faint glimmer hovered above. The still night of a new moon; such times were hard to fall upon.

"You feel it, don't you?" A gravelly voice cut through the silence. "This air is thick. The stigma of the wind besieges lost souls, carrying them beyond the boundaries of time."

"Master Hinju, you always make things more dramatic," a girl with shoulder-length black hair proclaimed, rocking back and forth in her spot.

Any means of a rebuttal were replaced by extended straight-laced humming before finally, "Now is not the time for remarks." Copper eyes opened to the sound of distant laughter caught in the indistinct gales, and a single glance at the source drew bitter silence. A stern expression coated his features as he gazed upon the group of fourteen seated around the open fire; no disturbances occurred, and he once more cleared his throat, running his fingers through the curly brown mop on his head.

"I have summoned you here today for your final examination." For a moment, chatter progressed among the group, some questioning what he meant by a 'final examination,' and after a second glance, silence took over again. "Moving on. The fourteen of you have advanced through your courses with ease, rising through the ranks of your respective classes. You were hand-chosen by your mentors to reach this stage in your lives."

"Master Hinju, what is the meaning of this?" One student piped up, a stalwart expression coating her pale features. "We've had plenty of tests, but an outdoor examination is rare."

"Curious as always, Leilana," Hinju replied, nodding. "That is correct—you have had many of these examinations, using your time to study magic and overcome obstacles placed before you. But how often does the Headmaster orchestrate your work?" Leilana grew silent, tucking a loose strand of her shoulder-length dark hair behind her ear.

"Master Hinju has a point," A boy with short blonde hair piped up from across Leilana, seated on a fallen tree trunk.

"This *is* the first time we've had someone like Master Hinju teach us," the beret-wearing boy with neck-length dark brown hair next to Leilana mumbled, laying a hand on his chin, amber eyes reflecting his uncertainty.

"Your examination on the night of emptiness will be a test of your overall skill level and valor." Hinju rose to a stand, extending his hand up towards the evening sky. "As Maesters and Arcana, under the blessing of an innovative and invisible moon, you will be guided by none other than yourself. I chose this night specifically for you to give your all." The students turned to one another in silence before continuing to listen to their Headmaster's words. "Two at a time, you will duel. The winners of each respective battle will progress towards the title that you each so crave—a chance to grow closer to becoming a Warlord."

Leilana's eyes widened at the statement, and she

clutched the golden-encrusted grimoire in her arms closer to her chest, the metal vines lining the book pricking her fingers. So, that was the prize for winning a duel. Seemed simple enough.

"Would anyone like to volunteer for the first battle?"

From the group of fourteen, the boy with neck-length dark brown hair tipped his beret and rose to a stand, confidence clear in his amber eyes. "I will."

"Ah, so the mighty Lancett Lune is our first up for battle." Hinju nodded in approval. "I expected no less. Do you wish to choose an opponent, or shall I have the stars choose for you?" Lancett briefly turned any signs of contempt on Leilana after looking at all his possible choices at least once, and the girl met his gaze before returning a small smirk. Lancett turned to Hinju once more, crossing his arms.

"I leave my fate in your hands, Master."

"Very well." Hinju closed his eyes and ran his fingers along the silver crystal at the tip of his wooden staff, the jewel illuminating a smoky gloom. The students never averted their eyes from the man, watching as the crystal's haze began to flow over the boy seated on the tree trunk. Once he caught notice of the beam above him, a grin upturned on his face, his blonde hair bouncing as he stood up.

"Yes!" he exclaimed gleefully before brandishing what appeared to be a rapier from the sheath at his side, twirling the hilt between his fingers. "I've always wanted to try my hand at fighting you, Lance! The day has come! I will bring your reckoning!"

Lancett laughed at the comment before he took hold of the sword at his side, pointing it at his opponent. "Take it easy there, Kindall. I will never become a villain. One day,

I'll be a Warlord. But right now, we're both amateurs in the field of magic."

"Begin!" Hinju commenced.

The two boys charged for one another at the call to battle, rapier and sword interlocking, the clashing metal harmoniously in sync. Lancett shoved Kindall back with his hand, causing him to stumble before regaining his stance in time to block an oncoming strike. Kindall thrust his hand out, minuscule shards of ice rushing through his palm, cutting into Lancett's skin before melting. Lancett's body became shrouded in flames faster than Kindall could process, the heat and cinders hazing his vision.

Kindall leaped from the line of fire and swung his rapier, sharper icicles accelerating from the tip of the blade. Lancett cut through the shards with his sword as he boosted himself forward off his right foot, ducking under another shard before slamming his sword onto the ground. Kindall barely had the time to react when a cataclysm of earth sent him off his feet and up into the air. He gripped to a tree branch and pulled himself up, anxiously bouncing on his feet.

"What in the world is he doing?" A male student with long black hair and red streaks pulled into a shaggy ponytail mumbled. Leilana's eyes narrowed as she kept her focus on the noble battle before her. Something about their method was a little profound. It was as though they were slowly beginning to seep into a fractured state of bloodlust.

Kindall held up his rapier with both hands and cast down a streak of lightning. Lancett cringed, the narrow impact sending quivers down his back. Once he had found an opportunity to strike, Kindall swung from the branch and pierced through Lancett's defenses, knocking him to the ground. He quickly regained his footing afterward and extended his sword forward as Kindall was rushing to him again, a swell of dark energy ensnaring the boy and locking him in place, hovering above the ground in a magenta-shaded bubble.

"Hey!" Kindall tried to slice through the bubble, to no avail. When that failed, he attempted to kick and punch it, and when his efforts came to nothing, he groaned and decided to take a seat inside of his solitary confinement, arms crossed in a huff. "Damn! I was so close!"

Lancett sighed of relief, falling to the ground, hand over his pounding heart. "That *was* close. I was afraid I was gonna run out of stamina..."

"Excellent work, Maester Lune. Victory is yours," Hinju stated, laying a hand on Lancett's shoulder. Within seconds, the torn flesh on his face and body began to mend and close as though the marks were never there.

"Thank you, Master," Lancett replied, grinning.

A girl with long lavender-shaded hair jumped to her feet, her hands curled into confident fists. "That was awesome, Lance! You're so strong!"

"That was impressive," Leilana agreed.

Kindall grit his teeth, anxiously rocking his right leg up and down. "There he goes again, winning the hearts of all the girls. Why can't I ever get that lucky? I'm handsome enough, I'm strong, and I'm fun and I'm confident too, just like him. Maybe I should change my hair or something..."

Hinju stepped up towards Kindall's little prison and patted it a few times with his staff, the bubble bursting and causing the boy to hit the ground face-first. Kindall sat up, nearly glaring at the man while tapping his finger against the dirt, his free hand still pressed against the ground.

"Vanity does not win hearts. Nor does it appeal to those that you do seek out for guidance—it shows that you have some weakness in yourself." He rested a hand atop the boy's head, and a warm light washed over Kindall's body, healing the wounds that he sustained during his duel. "But those flaws light a fire in your soul and force you to improve." Hinju extended a hand to the boy and once Kindall had a solid grip, he pulled him to his feet. "You did admirably yourself, Mr. Mandrison. Do not take this as a loss, rather as an experience."

"T-Thank you, Master. I will, definitely."

"That goes for all of you," Master Hinju continued, "Certain obstacles that you must face are not to be taken with a heavy heart. Every step forward is something that you are meant to grow from. Now, who would like to go next?"

One by one, the remaining students began to pair up with others or allowed themselves to be paired with someone based on the guidance of the fates drawn forth by Master Hinju's high prowess. Leilana felt satisfied watching the excitement of her classmates, knowing that the duel between Lancett and Kindall fueled their momentum. She wasn't much different in her emotions—seeing the strength and determination in every student that came before her only made her more anxious about who among them could stand as a Warlord. She flipped through the pages of her grimoire, resting a hand on a page.

Warlords, hand-picked by another Maester or Arcana of the same level, destined to rule as a protector. Few of them existed today, but many that were gifted with the power of magic strived to become one. Anyone with magical prowess had a chance to be granted such a title.

Any of them standing in this forest could be one right now and not even know it yet.

"U-Um, Leilana?" Leilana glanced up, finding the girl

with lavender hair reaching the middle of her back, her bangs covering her forehead, nearly reaching her cerulean eyes. Her cheeks were coated pink, rivaling the shade of her knee-length dress. "There aren't, um... there's only a few of us left. Do you want to pair up?"

"Sure thing, uh..." Leilana glanced up at the sky in thought before holding up a finger in realization. "It's Amelia, right?"

"*Amiria*," she corrected sharply, her face reddening more at the affliction of her voice. Sure, the pronunciation had its similarities, but the syllables differed. And that passion of wanting her name to stick was working its wonders in Leilana's mind. "Amiria Farone."

"Sorry, sorry," Leilana interjected, waving a hand in dismissal. "Didn't mean to upset you."

"O-Oh!" Amiria held up both hands and took a step back from Leilana, trembling a bit. "It's fine, you didn't! I-I'm sorry if I made it seem like I was angry, I'm really not, I promise-"

"Hey now, Amiria, no need to be so scared." Kindall wrapped an arm around the girl's shoulders, smirking. "Lei doesn't bite, not usually." Amiria held her arms behind her back and turned her head to keep from looking him in the eye.

"It's *Leilana*," Leilana said abruptly. "Not Lei, not Leila, it is Leilana. Live it, learn it, love it."

Kindall raised an eyebrow at her words as he set Amiria free and allowed her to run off towards Hinju to prepare for her own duel. "Geez, no need to be so crabby. It was just a little fun with friends."

"We aren't friends, Kindall." He jumped back at the proclamation. "We're students at the same school fighting for the same goal. That doesn't make us friends, does it?"

"Well, I, uh... I guess not...? But don't you think it's better for everyone that we tried to get along and be friends? You're right, we're all fighting for the same goal. Some of us are going to be Warlords someday, and we can all support each other until we get there. Right?" Leilana pondered his words before she cleared her throat.

"...I'm sorry. I've got a match." She stepped past him, and Kindall stared at her back a moment longer before sighing, reclaiming his spot on one of the logs.

"You really are just a kid after all," Kindall mumbled.

Leilana stood opposite Amiria, revealing her grimoire for her opponent to view. Amiria clutched the silver flute in her hands for dear life but kept her attention on the girl and even managed to narrow her eyes to try and stir up some intimidation.

"Come to think of it," Lancett whispered to Kindall, "I've never seen Amiria fight before. She doesn't seem like she'd hurt a fly."

"No, she doesn't," Kindall replied, retaining focus on the two. "But Amiria has skills that a lot of people don't understand."

"Begin!"

Leilana rapidly flipped through the pages of her grimoire and an array of fireballs shot out at the girl. Amiria put the flute up to her lips and closed her eyes, playing out a small melody on the instrument before reflecting the magic back in Leilana's direction. Leilana side-stepped out of the way, her eyes darting between the singed grass and Amiria herself, who was starting up another melody on her flute. She scoffed before flipping through the grimoire, stopping on a page, mumbling a scripture.

From the book, a pair of teeming hands cloaked in shadows emerged, grabbing the flute from Amiria's grasp and snapping it in half before her very eyes. Amiria blinked away the tears starting up as she stared at her destroyed instrument, collecting the fractured pieces. With each passing second, her eyes grew dark and clouded. Leilana outstretched her right palm, sending the hands propelling towards her. Before they could reach her, Amiria inhaled deeply and closed her eyes, belting out a single high note in a pitch of middle C.

The single note, prolonged over several seconds, caused the hands to shatter away. Leilana froze as the note progressed, the ground around her beginning to tremble before giving way under her. She let out a shriek as the chasm opened, reaching out a hand as she fell. Amiria gasped when she realized what was occurring, covering her mouth with both hands.

"Leilana!" Lancett raced forward, sliding on his side as he ran, grabbing her by the arm. Several other students rushed to his aide, helping the girl out of the chasm. Leilana laid a hand on her chest, finding it difficult to regain herself, her frame quivering from shock. Lancett gently placed both hands on her shoulders, forcing her to face him. "Are you all right?"

"Y-Yeah, just... just a little shaken up..."

He bowed his head, hands still on her shoulders, sighing heavily. "Good. I'm glad." Hinju was still in a bit of shock himself, his gaze reflected on Amiria now, who continued to put the pieces together in her mind about what she had done. After coming to his senses, he held up his staff, moving stalagmites of the earth back into place to mend the open crater, sealing it shut.

"I-I... I am so sorry, Leilana!" Amiria choked out, taking one step back after another. "I-I don't... I don't know what happened, I just...! I'm sorry!"

"It's okay," Leilana replied softly. "I'm not dead or anything."

"B-But-"

"Hey, don't beat yourself up over it," she interjected, "Don't worry. I'm fine. I promise." Leilana heaved a sigh. "Okay, maybe not completely true, I'm a little bummed that I lost so terribly, and so fast. After all that work I put into learning the concepts of the Lasette..."

"Remember what Master said," Lancett told her, smirking. "It's all a learning experience. You can definitely do better next time." She averted her gaze from him.

Hinju cleared his throat, catching the attention of the fourteen. "Without any more trauma running into our lessons, I'd like you all to return to your seats. I have another announcement that I would like to make." Lancett stood up and held out a hand to Leilana. Shakily, she managed to grasp it and was pulled to her feet, being led back to the logs.

Amiria found herself clinging to Kindall after the boy had managed to get her to sit near him to calm her antsy nerves, burying her face in his sleeve. She didn't want to acknowledge the faces that weren't even directed towards her. Kindall could only let her have her moment of solitude, patting her head occasionally to quell her further.

"I am proud of you all," Hinju spoke, "You all managed to achieve feats that I never imagined young Maesters and Arcana could, in many ways. Some of you are more proficient and honed to your skills than others, but now there is more you're going to learn."

"I thought this was supposed to be our final examination?" Kindall piped up.

"Recall what I said: this was the final examination on your skill level. But to truly advance to the title and responsibilities of Warlord, there is something else that you are to acquire. And to seek it out..." He extended a finger behind him, past the trees, beyond any of their eyes. "You must take your first steps through Adrylis. The world outside of this school."

"You want us to go to Adrylis, all by ourselves?" One of the students exclaimed, "That's nuts!"

"Not by yourselves, unless you so wish."

"What are we supposed to find out there?" Leilana asked.

"Warlords have trouble connecting humanity and magic as one. It is easy to lose yourself in your lust for power and understanding." Amiria covered her ears to block out the words, stifling a sob. "I wanted to evaluate where you stand in terms of this. And I must say, if what I saw during your duels was of any evidence, many of you are far from prepared to become Warlords."

"You're kidding," Lancett breathed.

"Therefore, I have your true final lesson in mind. The fourteen of you will be taking a pilgrimage throughout Adrylis starting next week. In the world, you will be seeking out totems that can be gathered from those that you encounter on your journey." He held up a chess piece, marked as the pawn. "These totems represent the elements of humbleness, passion, understanding, laughter, friendship, and love. They can take any form, be any material item, but it must be an item of importance to whomever you feel represents these totems you uncover."

"If we're supposed to be gathering elements in that fashion, why do we need the totems?" A female student asked, "Do they siphon magic from the person that owns the totem?"

"Not necessarily. The strength of the totem's owner is

granted of your own will, certainly, but it does not mean that they themselves possess magic like yours. In the end, the purpose of the totem is to grant you an understanding of others, their perspectives, how they live, and how they use magic in their own way. But you must choose your pawns wisely, for they will be the strength that carries you further, and it will be what gives you the opportunity to advance towards becoming a Warlord."

Hinju set the chess piece down in front of the stump he sat on, a smile glinting over his features as he folded his arms. "Travel anywhere that you'd like during your pilgrimage, then return to the school to inform me of your success. Ah, one more detail! Once you have five totems, the last totem that you possess must be *your* strongest element of the six. You cannot wield two of the same qualities in your hands—there is something in each of you that is more powerful than the people that you encounter. You also cannot find two of the same passions in the same person. Only you can decipher which element rules the heart of your chosen totem. If you cannot find where your true strength lies, then you will never truly become a Warlord. Remember this well."

"There are so many rules," Kindall whined. "How are we supposed to remember all of that?"

"Oh, believe me, I planned well in advance for this." Hinju waved a hand before a notebook appeared in his grasp. "I've taken down notes for you all and left them in your rooms, detailing each element for you and providing more information on the rules and regulations that I've just explained. You can interpret them however you'd like."

Kindall beamed. "You are amazing, Master."

"I know." Hinju winked at the group before venturing into the forest ahead of the fourteen. "I will let you all rest and prepare for your journey. Remember yourselves in this pilgrimage, my pupils."

"We're really going to visit Adrylis," Lancett mumbled, tugging on his front bangs with his index finger and thumb. "Never thought I'd be leaving this soon."

"I guess that's fine!" Kindall slapped him on the back, causing Lancett to flinch. "We're earning our freedom, and we get to become Warlords once we're done with it all! When are we ever going to get another chance like this again?" He stepped back, extending his arms, chuckling. "Come on, feel excited! Pep up, all of you!"

"Kindall, I'm convinced now that you're on something, and I want some," Lancett joked.

Kindall slumped before crossing his arms, smirking. "I'm squeaky clean. You believe me, right, Amiria?" Amiria remained silent, clutching his arm. "Never mind, this probably isn't the time to joke."

"Forget it. I'm gonna get some sleep," Lancett stated, waving a hand in dismissal. "See you guys tomorrow." Leilana gazed up at the empty sky, her mind wandering. Tomorrow was going to be a new day. The first day of what could become the first steps towards Warlord status.

"You should join us," Kindall told Leilana, snapping her out of her thoughts. "Lancett and I are going to be traveling together. We always talked about going off to see the world together once we graduate, and I guess we get the chance early."

"I have some things I want to study in the journal." Without another word, Leilana made her way through the depths of trees to return to the vast building.

"Man, I find it hard to believe that girl is fourteen sometimes, the way that she comes off." Amiria averted her gaze from Kindall, unsure of how to approach the new subject.

"In contrast, Mimi, you're a young and sweet fourteen. You can tell that by the way that you dress, and the way that you talk. You still get intimidated by little things, and you're a bit high strung."

"I'm not high strung!" she exclaimed, gripping to her dress. How had things suddenly become about her?

"Whatever you say, kiddo." He wrapped an arm around her shoulders, lightly shoving her ahead. "Whatever you say. Come on, off to the dorms, time for bed." She blushed at the gesture before glancing at the remains of the crater left in the middle of the ground.

Maybe this pilgrimage could be good for them all.

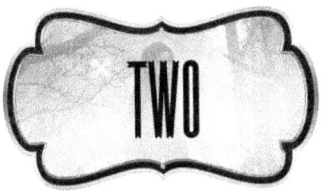

TWO

Queen Rira's heels were speedily clanking against the wooden tiles in Archbane Castle, doors flying open every few seconds, followed by shocked gasps or yelps. She didn't even bother to apologize or ask after those that she was disturbing, but the subjects of her kingdom couldn't find the time to question her frantic behavior before she was on to the next room. She wasn't like this often, but when her mood shifted from one of formality, there was only one cause.

Prince Remiel was causing trouble again.

Her blazing eyes locked on to a new target, a young man with sandy brown hair pulled into a low ponytail currently tracing over a worn cookbook.

"Solus!" Her booming voice cracked through his body like a whip. He raised his head and straightened his back like a board. It was never a good sign when she was angry. She practically glided to him, placing her hands on his shoulders, looking up at the taller boy. Solus couldn't help smiling as he met her incriminating stare, knowing that it wasn't directed at him.

With a velvety accent distinguishable to those that walked in his court, he asked, "How may I assist you, Your Majesty?"

"Have you seen Remiel?" she asked, her eyes pleading. "I've been looking for him all morning, but nobody seems to know where he went. I thought that he would be in the library studying, but his teacher said that he never showed." Her expression saddened. "His father is home, and he wants to see him, tonight is the gala, and I'm..." She sighed softly. "Oh, Solus, please tell me that you've seen him."

Solus laid his hands atop hers before gently removing them from his shoulders, as her grip was beginning to tighten. "I'm sorry, Queen Rira. I haven't seen him since our training session. Allow me to search for him and quell your concerns. If I see him, I'll come find you."

"Thank you," she beamed. "I'll keep searching around myself. Hopefully he hasn't gone too far." She continued down the corridor, and once she was clearly out of his sight, Solus sighed to himself.

"You can stop hiding now, Rem," he called softly.

From behind a nearby pillar, a young man with shaggy dark brown hair peered out, a bright smile on his face. He trekked over to the slightly older man, his hands firmly placed in the pockets of his dress pants. "Thanks for that, Sol."

Solus crossed his arms. "You know that I hate lying to your mother, Remiel. Is it that hard to tell her that you'd like to step out more often?"

Rem scoffed. "We've had this conversation multiple times. Ever since my powers started connecting with my aura, it's knock after knock." He held up both hands in a mocking manner, rolling his eyes. "'Oh no, Prince Remiel is forbidden from seeing the outside world, lest he loses control.'"

"I can understand her concerns," Solus began. "Your powers are dangerous."

"Dangerous or not, seeing my kingdom wouldn't hurt. Adventure is good for the soul. Going outside for a couple of hours a day isn't going to kill anyone." Rem took Solus by the arm, leading him towards a nearby window, extending his finger forward.

The kingdom of Linmus was littered with buildings and bustling crowds. The market was packed to the brim, and from his extended tower, he could see the forests stretch for miles on end. Further right was a cascading waterfall, his hidden passage into Adrylis. One day, he would walk through the water, watch the ripples disappear behind him. He could escape, if only for a little while.

"There's so much to see," Rem told Solus. "There's a world beyond this kingdom. And someday, I want to meet all my subjects. I want to learn from them and see how they live."

"The world is vast," Solus agreed. He wanted to sigh rather than tip the boundaries of their conversation, for the truth was far out of reach from his young master.

Rem laid his hands on the windowsill and watched the mid-spring chill graze the trees from afar. How he wished that he could kiss the leaves himself. "My father got to experience a life like that at my age, and so did my mother. Why shouldn't I have the same treatment? Why should I remain a prisoner in this castle for the rest of my life just because I was born differently?"

"Why don't we take a trip to our favorite spot?" Solus responded, to which Rem smiled softly. It was best to consider the little details in their plans, and they always shared their best thoughts until reaching the waterfall. Preferably with cream puffs, which added a moment's bliss into any details.

"How are we getting there without running into people? Surely we can't just walk out the front door."

Solus playfully smirked. "You know every nook and cranny; you tell me." Rem gestured towards an open door,

Solus trailing behind him. Rem shut the door once they were inside, running to a window and prying the latch open.

"Ever noticed that the castle walls are full of vines?" Solus shrugged, keeping an open mind on the subject. "My father used to tell me stories about how my mother would climb up to him. It was like he was playing the role of the princess, and she was the knight coming to rescue him. This is how they would meet before they were able to marry."

"So, your suggestion is for us to climb down the vines," Solus said flatly. "Isn't that dangerous? What if you slip and break your neck? Or better yet, you have magic to secure you. Will you be catching me if I were to fall?"

"Only if you're not careful, princess." Solus shot Rem a glare, but the young prince was already taking his climb onto the windowsill and blatantly ignored him. Rem turned around, holding out a hand towards Solus, his free hand behind his back. "Come on, what's the harm?" Solus stepped closer, wary of the distance between them.

"Please get down, Remiel," he warned.

"Oh, I think my feet are slipping," Rem egged on, his toes bouncing on the rim of the windowsill.

"I mean it," Solus snarled, holding up a hand in attempts to stall his prince's cruel intentions. This wasn't uncommon for either of them. Remiel was full of tricks, but Solus could dispel them just as easily. "Come down from there."

"You are not my father nor mother," Rem replied, both hands firmly placed on each side of the condensed space filling the window.

"This isn't the time to show off!" Solus tried to reason, noticing that the situation was becoming dire. "You'll hurt yourself-" Rem winked at him before jumping. Solus shrieked in surprise, racing for the window without a second thought, reaching out for Rem despite the increasing distance between them.

Rem hit the ground, but not in the form of a pancake like Solus anticipated. Instead, he charmed a barrier to manifest underneath his body, cushioning his fall. He was laughing the whole way down, loving the rush of wind across his face, kicking his feet like a toddler upon reaching the courtyard's cut grass. Solus's eyes narrowed, his knuckles going white from how tight his fists were clenched. So that was why he'd made such a risky jump.

"Come on down, Solus Brenner!" Rem called, though he was cautious about his volume in case someone else was around. "I'll catch you like you wanted."

Solus was reluctant for mere seconds before obliging, diving into the barrier that Rem placed at his side, patting his hand on the grass. Solus dusted off his clothes as Rem stood up, trailing over to him with his arms behind his back.

"You had nothing to worry about," Rem told him. Solus snarled a second time, pushing Rem hard, knocking him back to the ground. "Hey!" he whined. "That hurt!"

"Oh, you'll live," he hissed. "Though, you almost didn't. And for that, you can deal with a push. Now on your toes. We're leaving." Rem watched Solus make his way towards the castle gates and slip off to the left, pushing past some chipped wall plastering.

"Where does that way lead?" Rem asked, getting up to chase after him.

"Just a little path that takes us through a sewer passage," he replied. Rem's face paled. Sewage. They were going to be walking through sewage. "Oh, calm yourself, we won't be walking through water. I've had to take this way once to help Cyril fix some busted pipes."

"Not one of your better ideas," Rem mumbled.

Solus shoved him inside of the corridor and the two carefully descended through a barely-visible flight of stairs. "Far better than yours. Be quick about it. Just continue straight and we should reach the outside in no time flat. Keep your hand on the wall, it's quite dark."

Rem raised an eyebrow. "If you know this area so well, why have me lead the way?"

"You need to be a leader someday, so I figure this is easy practice. Eyes forward."

"Remind me why you're talking so formally?"

"You respond better to formality when you're taking orders. It's just the way of the world when you're royalty, you know?" Rem couldn't object. Still, it seemed like Solus was better at playing the leading role, whereas he was the rambunctious devil may care follower.

The sewers were damp and dark, and Rem decided to take Solus's advice once he'd reached solid ground again, his fingertips lingering over the cold walls as he trailed ahead, eyes forward. The running pipes were pouring into the drain, the sound reminiscent of an ever-flowing waterfall. These were the pipes that filled his bath, would be used to boil the meals he consumed, and provide aquatic energy to the people of Linmus. Any water that couldn't flow to the city returned to the catacombs and filled the waterfalls he so cherished.

Linmus was full of life. The citizens walked the streets, graced with protection from the kingdom, or invitation into the castle for those that were deemed worthy. Every waking moment was spent in preparation and excitement, every night a celebration for the royal family. A party city, the servants deemed Linmus; Rem saw it as a prison, an open captivity for the prince with untapped potential waiting to be unleashed.

The term Bloodlinch was vague in meaning, but it was something that he had come to hear about himself for many years. There wasn't enough knowledge, more than enough reason to push past the barriers that his lust for freedom opened. Linmus was vast, but Adrylis was everything that he had been missing. All that he needed was to run.

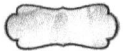

Rem took in a deep breath of fresh air once they freed themselves from the musty underground passage, stretching his arms up towards the cloudless sky. Laughter and merriment weren't out of the norm for the sounds that rose from the city's limits. Rem was marveling in the stone pathway guiding him into the land he cherished so, each step forward bringing him closer to a perfect alignment of brick buildings in a row of set columns, an assortment of fresh-baked goods and cooked meats filling his nose. The restaurants in their sight had people sitting outside at tables, awaiting their orders, and to their right, minstrels played lively tunes on their instruments. The citizens were raving about the gala set for that evening—anyone could tell based on their frantic banter and cheerful expressions alone.

January 19th, 1930. Today was his sixteenth birthday; of course, there would be a party. Not that his desire was to attend yet another event, but appearances had to be made. Another night of having his hair pulled out of his face, a polished coat and tie, more food than he could manage, and increments of liquor throughout the night to keep him composed, but not drunk, on the first night when he could legally touch the stuff. It was his own rite of passage.

He could already picture himself with Solus, sitting under the waterfall, carelessly chattering over a nice bottle of wine about what the future held for them. Solus was a year older, already able to drink, but no amount of sneaking could bring the young prince to take even a sip of his friend's drinks of choice. At least now they had no restrictions.

"Is there anywhere you'd like to go?" Solus asked him. When Rem was able to pull his focus back to his friend, Solus was standing with both arms behind his back, curiously watching over him. The midday sun was reflecting off of him, giving his light brown hair a fair glow and his emerald eyes an impeccable sheen.

Rem was already beaming. "Let's go to Kinstreak for cream puffs!" Solus chuckled, mostly to himself, as if he already knew that response was coming.

They took a leisurely stroll down the busy streets, narrowly avoiding the crowds with Solus expressing his pardons to those that they bumped into for them both. If anything, Rem caught the scent of the pastry shop's treats from several miles away, as if he were a hound on the hunt for prey. Down a beaten alleyway, they stumbled upon a small building with a wooden sign reading 'Kinstreak,' the bell chiming once the young prince had pushed the doors open.

"Phiran!" Rem called, looking about the empty shop. Solus shut the door behind them and took care that no one else was stepping in, lest his master causally flipped his lid about his identity. A bald, slender man with tanned skin emerged from the back room, having just finished some housework, which was evident by the dust on his apron.

"Oh, good morning, Your Highness, Solus," Phiran responded, tossing his apron onto the floor before going to fetch a new one from his closet. "It's been a while since your faces graced my presence. Come for more pastries, have you?"

Rem nodded frantically, lips moistening from the anticipation. "Cream puffs, cream puffs, cream puffs *now*." Solus laid a firm hand on the boy's head, a wordless call for patience. Phiran playfully shook his head. That was the prince's favorite snack, and apparently, it was a driving force for sneaking away from his charmed life.

"Very well then." Phiran gathered a bag of six cream puffs ranging in flavor before handing it off to Rem, who was searching his pockets for Nyte coins. "No need. Consider it a birthday gift." Rem nodded his thanks, taking a bite of one of the delicacies, his chocolate-colored eyes lighting up at the strawberry filling. Solus grinned softly. "Where are the two of you headed today? Seeing the sights?"

"Just having an escapade," Solus explained. "Remiel was looking to venture to the waterfall and have some free time before the gala preparations are complete."

"I'm so not needed," Rem responded, waving his hand in dismissal. "Why stick around?"

"You are certainly the poster of a rebel prince," Phiran stated, passing off a couple of glasses of water to the boys, to which Solus held up the glass in appreciation. "Let's hope that you don't go around causing as much trouble for your family as you did as a child."

Rem rolled his eyes. "I suppose that in time I'll become a model king. For now, a little freedom wouldn't kill anyone, especially not me." He turned to his friend. "Let's go, Sol. I want to enjoy these with a breeze."

"As you wish," Solus replied. Rem and Solus exited the tiny shop after bidding the man farewell. "Everyone in this kingdom treats you so kindly, even without knowing who you truly are."

This statement snagged Rem's attention before he could take another bite of his cream puff, causing him to pout. "I think it's just their nature. A lot of people here are nice, like Phiran."

"I've wondered for some time," Solus began. "How did you two meet?"

"Me and Phiran? He used to be a knight, but he didn't have much of a knack for the sword. My father lets him choose his own fate, and he discovered his love of baking." Rem paused to finish his snack, licking the remains off his fingers. "He quit the knight's round when I was eight after he got married and had a little girl, opened up Kinstreak, and the rest is family history. So, it worked out for the best."

"And now the crown prince is stealing away his business," Solus joked.

"No, I'm the one keeping the shop open!" Rem reasoned. "I'll give him all the support that he needs as long as he keeps making those cream puffs and keeps my identity hush-hush!"

"I'm sure that he will."

Solus and Rem were left to trail the ravine, climbing over hills to reach the waterfalls. Their years of working to the bone, training their bodies to achieve more heights and walk greater distances kept them with higher stamina than they carried in their youth. Upon reaching the waterfall, Rem went sprinting down the other side of the hill, sliding onto the sand and causing his clothes to tear on impact. Solus was about to ask after him, but by then, Rem was already stepping towards the water, tossing his shoes aside and dipping his feet into the icy liquid.

Solus thought about warning him about the possibility of the cold water, but once again, Rem was two steps ahead in realization, bouncing in his spot and occasionally lifting each foot up to regain some warmth. "Cold-cold-"

"You can always get out," Solus called.

"No way, I love it!" Rem held his breath and dove head-first into the deep pits of the water. Solus's mouth fell open, but instead of scolding the boy, he extended his arms in a half-hearted shrug and shook his head. Rem came up for air not too long thereafter, brushing his wet strands out of his face, glancing back at Solus. "You should come swimming with me!"

"I'll pass," Solus replied, chuckling. He knew that Rem related to the idea of freedom, so he'd let him milk it as long as possible. "Just be sure to dry off, you'll catch cold that way."

"With what, my personal wind machine?" Rem joked, shifting his body to drift afloat on his back. The waves crashing against his body, water flowing from the spring, the sounds of nature were hard for him to come by. Opportunities like this came as fleetingly as time. "Hey, Solus, you've been through Adrylis before, haven't you?"

Solus took a seat on the sand, his arms wrapped around his knees. "I've been down to Nilu, and I've also seen Kinsley once, but I never travel too far from Linmus."

"What's it like down there?"

"Spacious," Solus settled with. "There's definitely a lot

more to offer than what Linmus has." Rem grew quiet, and Solus realized the error of his statement; that would only push Rem further to want to leave the land he was born to rule. "But I love Linmus. It's not quaint or close-knit like some of the other villages, but there's never a dull day when you step into the market. Everyone here seems so happy in this city. And I know that you love it too."

"I do," Rem responded simply. "But I don't love chains. And I don't love my powers as much as I could." Solus sighed. There was no changing how Rem felt about being born as a prince. In his eyes, he was living as a prisoner. It was a duty bound by blood.

Rem shut his eyes, taking in the sound of the chirping birds hovering above. More than what Linmus had to offer, huh? "You know something? I heard long ago that there's a school off to the east that trains people our age to become Warlords. I've always wondered what it's like, studying magic."

"Maybe instead of becoming a student, you could become a teacher," Solus suggested. Rem scoffed at the thought. Something else that Solus would be better at.

They kept up their idle conversation for hours on end before the sun disappeared behind the night sky and Solus had to half-drag the soggy prince through town to return him to the castle, get cleaned up, and off to the gala. But it didn't take either of them long to consider that they wouldn't reach the castle without chaos from the wrathful queen, so they decided to take a pit stop at Kinstreak.

"Back again, just before I close shop," Phiran called upon hearing the familiar chime of the doorbells and seeing his two most frequent customers. "Cream puffs not enough for you?"

"Not that," Rem responded, shaking out his still dripping hair. "Do you happen to have some dry clothes I can borrow?"

"No clothes in pipsqueak prince, size, sorry," Phiran stated. "But I can provide you with towels, or jet-dry your hair with my wind magic."

"Pass on the towels," Rem laughed. "I'm in a rush. I was supposed to be back at the palace by now. My parents are expecting me for the gala, and the last thing I need is to run into the angry queen."

Phiran resisted the urge to roll his eyes. Somehow, Queen Rira was always putting up with these antics, but that didn't change their relationship. "Oh, very well, the easy tactic."

Rem outstretched his arms in preparation for the burst of wind to strike his body when a rumble rocked the tiny shop. Solus clung to a nearby table to steady himself while Rem kept his feet planted on the ground, his body rocking to-and-fro. Phiran merely placed his right hand on the counter, his free hand laying over a half-full glass of water to keep it from spilling onto the freshly cleaned area.

"What in the world was that?" By the time that the question had escaped Solus's lips, Rem was already starting out of the door, nearly being bombarded by people screaming and running for cover. He stepped back slightly, grabbing the arm of one of the men racing by.

"What's going on?" he asked.

"Let go! I have to go, my family!" The man cried out

before prying his arm free, sprinting off in the direction of the vast kingdom. "My children are at the castle!"

"The castle?" Rem repeated, mostly to himself as Solus ran to his side. Rem's eyes darted up to the palace in the distance, his stomach dropping at the new sight.

Archbane Castle was up in flames, the cinders hovering beyond the surface of the crumbling world. Rem couldn't hear Solus asking after him, his ears fine-tuned to the imagery of splitting wood and people around him panicking while rushing to safety. His mind was racing faster than his beating heart. Just this morning, normality was the only constant. He could still smell the rosewood on the polished furniture, likely ashen by now. The clean-swept carpeted floors were probably stained with blood and scorned by flame. The glass windows, once brimming with morning light and starry skies were shattered.

"M-My parents, they..." Rem started forward, but before he could get beyond the border, Solus was right at his heels, grabbing him by the arm. Rem's muscles tightened at the secure grip keeping him from moving another step, his fingertips curling into a fist. "Let me go."

"It's not smart, please don't go," Solus said firmly. "You don't know what could be happening inside. You could be killed."

"My *parents* could be killed!" he shot back, whirling around to face his friend, tears brimming in his brown eyes. "There has to be something that I can do!"

Solus put his hands on his shoulders. "Live, Remiel. You must live. You can't afford to think negatively about their fate."

"Both of you, come inside," Phiran called, to which Solus began half-dragging Rem back towards Kinstreak. The young prince couldn't avert his eyes from Archbane

Castle, his thoughts heavy on his parents and the other servants. There were bound to be so many people hurt during the gala.

Phiran was hovering about the kitchen when Solus and Rem stepped back into the shop, packing a bag of provisions. Solus watched him curiously, his hand still firm on Rem's arm. "It isn't safe for either of you on the streets anymore. I'm going to take you down to Nilu. I have a partner I keep in contact with, his name is Laikros Olen. You should be safe there for a while."

"What about your family?" Solus asked. "Shouldn't you be searching for them?"

"My wife and daughter should already be heading in that direction if they're out of danger, but I can't tell how far the chaos could be spreading. I doubt that they've claimed only the castle." There was a bump against a nearby wall followed by glass hitting the floor, which snapped Phiran's attention back in place. Someone was here, and they weren't being friendly.

"What was-?" Rem began, but Solus covered his mouth with his hand, putting a finger to his lips. Phiran gestured towards the back room, pushing Solus slightly ahead. "Phiran-"

"No matter what happens, don't come out of this room," Phiran warned them softly, handing Solus the bag of provisions. "If anything goes wrong, take the back entrance and run. Get as far away from Linmus as you can, and don't look back."

"You know something, what's happening?" Rem whispered.

"Just do what I say."

Phiran closed the door gently to keep from drawing attention, and by the time that he emerged from the kitchen to return to the front entrance, there was a group of five swarming the area. He picked up the overturned glass and used the handkerchief in his back pocket to clean the spilled water.

"I was expecting customers after hearing all the ruckus, but I never imagined that I would step in and find a bunch of mages in my wake."

Maesters and Arcana. He could sense their powers, far greater than his own magic. Their auras practically leaked onto the floor. They held a grasp on this siege, a declaration of war. One of the Maesters stepped up to his counter while the rest stood back, slamming a hand on the wood, leaving behind a visible singe. Phiran didn't even flinch at the gesture, though his eyes narrowed at his polished work going to waste.

"We've gathered intel about you, Phiran Reinsley. Former Knight of the Archbane Castle, now running a pastry shop. You've got a lot of connections to the royal family."

"So, you opened up a book on the knights and came to say hello," Phiran replied, wiping off the glass before setting it face-down on the counter. "How may I help you ruffians this evening? It's topside that I get many guests, but now I have a party to entertain."

"Where is Prince Remiel?" At the sound of his name vibrating through the walls, Rem cracked the door, peering out, Solus hovering just over him with his finger-tips lingering over the wood just in case they needed to slam it shut and break away. They were just out of sight, and no one in the room seemed to pay attention to the door.

Phiran gave a shrug. "I could not say."

"He frequents this place," the Maester growled. "I

would expect that this is the first place that he would run to when he's caught with his tail between his legs."

"Are you certain that he isn't chained down at the castle? After all, it is his sixteenth birthday, and he was to be present at the gala in celebration."

An Arcana with blonde hair styled in two lengthy pony-tails held together with red bows seated in a booth cleared her throat to steal Phiran's attention. "According to his dearest daddy, he never arrived at the shindig." She held up both hands in lieu of a shrug, smiling. "So, our master sent us to search for him."

"Farís, you're not supposed to give away our mission," the Maester at the counter hissed. "That's the first rule of being in the Order of Helix."

"Whoopsy-daisy," Farís giggled, twirling some hair through her finger.

"Order of Helix," Solus mouthed the name to himself.

"So you are just a band of misfits looking for trouble," Phiran droned. "You won't find anything but pastries here, sorry to say. Now get out of my shop."

The Maester stepped closer to his face, pointing his index finger and thumb at the man's head as if pointing a weapon. Phiran's eyes darkened as the Maester's index finger began to emanate a crimson glow, shutting his eyes as the heat that he conjured began to rise to his skin.

"I'll ask you one more time, old man. Where is Prince Remiel?"

Phiran spat in the man's face, wiping the remains off his lips with his handkerchief. The Maester was taken aback momentarily, snarling at the shopkeeper.

"I will never tell. I will ensure His Highness's safety to my dying breath."

The Maester smirked, his teeth bearing an eerie mix of

rage and content at the words. "That's going to happen a lot sooner than you'll ask for, old man."

He pointed his index finger and thumb at the man again. Phiran cast wind magic on the handkerchief rather than defend himself from the attack, sending the last piece of his embodiment towards the open door. The Maester fired off an inferno that quickly consumed Phiran's body. The man was reduced to a thin crisp, his bones barely left intact before they too were reduced to ash. Within seconds, there was nothing left of the man himself.

Rem's eyes nearly shot out of their sockets, and he fell backward. "Phi-!" Solus covered the young prince's mouth as he screamed cries of protests. Rem was close to hysterics, which was bound to draw their enemies to them if they didn't leave *now*.

"There's nothing we can do," Solus told him gently.

Rem's hands found the handkerchief, slightly singed from the fire. He beheld the sight of it, holding the cloth up to Solus. "H-His family, they-"

Solus shook his head, pulling the boy to his feet, closing the door, using his foot to kick off the doorknob on their end. "It won't be long before they realize that we're here. We need to go, Remiel. There's no place left here for us that's safe. He wanted us to leave no matter what. Don't allow his sacrifice to be in vain."

Rem drew in a deep breath, allowing his mind to regain some sense of reason. Solus was right, they couldn't run far if they were left lingering around for too long. They couldn't be left to mourn without running the risk of losing their own lives.

"Where do we go, to Nilu?" Rem asked, pocketing the cloth as he followed Solus through the back room, keeping close. He could hear the doorknob on the other side rattling, followed by frustrated chatter from Phiran's killer.

Solus tugged on the rather rusty doorknob to the back door before he managed to pry it open. "We can find Laikros Olen there. It's a start if anything." Solus peered out into the town. There was no view of the homes, but there was a straight walk to the hills. From there, their waterfall would come into sight, but instead of traversing towards it, they would instead need to break to the left. "We can reach the forest from here as long as we keep out of sight. Hurry."

Rem gazed over the room a final time, swallowing. There were so many memories tucked away in just this shop that he could barely keep them in one place in his heart. But now there was no Kinstreak, no Archbane Castle... no home.

Linmus had fallen at their feet, and he was powerless to stop it.

THREE

They roamed the forest for half a day and passed through the grassy terrains and ashen lands that carried them to Nilu. The scent of burning wood and smoke smothered the air, which practically nauseated Solus due to the pressure building around his lungs. In contrast, Rem kept his gaze on the smoky clouds hovering above the tiny town, daring to release the tears of the sky in lament for the fall of his kingdom. Surely the news had traveled here by now, and maybe even further beyond the border. Solus took him by the arm, inquiring about the home of Laikros Olen in place of his distraught ward. It didn't take long for someone to guide them to one of the larger cottages in the mining town.

When the door flung open and a man with a clean-shaven head and a long dark brown goatee stepped out, it took both boys by surprise. The man frowned at the sight of them, and without a word, allowed them to enter his humble abode.

"The King and Queen have passed," Laikros told them upon sitting the young men down at his dinner table. The two had no knowledge beyond the initial attack, but eventually, they were going to know. Why withhold it and waste any more time?

Rem's breath emerged like a trivial gasp caving under the weight of his lungs. Solus remained silent as he watched the Prince's expression warp from a static calm to visibly shaken, right to the point of collapse. Neither of them had considered the inevitable, but to hear it now, when they had barely eaten, hadn't slept, and sat in silence in the same cramped room waiting for more information, neither of them could process the ordeal either.

"The council members in Linmus have discovered the truth about your ordeal, Highness," Laikros continued. "They know that your mother is an Arcana of exceptional skill and that your father is a mere human. They know that you're a Bloodlinch."

The words didn't seem to reach Rem, for he was lying face-down on the table, forcing back the tears that were rushing to him faster than he could process. He swallowed down his sobs. It didn't matter what he was, or where he was going to end up; all that mattered now was who he had to become without his parents, and that was going to be the biggest mishap of all.

He was King now. A King trapped in an unbreakable rut, all while needing to reclaim his throne, unsure of how to return to Linmus unharmed. Was there even a way back? And what about their corpses? Were they still inside of the castle, or did they become ash and smoke along with the others that were caught in the blaze?

Solus outstretched a hand to lay on his back, knowing that the comfort wouldn't amount to much in easing his mind, but hoped that it could at least show a means of support. Now it was down to the two of them. But maybe that was all that they needed. One person joined at the side of another was better than none in the end.

After a few minutes of silence and noticing that the young prince was growing tired, Solus led Rem to the upstairs bedroom and let him sleep off his agony. Rem didn't take long in passing out, the tear streaks still fresh on his face. Solus gingerly wiped them away as best as he could with his hand, staring down at him before exiting the room, closing the door behind him. Laikros was still seated at the table, waiting for him to return.

"I wanted to know more about what happened. What about Linmus itself?" Solus began. "How are the citizens, the town?"

Laikros folded his hands, sighing. "There were a few survivors from the kingdom, but I've no idea if they were able to make it to safety. No one knows that Remiel has escaped. For now, he is safe, but there is no telling for how long."

Solus lowered his head, swimming in his own thoughts. He was conflicted about the state of the kingdom himself, but he couldn't allow himself to become distraught like Rem. Someone had to keep a level head about where they could go from here. Laikros was right, it wasn't going to be long before someone put the pieces together and realized that Rem was alive. His enemies would return for his head, even with him as a guard. He was no knight, however, and his swordplay could only carry him so far. Eventually, Rem's scornful Bloodlinch powers would become more than a concealed trump card, and there would be no end to the chaos.

"It wouldn't be smart to remain here," Solus concluded. "He wished to visit Magiten Academy and become a student there. Maybe I could lead him there, and the mages can guard him against harm. They wouldn't need to know the truth about his identity."

Laikros scoffed at the idea. "Proper training is what he needs to hone his skills, but Magiten Academy is not where he can receive it." Solus raised an eyebrow. Wasn't it better that he learned about magic in a place specializing in it? "He has been away from the world his entire life. The best training is experience. That is how many of us become stronger."

Solus crossed his arms. "I don't know how much that Rem can handle all at once. He has always wanted to see Adrylis, especially after hearing stories from his mother about her travels, but I'm not certain that he's ready."

"There is balance within this land, and Remiel resonates with it as an heir of the Vesarus name. He will have to become ready to uphold his title. With you at his side, I imagine that challenging his fate will become easier. There is much for you to learn as well, Solus."

Solus managed to smile. "I suppose there are a lot of memories I need to regain. Maybe seeing the sights will help us both and take Rem's mind away from Linmus for a little bit."

Blending wonder and war to escape the reality of their tiny world being twisted in the gales; it was almost childish a thought, to be left forlorn, alone, and still desiring opportunity at a heel's click. They were running away and pushing forward, all at once. In a single night, they were forced to become better adults not only for themselves but for a kingdom that needed to have their prince back once he was prepared to step up to his throne. For now, turning in the other direction probably was for the best.

The sun disappeared behind the clouds hours later, and rain streaked the skies, thunderclaps giving off mighty roars. Solus was exhausted, taking a place in the spare room alongside the still sleeping Rem, but couldn't bring himself to fall asleep just yet. Instead, he took to staring out of the window, watching heaven's lightning bolts pierce the ground.

Seeing the world through a closed window in a small town held more depth over peeping from a castle tower.

They were far closer to the ground, but a long way from familiar land. Any step forward would have to be carefully placed from here on.

"Do you think that they were in pain?" Rem whispered from the comforts of his blanket. Solus clenched his fists, the cool texture of the windowsill now a distant sensation.

"You can't think about things like that," Solus urged, all without bothering to steal a glance at him. "Never think of what happened, only think of the love that your parents had for you. Never allow the bad memories to outweigh the good. It will keep you from crumbling."

"Is that how you felt when Cyril died?" Solus visibly cringed but managed to keep his cool. That was always a touchy subject, the death of his adoptive father just one year prior to this thin thread of catastrophe. "I'm sorry," Rem said softly. "I just haven't felt this alone in a long time. I know you're here, but... things are different, you know?"

"You feel burdened," Solus concluded, his voice over-lapping with the cry of thunder above their head. "Such is the role of a troubled prince."

Rem sat up in bed, the thin blanket wrapped around his body. He was shivering a bit, clearly not used to so little comfort. "I want to go back to Linmus. I need to know who did this."

"We can't afford that risk. For now, we need to stay out of the shadows to avoid you getting into any more danger." Rem thought of Phiran's handkerchief in his back pocket. So many people had already died on his behalf, and more would follow. Solus found the momentum to face his friend, his eyes full of remorse as he stated, "You and I aren't strong enough to handle the force that is waiting for us in Linmus. How can we go back to lose our lives?"

"Then what are we supposed to do?"

Solus was unsure of how to handle the consequences. Trained as they were, they were still children that had never seen Adrylis for all its worth.

"I don't know," Solus admitted. Somehow, Rem knew that there was no proper answer, but he wasn't going to hold it against Solus.

"There's no point in trying to run away. I'm going to take back my kingdom," Rem stated firmly. "I will become king, even if it takes years to step up to the plate. We can find a way to return to Archbane Castle and keep ourselves alive long enough to take down the person who broke down our walls and killed so many innocent people."

Solus folded his hands. "We need to come to an agreement, Remiel. Returning to Linmus is a death sentence. Olen suggested that we travel around Adrylis and gain some experiences of our own." Rem's eyes lit up like roman candles, and Solus grinned at the sight. Remiel's depression escaped his thoughts with the realization that he could execute his birthright. He could take Adrylis by storm just as his parents did.

"We can really see Adrylis?"

"We can," Solus replied. "But we have to keep on our toes if we are to explore. And we should help as many people as we can out there. Who knows how far the enemy may have spread."

"We'll find a way. I'll make sure of it."

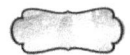

Leilana must have read through the notes that Hinju provided half a dozen times now, and she still couldn't comprehend melding human emotions with magic. There was so much about the concept that seemed off-putting. The radio on her desk was blaring, the discussion heavy on news of the kingdom of Linmus. The details were nearly lost before she decided to acknowledge the static-filled device.

"It has been five days since the kingdom of Linmus was struck. No one is certain of the circumstances, and there appear to be no survivors from the castle grounds, with few having fled the city limits. Among the fallen are King Somano Vesarus and Queen Rira Lurin-Vesarus. The only remaining heir to the throne, Prince Remiel, has been declared missing-"

Leilana reached for the dial of her pocket radio and turned it down to a lower setting, continuing to look over her notes. She was stumped on the field of laughter. There were so many interpretations that Hinju could have specified for his notions, and instead, he stuck to the most literal statement.

Laughter is the expression of true happiness. Encountering someone that may possess the totem of laughter is most evident in how they carry themselves—they walk in the present, ignoring the past and looking to the future with open arms.

Come on, seriously? How many people still had reasons to laugh and be merry with war at their doorstep? How could they live a life where the future wasn't even guaranteed?

Closing the spiral-bound notebook, she turned the radio up to listen to the news about Linmus again to find infomercials about 'the land of sunny springs, Kinsley' playing. They were holding a formal to shed some light in the world of chaos. It wasn't the first time she had heard of Kinsley, but from acquired knowledge, it wasn't her ideal vacation spot. Too much sun was bad for the skin.

She laid her head on her desk, giving a passing glance to the open window, where the school's pride stood gallantly in the form of a mahogany tree. The skyline reflected a melodious blend of ginger, rose and amber, the premature light hovering over Adrylis promising a bright start to this pilgrimage she was granted. She turned to look over her room. It was minuscule but fit for one due to its custom options. Her floor was scattered in paperwork here and there, the wall space taken up with quotes she had written down from her professors:

'Inspiration is everywhere.'

'Magic stems from the comprehension of others.'

'Happiness is not one note.'

Every moment spent in determination, every step in any direction held meaning. That was something she had come to learn through her time cooped up in this room, bound to her elements, spending each day diligently reviewing magical spells and the mystic word of Lasette. This would be her last time in this room as a student. When she set foot in this tiny space she called home again, she would be either a Warlord or a failure. She didn't want to consider being trapped as a lowly Arcana for all eternity. Such a fate seemed too cruel with so much possibility at her doorstep.

She wondered if anyone else was awake already and feeling as uneasy as she was. They had all lived outside of this school at a point before awakening to their magic, but not one of them seemed to look back on life outside of the walls that bound them to new purposes. There wasn't a place for her to question what lied beyond before now, but curiosity was overwhelming.

What would be the first place she visited? And where would her pilgrimage come to an end? What people lived in Adrylis, and what totems did they carry within their souls? How was she going to be able to pick just one representative for each of the five she had to gather?

"Hey! Leilana!" Fervent pounding on her door fully threw her away from the lingering thoughts. "You up yet? We've gotta get out there and see the world!"

"You're being loud, Kindall, she might still be asleep." She recognized the smooth, calming affliction of Lancett's tone, contrasting Kindall's low, penetrating pitch merging with his spontaneous behavior. "See? I don't hear anything."

"Uh, oops. I guess I screwed up?"

"I'm not asleep," she settled with, cutting through the silence. She swung her hand out carelessly, the door unlocking and opening with a soft creak. Kindall was the first to peer inside, beaming. Her forehead puckered at the gesture. "What are you doing here?"

"We came to see if you were gonna take us up on the offer of joining us on our lengthy pilgrimage."

Leilana still didn't feel surprised that they had decided to travel to Adrylis as a pair. They were always together, from the very day that she encountered Lancett in class. They spoke of random topics, laughed together, and argued with one another. Yet, they never physically fought before yesterday, and though both were versed in their own magical abilities, Lancett held less regard in holding back for the sake of his friend's safety.

Master Hinju had said that Warlords needed to retain a sense of humanity to keep the magic they were blessed with from consuming them. But what did humanity have to do with magic?

"We would love to have you along for the ride," Lancett continued, "It would be nice to have someone among us that's more, well, dignified."

"You want me along to keep you on track," she concluded, her hands resting on her hips now. "You really aren't capable of that on your own?"

"Well, it's not that we can't," Lancett started, watching Kindall scrutinize every detail in the girl's room while stepping further inside. He snarled to himself, grabbing him by his shirt collar to hold him back while Kindall outstretched his arms, whining as he fought to progress forward. "It's not really asking a favor. Opportunities like this don't come along often, and it's best spent with friends."

'Friends.' That word didn't seem as slack coming from Lancett opposed to Kindall.

"We can nurture ourselves as Arcana and Maesters," he continued, "And who knows? Maybe all of us can become Warlords together."

She batted her lashes, genuinely pleased by his response. "I guess it can't hurt to tag along."

"How do you do that, Lance?!" Kindall questioned, which took Lancett and Leilana by surprise.

Lancett held up his hands in defense. "D-Do what?"

Kindall furrowed his eyebrows, his mouth set in a hard line. "You've always been so great with girls! They never say no to you, and it's not fair! Teach me!" Leilana was appalled at the sudden change of pace in the conversation, her attention darting between the two boys before settling on Lancett. She reached for the tote at the foot of her bed.

Lancett upturned his lips into a small grin, holding back a laugh. "There's nothing to teach you." He held up his index finger, stating, "In this case, you either have it or you don't. What more can I say?"

"What is this 'it' you always speak of?!" Leilana's mouth curved into a wide smile and she found herself laughing. The action nearly shocked Lancett and Kindall, but they themselves began to grin as well. Kindall placed his hands on his hips, shifting his weight onto his left leg. "What's so funny?"

"You two are so strange."

"And that's funny?" Lancett asked, "This is how we normally are. If you think this is entertaining, tagging along with the two of us is going to be a riot."

"You know, if we're gonna get a move on, I wanna do it before the crowds roll in," Kindall stated, "The future is bright, there's a cool winter breeze, and it's a brand-new day!" He grabbed both of his companions by the arm, leading them out into the hall. "Lady and gentleman, today we begin anew and take our first steps forward to becoming dignified Warlords!" He extended a finger to the ceiling, voicing to no one in particular, "Today, we are blessed by mages of the Arcana, Maesters of salvation!"

"Not yet, Kindall," Lancett pointed out. "We're in the prime of our youth, barely adults."

"Details, excuses!"

Leilana shook her head. These two certainly were energetic despite it being so early. Their bouts of optimism were making a mark already—a few of the students down the hall from her room were up and throwing things at them, shouting slurs of swear words and wishes of failure, but the two boys didn't seem to have a care in the world. Words of discouragement weren't uncommon for jealous onlookers, and a lack of well-wishing was a thing of the past. She clutched her grimoire in her arms, eyes to the floor. Sure, it was nice to be among optimism, but that didn't make it any less embarrassing.

"L-Leilana!" A familiar high-pitched voice rung out. She glanced back in time to notice Amiria racing up. In her hands, she carried a navy-blue tote, likely holding a change of attire, clothed in a knee-length dress of the same color. Her violet hair was tied back into a bun with a white bow, not a single strand out of place. "G-Good morning!"

"Mimi!" Kindall beamed, holding up a hand in lieu of a wave. "You made it!"

Leilana gave Kindall a passing glance. Did he know that she would be arriving? Funny, she hadn't been here when they first arrived to convince her—maybe she slept in?

"Good morning, Amiria," she began, raising an eyebrow. "What's-?"

"I wish to travel with you!" Amiria exclaimed, her face retaining a rosy shade, afflicted due to her pitch. Leilana blinked, surprised by the sudden proclamation. "I'm sorry, that was so out of the blue, it's probably hard for me to get a response! I tend to get kind of antsy about situations like this!"

"Like that's not obvious," Lancett mumbled.

Amiria scratched her right cheek with her index finger while her mind worked in overdrive to gather her thoughts. "W-What I mean is... I felt inspired watching you in class, getting to see how persistent you are, and getting the opportunity to duel you yesterday was so surreal! It would be an honor to stand at your side and help you to become a Warlord! I hope that I am worthy of the same!"

Someone believed in her. She stood out in the eyes of a single person, someone that was more skilled and unique with magic than she herself was. That was rare, she had to admit.

"You do realize that Leilana is going with us, right?" Lancett asked Amiria, causing the younger girl to jump. "The two of you would have ended up on the same team regardless."

Her lips parted before she covered her burning face with her tote, whimpering. "Then I made that speech and prepared all night for this moment for nothing?!"

"Hey now," Leilana began, stifling a laugh as she pulled the tote from over the girl's face to look her in the eyes. "I wasn't going to turn you down. The way you handled this was different though. Last night's duel was impressive, and I was curious about what other skills you possess. I'd love to help you work towards becoming a Warlord too. I think you've got talent."

"The sister of Ennis Erovina thinks *I* have talent!" Amiria squeaked. Kindall didn't hesitate to grab Amiria by the arm and begin to lead her outside. "How unbelievable, and here I believed that I was destined to break everything with this voice, it's so-!"

"What was that about?" Leilana whispered to Lancett.

"No idea. I'd say take it as a compliment."

"Eh, point taken."

The first steps out of the school grounds exuberated Kindall, for he practically dashed for the forestry and climbed as high as his feet and body would allow. He inhaled deeply, shutting his eyes. "Just listen to those birds sing! Don't they sound so happy?"

"You're going to break the branches," Leilana called,

and as if on cue, the branch under Kindall's feet snapped, sending him falling to the ground. Just before he impacted, however, he held up a hand, his face levitating centimeters above the dirt. He sighed in relief before contorting his body into a more upright position, his feet touching land. "I warned you."

"Are you all right?" Amiria asked, looking the boy over from afar, her fingertips clutched around her tote's thin strap. "You're not hurt or anything?"

"Not a scratch!" He held up a finger, wagging it briefly. "Levitation spells, definitely one of my fortes. Different from my buddy Lance over there, but I have it down packed!" Amiria shook her head at his comments, giggling. Somehow that wasn't surprising—boiling confidence spilling out onto the pavement, even in the face of danger.

Leilana averted her gaze towards the oak treetops, watching the birds soar beyond the brimming sunrise. The further that they traveled, the scarcer such sights became. It was as though the walls that held them in place were crumbling like a sledgehammer to cobblestone. They weren't fruits of labor, but they did act as monumental pillars of solitude and isolation. The one-hundred students of Magiten Academy were always sheltered from the world, hidden away to conceal the powers that they possessed. And now they were breaking free of their own will, prepared to become something far greater than mere mages.

"You look distracted." Leilana nearly jumped at Lancett's sudden statement but retained a sense of calm. "Thinking about the future?"

"Not so much the future as the past. It's something to adjust to, not being able to look back and see that the school is right there. Also, that was a random conclusion to make."

Lancett shrugged a single shoulder, grinning. "We may

not be joined at the knee, Leilana, but you can be an open book when it comes to your thoughts reading on your face. You don't have to speak for some people to feel like they understand you."

"You got all that from a single look," she specified in a deadpan tone.

"Open book," he repeated, chuckling. "Keeping things to yourself like that all the time is bad for your complexion, and one day you're going to have someone in your life that represents your totem of love. It means that you'll have to play a different hand in expression."

"Ah, the totem of love," Amiria swooned. "Master Hinju interpreted that we're all destined to fall in love with someone. It sounds so romantic." A few feet behind her, Kindall was pretending to gag, and Leilana rolled her eyes. "I hope I find someone to love." She glanced back at Kindall in time for him to retain a straight face, peering up at the trees as a wide grin spread onto the girl's face. "Right?"

"I guess. I'm not into that mushy stuff. If I find someone, I find someone, and if not, well, that's life in a nutshell. Can't go into these things with an open heart, sadly." Amiria got downhearted by the proclamation but continued to smile as if she hadn't heard him.

"That's the least optimistic thing I've heard him say yet," Lancett breathed.

"Me as well," Leilana agreed. "Anyways, Amiria, you seemed to interpret the notions of love as 'falling in love with someone.' What else did you consider from Master Hinju's notes?"

"Hm, well, the only one that I didn't understand was, ironically, understanding," she stated, tapping her chin with her index finger. "I think that there's such a broad meaning that it's hard to put my finger on any one interpretation."

"I thought the same!" Kindall exclaimed, facing the group, his back was turned to the array of fields lining their path forward. "It's like Master Hinju was trying to test our intelligence in tandem with our magical prowess. Kind of burns down the soul a little."

"O ye, of little faith," Lancett indicated, earning a glare from Kindall. "It's good for us to build some strength in our mind as well as our bodies. We need both to properly succeed as a Warlord."

When the sudden scent of what she deciphered as rotting wood plunged into her nose, Amiria inspected the road onward with confusion, the conversation of her companions growing distant. The forestry was barren. The fields were abounding in jaundiced grass blades, dying weeds covering the ground. The sight was a far cry from the lush scenery filling the school grounds. There were no signs of life in the forest anymore—no birds, deer, not even bugs. It was horrendous. It was as if they had stepped into a whole new world. The sight frightened her.

The world was spinning, spiraling out of control faster than she could process. Even standing up straight seemed to sway her from any potential regulation of self-control. A firm hand on her shoulder steadied her, her vision clearing from the haze of disdain.

"Don't look so worried," Leilana told the girl. "This is just the start of the journey. I'm sure that the rest of Adrylis doesn't look like this. Maybe the area is just poverty-stricken?"

"According to the map we were given by Master Hinju, the closest town is called Paluna," Lancett stated, now gazing over a miniature-sized map inside of his journal before holding it up to the three. "Anyone here heard of it?"

"I have before," Kindall piped up. "There are a few

places in Adrylis that are really big on worshipping the Warlords. I think Paluna might be one of them."

"A Warlord worship town," Leilana repeated, her mind wandering. Such an atmosphere may have been rare to come by. "Do you think that they'll respect us for wanting to become Warlords? I mean, we are on an official pilgrimage."

"They just might! We'll get all kinds of praise for what we're doing!" Kindall beamed. "I say that when we get there, we chill out for the night!"

"Sounds good to me. We've been walking for..." Lancett allowed his gaze to waver over the sun, now high in the center of the horizon. "I'd say about three hours now. We should at least stop for a break. I made lunch, that way we could actually take the time to sit somewhere."

"I'm fine with a break," Amiria admitted, kicking off her shoes to carry in her hands. She wiggled her toes, enjoying the warmth of the dirt between them. "Flats weren't the best choice for this trek."

"Where are we even supposed to sit?" Kindall inquired, "There's nothing but dead grass everywhere. It's not going to be comfortable." As he spoke, Leilana was flipping through the pages of her grimoire, his voice hardly reaching her. Kindall took comfort in the sound of flapping paper before continuing, "There isn't even any shade from the sun now that it's near the afternoon. And it'd be too much work to turn back and look for some trees to sit under."

Leilana held up her index finger, closing her eyes and moving the joint about the thin air. "Pe... an... re..." Amiria blinked a few times at the soft syllables being spoken.

"What is she doing?" Lancett whispered to Kindall, an eyebrow raised in contempt.

"I'm not sure."

"Well, what's she saying?"

"How would I know?"

"An... so... oh... lien..." Leilana held up the grimoire, and from the fair-sized book, a parasol emerged, soaring upward before sticking into the ground upright, the umbrella flying open. "There. That's better."

The sudden action took the three by surprise, and Kindall dashed over to the item, looking between the parasol and Leilana. "What was *that*?!"

She closed the grimoire shut with her right hand. "Magic. What else would it be?"

"You mean, you *made* that?" Lancett asked, still in awe. "You made us a parasol?"

"Sun is bad for your skin, correct?" She took a seat under the parasol, running her fingers along the amber shards. "The grass here may be dying, but it's soft enough to rest on. Why don't you join me? There's plenty of space."

"I wanna know how you did that! Is that grimoire really that nuts?!" Kindall exclaimed.

"It was an heirloom," Leilana settled with, setting the book next to her before leaning back on the grass, arms folded behind her head. Lancett decided to take a seat next to her. "I can make another if you prefer it, Kindall, Amiria."

"N-No, it's fine," Amiria replied quickly, "I like the sun! It helps the plants to grow! I want to help the land to flourish again! I'll give them water too! I'm going to see if I can go on ahead to find some!"

"Do you want me to go with you?" Kindall asked, already up on his feet to follow her. "I don't want you getting into trouble."

"It's fine!" she called back, taking off down the beaten path. Kindall watched her for a few passing moments until her frame was out of sight before reluctantly chasing after her.

"Where are you going?" Lancett called.

"Don't worry about it," he replied, "I'll be back soon! You two hold down the fort while I'm gone! And no flirting!"

"Flirting?" Leilana repeated, "What in the world...?"

"Those two have some serious chemistry," Lancett joked. "Maybe they'll be the ones to get the love totem first at this rate."

"What?" Leilana raised an eyebrow. "I don't see it. Those two? I'm not sure what to think about love. They care about each other, but..." Lancett chuckled his response.

The scenery filling Amiria's line of sight gradually grew with a myriad of tawny grasses and dying trees, but now a few buildings were in sight; it seemed to be promising in her eyes. Maybe they were closer to the town of Paluna than they initially believed. If this was how Paluna's surrounding region was being treated by the people left to maintain it, she could only imagine what energy could have been drained out of other lands in Adrylis.

She stooped down before some wilted flowers, cutting through them with a dagger, finding them to be more of a lost cause. After she had peered enough through them, she tenderly fiddled with the scrunched-up leaves, humming to herself. She allowed herself to caress the weeds for a few more seconds, a mint-colored aura seeping from her fingertips. Gradually, the minuscule leaves began to regain a healthy shade of green, thriving and blooming into the land that she hoped for. She wasn't skilled yet in trying to heal and restore. Maybe it was a petty delusion, but for her, a beautiful lie with little effort was the better option to help others grow.

A change of scenery could help at least one person, right?

Kindall watched as she continued to work on healing several other flowers and plants in the vicinity from behind the rotting trees, smiling almost sympathetically at the effort she was putting in. Bit by bit, he watched as the scenery around him began to transition from disparity into a valiant form of prosperity, shaping the trail to Paluna with ease. The area was blossoming with every passing second. She held up her hands to caress the flowing squall, causing the trees to rattle. The gusts blew gently, and down came some leaves, which stuck to Kindall's hair. He didn't seem to mind it in the least.

It was impeccable that Amiria found dedication in such minor actions and remained humble about the situation at hand—he could only hope that others thought the same of her when they reached Paluna. How could they not love her? A little high-strung and snippy at times, sure, but her pure heart was unmistakable. Her soothing melody appeared to pass over the stiffening winds before suddenly stopping. Kindall found himself muddled by the distorted words and jumbled mess swirling in his mind, curious about the language and clan that she hailed from. And yet, he felt so entranced by her.

"Are you going to just keep watching me, Kindall?" she addressed him in an almost stern manner. Kindall visibly cringed. So, she knew that he was watching her. "It's not hard to tell when you're up to something. Your footsteps thud like a hammer to stone."

"Hey, don't read my mind!" he exclaimed, peering out at her. She wasn't even looking in his direction, continuing to restore the flowers to life. "You didn't read my mind, did you?"

"Nope. That's not my field at all. Why did you follow me?"

"I was worried about what you were thinking, but now I see that you're playing nurse." Amiria tucked a strand back into her loosening bun and wiped away some sweat, giggling. "You did this place justice." He nodded, allowing his gaze to waver over the fields, brightened anew.

"I didn't think that we should be the only ones with something worth looking at. We were living isolated, surrounded by flowers and trees, and yet, the moment we step out, we see all this desolation and sorrow. People are unable to care for their land. And magic runs dry..."

"I'm sure that there are many people outside of the school that will be glad to see it," he interjected, "And I'm sure that people will be grateful to you for it." She rose to a stand, smiling at him. Behind her smile, Kindall detected a hint of anguish.

"I would rather people not know that I exist." Without another word, she turned back, anxious to return to her two other companions.

Kindall's smile faded. His mind wandered on every possible meaning behind her words; there wasn't much that Amiria let on about herself, but then again, no one ever seemed to thoroughly connect with one another in the school.

Maybe some things in life were just meant to be a mystery.

FOUR

Upon arrival in the dusty town near dusk, the four students stumbled upon pillars lining the entrance to the town, doused in dripping water with the emblem of a sword cloaked in a hazing fire embedded into the might of the pillars. Further down the line stood stone monuments standing as tall as the average man.

"Look at those!" Kindall exclaimed, pointing to the monuments as he continued walking ahead, rubbing his palms together. "They're practically washing their hands with the blood of the Warlords and bathing in their magic! I can feel their aura just swirling!"

Lancett visibly cringed. "That sounded a little darker than I think you were hoping for."

Amiria hovered over one of the monuments, admiring the craft. The woman carved in stone was wielding an axe, her long hair flowing through an uncharted wind. Her eyes were blazing with passion, but deep within, Amiria could sense pain, evident by the thin streak of tears embedded in stone. Gazing up at her, she could still hear the shrieks of terror passing through the woman's throat, see the blood on her lips and feel the writhe of her tearing flesh. Warlords could never truly be healed from their suffering. It was something beyond her comprehension, even if she now possessed the power to mend it.

"Peculiar," Amiria mumbled. "How much free time did these citizens have on their hands to craft these?" Lancett followed her line of vision. "You can still see the tears rolling down her face."

"It's haunting," Lancett agreed. "We're the ones that carry their will, and I don't feel nearly as connected to them." Amiria examined the metal plating at the center—information on the former Warlord. This woman had been called Anise Kinsley. She was likely the first Warlord bound to the realm that was to become Kinsley.

Leilana allowed her gaze to waver over the shrine furthest from the entrance before opening her grimoire, flipping through the pages and stopping on one entitled the 'Age of Ruin.' The people of Paluna seemed to carry each Warlord down a stroke of heritage and expansion. At the start of the line stood the original seven Warlords, chosen merely by fate, carrying out their assigned duty to guard the lands of Adrylis with an open mind and a fractured heart. Those that died to restore the world from a time of desolation and crisis.

And as time went on, they only moved further down that thin red string, the only end goal in sight to keep from falling into oblivion.

She spun the words of the Lasette into the air of her condescending mind. She knew of the 'Age of Ruin,' but to a limited degree. The remains of the tale were something to be interpreted over time by those that wished to learn it through experience.

"Ennis Erovina is here too," Kindall called, which snapped her out of her focused state too easily. "Leilana, you've gotta see this! Look, look!" She made her way over to the statue that Kindall stood before, pointing vigorously. Leilana clutched the Lasette to her chest, gaping at the shrine's monument. High and mighty stood a man, much smaller than those that came before him in size, carrying a trident over his broad shoulders.

"He has your face," Kindall stated. Leilana almost took offense, thinking that he was specifying that Leilana possessed masculine features, or that Ennis had possessed a femininity to his facial structure that mirrored hers. But after contemplating his words, she realized that he could have meant that they had a displacement about themselves that rivaled one another.

"You mean her passion?" Lancett asked.

"No, I mean that he looks kinda girly."

...Statement revoked. He was a simpleton after all. Leilana couldn't help but sigh. Lancett slapped his palm against his face and sighed heavily, pinching the bridge of his nose. Amiria was dumbfounded that something so insignificant could slip past the cracks in his mind. Maybe they gave Kindall far more credit than he seemed to be worth.

"What? What's with your faces? Did you step in something?" Kindall asked. "Do I have something on my face?" Lancett nervously chuckled in response before ushering the two girls off in the direction of the village. Kindall outstretched a hand towards the three, a bit astonished. "H-Hey! Lance! Don't steal the girls again!"

"I'm not stealing anyone!" Lancett called back, continuing to laugh. "Hurry up or you're going to be left behind!" Kindall groaned loudly before running after the group.

Within seconds, straw huts and a wholesome display of decorations resembling hanging lanterns besieged their vision. Lancett's eyes bore into the flames, and he closed his eyes, listening to the slender wood crackling. The afternoon sky was becoming cloaked by a modest auburn shade. Off in the distance, Amiria caught a glimpse of vast silver shrines, unhindered by even the blackest night, and the entire area gave off an emanate glow despite the setting sun. The wind lightly blew through the straw huts, and in the center of the town stood the residence of the leader. It was far larger than the other huts, and dozens of people were standing just outside of it.

Paluna wasn't absent of people, at least, for women of all shapes and form, many men, and children guided by their parents were forming a crowd. Leilana's gaze locked on a small girl with pointed ears concealed under a thin hood, the child's expression fearful and lonesome. The child's eyes were a shade of cerulean, the irises reflecting a smoky haze as she looked up towards the sunset. Alongside her were two adults with the same features, the woman grabbing the child's hand to lead her away once she had met Leilana's stare. That concerned her—was she subconsciously incriminating?

"Nymphs...?" There certainly were some unique people walking through Adrylis.

"This is already eventful," Lancett stated, looking over the town for himself. "I always believed that nymphs were bound to the forests or groves or mountains, based on legends. But they're walking around Paluna like there's nothing to it."

"Well, there's still a lot that we don't really know about anything outside of school," Amiria stated, "The laws must vary depending on where the residents, um... reside."

"Do you think it's better that we try asking around?" Lancett inquired. "Surely, they must know that students will be dropping in from time to time for their examinations."

Before Amiria could muster up a response, she was

suddenly seized by a larger man, binding her arms behind her back. She was quick to let out a shrill high-pitched note, causing the man's ears to burst and for him to release his grip on her, blood seeping down the side of his face. He was yelling and cursing, the white noise ringing as he tread back, clutching his wound. She covered her mouth with both hands, stepping back towards Lancett, shielding her by wrapping his arms around her, asking her to confirm that she was all right. Amiria didn't reply, gripping to his sleeves with both hands as a form of comfort. Leilana was flipping through the pages of her grimoire, the book now hovering several feet above her at the ready.

"Hey, what's your problem?!" Lancett bellowed.

"We come here in peace!" Kindall hissed, taking hold of his rapier, extending it out in front of the three in a protective manner. The rage of his burning mind replicated into his sharp, polished blade becoming streaked in a thin sheet of ice. "Don't wanna be in pieces just for trying to rest for the night!"

"Arcana and Maesters," one of the men mumbled, "Rare are they to find out here..."

"But they aren't Warlords," another spoke, "So, they aren't of much use. They aren't magically inclined enough to be able to guide us."

"Hey, we may not be Warlords, but that doesn't make us useless!" Lancett countered, "We are on a pilgrimage to *become* Warlords! And from what we have seen, this town supports our cause too!"

"W-We don't want to be of any harm to your country," Amiria piped up, her hands folded in front of her to quell any lingering anxiety that she possessed. "If you want us to leave here, then we're more than happy!"

"They attacked you, and you reacted to it," Leilana

reminded Amiria, "I doubt that they'll let you go in peace now that we've been put on a pedestal of devastation."

"Well, do we run?" Amiria asked in a hushed tone, noticing the villagers of Paluna drawing nearer to them, trying to condense them in one area and surround them. The fury mounted between them all seemed to be progressing over time, even more so now that they were talking amongst themselves. It was making her nervous and a bit queasy.

"That will put us in greater danger," Lancett stated, taking up his sword as he took a step back, one arm still wrapped around Amiria. "We could always fight our way out of this and hope for the best."

"But that's inhumane," Leilana interjected, the haze around her grimoire began to illuminate in a broader manner before dropping back into her hands once more. "As easy as it could be for us, we can't go around picking fights with random people."

"They may hold the key to ending this war in Linmus! They say that they need more magic to restore the kingdom!"

"Magic...?" Kindall breathed, taking in the words of those around him rather than the overshadowed statements of his comrades. "Wait, *war?*"

Lancett gripped the hilt of his blade with more force. "We've no other choice-"

"Halt." The thunderous voice expurgated through the wrath of the citizens of Paluna, and from the crowd stepped a man with shoulder-length graying hair and a beard littered with strands of the same color. In his hands, he carried a staff. Leilana eyed the prayer beads wrapped around the crystal jewel, hanging to the ground.

"M-Master Kosmin," one of the villagers whispered.

Many began to bow in the man's presence, dropping all the negative emotions that had once swelled and prepared to burst.

"That was unexpected," Kindall settled with, relinquishing his weapon to rest in the sheath on his back. Leilana was still flipping through her grimoire, unable to let her guard down for even a moment in case that these people decided to turn against the grain of dignity that they had for this man.

"These children are not Warlords, indeed, but they are to be treated with respect. They are guests in this town." Some of the people in the crowd began to converse with one another, all with some sense of confliction. Lancett watched them scour and writhe in their confusion over their leader's words, an almost amused expression on his face.

"But Master! They are Arcana and Maesters, not worthy of standing among their ancestors just yet! There is so much that they have yet to comprehend!"

"That is no manner of yours. All Warlords start in similar positions before growing to become more proficient in the skills that they have been granted."

At that moment, the young girl that Leilana had kept her attention on earlier stepped forward from the crowd, making her way towards Kosmin. Wordlessly, she glanced up at him before removing her hood, revealing her pointed ears and shoulder length wavy curls, every strand out of place, yet styled with peculiar intent.

The girl looked to the crowd. "Master is correct. Harming children that only seek to achieve their goals is shameful. I wonder just how far you all are prepared to handle yourselves. Would the fates be pleased with the idealism that you have shown today?"

"Yino, please don't strike fear into the people," Kosmin

stated, tapping the girl on the head with his gentle fist, causing the child to reach up her hands and shield her now exposed skull. She grinned playfully at Kosmin before pushing his hands away as he tried to strike again. Amiria grew pleased at the sudden change of pace, smiling tenderly at the two. "You, girl."

"Y-Yes?!" Amiria jumped at the sudden address, his eyes glaring into hers. There was no sense of malice or anger behind his gesture, however, which eased her progressively.

"Your power levels are astounding," Kosmin stated, "I've never heard of someone that uses their voice to control their magical energy."

"She did kind of blow out someone's eardrums with that scream of hers," Kindall admitted, "So she's got skill if nothing else."

Only then did Amiria realize her actions, her eyes widening. "I *did* do that! I-I'm sorry!" She lowered herself into a bow, her hair slipping out of its bun, curling over her left shoulder. "I didn't mean to react in that manner." She considered the crowd behind her and allowed her attention to shift to them. "I'm also sorry about accidentally hurting that man, h-he startled me!"

"You don't need to apologize, Amiria," Lancett told her, "You were defending yourself. You thought he was going to hurt you, and you had a right to that."

Contrary to his words, Amiria still bowed to the crowd of people. "I know that it was an act of defense, but please, I ask forgiveness."

Leilana peered into the crowd as well, watching their once tranquil expressions in the presence of Kosmin and Yino revert to a state of misunderstanding. Their noses could have turned up in approval and still she would not have gained any momentum. But Amiria seemed to thrive on the kindness of others—even if it wasn't being shown in front of her.

"This is no place for talking," Kosmin called, "Come, join us at our shrine."

Amiria's eyes traced over the crowd once more at his words, and behind their calm demeanors, she could sense overwhelming anguish and frustration. Her gaze locked on the man she had harmed. He was talking with his family, all the while holding his little girl in his arms, kissing her cheeks and nose affectionately and assuring her that he was fine. The woman at his side was clinging to his arm, fighting tears, and the teenage boy next to her had been rubbing her back to ease her mind.

Warlords have the trouble of connecting humanity and magic as one. It is easy to lose yourself in your lust for power and understanding.

Becoming a Warlord meant ample responsibility. It also meant that in a search for a greater strength, that people could become hurt or corrupted by madness. Everyone on the path to greatness had a chance to be consumed by that immensity or could even become lost to time.

Leilana rested a hand on the girl's shoulder, causing her to look up, straightening her back. "Come on, Amiria. It's better that we don't stick around. Trying to apologize is going to be lost on them."

Amiria interlocked her fingers with Leilana's, her eyes averted to the ground, a light shade of pink blanketing her features. Leilana found herself staring at the right side of the girl's face, clearing her throat. She supposed that she didn't mind the gesture—Amiria was always going to Kindall for comfort. Maybe she was just switching things up.

They followed Yino and Kosmin, hand in hand the

entire time, Kindall and Lancett a few feet ahead of them whispering and joking. What about, Leilana didn't bother to decipher.

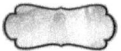

The four trailed closely behind the leaders of Paluna along the beaten path leading up to the shrine. Lancett found himself gawking at Yino in particular—the girl appeared to be much younger than any of them, and yet she was standing at Kosmin's side as an equal. Maybe she was his daughter or some other relative based on her traits. She was a nymph, or at least in relation to one, which included features that Kosmin seemed to lack due to his more human adept. Still, she seemed capable enough to care for this town; her aura spoke it so.

Along the way, Amiria freed her hand from Leilana's, stopping to restore some dying flowers to life, using the water from her canteen to quench their thirst. Leilana looked on with wonder, curious as to how she could give up supplies that she was limited to, all to save a few plants. Then again, Amiria carried a sense of generosity that went unmatched by anyone she had known despite their short time together. There was little chance that she herself could ever hold such an impact over trivial and seemingly unnecessary actions.

"Where are we going?" Kindall piped up, "I mean, the shrines are up here, but what exactly are we doing? What do you want with us?"

"I am a landmark in your pilgrimage," Kosmin stated, pressing his staff into the ground with every step that he took, using it as a leverage for his movement. "You are the first group to arrive today. I figure that after coming all of this way, it will be good for you to learn more about what is to come."

Yino looked back to the group, grinning. "Master Kosmin specializes in reading tarot cards, something that he uses alongside communicating with the fates."

"Oh!" Amiria beamed. "I've always wanted to have a tarot card reading! There are so many endless possibilities behind them."

"What are tarot cards?" Lancett asked.

"Cards that spin the future," Kindall replied, waving his right index finger in a circular motion. "But I'm sure that you'll see it in more detail soon."

Kosmin wiped some dust from the metallic doors, and Yino wrinkled her nose as if to brush it away before sneezing. Kosmin smirked down at the girl and patted her head. She pouted, turning away from him. The four followed in line with the Warlord and apprentice to discover a single room shaped in a circular motion, a six-pointed emblem in the center of the floor and several unlit lanterns hovering aimlessly without magical aid. Off to the right of the entrance were a vast accumulation of documents and books set up on a shelf. But what seemed to overpower the sight of the room was not the sensation of mystical energy, rather the soil that ravaged the entire area.

"I take it that no one has used this place for some time?" Lancett concluded, wiping a myriad of dust from the wall with his index finger.

"No, not necessarily. Paluna rarely has unknowledgeable visitors dropping by." Kosmin spun his staff once, an essence of flames hovering over the dim candles inside of the lanterns. One by one, illumination besieged the room.

"You might want to cover your noses and eyes for this next part," Yino warned, plugging her nose and shutting her eyes. "It's gonna get messy." Amiria and Leilana didn't hesitate to obey, but Kindall and Lancett stole a passing glance at each other before doing the same.

Kosmin nodded at the progress before a spiraling whirlwind emerged from his staff, gathering all the dust at once from the walls and windows, propelling it to the floor. Once he had achieved this, he retrieved a broom hidden behind a curtain, sweeping the contents outside.

"That's useful," Lancett mumbled, brushing some dust from his blazer.

"But annoying," Leilana pointed out, dusting off her skirt as well.

"You think that's bad, imagine what his house is like," Yino piped up while gathering the remains of the unclaimed mess. "Trying to talk him into cleaning before all of the dust builds up the way that it did here is a pain. And it never works out."

Kosmin gave a hearty laugh. "Oh, come now, you know that it is more fun this way!"

"Senile old man," Yino scoffed.

Once the cleaning had come to an end, Kosmin had the four teenagers take a seat around the condensed space, gathering his pack of tarot cards.

"There is much that you will need to know about yourselves before you are going to be able to establish yourself as Warlords in the future. I am here to give you an idea of what you can expect from yourself as you begin your journey. But I warn you, you may not like your results. However, in light of what you receive, know that there is a way to overcome the obstacles hindering that potential line. You can always change what the future has in store for you, bit by bit. The smallest action towards brightening yourself begins with that single step." After shuffling the cards, he set the deck down in front of him. "Now, who would like to go first?"

Lancett held up a hand. "I will. What do I do?"

"Lift the cards in your hand and shuffle them," Kosmin began, "Yino, watch closely. This will one day become your duty." Yino gave a small nod and took a seat on the floor. Lancett took hold of the deck and closed his eyes, listening to the sound of the thin paper rustling against one another before setting the deck down in front of him. "Cut the cards and think of a single question about yourself or about your quest that you have in mind. We will be working with only the Major Arcana cards, which contains twenty-two full descriptions."

"Arcana, huh...?" Kindall mumbled, glancing over at the girls. Amiria was deep in thought over the tarot cards and the meaning behind each of them. There was an array of possibilities, and any cards that the fates placed over her head could change her set path at a moment's time.

Leilana's eyes never left Lancett, curious about what the future could hold in store for him. He possessed an aura of mystery through his sheer kindness, and he seemed to understand his own personal mission greater than any of them, likely due to his superior age and desire to seek out a greater purpose as a future Warlord. Once Lancett was finished cutting the cards in half, Kosmin began setting them into a three-spread group from left to right.

"What I am setting up will be simplistic: this spread shall determine your past, present, and future, in no particular order. You may choose which card you would like to see first."

Lancett decided on the card furthest left, holding it up to Kosmin. "Um, the Chariot?"

"And you received it in an upright position. This is a good sign. The Chariot in an upright position represents willpower and determination, crucial to your present spiritual journey." Kindall gave a small nod. Those traits sounded spot on for how Lancett's personality. "Choose again." Lancett drew the middle card next, holding it up. "Ah, the upright Wheel of Fortune. You will face a formidable turning point and have good fortune in your future."

"Man, he's getting some good cards," Kindall whispered to Amiria, who nodded in agreement.

"I guess all that remains is the past," Leilana stated as Lancett took hold of the final card in his grasp, scanning over the image it presented.

"Hermit?"

"Reversed Hermit," Kosmin stated. "Tell me, Lancett, in the past, were you lonely and isolated from others for any particular reason?"

Lancett shook his head. "Not really. I've always had Kindall by my side, so I was never truly isolated from people. But there's so much that I don't know about myself just yet."

"Then perhaps your journey into self-reflection will begin with knowledge of your skills. You all walk different paths, retain different perspectives, and you will come to terms with the realization of self as you progress." He looked at the remaining three. "Which of you would like to go next?"

Amiria glanced up at Kindall for approval, and the boy gestured wholeheartedly for her to venture ahead of him. "I'd like to."

"Same as Lancett, shuffle the cards and then cut them in half. I will deal your hand for you." Amiria lifted the cards, but the moment that she attempted to shuffle them, they flew out of her hands, hitting the floor all at once and startling her.

"I-I'm so sorry!"

"It's quite all right," Kosmin replied, chuckling as he gathered the cards in her place. "I should have considered that not everyone is able to shuffle cards professionally. You can shuffle them in any manner that you like, so long as you know that faith is in your hands alone." Amiria settled with flipping the cards one after the other before setting them down again, keeping her hands free from the pile after cutting the deck in half. "Pick your poison, my dear."

Amiria took possession of the card in the middle. "Ah, it's the Empress. Upright." She glanced up at the ceiling, pondering on the meaning behind it. "Hm... I think that it was beauty and nature that coincide with the card, right?"

"You have done your research, Amiria."

"I used to experiment when I was figuring out my powers," Amiria admitted, smiling sheepishly. "Turns out I'm not very good at reading into them though."

"So, what does it mean?" Kindall asked.

"The upright Empress tarot card represents creating beauty with your life's essence and balancing the qualms between both genders." Amiria stared at the card in his grasp as he held it up for the three behind her to view. "This is your present self. Next card." Amiria reached for the card on her right and then held it up.

"Reversed Strength," she told them, forcing back the lump forming in her throat.

"This represents weakness and self-doubt, something that you have carried in your past." Kindall didn't seem too surprised, but he could see that Lancett found some hesitation in the resolution. Leilana decided it best to keep an open mind about the entire ordeal.

"I suppose that's true..."

Kosmin leaned in closer towards the girl, tilting her chin to meet her hesitant gaze. "That disposition is something that still hinders you, but there is no need for concerns. This opportunity is meant to help you to improve and retain your humanity."

Amiria managed a small smile. "I'll try my best to uphold this. Maybe this last card can give me an insight into my future." She took the last card and held it up. Her smile faded away almost immediately, and she handed it off to Kosmin without a word.

"What is it?" Kindall asked, leaning forward to try and see what was troubling her.

"The Tower, Upright," Kosmin stated after looking at the card for himself. "It represents disaster and sudden change. It can be a physical destruction to those that are given this card. There is no telling how soon or far off that this prediction could be, and it can easily be transformed. No form of agony is ever set in stone." Amiria scrambled back to her previous spot.

"So, you can give negative propositions like that," Yino piped up, finally allowing herself full immersion in the moment. "And you expect that the person can just go with it."

"I did forewarn that they may not like the predictions provided to them. Acceptance is a virtue that every person must one day follow. It is just how some things must be. That is why they were assigned seek the truth. And then one day, they can ascend beyond even my power."

Yino nodded. "I'd like to believe that as well."

"Kindall, do you want to go next?" Leilana inquired.

Kindall pondered her inquiry before shrugging it off, smiling. "Nope. I don't want a reading. I'm going to try to figure things out on my own."

"Are you sure that isn't dangerous?" Lancett questioned. "It never hurts to have some idea of what you're getting yourself into."

"Well, no, it doesn't *hurt*, but I think it's best that I don't bind myself to what my future could hold. Life is more fun when you're surprised by it rather than having it spelled out for you at every turn. It doesn't work that way." Amiria grinned at the proclamation. Things could always change. That gave her hope.

"I guess I'm up then." Leilana crawled over towards Kosmin and planted herself in front of him. Once he had handed off the deck of cards, she began to shuffle them, setting the deck on the ground, cutting the cards.

"Where would you like to begin, Leilana?"

Leilana decided to start from the right after observing that Lancett had gone to the left and Amiria had taken from the middle first. On the card were groups of naked men, women, and children rising from graves, praising an angel up above. The sight almost disturbed her.

"Um..." She eyeballed the words on the card before reading aloud, "Judgment?" She held it up towards Kosmin, who nodded.

"And it is reversed. This shows a sense of self-doubt and a lack of self-examination—you find it hard to concern yourself with change when the world around you has little to offer in a productive development." Leilana considered his words, looking down at the card once more, tucking a loose strand of dark hair behind her ear. "It is a mental state of compromise due to your past experiences." Leilana grew disheartened. "Your expression tells me that there is something that you are forgetting. You don't know much about yourself."

"No, I do not. I entered the academy with my older brother Ennis five years ago, and we relied on each other in hopes that I could regain some old memories."

"You cling to your past," Kosmin concluded before gesturing to Leilana to seek another card. She decided to move towards the left card this time and flipped it over. "The Fool, upright." Leilana almost glared up at the man, finding the term offensive, but caught herself in the action and remained calm. "The Fool is a card that represents endless potential, and it is the start of a new beginning. But there is no determining outright if this card can guarantee your present or your future because it can occur at the end of your journey."

"Then, she doesn't have a clear future?" Lancett asked.

"The Fool Arcana is rare to uncover, and something that shouldn't be tested lightly," Yino piped up, "Not many are able to draw it and follow through. It shows that there may be more to you than even you might be able to understand yet. Be its guide—do not allow yourself to play the Fool, rather allow the Fool in you to sway you from temptation."

Leilana's fingers wavered as she reached for the final card, quivering. It was scary to consider that she already walked down a path with no future or a set present. How in the world was she supposed to find out if her future was in a secure state when she didn't even know if the present was?

"Leilana," Lancett suddenly stated. "You don't have to contemplate on it, you know. You could figure it out on your own like Kindall is." Leilana glanced up at Kosmin for confirmation, and the man gave a small grin.

"If there is no set path that you wish to seek, you are more than welcome to walk blind. Kindall was correct—it is far more entertaining to have a clear mind and reflect on what your future could become without the guise of the Arcana cards following you. If you'd like, you can turn your back on your final card."

Was it right? Would it be better to go in blind?

Leilana drew back her hand, staring at her empty palm before averting her attention to the already flipped cards at her side. The Judgment, and the Fool. Self-doubting with untapped potential. Some of it didn't add up to how she was as a person... but for all that she knew, this could have been someone that she was in an unclaimed past, or even someone that she would become somewhere down the beaten path.

The road would be turbulent. But there was no better teacher than experience.

"You are all welcome to remain here for the evening and recuperate before setting off again tomorrow. We will provide you with a meal and a place to rest your heads," Yino stated.

"I think we'll be fine up here, actually," Leilana replied, "We're all kind of comfortable being surrounded by the sanctified atmosphere, and Amiria seems drawn to those books you have." She gestured over to the girl, who had begun to scour through the pages of some of the documents left untouched, still lingering in dust. Once she had opened a file, the substance flew up into her face, and she broke into a flurry of sneezes.

Kosmin chuckled. "Well, you're welcome to them. Unless you happen to be allergic to an indecent amount of dust, in which case, don't do that. That could be disastrous to your health."

Amiria sniffled, and Lancett fumbled through his bag before holding up a handkerchief to her. Amiria nodded her thanks before wiping her nose, which gradually reddened the more that she pressurized it. Kindall couldn't help but laugh, complimenting on how adorable she looked with a little more color to her face. Amiria's face only reddened more before she shoved him onto the floor, crossing her arms in a huff.

"Thank you for your support," Leilana told Kosmin and Yino, arching her back to lower into a bow. "I think that the others appreciate it as well. We will use your advice and your predictions for our futures to the best of our ability."

"I wish you all luck on your journey. Yino will return with your dinner." Kosmin rested a hand on his chest and gave a nod. "May the fates secure your pilgrimage."

FIVE

The moon was high above the shrine, the singular noise in the room stemming from Leilana's radio, tuned in to an earlier update on Linmus. From what she had gathered throughout the day, the kingdom was attacked by an opposing force nearly a week ago, the king and queen slaughtered, and the remaining heir declared missing. Linmus was besieged by war, and slowly the bloodshed was seeping into Adrylis. It was only a matter of time before it reached them. Leilana couldn't fathom most of the details, but secretly, she was hoping for the best in relation to the prince, that he was safe from harm.

No one deserved to lose everything in the blink of an eye.

She rested her palms under her chin as she tuned in to the announcements, turning the dial to lower the volume when she noticed that Kindall and Lancett had fallen asleep, nestled under the blankets they were provided by Yino. She couldn't help but grin at the sight. They had progressed far in such a short time, and they were well on their way to starting their personal journey to see the world together. It was a shame that they likely wouldn't get to see Linmus now that the kingdom was being blocked off from any potential travelers.

She eyed the map in her journal before discovering Linmus, one of the largest countries on the map. It was furthest north from Paluna, a month-long trek from their location, and that was without rest or the need to travel over the ocean by boat. To the west of Linmus were regions like Kinsley and Elucia that bordered the coastlines, where she felt that Kindall would probably want to visit most.

Brushing away the possibility of having to see the ocean, she turned to Amiria, finding the girl still devouring the books and documents that Kosmin had left behind. Amiria was flipping through pages slower and slower, indulged in the newfound wisdom. Dark circles were forming under the younger girl's eyes—she probably hadn't willed herself to blink, not wanting to miss anything that could be potentially useful for her research.

"Did you know that Warlords eventually lose themselves ...?" she whispered to Leilana, barely catching the girl's attention. Leilana blinked away whatever sleep was forming, providing her full and undivided attention. The last thing that she wanted was to keep the girl in the dark and make it seem like she wasn't listening.

"What do you mean?"

Amiria's hands were trembling as she gripped to the flimsy paper, and Leilana grew concerned. The girl was always high-strung and antsy, but now there was a touch of agony in her gestures as well. "Every Warlord that rises will become consumed by their power no matter how much energy and strength they put into maintaining their peace. Humanity is always changing, and they are not always able to keep up with the status quo due to their isolation from reality."

Leilana raised an eyebrow. "That's not true, Amiria. We're not like the Warlords of the past."

"How did Ennis Erovina die?" Amiria asked without missing a beat. Leilana's lips parted, unsure of how to address her question. "Do you know? Do you know how your brother lost his life? Do you know what stressed his body to extremes? Or were you blind to it?"

"Amiria," Leilana continued. "I think you need to calm down."

"I'm calm, I just asked a question."

The forceful statement stunned her. "I'm not sure what happened to Ennis. I was left behind at the academy with nothing but the grimoire he gave me, and he never returned. He became a Warlord not long thereafter, and we never got the chance to speak again. I don't know how he died, and that's just something I have to accept!"

Without warning, Leilana slammed her clenched fist onto the floor. The action startled Lancett from his sleep, and for a few seconds, he was shouting obscurities surrounding a failed midterm, holding his spinning head once he'd regained himself.

"What's going on?" Lancett called only to receive no response.

"Did you ever wonder why you didn't hear from him after he became a Warlord?" Amiria slid her documents over to Leilana upon reaching a certain page. "These were written by other scholars, and by Warlords themselves. They were gathered by Kosmin and arranged into these books and folders. I didn't go through them all, but I did find words of meaning."

Leilana lifted the folder from the floor and skimmed through the pages. Lancett was quick to rise to a sit, wiping the sleep from his eyes before approaching Leilana, glancing over her shoulder to read over the words as well. Leilana waved her hand over the page, allowing the words to hover above them.

"What language is this?" Lancett asked.

"It's Minsuran," Leilana told him, "This is the language

that Ennis Erovina spoke and signed with. It is not common-fold for many to understand. It's a dead speech—one that I happen to be able to transcribe."

"I figured that if anyone could, it would be you," Amiria implied.

Leilana's eyes averted to the floor. Sure, it was no real secret in Magiten Academy that she was the last living Minsuran, and its sole heir, but there wasn't much recollection to be had for her fallen country. Minsura fell to chaos long ago. Only she was left to carry it on her shoulders. The burden was heavy, but hers to bear. Still, no one in Adrylis knew the fact, and she preferred that it stayed that way until she came across the Prince of Adrylis. Together, they could make peace. Or so she hoped.

Amiria crossed her arms, planting herself on the floor once more, gripping to the sleeve of her dress. Her hands were burning, and she couldn't make the pain dissolve. Leilana was unnerved by the girl's sudden personality swap but allowed her fingers to graze over the unspoken words, reading them aloud for the sake of her allies.

There is much about this world that I do not understand. Humanity has become so fickle, so intangible.

I was given a duty, sent away from my home life to try and uncover the truth behind human emotions, guided by the voices of the Warlord Luminos. He utters often that there is more to uncover than merely an observance. We are always meant to work from the shadows, yet interact with those that follow our words and depend on our powers to survive.

"Then, he could hear the voices of the Warlords from the past?" Lancett decided on after listening to the interpreted words. "Maybe that was his power. Every Arcana and Maester possesses a special skill unique only to them."

Time is escaping me. Walking this path aches my feet

and burns my blood. How long has passed since the day that I was initiated as a Warlord? How long has it been since I last saw my young sister, heard her laugh, basked in her smile...?

Leilana gripped to the papers for dear life, nearly ripping them to shreds, her eyes narrowed in contempt. "Did you really? I'm not certain how true it is anymore."

Lancett reached up his hand to comfort her, wanting to lay it on her shoulder, but he couldn't find the right momentum and didn't want to wind up upsetting her. He lowered his hand and watched as the words scribed by the deceased Warlord began to take shape once more.

I think of this life often.

It is difficult to maintain some stability when every day feels endless, even pointless. There is nothing left to experience.

Most at my age would be building relations, settling down, starting families, but I can find no relations to form— there is no hope of me coming to terms with a humble life knowing that supremacy will follow me over several lifetimes.

The expectancy of a Warlord is condemning. I am left to seek knowledge and understand only a simplistic ideal of how the people of Lunare behave. While more enter this world, and others exit the plains through demise or travel, there is little room for change.

I am trapped in a realm of stillness and stagnancy.

"The life of a Warlord couldn't possibly be that stagnant," Leilana scoffed, slamming the documents closed with her right hand. Some dust flew up into the air, and Lancett had to cover his nose to keep the substance from reaching him. "Ennis was never good at keeping peace with himself. So easily bored by everything. He would have never made a proper Warlord. Why are you showing me this, Amiria? What's your purpose? And why are you behaving in this manner?"

"Do you understand what being a Warlord means?" she pressed on, her hands continuing to fidget about the paperwork before she finally threw them down, tears filling her eyes. The gesture woke Kindall halfway, and he struggled to regain his vision. "This isn't a journey about seeking the truth behind the growth in Adrylis, o-or even about gathering totems to fuel our magic further! It's about cutting off our own emotions while in search of the real goal in mind— becoming trapped in madness and lust for something greater."

Leilana slowly shook her head, hardly able to process the words that were coming out of the girl's mouth. "You're thinking that becoming a Warlord means becoming inhumane?"

"But that's everything that Master Hinju was against!" Kindall exclaimed, now up on his feet. "He wouldn't send us off on this pilgrimage to build relationships with other people in this world if the end goal was to cast aside who you are! That's not what being a Warlord is about! You know that, Amiria!"

"I thought I knew that!" she countered, taking a step back from the three. "But how they spoke, the things that they all wrote, how can you just ignore the way that the Warlords must have felt?!" She pointed to the door. "I saw the statue of Anise Kinsley! I saw the tears etched into her face. There was a reason why she was crying, why she was so miserable! I want to know more about why that was, and why she suffered so greatly! Moreover, there is a war at Linmus's doorstep! There are people out there that are worse off than we are, people that we can help! If in the end, all that goes towards this path we seek is a life of desolation and pain, then what's the point in trying to go along with it?"

"We can't just abandon this pilgrimage, Amiria!" Lancett exclaimed. "This is all that we know, and it's our only chance to truly be able to make a change!"

"This isn't the only way though!" she cried out, "We don't have to be Warlords to watch over Adrylis! I... I know that now!" She frantically shook her head, her palms beginning to ignite a tint of amber. Lancett slightly grasped Leilana's arm as she prepped a countermeasure to guard any potential strikes. "I don't want to die in vain like they did! And I don't want any of you to either!"

"Amiria," Kindall began, stepping towards the girl. "You need to calm down. We're not against anything you're saying. We just want you to understand that what you've read in those documents may not be what could happen to us. The Warlords, they weren't all capable of clinging to their humanity." He gestured to Leilana. "Ennis Erovina was someone that possessed more talent than compromise. I just want you to understand that we're different from them."

He reached out his hand towards her, managing a smile. Amiria took a step back, her shoulders unsteady as she looked down at his open palm. "Please. Believe in me." She shut her eyes tightly and then slammed her foot against the floor, the paperwork and books lighting up in flames. The fire spread rapidly, consuming the fabric cloths and expunging the walls, setting off infernos. Lancett knocked Leilana to the ground as a chunk of the ceiling broke apart, narrowly keeping the girl from avoiding it, his foot becoming crushed under the weight.

Leilana quickly sat up upon hearing his cry of pain.

"Are you all right?!" He glanced up at her and then down at his foot, trying to find his way around the haze of the flames, but his eyes were beginning to water. He attempted to push the plastering away to find that the material was thick and heavy, barely out of his reach to move aside.

Leilana acted quickly and flipped through the pages of the grimoire, mumbling a few letters of the Minsuran alphabets while attempting to sign the words in the air before breaking into a fit of coughs, hardly able to keep her concentration with the growing flames interfering. Every inhale needed to shield the dead language was stripped away in an instant, consumed by the fire building in the heart of the girl that held such admiration for her.

Lancett reached out a hand to lay on her back before covering her mouth and nose with his sleeve "Kindall!" he choked out, "Amiria!"

Amiria whimpered as she stared shockingly at her hands, trying to shy away from the chaos, but finding that her feet were unable to move, plastered to the spot where she stood. She couldn't find the exit no matter how much she looked, and when she held up a hand to try and brush the smoke away, she found that it was ineffective. Her lips parted, but as she attempted to belt out a note and open a path or even dispel the flames, her words became choked and lodged in her throat.

Kindall was coughing harshly, trying to maneuver through the rising smoke before he noticed Amiria's violet hair peeking through the miasma. He brandished his rapier and tried to cast forth an ice spell in attempts to negate the magic and disperse the flames, but when none conjured forth, he concluded that his energy was minimal in comparison to Amiria's rage-induced attack. She carried more potential than he had, even if hers was stemmed accidentally. He could hear her hacking away, reaching out a hand and grabbing her wrist, gripping it tightly. She inhaled a sharp gasp before meeting his gaze.

"I-It's okay to be scared. *I'm* scared. I'm scared of a lot of things. I'm scared to know my future; I'm scared of remembering my past." He wrapped his arms around her, pulling her close to his chest, his lungs beginning to cave under the pressure of the smoke, his eyes blinded by the blazing heat. She blinked a few times before allowing her head to rest against the warmth of his chest. "But I know you, Amiria, and I know that if anyone possesses the power to overcome themselves, it's got to be you."

While he spoke, his attention split, working to try and uncover the entrance. There were no windows and only one door that would lead outside. Through the blaze of heat, he noticed the faint glimmer of the moonlight being held away by the door to Paluna. He grabbed her arm and then pushed her towards the door, causing her to stumble.

"K-Kindall!" she coughed, reaching out a hand towards him.

He waved a hand of dismissal before clicking his tongue once. "You be careful, now!"

He dove into the miasma to reclaim his two friends, accidentally tripping over some plastering from the ceiling. He managed to catch the glint of moonlight hovering above, reflecting off the polish on his rapier. But there was a touch of another source as well. He tilted the blade left every so often until another glimmer mirrored his view— Lancett's sword, coated by the moon. That would be his guide.

Over the crackling flames, he faintly heard Leilana's cries and Lancett's brisk coughs, moving towards the direction where the resonating sounds seemed to grow strongest before finally discovering them, his eyes widening. "Lancett! Leilana!"

"Where's Amiria?!" Leilana exclaimed.

"She's safe," Kindall said quickly.

He knelt next to Lancett, gesturing towards Leilana to help him grab the other side of the plastering trapping him, and the two managed to push it off with their combined strength. Lancett tore his foot free, covering his mouth and nose afterward to mask the agonizing pain lining his features in tandem with keeping from inhaling any more smoke. The more that he peered into the haze, the more clouded that his vision became until he lost consciousness.

"Lance! Stay with me here! Lance!"

When Kindall received no response, he grabbed Lancett's arm, pulling him to his feet, supporting him over his shoulders. The boy was little more than dead weight, but being a dead *weight* was an improvement over being plain dead. He reached up a hand to cover Lancett's mouth and nose, keeping a grip on him. Leilana was horrified by the sight, her hands rushing up towards her mouth and nose. Things had escalated quickly in the endless minutes they spent trapped in this condensed space.

"We need to go too, or we won't make it. Go, follow the moonlight. It should get you to the entrance. I'm right behind you...!" Leilana slowly shook her head, still in shock. Kindall grit his teeth before forcefully shouting, "Go, Leilana!"

She took a few steps back, the broken ceiling temporarily cleared out the smoke enough for her to glimpse at the entrance at the end of the room. Her designated path, right in front of her. Her eyes were red and puffy from the smoke, which struck a chord in Kindall's unsteady heart upon seeing her dagger-like expression.

"You better come back." And then, she was gone.

Kindall's breathing became labored as he carried Lancett, each step extracting a wheeze. The pathway was becoming disoriented, and he felt himself drop to his knees, vomiting into his hand. He drew back his palm to find it covered in a ravenous liquid. That only led him to spill the contents of his stomach again. The world was spinning; his head was pounding. His lungs ached. Breathing itself was becoming a challenge, and that led them to shorten until he was gasping for air. Shakily, he rose to a stand, his grip on Lancett tightening. He forced himself to take wider steps until he reached the entrance. The moment he had stepped out of the frying pan and into the light, he collapsed to the ground, Lancett lying next to him.

Leilana, waiting at the entrance for them, ran to his aide, carefully flipping Kindall over, allowing his head to rest on her lap. His lips and face were tinted blue, his breaths rapid, his crimson-shaded eyes beginning to gloss over. Her own eyes were filling with tears, and she clutched his hand while running her fingers softly through his soot-covered blonde hair, forcing back her coughs. "K-Kindall, it's going to be okay, we'll get you help...!"

His loosening fingers laced with hers. He could barely look at her without vomiting, the black liquid spewing over his clothes, constricting his lungs further. She rested a hand over his eyes to shield out the world as his system began retaliating against him in overdrive. He erupted into spasms, every slight movement racking him with pain.

Lancett's eyes flew open, and he shot up, gasping for air. He scrambled to his feet upon seeing Kindall and Leilana, limping towards the two before dropping down in front of him. His hands trembled as he reached out towards Kindall, his lips parted in disbelief. Before another word escaped him, Lancett noticed a faint aura surrounding the boy, a radiance springing from his throat.

"Kindall, y-you-" Kindall's vision was fading, his mind slipping through an inescapable black hole. Shakily, he extended a hand towards the dulling light, ripping the crystal pendant from his neck.

"It's not much," he stated, his voice rusted and hoarse from the smoke that besieged his lungs. "But I want you to know that I never... I never stopped be... believing in you..."

Lancett shook his head slowly. "Kindall, please stop."

He coughed, the black liquid streaming down the corner of his lip. He inhaled shakily, a tired smile curving onto his face. "You're my best friend... and I know that you'll... make it..."

"I'll do my best, I promise," he choked out.

"Good... you... you be good... now..." Kindall's breaths began to slow before finally ceasing altogether, his head still cradled in Leilana's lap. Amiria, hiding behind the trees, covered her mouth with her hands, stepping away, trying to erase the sight. Leilana shielded her eyes, trying to wipe away the tears, the sudden turn of events too overwhelming for her. Lancett held the pendant in his hands, a surge of enlightenment rushing through him.

You have ascertained the temperate of a pure heart.

Through this wandering soul, you have gained the totem of friendship.

He could still see Kindall's face brimming through the cracks of his troubled mind, his bright smile eclipsing the darkness. He couldn't turn away from him. He couldn't stop shaking, refusing to accept the inevitable. His final words lied in calling him his best friend. In the end, he still found hope in the boy called Lancett, someone that had grown next to him from the moment that they took their first steps into the academy. Now, he would no longer laugh, or cry, or find the momentum to help others. He wouldn't be able to hear the voices of his friends, now lost to the wind.

Kindall had saved Lancett's life, and it had cost him his own. And it was something that he was going to have to live with for the remainder of his days.

"There's such irony that he didn't choose a path to walk. He was the only one of us that didn't accept his prediction. He had to have known." Lancett clenched his hand into a fist, slamming it on the ground. "Why didn't I see this coming...?"

"It isn't your fault," Leilana stated, stroking soot-stricken Kindall's hair while trying to fight back tears. "You didn't know. None of us could have known. Don't beat yourself up over it. He did it to save you—to save *us*, and he didn't have to..."

"He didn't," he mumbled, "But the facts remain. He didn't deserve an early end."

"Do you blame Amiria...?"

Lancett allowed his mind to wander, recalling the girl's set prediction. She was given the card of 'Tower' as her guide into her future, and she knew in advance that she needed to be prepared for any signs of the card's weight, whenever and however they should arise. Something for her had been set in stone to be her downfall in this lifetime; something that would wound everything that she could have ever known and unravel before her. That was the last thing that either of them would have wanted her to suffer through.

"No form of agony is ever set in stone."

"Leilana, go after Amiria, and bring her back," Lancett told her softly, causing her to glance up.

"'Bring her back?'" she repeated, "What do you mean by that?"

"I mean it in every sense of the phrase. Amiria is kind-hearted, but she's also gullible and puts too much pressure on herself. She'll lose everything if she's left alone. This was just the first step; she'll succumb to whatever fears are welling in her. That was what Kosmin predicted for her during his tarot reading. Clearly, not having a reading done can be just as demoralizing to one as having a reading with a dangerous outcome thrust upon you. Maybe that's why she drowned herself in the knowledge of the Warlords and ended up causing this incident."

Leilana shook her head slightly. "No, Lancett, you don't mean that. You *know* that isn't true. Amiria would never intentionally try to hurt anyone. She's too good."

It was a coincidence that Kindall didn't have a reading and reaped the consequences of it—it had to be. There was no way that Kosmin's predictions could have all come true so soon.

"Just..." He held up a hand, resting it on her shoulder. "Just trust me. I know it may be a coincidence, but that doesn't quell my concerns. Amiria is important to Kindall, and she's important to me too. But if there's anyone left that can try to help her, it's you."

"Why me?"

He managed a grin. "I've always seen potential in you. You weigh your idealism on your shoulders, and from what I have seen, that observance is going to carry you through many trials."

"You hold too much faith in me sometimes." Lancett rose to a stand, carefully lifting Kindall's corpse up from her legs. The bulk of his body felt like a weight from her, but she couldn't help feeling like she played a part in the situation coming to this. He seemed so peaceful in his expression now that his discomfort and agony had ended abruptly, and she couldn't help watching him be taken away. "What are you going to do?"

"I'm going to find a place to lay him to rest. It's the least that I can do." She caught the faint glimpse of irritation on his face when he specified, "I trust that you'll make haste?"

"I'll do my best."

SIX

"Did you know that Warlords eventually lose themselves?"

Amiria was gripping the hem of her dress, sitting on a bench at the foot of the shrine overlooking the village. The lanterns that filled Paluna were burned out, smoke still rising from the poles. The sight made her reminisce about the fire and flames that had started up in the shrine. None of them could disperse them with the powers that they possessed, and none of her friends had possessed the right momentum to try and stop her.

Still, she could see the determination in Kindall's face as he reached for her. He fought for her freedom against her overpowering rage. She hadn't wanted to harm him—he was the last person that she had ever wanted to hurt. But now things had taken the worst possible turn. She killed him, even if the real cause was the fire boiling down her sanity. She was responsible for the death of someone she had thought to be her closest friend.

She could still see him resting peacefully, his face scarred by burn marks, his throat, and hair engulfed with soot and grime. The chemicals from her flames intertwined with the paper burning. His expression was already starting to shift from one of gentleness and hope to a tinted malice. She could see the blood coating his body, the flames blazing behind him. Still, he had extended his hand to her and smiled, as if the danger behind him was nonexistent. All of her past actions were a relic of his past.

"Believe in me."

"I wanted to believe in you... but I can't even trust myself. How can I ever hope to find my solace in you anymore anyways? I let you die."

"If anyone possesses the power to overcome themselves, it's got to be you."

She stifled a sob, her head sinking further into her knees, but she willed the falling tears to cease. This wasn't the time to cry. Not in this place, where anyone could see her, fault her, judge her.

Not this time.

"Amiria?"

A familiar voice plagued her senses. She jumped at the sudden call, her thoughts running away with her. She hadn't even turned around, but she knew that Leilana had been the one to make her way up towards her. It was an impending outcome, knowing that she would be here to drag her from the darkness. There was no other with the potential to ease her thoughts, but every ounce of concern and fear rising in her spoke otherwise. Leilana was gripping to her right sleeve with her left hand, finding it hard to lock gazes with the girl, her expression contemplative. So, even she had a hard time searching for the right words, Amiria thought.

"What is it?" Amiria settled with, her mind regaining some stability.

Leilana faced her, but Amiria quickly deciphered that it was an expression tinted with concern and disappointment. She was judging her. She may have been silent, considering the right approach without being too harsh, but the level of judgment was evident. Then again, Kindall's fate was her responsibility—how, logically, could anyone keep from arbitrating her?

"I want to talk," Leilana explained, "And I want to do it without making you feel trapped in a state of confusion or anguish. We all lost someone dear to us."

"What do you know?" she scoffed, surprised by the shape of her own words. She had never known herself to sound so spiteful. Never until now did she have the heart to be so blunt and cruel. It confused her further. "You didn't even know him that well. How can you call Kindall dear to you?"

"I may not have been as close to him as you and Lancett were, but I had the fortune of spending time with him. I got to experience through both of you how exceptional he was. He always looked at life with anticipation and saw the silver lining in every step that he took. It's rare to find someone that lived with such momentum." Amiria remained silent, openly absorbing her words, resting a hand on her forehead and brushing some sticky soot-strained strands from her face. There was more to Leilana than what met the eye. She was *too* perceptive. "I ask that you not judge my feelings before hearing my thoughts again, Amiria."

"Then, will you hear *my* thoughts?" she asked.

"That's why I'm here. I want you to open up to me, even if you feel like you don't have anyone that you can lean on. I don't want you to feel lost."

"It's too late for that," she admitted, able to face Leilana head-on, managing a smile. Leilana cringed; it *seemed* genuine, but she couldn't deny that it was forced. "I already feel as though my path is tainted black. I threw myself deeper into the fire, literally and metaphorically. I killed my friend."

"Don't say that," Leilana warned.

"I killed Kindall," she repeated, this time with less gusto, her words becoming choked on tears. Leilana inhaled deeply at the proclamation. "But this town killed him as much as I did."

Leilana rose an eyebrow at the change of pace. "What?"

"This town," Amiria began. "The people here cherish the Warlords more than the wellbeing of others. The moment that we entered, they tried to attack us, deeming us unworthy of their support." Leilana no longer felt confident trying to reach out to the girl. Lancett *had* put too much faith in her abilities of persuasion. "It doesn't seem logical to drag someone under if it means that you'll be saving yourself instead." She glanced over her shoulder, smiling at the girl. "That's something that we've been trying to avoid all of this time. Isn't it?"

Far too late to convince her of anything. She's already gone.

"Amiria..." Leilana stepped forward to the girl. Amiria wordlessly turned her back and allowed her gaze to hover over the town of Paluna. The smoke filling the lanterns was beginning to dim; her concentration heightened. "What are you planning to do?"

She lowered her head and closed her eyes. "I don't think there's a place for me to tell you. At best, you'd try to stop me, and I would have to keep you from achieving that. And at worst..." She stopped herself, clearing her throat. "You should go back to Lancett. I'm sure that he would value your company more. He did just lose his best friend. I'm sorry for dragging you down with me, Leilana. I hope that you succeed in your pilgrimage if you wish to continue moving forward. But this is where I call things done."

"Don't do it, Amiria. They aren't worth risking everything for."

"I know they aren't," she explained before turning her gaze on the lanterns again. She narrowed her eyes, and one by one they lit up the town. The sight took Leilana by surprise, and she watched as people began to clamor about the area, confused and concerned. "But this town took him away. Now it must die with him." Her eyes expanded, the glare hindering her features remaining.

Leilana's mouth fell open as the first of the lanterns tipped over at the will of their commander, kindling the lush grasses. A man had been in the line of assault, the cinders brushing up onto his shirt. He swiftly worked at brushing them away, but as he stumbled to avoid any further mishaps, a second lantern fell before him, striking his back. The lantern collapsed on top of him, setting his body ablaze. Leilana gasped sharply at the sound of his blood-curdling screams followed by the protestant cries and screams of others, covering her mouth with both hands.

Amiria hadn't so much as batted an eyelash at the scene unfolding before them, her expression cold and unnerving. This was what she desired most. Leilana had never seen such a confident expression. It held so many questions; was she always this intent on doing others harm, or was it simply something that stemmed from the rage and grief that she had been enduring?

"Amiria!" Leilana snapped, pushing the girl to the ground, which caused Amiria's concentration to break. Numerous lanterns bathing the town in light, in a false solace, tumbled like fell trees, spreading along the grass and engulfing the straw huts. Leilana's heart dropped to the pits of her stomach before she turned her irritation on the younger girl.

"What have you done?!"

Leilana held up a hand, slapping the girl across the face with as much might as she could put behind her strike. Amiria's hand flew to her throbbing right cheek. It took her a few seconds to process what had occurred before she found the momentum to face Leilana, who was fuming at the selfsame sight of her. She had seen this expression many times. The years became wasteful. Amiria watched her rise above the ranks, noticed how Kindall and Lancett naturally flocked to her with knowledge only of her battle skills and her prowess with the grimoire called Lasette, an inheritance from Ennis Erovina. In contrast, they had seen Amiria herself as someone full of potential, but too humble and misunderstood to truly make a difference, the near opposite of Leilana.

Maybe they didn't see her as a friend, or even an asset to their journey. Up to this point, she had either slowed them down or hindered their progress. She had caused Kindall's death all because she couldn't accept the knowledge of the Warlords' suffrage.

She had come to admire the way that Leilana could take charge of a situation. These thoughts had grown twisted over the single day that they had spent together. All that she knew about Leilana Erovina unraveled like a red thread snagged around her throat, constricting her. Betrayal. Urgency. Protection. She wasn't sure which underlining emotions were winning out. Her expression turned grim in a manner of seconds and she rose to a stand, her body swaying left to right in a paced motion, her hair sinking over her eyes.

"You're leaving me with no other choice, Leilana."

Leilana gripped to the Lasette with both hands before allowing the book to drift above her, the pages turning one after another as the gusts of wind and ash rushed through them. The girls faced one another from opposite ends of the spectrum, one of madness, the other of fury.

"I'm not expecting to walk out of this. But I will make you pay for your actions, Amiria. For my sake, and for Lancett and Kindall. I'm disappointed in you. *Kindall* would be disappointed in you."

"I know he would be." She curled her hand into a fist, inhaling deeply before drawing out her breath, her voice reverberating as she proclaimed, "But he isn't here anymore, is he?" Leilana forced back a snarl. Every statement she made, Amiria seemed to hold less regard for what she had done.

The Lasette suddenly stopped on a page, a pair of hands swarmed by shadows seizing Amiria, grabbing her and lifting her from the ground she walked on. Amiria glared down at her before preparing to belt out a note. Leilana willed one of the hands to cover the girl's mouth before slamming her to the ground, causing her to skid, the hem of her dress tearing to shreds.

"He's here," Leilana hissed as Amiria was working to clear her vision, resting a hand on her head. "He will *always* be here."

Amiria slammed her fist on the ground before the earth underneath Leilana began to give way. The moment that the girl felt her foot begin to sink, she pressed her hand to the ground and flipped back to steady herself, landing on the other side of the crater separating them. Once she had regained her footing, she held up a hand, shadowy illuminates spewing from the Lasette, plunging through Amiria's body, knocking her back a few inches.

Leilana could hear people shouting behind her, trapped in Paluna's cinders, to a fate that no Warlord could ever correct. She bathed in the infernos that torched their skin. She could taste the ash filling the air and feel the blood seeping between her fingers. The Lasette was cursed, weakened, and conflicted; that was something that Amiria carried within her. The spirits that no longer found resonance in the world of Adrylis would haunt her. A curse that would never be lifted from her burdened mind.

Amiria's body was swimming in a fervent state of misperception and mental collapse, consciousness escaping her in pieces. She allowed her gaze to waver over the town, the scent of ammunition and rotted flesh in full bloom. She groaned as she stumbled forward into the chasm. Leilana grabbed the girl's arm, nearly falling in herself. Amiria dangled on as Leilana tightened her grip, pulling her back onto steady ground. She laid the girl out across the dirt, and then she hit the ground herself next to her, sighing of relief —they were both rather petite girls for their age, but combining two weights amounted to more than she could manage at once.

The Lasette dropped from the air, the golden metal lock sealing it closed clanking against the ground first. Leilana rested a hand over the grimoire, and for a moment she swore that she felt another hand resting on hers. Right as she was prepared to turn Amiria's way, a sudden kick to her right side sent her reeling. She cried out in pain as she skidded across the ground, clutching the aching wound before allowing herself the opportunity to locate the source. Amiria was up and about, her breaths so aggressive and substantial as she stepped forward that smoke was almost pouring from her veins. Her eyes were brimming with detestation as if the girl had no morality left in her soul.

"A-Amiria," Leilana choked out.

"Are you so frail... that one kick brings you to your knees?!" she screeched before jolting the girl in the stomach, causing her to double over. Leilana shakily inhaled, reaching for the grimoire. Amiria slammed her foot against it before kicking the book away, just out of her reach. Leilana was horrified, watching her grimoire tumble away. She hadn't been without it since she had received it. Amiria grabbed the girl by the collar of her shirt, bringing her to her eye level.

"D-Don't," she whispered, for that had become all that she could manage. "Amiria...!"

"Go to sleep, Leilana. This is what you deserve for interfering."

Before Leilana could retort, Amiria let out a single shrill note, which straightaway knocked the girl into a state of unconsciousness. She dropped the girl to the ground, watching her slump over. Amiria brandished the dagger that she had previously used to cut the wilted flowers on her way to Paluna from the tote at her side, brushing away the residue of damaged leaves and grass to the best of her ability. Now, she harbored repentance that she had ever wanted to grant the first citizens she would encounter on her pilgrimage a modest wish of a little joy; they hadn't desired the same of her.

These spells...

What's even the point of trying to live a humble life among people anymore? What's the point in trying to understand them, or learn how to love them, or anything like that?

It's not worth it. It's not as though others will grant the same courtesy to you.

She stood above Leilana, turning the girl's face in her direction. She caressed her cheek tenderly, her eyes filled with a sense of longing, reminiscent of the nature she had treated the flowers with.

"*You* are my flower," Amiria whispered. "You were the first one to truly help me blossom into something more. I wanted to catch up with you for so long. I was glad to be able to fight you, and to stand by your side." She gripped to the dagger with both hands. "Now it's time that I surpass you."

She lifted the blade above Leilana's chest, her fingers lacing firmly around the hilt. She swallowed, sweat rushing down the back of her neck. The flames were crackling in the background. The screams had silenced. The people of Paluna themselves were no longer a factor. Contrary to how hesitant she wanted to become about this decision, it was set in stone carving. There was no way that turning back would be an adequate option. Leilana would return to this hectic world in due course, and they would have to do battle against one another a second time.

She couldn't take that chance.

She closed her eyes as she thrust the blade downward.

Abruptly, a sword clashed with the dagger, slicing through her hand and knocking it away. She yelped as she clutched the wound, scarcely noticing a collection of small droplets starting to streak down Leilana's face. She froze when the blade came into her line of sight inches away from her throat.

"That's more than enough from you," the resounding voice thundered through her, her body shaky at the indication of frustration behind his demanding words.

Her eyes marginally glinted to the left, and through the moonlight, basked under the still of the night, she caught the silhouette of a young man. She could only make out his shoulder-length ponytail and the glasses shielding his eyes. She nearly confused him for Lancett, noting to herself that the two withheld similar auras and determination behind the power of their weapons before realizing that their appearances had differed too greatly to ever mistake them.

"The fires grow fiercer," he continued. There was a clear indication of an accent, evident by the elongated enunciation of each vowel he spoke. "And there are few left to explain the occurrences due to the severity of their injuries. We will assure that they will pass on in peace. You are the only one that remains—tell me what happened to this town."

"I-I don't know!" she exclaimed without thinking. She couldn't keep her composure no matter how much she willed herself otherwise. "I'm not sure what could have happened, I-!"

"Are you lying?" he interjected. "Because I can see your sweat."

"Yes," she admitted, resting her hands on the dirt, tears filling her eyes.

He gestured his sword down towards Leilana's unconscious form. "Did she do this?" Amiria opened her mouth to speak, shaking her head sluggishly, any expended energy lost, all at the hands of this one man's quick succession. "I see. If the fault does not lie with her, then did *you* do this?"

"Yes," she repeated, much faster this time around.

Swallowing her fear, she began to sing softly, stringing together the intangible words. As the man drew in closer, curious about what actions she was taking to get herself out of this mess, her head whipped around, the notes themselves overtaking him. He covered his ears, gritting his teeth, his eyes flaring with annoyance when his sword slipped from his grasp. Now she could marvel at her accuser. His shoulder-length ponytail was a sandy shade of brown, his emerald eyes radiating under the flames.

"What in the world...?" he mumbled to himself, never turning his gaze from her. Amiria dashed away from him once he had dropped to his knees, the pitch too abnormal and excessive for him to bear for too long.

Once Amiria was out of sight, he let out a small groan, his palms firmly on the ground. He may have lost his target, but at least now his ears could stop ringing and regain some stability. He stole a glance at the girl lying unconscious only a few feet away, the imagery of this songstress attempting to steal her life still fresh in his mind. He was fortunate enough to have stumbled upon this town in hopes of seeking shelter for the night. Sure, he hadn't gotten his wish, but in the end, he had secured one person's sunrise. That was at least a plus to the ordeal.

"Solus!" Another male called out, running up to him. In his view came familiar messy black hair hanging just past his neck, covering his brown eyes until he had brushed them away and tucked them behind his ear. He was panting a bit from the jog but kept his stamina. "A-Are you okay?"

"I'm fine, Rem," he replied in a straightforward manner before jumping to a stand, brushing off his dress pants and gathering his sword. "Did you find any survivors?"

Rem straightened himself before holding up his left index finger, his free hand resting over the sheath at his side. "Not really, no. What about-?" Rem glanced past Solus and noticed the foreign girl lying on the ground. "...You?"

Solus stepped towards her, lifting her off the ground slightly and checking her over. He rested his ear against her chest, sighing of relief when her heartbeat emerged at a normal pace. "She's alive, just unconscious." The injuries that she had sustained seemed more minimal than most that he had seen on the way over to this spot, but they still had their weight. "Come, Rem, lend me your healing. It might come in," Solus stifled a chuckle, stating, "Handy."

Rem scoffed at the horrendous wordplay, resisting the urge to laugh. "Oh, throw me a bone, your jokes are so not funny."

Rem leaned over the girl, pressing his hand to her chest, his hands grazing over the punctured wound. She flinched at the sudden contact but didn't awaken. Solus rested a hand on the girl's forehead to quell her, and she seemed to respond. After being certain of what he was working with, Rem's hand began emanating a teal glow, bathing the girl in a healing light. He retained his focus, keeping his gaze locked on the girl for any signs of physical change. The color began to return to her face, and her muscles settled from the agony she had been facing, which relieved both young men of their qualms.

"There. That should be a little better on our conscience. I guess we'll know how she's actually feeling once she's awake," Rem stated.

Solus nodded at his words as he pulled the young girl onto his back, keeping a secure hold on her by tucking his arms under her knees, her head resting on his shoulder. Her body smelled of ash and grime, her hair a bit charred and her clothes ripped. Still, it hadn't been hard to tell that she was defending herself thoroughly after taking a mental note of the injuries that her opponent had acquired. It was rare to find someone that could handle themselves against a songstress of that girl's caliber. Hell, he was amazed that he himself could withstand it long enough for her to escape and not be injured in the process.

"Hey, check this out," Rem called, holding up the Lasette towards Solus.

He raised an eyebrow. "And what is that supposed to be?"

"Looks like some sort of book. Might belong to her." He flipped the book between each of his hands. "It's kind of heavy. Must have a lot of information beyond its pages."

He messed around with the golden lock before finding that he couldn't pick it, shaking the grimoire in his grasp a few times. After no success, he decided to carry it, eyeing the illustration of an owl clutching a wrapped scroll, soaring through the air. Lining the image were twenty-six odd symbols. The words were unfamiliar to him, and he assumed that they wouldn't stand out much to Solus either. The symbols were likely the language of the book's keeper.

"But I admit, the cover design is intricate." He ran his finger along the book, the metallic bearings rough on his hands. "Must have been passed down through several generations before it found its way here..."

Solus playfully rolled his eyes. He didn't appear surprised that Rem had taken an interest in something that related to an ancient era. "I don't think that you should mess around with it too much," he began, "It isn't your book to own."

"Well, certainly not," Rem replied, stepping towards the girl, placing the grimoire back into the tote at her side. "But if it won't be mine, then we already know that it belongs to our little captive. She must have been carrying it with her and used it to defend herself. Maybe she's a mage too." Then he paused, noticing Solus's face light up at the mere mention of the word. "Wait, you didn't hear that."

Solus chuckled. "She's a mage."

Rem slumped at the statement. "Oh, great, I've started something here."

"She may even be an Arcana."

"An Arcana?" he groaned before straightening himself. "Don't tell me what you're thinking, because I feel like I already have an idea. We're bringing her with us, aren't we?"

Solus was already starting towards Paluna's scorched remains. "I don't see why not."

"Sol, come on, we're not supposed to be involving other people!" Rem exclaimed, dashing off after him, all the while glancing around to see if there were others that could open their lips. The moment that occurred is when he could put his sword to better use. "If anything, I'm not supposed to be seen by anyone or acknowledged in case they catch on to who I am!"

"That's fine. I'll assure that anyone that is perceptive in that manner is dealt with accordingly. That is my duty as your servant, and one of the Brenner name. But you must understand that we come from a different lifestyle—we may need to rely on others that know Adrylis better than we do, all while balancing our identities. You cannot be naïve to the situation, contrary to your upbringing."

"I wasn't intending to be naïve," Rem tried to reason. "I just want to keep some order in this situation. I can't afford to have my identity run with me."

Footsteps, slow and purposeful, crunching against gravel. Hushed voices, an unknown topic rising to the surface. The action was becoming repetitive, and though it wasn't of heavy influence, it was enough to help Leilana realize that she was being carried. This wasn't the first time she had been carried on someone's back, but she knew that this sensation was foreign enough for her to wonder just what had caused the tables to turn this way.

Leilana stirred at the movement, reaching up her hand slightly to lay on a strong shoulder. They were much too broad to belong to a woman. A man, then. She nestled further into the warmth that this mysterious person emanated. He stopped walking, and the gesture caused his hair to tickle her nose, which began twitching at the contact until she let out a small sneeze. Her eyes snapped open and she met the sight of emerald eyes shielded by a pair of frames, the irises reflecting a delicate shade of caramel under the light of the building flames.

Oh great, so she was still in Paluna. But at least she was alive, somehow.

"Good morning," he told her with a smile plastered on his delicate face. She wanted to retaliate that it wasn't morning, but she held her tongue instead. "You look confused." Did she really? She couldn't see her own face. "You probably have a lot of questions."

"I think I'd like to start with 'who are you,' to be honest."

"No time for that." Another young man stepped past Leilana's line of sight to walk ahead of the one carrying her. "We need to leave. There's no point in burning to a crisp ourselves."

"Rem, please don't walk too far ahead." Leilana was staring at the rather abrasive young man's back for some time, but before she could bring herself to inquire about who these strangers were, she slipped back into unconsciousness.

"Solus, hurry up, we don't have time to lose," Rem called. Solus sighed. He supposed they would end up keeping this girl prisoner anyways.

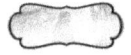

Lancett was kneeling before a covered dirt patch, Kindall's rapier planted into the ground next to it as a headstone. He regretted leaving him behind so easily, but he would have to continue moving on for them both. He couldn't bring himself to tears, the shock of his best friend's sudden passing weighing too heavily on his mind. He rested his hands on the mound of dirt, wondering if he dug deep enough, hoping to touch him once more and pray for his eternal peace.

There was so much now that he was left to consider regarding his pilgrimage, the Warlords, and seeking the truth. The world was already beginning to collapse, and all that he had come to know beyond the security of his tiny school never amounted to anything but temporary solace.

Adrylis differed—Paluna was full of magicless citizens, guarded by a Warlord, marveling in the grace that the man provided his followers with. Linmus itself was not ruled by a single Warlord, rather by a monarchy that was comprised of powerful Arcana and Maesters in the direct lineage of Warlords. Arcana and Maesters of his age group were the most prominent fighters, still young and agile with gifted spirits, the perfect candidates to become a successor.

But already, their numbers were dwindling from the first night alone, and a country was burning away, no resolve left for him to fight. The ash-filled wind kissed the trees, smoke rising beyond the clouds. Soot was raining down on the tarnished land. Was Adrylis truly such a damaged place?

"There's still hope," he tried to convince himself, rising to a stand. His right foot was swelling, but the pain was minimal compared to the further damage that he could have sustained. Maybe he just hadn't processed the injury with everything crumbling. "There's something that can be done to make things right, isn't there?"

His thoughts were promptly cut off when he noticed Amiria race into the trees with her tail between her legs, limping and stumbling over her own feet with every meter forward. She was troubled, that much was certain. But her presence here meant that Leilana had failed to shield her emotions from running rampant. His mind tore at the idea of chasing after Amiria to try and talk to her or going to look for Leilana and ensure her safety.

Kindall's face emerged in his mind. His best friend was attached to the broken girl, his love for her budding like the flowers she so adored. With him gone, the duty to protect her naturally was going to fall into his lap. But the care he had for Leilana left him too conflicted with obligation. Either decision was going to leave him trapped in regret for a long time coming.

With grit teeth and a good stomp on the dirt to temporarily ease his frustrations, he decided to go after Amiria. He wasn't sure how far that she would travel in such a short time, but he would find her again. And he would see Leilana again as well if the fates would allow.

This wasn't the first time that flames of indignation had taken away something of importance to the world, and it certainly wouldn't be the last time that lives would be swept away like ashen ruins, lost to the winds, guided to a better place by the fates of humanity. But to comprehend that the town of Paluna was no more was inconceivable. And it had been by her own hands.

Amiria didn't sleep that night. Kindall's face, Leilana's virtuous decision and the elegant stranger's sorrowful words were fresh in her mind, tormenting any solitude that she could have regained in a single night. It was too soon to think about moving on. She had run from her discomfort for hours on end before taking refuge in a cave as far away from the town as possible.

She drew herself closer to the fire luminously burning over some firewood, listening to the wind rushing through the trees outside. She went through her tote, pulling out the notes from Master Hinju, deciding to look over them a second time.

"'The totem of love,'" she croaked out, having hardly spoken a word after her escape. She didn't even bother to clear her throat. "'Love is the emotion affiliated with deep affection, where one develops a close bond with another.'"

Leilana crossed her mind. Did the two of them have a close relationship? She wasn't certain of that, knowing that now the girl resented her for her actions against Paluna. It would take time to restore any confidence to approach the girl, even if the admiration she held for her had fizzled out.

"'Love can be found and reciprocated in several forms. It can be uncovered in a parent, a friend, and even a lover.'"

Lancett and Kindall's relationship reflected well on the aspects of friendship, but they also seemed to correspond with love. They were joined at the knee. She couldn't recall a day during her lessons when they were apart, laughing and smiling together.

"'Love is unpredictable. And it is the most powerful spell that any budding Warlord can have. When you discover it

*for yourself, the world will turn in your favor once more. You
will have no fears.'"*

Amiria sighed before closing the journal. After
beholding the cover and signing off on it with her name on
the label, she tossed it into the fire. "You never make much
sense whenever you got into a poetic frame of mind, Master
Hinju."

For a while, she watched the pages shrivel and burn
away as if they were nonexistent. Everyone had been so
excited to start this journey, but now hers was officially
beginning, away from prying eyes and hurtful words.

Now, she was free to carve a new path without the limitations of her magic. It could be contained so long as she
didn't allow herself to think like a Warlord. She couldn't
lust for power; she couldn't bring herself to fight for this
world. It was a matter of survival from here on out.

The sun was rising high, the sky tinted orange and red.
The world continued to ascend to the next moment of gratitude and solace, just as it always had, and always would.
Surely the world wouldn't miss someone like Kindall. There
was more to life. It was easy to assume that. One life was
nothing when amounted to many. But that didn't change
that he was no longer around to make an impact. She had
stolen his bubbling optimism, his chance for recognition.
She snatched away his dream of exploring Adrylis alongside
Lancett from directly under his nose. She covered her ears
and hid away her tear-streaked face.

"**I don't want you to feel lost.**"

'Lost.' Such a funny concept, a trivial word, an unnat-
ural feeling. This was the last thing that she could have ever
considered after coming this far, having the opportunity to
see Adrylis for herself. To think that this world held so
many secrets outside of their sheltered academy, several

pieces locked away in the shreds of lost memory and reasoning that were waiting to be claimed. If becoming a Warlord and discovering human emotion was out of range, then maybe those mysteries of Adrylis and the purpose of the Warlords and their mission were in her grasp in place of it. And the moment that they were attainable, everything could become clear again.

That was something to hope for, at least.

SEVEN

Leilana woke once more to find that the night had slipped away and transcended into a new day. The sun was hidden behind rolling storm clouds, peeking out every few minutes, evident by the occasional shade covering her. She kept silent, continuing to rest her head on the shoulder of the long-haired stranger that she'd given a single glance at since her turmoil in Paluna, her throat dry and her muscles too stiff to chance fighting back. She couldn't afford to make any sudden movements. It didn't seem like he was particularly harmful or malicious, but she had been wrong in the past about deceit and how others offered it in a guise of trust.

The lengthy red ribbon holding his ponytail in place brushed against her face constantly as he walked, making her plan to keep still more difficult. She withheld her sigh, shutting her eyes. His shoulders were strong and clinging to his aura relaxed her; he reminded her briefly of Ennis, at least in stature. Not that it made him any more trusting— she didn't even know his name or anything about him. All that she had to go off of was that he provided an escape route from a burning village.

"You're awake, aren't you?" he called in nearly a whisper. She almost jumped, but surely, he felt her body tense at his acknowledgment. He didn't bother to look at her, but she noticed his cheeks curl upward as if he were smiling. "Can you stand?"

There was no point in hiding anymore now that he knew the truth. "I think so."

He allowed her to touch base with the grass, and though she felt she would stumble, she caught herself in time to exchange glances with him. He was at least half a foot taller, definitely older, but he still had a youthful expression and facial structure. Maybe he had just a few more years of experience in this life than her. He rested a hand under his chin, his free hand resting on his hip, appearing inquisitive about her current demeanor before shrugging it off. Crap. Had he noticed?

"Um, about what you did back there," she began. "Thank you for saving me."

"Of course," he replied with a subtle nod. Leilana was taken aback by his peculiar accent. She had come across many people in Magiten Academy over the years, but none of them carried such an indistinguishable trait. "Though, I suppose it was more coincidental than anything."

"So, it's mere coincidence that you carried me away from Paluna? I have a friend there that was waiting for me. I'm not exactly sure of our current surroundings." She rested her index finger on her chin, averting her gaze up. "If anything, I could call this a kidnapping, could I not?"

The tables had turned all too fast. The young man held up his hands in defense. "N-Now hold on a moment, let's not be too rash-"

"That's not how you talk to someone that saved your life," A second voice snarled. A young man with neck-length shaggy black hair pushed past his friend, hovering over Leilana. She folded her arms behind her back and shifted her weight onto her left leg, her gaze ensnared by his vigilant brown eyes. He practically jabbed his finger into her chest, which did little to break her balance. "If anything, you should be thanking him for carrying you after I healed your injuries."

"Thank you for your kindness," Leilana responded. "But is it wrong to be a bit suspect?"

The light-haired man laid a hand on his friend's shoulder, mustering up a smile. "No need to be snippy, Rem. She doesn't know anything that's going on."

"And she hasn't given you a chance to explain it either. She was the one being rude."

"I wasn't being rude," Leilana interjected, both hands on her hips, shifting her weight onto her right leg instead when her left leg became a bit stiff. "If anything, I was humoring him. Then again, it's easy to mistake the two traits before they mesh into a single quality: sarcasm."

"Are you making fun of me?" Rem hissed.

"Am I?"

"Are you?" he countered, taking a step forward, his hand curled into a fist. Leilana almost laughed; he was trying so hard to be intimidating and it was still falling just short of the mark.

"Oh, gee, I don't know," she said smoothly. Rem grit his teeth at the proclamation before turning away from her, his focus locked on the ground from the corner of his dominating sneer.

"Sorry about him, he can be a bit... I suppose that aggressive is a close enough phrase. My name is Solus. And this is-"

The man now known as Solus peered over his shoulder, pausing when he noticed that the friend he was set to properly introduce stepped several feet away to plant himself on a bulky rock. Rem had his arms crossed, his dark hair sinking over his eyes. Leilana glanced past him to examine the sight for herself before once more turning to Solus in anticipation of his reaction. Solus's shoulders slumped, his eyes narrowing in disappointment.

"Correction. That *was* my friend Rem."

"Solus and Rem, huh?" She placed her hands behind her back, peering off towards the trees in their pathway rather than in Rem's direction. "What peculiar names. Mine is Leilana."

Solus couldn't help but sigh at the twist of events. They hadn't even gotten past the stage of introduction and they were already at each other's throats. It was strange, but he didn't know Leilana at all, so he wasn't in any place to judge her 'rude' behavior. He hadn't seen her as such, rather a bit troubled because she was in the presence of two people that she knew nothing about, people that were claiming that they saved her life.

And he knew Rem, acting as his sword, too deeply to ignore his distress. There was little fault he could find in any statement that his prince could spew, no matter how incredulous the details or biased the development and basis of his words seemed to be in the eyes of others.

"Are you on her side?" Rem spoke up. Leilana's gaze narrowed. Certainly, he knew that she was still listening, even if she was attempting to ignore his antagonistic banter.

"Well, I'm not really on anyone's side. This argument is barely considered an argument. You're certainly making me question my logic here," Solus admitted, brushing some strands of hair out of his face. "I'm not sure what you want me to do. Am I acting as a mediator for the two of you?"

"I suppose that's the case," Leilana told Solus, which caused Rem's head to snap back towards her. "If you're willing to uphold it, at least."

"You'd be smart to keep your mouth shut about the situation," Rem warned.

"And why's that?" Leilana countered. "Because you say so? What gives you the right to order people around?"

Solus's eyes kept darting between the two, his parted lips alone mirroring his desire to interject, but finding no momentum to cool their heads. Before either of them knew it, Rem had grown eerily silent, his racing mind practically up in flames. Leilana withheld her smirk when he scoffed a reply and turned in the opposite direction.

"The next town over," Rem began, his voice regaining some levity, "that is where we're dropping you off." He stopped short while walking. The moment that his footsteps ceased, Leilana could see a firm illumination engulfing his body. Her eyes widened. She turned her attention to Solus, who calmly returned the gesture before addressing Rem's firm statement again. He didn't seem to notice the aura surrounding Rem's body, which rose an underlying issue in her mind.

You have taken the first step.
Breach the path of understanding.

Her eyes darted around before she found that it was something else that Rem and Solus hadn't taken any note up. Which meant that the voice was something meant only for her. She reached up a hand towards her head, the unfamiliar voice spiraling through her mind. It seemed to consume those passing seconds. They made her head spin.

"I promised Solus that we would guide you passage until then," Rem continued, though the words barely reached Leilana's senses. "After that, stay away from us."

She curled her tiny hand into a fist but kept it concealed behind her back. The way that he handled the news was cold, but what place did she have other than to agree? "Understood."

"Try not to slow me down."

"Please forgive Rem," Solus said lowly to her once the boy was out of earshot. "He can be socially selective, and that trait has amplified as of late. I wish that I could explain things, but he isn't normally this aggressive."

"I'm not worried about it." But only because he seemed to play a part in her pilgrimage. That meant that even if he disagreed with her being around, she would have to find a way to break down his walls and pick his brain eventually. She could save him for last. "So, where is the closest town from here? Do you have a set path?"

Solus forced a nervous chuckle, tugging on his front bangs. "Honestly, we're just winging it and hoping that we are led in the right direction."

"I think that I can help with that."

"Really?"

She went through her tote to uncover the journal that Master Hinju had provided each of his students with. Among the contents was a map, but it was so poorly crafted that anyone reading it would have the narrowest of ideas of what Adrylis held in store. Solus glanced over her shoulder at the art and stifled a laugh. That only confirmed her thoughts. The idea of having to work with this atrocity of a guide made her stomach turn. Master Hinju could not be a master of every trade he attempted, she supposed.

"Okay, plan B," she mumbled. After crumpling up the paper-drawn atlas and ensuring that it will never return to her line of sight by stomping it into the ground, Leilana opened her grimoire and flipped through a few pages before allowing the book to drift several feet above her. She held up a hand and began to sign a few letters, mumbling, "Mal... An... Pe."

Solus raised an eyebrow when a map floated down from the book like a feather caught in the morning breeze, falling into Leilana's hands. She looked it over once, turning it every which way before nodding, passing it off to Solus. "I may not be an artist, but making one this way could be useful."

"I'm curious about how you can create a map with so little information on Adrylis engraved into your mind." He stole a glance from her and smiled. "But who am I to go against a rising Arcana?"

Leilana cleared her throat, taken aback by the cordiality in his smile. She leaned in closer to him, allowing her gaze to hover over the map. The detail into the art was broad, and she could mark off every tree, every stone. Maybe the Lasette had prepared her for this journey in more ways than she could imagine. "The closest town from Paluna is called Kalonia, off to the west."

He didn't seem surprised by the sudden subject switch, deciding it better to act on her words. He glanced at the map and uncovered the landmarks surrounding them. They had passed several mahogany trees, but upon following the morning light once the sun had risen, they had been walking in the opposite direction. "We've been traveling the right way, at least."

"Are you two coming or not?!" Rem urgently called, which rose awareness in Solus. "We have a problem-!" A sudden cry of pain made Solus rush into action, drawing the broadsword at his side. Leilana outstretched out her arms, the Lasette falling into her possession again, taking off after him.

Rem fended off a wolf-like beast with his saber, the blade clamped between the razor-sharp jaws. He pressed his right foot to the ground, pushing the wolf back to get a clear glimpse at it. The beast was cloaked in shadow, a crimson miasma spewing from its back and hind legs. It grew to nearly twice his size when it leaped up to pin him to the ground. Rem's back slammed against the dirt, colliding with some overturned stones, hindering his means of defense for only a passing second. He screamed, his limbs fighting against him, but he prevailed in regaining enough momentum to prolong his life.

The beast was snarling as it gnawed down on the polished weapon. He could hear the metal beginning to crunch under the pressure, and he placed both hands on the hilt, his eyes slipping between brown to a shade of amber that rivaled the sunlight. With a yell, he thrust the beast back, electrical pulses surging from the shadow's body. Rem shot to his feet, sword at the ready, watching as the wolf began to convulse from the internal shock before splitting into four separate forms.

He swallowed, taking a step back before gripping to the hilt with both hands, extending the sword in front of him. "That is not a good sign." He swung, casting a wave of magic over himself to heal his weary body, the back injury he had sustained now a relic of the past.

"Rem!" Solus called, emerging from the trees. His speed was heightened, maximizing his level of strength, cutting through one of the shadows set to leap at the younger man. Its head hit the ground before dissolving into nothingness, and Solus whirled around, knocking one of the other shadows back into the trees. "Can you fight, Leilana?"

"I've got it covered!"

Leilana extended a hand forward once she had opened

the grimoire to the right page and mumbled an incantation, the Lasette releasing a wave of flames upon her target. When the burning insignia wasn't enough to subdue its rage, she lifted her hand and then thrust it in a downward motion, the Lasette conjuring a bolt of lightning that plunged through the trees, causing the beast to convulse and dissipate much like the first.

She allowed her gaze to waver over the ethereal remains left among the trees. She could almost see the timbre of the shadows uniting with a mental flux. Among the obscurities of the corrupted wolves, she glimpsed the expression of the person that controlled them. His free-flowing hair, his cold, unnerving eyes...

Her fingers twitched, and she flexed them to keep some sense of gripping to reality.

Rem and Solus met at one another's side, looking over their remaining two opponents with some contentment, their backs nearly pressed against each other. The wolves were crouched low, set to attack at any given moment, guttural snarls filling the air and cutting through the silence. Solus's fingers drummed over his sheathed sword while Rem had taken up an early veil of defense and held his own weapon in his right hand, resisting the urge to twirl the hilt between his fingers.

Rem smirked. "I have to admit, it's been a while since we've been put in a fix."

"Would you really call this a fix?" Solus responded, eyes lingering over the wolf in his path. "It doesn't seem complicated unless you consider how they could have ended up this way."

"So, it's not just me thinking we're being hounded then. Best to take out the little spies." The two charged towards their respective opponent, reaching up their blades in a simultaneous motion before cutting them down, the beasts vanishing upon contact.

Solus sheathed his broadsword once more. "Geez, Remiel, how did you allow your guard to drop so easily against one little wolf?"

Rem chuckled. "Hey, that 'one little wolf' packed a hell of a punch. Or, uh, claw."

"Are you guys all right?" Leilana asked after reaching the two.

"We're fine," Solus assured her while Rem turned up his nose and listened to the metal scraping against his sheath. Harmonious and satisfying a chime. "How did things go on your end?"

"It went down to a little blast of thunder from the heavens," Leilana said proudly, crossing her arms. "I'd like to say that my first battle against an outside force was a success."

"I take it your magic is pretty adequate then?" Rem asked.

She extended the Lasette forward. "I've trained to wield this grimoire. I certainly hope that my magic is adequate now that I'm using it more frequently."

Solus rested his hands on one of each of their shoulders, his grip almost forceful. "All right, before you two attract more unwanted guests, I say we take our leave." The gesture sent chills down Rem's spine and left Leilana somewhat concerned for both of their well-being. They knew little about each other, but he seemed to emanate a sense of calm far beyond any storm that he could execute.

"Yeah, yeah, all right, we're going," Rem stated.

It was reminiscent of Lancett. Wait. Lancett. She almost forgot him. Was he still in Paluna? She wasn't sure if she could trust Rem with her concerns. Maybe she could ask Solus instead before they would have to part ways if they knew of any survivors in Paluna. He could have been one of them, and if he was... where was he now? Was he alone, or maybe he had found Amiria?

Amiria...

"I'm sorry for dragging you down with me, Leilana."

She had to be broken up over Kindall's death and took the ache brought on by the incident in a different manner than even Leilana herself could have predicted. Such a fragile and humble person turned bitter all from a little knowledge that had overstepped their boundaries. The memories were encircling her faster than she could process.

"Leilana?" Solus called, already ahead. She jumped at the sudden address and continued after them. Solus's expression read a sense of concern, while Rem's was trapped in a virtually lackadaisical sense, still in a state of bliss from his battle. He was glancing around the area in anticipation of more. It was a strange blend of emotions from her temporary companions, and it made her a bit uneasy. "Are you all right? You seem concerned. Do you want to talk about it?"

"It's nothing, I'm fine," she responded a bit too speedily. "Please don't let it burden you. If anything, I think I'm just tired."

"Tired?" Rem repeated, almost astonished by her demeanor. "But you just got up not too long ago, and it's still early. Not used to the heat of battle at all, I see."

Solus tilted the girl's chin, looking her over for himself

before examining her features. There were traces of dark circles under her eyes, her face a bit sunken. Her skin was pale, and the light of the sun did little to mask the exhaustion. "Well, we have to consider that she was *unconscious*, not asleep."

He raised an eyebrow. "There's a difference?"

"When you are asleep, you are easing your mind and reflecting on events of the day, about future ambitions or even fears, which reflects our dreams. When you are *unconscious*, it is your body's way of coping with pain. She was involved in a hefty ordeal, and she did just begin a pilgrimage of her own on the wrong note."

Rem considered Solus's statement, glancing at the ground, then up at the sky. The sun was beginning to drift to the west, near the center of the atmosphere. To him, that meant that the afternoon would be approaching soon. "I'm taking this as a 'you want to stop and let her rest' sort of diagnosis."

"It's all right," Leilana piped up, "I don't want to slow you down. I don't mind waiting until we reach the next town like you wanted. Then I'll be out of your hair-"

"As much as I didn't want to have to stop yet," Rem began, effectively cutting her off. "Solus is right. I'd feel guilty if we kept going and you ended up passing out from exhaustion. That wouldn't be very chivalrous of me, or wise to any of us if anything were to happen to you."

Leilana averted her gaze to the ground, not sure how to take his words. It didn't seem to strike a chord about how he truly felt; it seemed like he was obeying for Solus's sake rather than hers. Then again, what could she expect? She didn't know anything about either of them or what their goals were. She was just a pebble in their shoes.

"So, let's get out of the open, find a place to rest."

By the time that she looked up, Rem was kneeling, his back to her. "What are you doing?"

He glanced over at her in the corner of his eye. "Well, you won't get very far walking by yourself if you're that tired. I'll carry you. Solus can scout out the area to make sure that we won't run into any more wolves or creatures or anything. Trust me, he's more than capable of handling things on his own."

Solus rested a hand on his chest and bowed. "Indeed I am. I shall put your fears to rest."

The reaction that Solus presented left her confused—it seemed a bit too formal for someone to behave in that manner towards a close friend, but she supposed that Solus had a different demeanor. Leilana approached Rem and wrapped her arms securely around his neck, allowing herself to be lifted off the ground. Rem tucked his arms under her legs and started after Solus.

They trekked through the forest for over an hour, and still no Kalonia. Solus was keeping up the front, cutting down any enemies in sight before they could sense Rem's budding aura, clearing him to move forward once they were out of their way. The actions impressed Leilana—Rem was skilled, but Solus seemed to be more rounded with a sword and carried out his duty as a servant and guide with ease.

"Geez, kid. You need to eat more; you don't weigh very much," Rem's voice cut through the lengthy silence. Leilana was surprised that he was acknowledging her in such odd fashion, but after some thought, she assumed that this was his way of getting her attention, which was somewhat of a change from starting an argument. There was some form of trust, perhaps.

"I eat enough," she retorted, "I still have plenty of time to grow."

He shrugged his shoulders lightly at the proclamation. "True. I guess you are still a sap. You're, what, twelve and a half? Three quarters?"

"Fourteen," she corrected.

"Seriously, you're only two years younger than me? I thought you were some preteen. Then again, I guess girls are a lot shorter. And you've got room for a growth spurt, maybe even gain a few inches and increase your magic range."

She scoffed under the guise of a breath, her eyes already starting to fall shut. Since when was Rem's body so warm? Or maybe the sun was a little higher up and shining down on them?

"Are you really going to criticize my potential based on my height?"

"Well, height does play a factor in how you fight. If you're tall, it makes you a little more sluggish, but then you can put more power into your swings, and you gain range. And when you're short, you-" He paused when she suddenly rested her head on his shoulder, her hair brushing against his face. He cleared his throat, rolling his eyes. "You, uh... you feeling okay? Moving too fast for you?"

"No," she replied, carrying less energy than she previously had.

"Uh, which one are you saying no to, exactly?"

"The second one," she settled with, nuzzling into his shoulder. The gesture sent quivers down his spine. He was used to carrying people. He had carried soldiers off the battlefield after Linmus's destruction, carried children about the kingdom while playing... but this sensation was different.

He was bringing a single girl to safety. Solus was right, she was going through her own tribulations early on, but so were they in losing their kingdom. Their meeting was coincidental. That was the only relationship between them, and he wasn't going to bring himself too close to her. After all, they had already decided on leaving her behind to develop in a better place.

He leaned back his head, a slight fluctuation of heat rushing down the back of his neck. He stopped short, setting Leilana on the grass before resting a hand on her forehead, confirming his thoughts. "Hey, Solus?" he called, "Solus!"

Solus glanced back from further ahead. "Something wrong?"

"I think we might have a new problem. How close are we to a rest stop?"

"I'm going to check up ahead!" Solus replied, "Can you handle yourself for a few minutes?"

"Who do you think I am?" Once Solus went off on his own, Rem sighed. Leilana met his gaze, retaining her typical stalwart expression, which came to show him that she either felt nothing or cared even less about herself than she seemed to let on. "I'm going to ask again. Are you feeling okay?"

"Fine," she responded with a shrug.

"I don't like being lied to, Leilana, and you're already high on my list of 'what do I feel about you,'" Rem warned, pointing a finger at her. "You have a fever."

She blinked a few times. "No wonder I feel so tired."

His eyes narrowed in discontent, closing his lips shut to avoid any means of disrespect.

"I found a cave up ahead!" Solus proclaimed upon returning to his companions. "We should be able to rest there. What is going on, exactly?"

"Leilana has a fever. I think it's stress related to the pilgrimage, and Paluna, all that jazz, we know the story, why repeat it?" Rem knelt to the girl and allowed her to climb onto his back, struggling to raise the second time, his legs aching from the constant movement. "Where's this cave?"

"It's further ahead-" Solus shook his head. "I can't keep silent. Rem, are you sure that you don't want me to take over? I can carry her for you."

"It's fine, Sol, I can handle things," Rem replied, walking past him before stopping short. Leilana peered over at Solus herself, blinking a few times at the concern reading in his eyes. "Um, lead the way." Solus playfully rolled his eyes.

EIGHT

The gears in Rem's mind creaked and curved in numerous directions as he blankly stared at the cave entrance, his back to Solus and Leilana. His shift was strenuous, but he knew of the risks in the area thanks to Solus's intel. The only sound filling the tight space was Leilana's labored breathing as she laid asleep. Solus hovered over her, pressing a torn rag to the girl's forehead to ensure that it wouldn't slip off in midst of her slumber. The afternoon sky gradually became shrouded in grey, miniscule electrical sparks surging from the veil coating the cave's entrance. Rem grinned in satisfaction at his work; at least he had beaten the rain. He returned to Solus's side once he was certain that his barrier was secured for the night, crossing his legs and shifting his weight to his hands after leaning back.

"So, how's our captive faring?"

Solus kept his lips pursed a moment longer, laying a hand atop the girl's head before stating, "Her fever isn't high, so it's likely that she'll be able to sleep through the night. Not a bad call on stress as the primary cause. Resting will be enough to carry her to Kalonia with us."

"I see." Rem outstretched his arms as he laid back, gazing at the stalagmite-crafted ceiling. "Well, I guess it's not a bad thing. She's not the only one that could use a little break."

"Solus," Leilana suddenly called, leading both men to turn, watching as she rose to a sit.

"No, it's all right," Solus stated, resting his hands on her shoulders. "You don't need to get up."

"Do you know anything about a boy named Lancett?" Solus lost his focus on keeping her from pushing herself, and she brought herself to a full sit, resting a hand on his. "He's... he's around your age... he was with me in Paluna..." She blinked a few times. "O-Or maybe you met a girl, her name's Amiria. She has long hair, it's a unique shade of lavender-"

Solus sighed, grasping her hand now. "I did run into a girl. When I found her, she was preparing to kill you. She had a dagger to your chest, and she was going to stab you in the heart. There is no doubt in my mind that if I hadn't been there to stop her, you wouldn't be here."

Leilana glanced down at his hand to keep herself from tracing his eyes, to uncover some form of a lie beneath the surface of his words. There was no way that Amiria was capable of something so sinister. But he had no reason to lie to her.

It wasn't a dream.

"Lancett went after her," she whispered to herself, a slight grip on her hair, her eyes brimming with tears. He had abandoned her, but she supposed that it wasn't in vain. He was far closer to Amiria than he was to her, and even if he weren't, Kindall had been. Lancett didn't take Amiria's betrayal lightly, and he seemed adamant on the idea that it was his duty to bring her back under consideration of his dead friend. There was some form of morality seeping through the cracks.

Solus was unsure of how to comfort her, the details of her expression lost on him. They didn't know each other well other than a first name basis, and yet, he felt compelled to try and stop the tears before they could fall. He was far used to cheering up someone who cried, having known Remiel's pains, rare as they were to come to the surface. He settled with continuing to hold her hand.

"You should get some more rest," Rem piped up for Solus as if reading his thoughts.

Her tired eyes were already falling shut, and both boys knew that she had been fighting the ordeal for some time, but no pain compared to her lust for information. "But I..."

"It would be better if you didn't reflect on what happened," Solus explained, "It'll make things worse. Please, get some sleep." Leilana wanted to retaliate but found herself resting her head, drifting off moments later. Solus was relieved that she heeded his words, even with newfound information.

Maybe Lancett was safe, and they could take pride in at least one of them being in good hands.

Drip. Drip. Drip. Raindrops hitting the cavern nook became a routine reverberation, and it was driving Solus senseless to merely endure. There wasn't much that he could do in his mundane state. Rem had fallen asleep after finishing his shift, having hardly done so in the last few days, and Leilana was sleeping through the hours with ease, her fever fluctuating in temperature now and again, but time could heal the ailment. That left him with silence from his companions and only the rainfall to keep him company. Even thinking things over seemed to be too far out of his normal variety of distraction.

He wasn't sure of the time outside anymore now that

the sun was eclipsed by the overcast clouds, and he decided to use Leilana's radio to uncover any details that he could; time, location, maybe even information on what was occurring in Linmus, recalling that Leilana mentioned hearing about the terrorist attack on the kingdom through the device.

He flipped through the dial and adjusted the volume and antenna as much as he could, but through the static and warbled noise caused by the rain and the lack of power in range, he didn't have much luck. He narrowed his eyes in disappointment before deciding to try again. A few minutes went by before he could make out even the most insignificant of voices behind the static and he pulled the radio further into the cave, taking a seat at the far end. He turned the dial a bit to the right and the voice of the announcer came to fruition.

"-Statement from Laikros Olen, a former knight of the round detailed the tragic event."

"The night of the fall of Linmus, the assailant reportedly set fire to his own room and lured out servants before decapitating them with a thin blade. Once any witnesses were out of the way, the assailant moved on to every room, scoping out any potential subjects that could forewarn the unsuspecting King and Queen." Solus narrowed his eyes in thought.

"Sol?" Solus glanced over upon hearing Rem's voice, managing a grin. Rem was sitting up, rubbing the residue of sleep from his eyes. "What are you listening to over there?"

"I borrowed Leilana's radio. I was curious to see if there was any news on Linmus." Rem crawled over to Solus and took a seat next to him, lying on his stomach and supporting his head by resting his hands under his chin.

"Anything useful?"

"So far, it doesn't seem any different from rumors around towns we've crossed on the way here. Apparently, they got a statement from Laikros Olen."

"Old-Man Olen, fighting for justice up until the end," Rem mumbled, nodding. "Makes sense that they were able to track him down." Rem could still see the man's face, his clean-shaven face and patched left eye covered by his long white hair most evident in his memory.

Solus was still tuned in to the broadcast, trying to pick through any valuable information, but there was little that seemed to stand out that he hadn't already heard or saw for himself. They had already moved on to infomercials about new drinks and snacks that would be making a debut in the city of Kinsley. The world seemed to love talking about that place in a high light far more than they even considered speaking of Linmus, and that place was the kingdom itself.

"It doesn't seem like Olen has let on to the press about you being alive," Solus stated while turning off the radio. "That's a good sign, at least."

"Let's just hope that it keeps up for a while. The last thing I need is some rumor going around about the walking dead Prince of Linmus."

Solus chuckled. "I admit, that would be a worthy story. I think I'll create that in about five years as a sequel to our current tale."

"Can we get through this one first? And did you just imply something?"

Solus playfully rolled his eyes. "Moving on."

He abruptly paused when a diminutive whimper passed through his ears, his attention rushing to Leilana. The girl was tossing and turning in her sleep, grasping the thin blanket in her hands, sweat rolling down her face. Rem was quick to rush to her side, rubbing her back to ease her. A pale aura was engulfing the girl's body.

"There is more to magic than you can comprehend."

The meticulous affliction of a man rang through Solus's ears, catching him by surprise. His gaze landed on Rem, who didn't seem to acknowledge the new encouragement. Next, he found himself watching the barrier surrounding the entrance—the electrical sparks were becoming less tangible due to the rainfall striking it. Rem's spells weren't skilled enough to hold for extended periods of time just yet.

The Lasette flew open, the brass concealment smashing against the ground, drawing silence. Solus and Rem were both stunned by the involuntary lock-picking as if the grimoire itself had a mind of its own. Leilana moaned, reaching out her hand, her fingers fervently twitching. Solus and Rem glanced at each other before their eyes landed on the grimoire again, uncertain of what the meaning of this situation revolved around. Never had the Lasette opened to them, even by accident. And they were both certain that Leilana had regained little influence over the situation.

One by one, the pages turned until each of the thin papers lining the book was flipping at an increased speed.

"I'm not getting this," Rem admitted. "Why and how is the book acting on its own?"

"I feel the same." Solus rested a hand on the grimoire's open page once it had ceased. There lied the image of a crystalline orb shrouded in a magenta shade. "Maybe it's a sign that there's something we're meant to see."

Rem leaned in closer to him to try and examine the words for himself, his nose scrunching in disappointment. "What am I reading?"

"I'm not certain," Solus replied after looking the scrambled words over a few times.

The letters were twisted in an odd fashion, some upside down, others turned to the right. It left Solus in a conflicted state on how to translate. He had studied several languages over the years in preparation for a time like this, come to comprehend the differences of others based on affliction, patterns, and even phrasing. But never had he stumbled across such a complexity.

"I feel that what lies in this grimoire is a dead language."

Rem raised an eyebrow. "A dead language? What, can only the dead read it?"

Solus stared at him in disbelief before placing his thoughts in a place where he could translate 'Rem speech.' After considering what the boy could have meant, he gave a nod. "I suppose that's not far off, but that wasn't what I was jumping at. A dead language is a combination of words and dialogue not commonly used anymore. It may have understood by olden Arcana and Maesters, but times have changed, and as we evolve, so does everything else, including the way that we address linguistics."

"Oh, wait!" Rem piped up, "I remember symbols on the book cover that looked like this!"

Solus took note of this before marking the page with his thumb to hold it in place, leaving a noticeable indent to leave the book open just enough. He could always correct it later for Leilana's sake—he didn't want to end up getting chewed out for potentially wrecking her grimoire. He examined the cover, squinting his eyes. Rem ran his fingers along the symbols for himself.

"See that? There's twenty-six symbols lined up in an order, just like in our alphabet. I think that may be the book's language!"

Solus recalled Leilana's gestures and phrasing before connecting the words and symbols, giving a small nod. "I understand now. So, she hails from a country that speaks Minsura."

"You do know it then?" Rem asked.

"I've heard of it in passing, but never much aside from the name. Definitely a dead language."

"Does that mean that we've come to a dead end?"

Solus chuckled. "Certainly not. I have an idea. It will be time-consuming, but effective."

He handed the grimoire to Rem, stepping towards the soundly sleeping Leilana. He rested a hand on her forehead and wiped away some of the sweat with his sleeve, finding that her fever had broken. That was a relief; the worst had come to pass. He cautiously stepped away after claiming her tote. He closed his eyes to manipulate himself from thoughts of invasion of privacy until he grazed her journal. He slipped his fingers through the bag a second time to uncover a calligraphy pen, then began to recreate the symbols on the book cover on a sheet of paper, writing the translation of each letter from their own dialect above the symbols. Once he had finished, he returned to his marked page and thoroughly examined the description above the image.

Something about the orb's image stirred up old memories, and Solus wasn't sure why. This was the first time he had seen it, but the energy resonating in the image alone struck a chord with him.

"Now that I think about this, can we translate a dead language with just the book cover's alphabet alone?" Rem inquired. "I don't want to wake Leilana, especially if we end up struggling to try and comprehend all of this."

"We'll do what we can," Solus replied, "even if we have to translate one letter at a time."

"But won't Leilana be mad if she sees us reading the book?"

"The life that we are blessed with is full of hazards, Remiel. That is why we are born and raised in a concrete manner—to live for a mistake or two in the long run."

Rem's eyes narrowed, his expression conflicted. "Are you specifying that you're afraid of her waking up too because you don't want to face her wrath?"

Solus began to scribe the words and translate each individual letter, writing them down in the journal. Quite a few minutes had elapsed before he prudently tore the first lengthy page from the journal, making sure that the crests along the sheet were even and that noticeable tears weren't made. Maybe Leilana wouldn't catch on.

"All right, here we go," Solus began, beholding the paperwork. He had jotted down the words in a hurry, so his handwriting looked a bit scrambled and even jumped out of the lines at times, but what's done was long done.

Rem rested his palms on the ground and leaned back in his spot, knowing full well that he was in for a lecture. "Whatcha got?"

"This picture inside of the grimoire is the Orb of Concord," he read the large letters at the top of the page first, written in a bold face with the pen as thoroughly as he could manage. He inhaled before interpreting the translated passage aloud for Rem.

The Orb of Concord is a collection of crystal shards merged together by the lost souls of Warlords. It is said that those who amass its energy carry the will of these Warlords and are

granted not only the powers that they possessed, but the knowledge cradled in the weight of each generation that they walked in.

Solus paused, glancing at Rem, who was now staring at the ground, taking the passage into consideration. There were questions; Solus could tell that Rem was considering asking them. But neither of them truly knew what answers would lie beyond the grimoire that the girl they met by coincidence wielded with ease. Rem met his gaze as if ushering him to continue granting him the knowledge he craved. And so, he did.

However, this comes at a hefty toll—only those that the Warlords deem well-intentioned can harness their resolve, and such worth is laid only in those that possess magic of the highest pedigree.

"That sounds like Old-Man Olen's speech from when we first arrived in Nilu," Rem noted, recalling the information. Solus knew it well. It was hard to erase the memory of being told the fate of the only home one could ever know. "Why was I born a Bloodlinch?"

Solus paused before setting the paper aside. So, Rem stopped listening to the translations somewhere in between. He wasn't surprised. The young Prince did have his mind wrapped around other places. It didn't matter to him; they could always come back to it at another time.

"Laikros says that a Bloodlinch is considered an illegitimate child of an Arcana or Maester and a human that possesses no magical prowess. But you know the story. Your mother is an Arcana, and your father was a man bred to become King. Their relationship was a damned one, but they had you."

Rem shot his adversary a glare. "Way to chalk up the phrase of 'you shouldn't have been born' to a new level, Solus."

Solus held up his hands in defense. "Pardon me. The words belonged to Laikros, not me. Continuing... he believes that the motivation and supremacy that your mother carried as an Arcana is why you were born with magical energy—it's a rare trait to have from the moment of your first breath."

"Magic isn't that uncommon in Adrylis. Why does it make me any different?"

He folded his hands now, clearing his throat. "Most have their magic thrust upon them at a young age, if at all. It was my duty to make sure that I knew as much about you as possible—it is what my father wanted me to understand. Your magic was always unique. I'm not definite on the consequences of magic yet but being born with the skill would have made you a target when you began showing signs of possessing them. Your parents kept that secret from even you."

"So, they couldn't tell me, but they told you," he said flatly.

"I'm supposed to protect you," Solus reasoned.

Rem pointed a finger at him, his face set in confidence. "You listen here, Solus Brenner. That was your duty but now things are different. Now it's just us. We protect each other." He grabbed the sheet of paper and allowed his eyes to scan over the words for himself.

Solus sighed, knowing that he couldn't accept no for an answer. Rem always did have a sense of justice in his blood, defying the odds and craving battle. Always with a grin when he picked up his sword. "I know that face." Just like now, he was wearing that eager grin, but his eyes were bright with a thoughtful haze. "You're wearing your thinking cap, aren't you?"

"We're gonna need this Orb of Concord if its power has the potential to bring down a colony when used for good intentions. It may be our only chance to take things into our own hands."

He closed the grimoire shut and handed it back to Solus, who walked it over to Leilana's side on the tips of his toes to keep from rousing her from her slumber. She stirred at the movement before returning to sleep. Once he had finished his duty, he reclaimed his seat next to Rem, folding his hands while considering his words.

"Therein lies the problem though, Remiel—nobody knows where to find it. It has been hidden away for more generations than either of us could count back, and I'm certain that others before us have tried to find it and had no luck."

Rem's face held no hesitation, a soft glint in his brown eyes. Solus cringed. Oh no. He knew that look as well. His mind was made up already, wasn't it? The wheels of his mind swerved in every direction. There had to be something that he could break down for him. Anything.

"That shouldn't be an issue," Rem stated. "It may be hidden, but it's not impossible to find. Someone had to have found it to be able to hide it again."

Solus's leg was anxiously bouncing. "We could search around every corner of Adrylis for the rest of our lives and never track it down. And even if we *do* manage to find it, you might not be able to use it. The Warlords of the past might not see you as someone that's worthy enough to use the Orb. You-you do understand that, right? Would you really want to take a risk like that?"

"Hey, think about it. We'll just have to try our best, right?"

"Oh," he elongated the vowel in the simple word for a few seconds before stating, "I suppose."

Rem smirked in satisfaction, holding up a closed fist in a silent victory. "Don't make a big deal out of it, Sol." He wrapped an arm around the man's shoulders, shaking him in the process. "We'll be able to handle anything!"

Solus couldn't help but laugh. "If you say so."

All the while, Leilana was watching over the two, turned on her side to face their backs. They had no idea, and maybe it was for the better for them all that they didn't. The two continued in their banter for some time now that their plans had been laid out onto the floor, and she rolled over onto her left side, returning to sleep.

NINE

"I see that you're feeling better today," Solus called after waking.

Leilana was sitting up in her spot on the floor, the blanket she was provided wrapped around her shoulders. She had hardly acknowledged him, her attention set on the morning sun. The rainwater was a fresh scent, and the aroma was pleasing to her reemerging senses. She wanted to step out but decided in the end that it was better to wait for Solus and Rem. She knew as much about Adrylis as them and being separated could have put them all in danger. Unwise.

The barrier had since fallen, and Solus found it fortunate that no beasts or people had seized them in the middle of the night despite the three of them all being asleep at relatively similar times. He crawled over to her, claiming the empty spot at her side. Still, she didn't turn to him, staring instead at her fingertips clutching the blanket.

"Are you thinking about something?" He wasn't sure if he wanted to intrude on her thoughts, but he didn't want her to be left alone in whatever darkness was plaguing her mind. She stole a glance at him at long last, and Solus noticed a hint of discomfort in her expression.

"Kindall." Solus raised an eyebrow. "He was a friend. Someone that was lost in Paluna." Solus continued to listen, not daring to interrupt her while she spilled the goods. It was important to her, so why hold back any chances? "I keep seeing his face, covered in soot, his lungs caved in until he couldn't breathe anymore..." She was staring at her empty hands again, raising them closer to her face, as if peering through a looking glass that withheld no reflection. "And I held him in my arms until he went." She rested her hands on her lap, an audible slap filling the cave, echoing for a subsequent moment before fading away altogether.

Solus folded his own hands, drawing in a breath as he attempted to address the manner in a non-damaging way or a way that seemed to be too insensitive. Death was always a complicated subject to discuss, but the process of it was forever going to be inevitable. "...Leilana... have you ever seen someone die? Before what happened to Kindall?"

"No," she said softly, "nobody ever got *really* hurt at the school, and no one ever died. They talked much about that topic. They treated it as though-" She swallowed, her eyes beginning to widen. "As though those that die never existed at all, not that they lived and then ceased to exist. That's why they never spoke of Ennis..."

"Ennis?" Solus repeated, "Are you referring to Ennis Erovina, the fallen Warlord?"

"The very one."

That name brought back more memories than one. He took pride in having the chance to know Ennis Erovina, but they had met only once in his short life, just before his pilgrimage came to an end. Solus's own statement towards the rather enigmatic budding Warlord left a mark, but it was shaped in a different light, and now he brought his own words down on himself like a hammer to stone. How times had come to change.

"Don't let your sister down come morning light, when all is said and done," he mumbled.

Leilana raised an eyebrow at the nearly concealed

words. "What's that mean?" Solus returned her expression, no longer masking his smile.

"He and I had the opportunity to meet once. He mentioned a girl, his younger sister. She was someone that he fought for, to make a home with her." He stared at Leilana, noticing the sense of sincerity in the girl's expression. "Leilana, that girl is you, isn't it?"

Her lips upturned into a smile. "It would be ludicrous to compare me to my older brother. I was never as special as he was. I never knew he thought so highly of me, especially when I look at myself. He got to take his pilgrimage after training for only a year. Our Masters called him a prodigy."

Solus cleared his throat, giving a small nod. "I'm sorry about what-"

"You don't need to apologize," she interjected. "As time passes, people expire. it's something that can't be helped, and it's an inevitable aspect of this short existence we are given. Ennis used the time he was given to make a difference and gain a title that would outlive him."

Solus considered her words before piping up, "I heard a rumor about Ennis Erovina long ago. He entered Archbane Castle in Linmus with a premonition of demise—the kingdom's destruction. But the royal family didn't believe him and sent him on his way. That was his quirk; he could foresee certain incidents." He sighed, brushing some hair from his face. "Good gracious, why *didn't* they heed his warning...?"

"In the end, the decision still rested with the royal family. They chose not to follow the will of a Warlord, and they didn't prepare for it. They had their enemies, and they also had their allies. Some people can become too clouded by lies to uncover the truth between those at their side and those with a knife pressed to their back, ordering them to walk forward."

Solus was impressed by her logic, curious about what she would uproot next. She may not have been conditioned to the ways of the world, same as him, but she certainly knew her way around people. Maybe that was why she was chosen for the pilgrimage—she carried herself in a manner that rivaled her brother. They both seemed set on what method they took towards approaching their pilgrimage, but each step could unravel what fate had in play for them. Then again, Solus knew little about what they were meant to do; every pilgrimage differed.

"At the same time," Leilana continued. "How could they have known that things would come to this?" She leaned back in her spot, continuing to gaze at the budding horizon. "There is a lot to consider when stepping into a new day. The future is always changing, and nothing is set in stone. Warlords can provide readings and offer a small sense of what is going to occur down the line for you." She cleared her throat, stealing a glance at Solus, who grinned in response. "That is something that I've come to understand after having a tarot card reading, at least."

"I think that it is good progress," he stated, "Even a small hint can turn the tides."

"Why are you two being noisy so early in the morning...?" Rem whined right before a stone hit Solus in the back of the head. He reached up a hand to rub the aching spot, glaring at his friend. "Trying to sleep here." Rem rolled onto his side and pulled the blanket over his head.

"Good grief, he can be such a pain," he mumbled.

"That was a bit rude. Does he do that often?"

"Rem has a habit of being moody when woken up. So

yes, this isn't uncommon for him. I'm choosing not to retaliate due to a rather unfortunate time period. I would be wrong if I found no sympathy in the manner."

"Terrible fate or not, that still doesn't give him much right to behave like that. The two of you are friends, and you're doing your best to help one another."

"Pay it no mind," Solus replied, his irritated expression wiping away into a satisfied grin.

"All right. I guess I'll just take your word for it."

"Grand choice. Now that we've established that, what do you say that I look around for breakfast, and you can remain here with Rem while I am away?"

"Breakfast?" Now that he mentioned it, Leilana's stomach was growling audibly. The action made Solus laugh uncontrollably, and he wasn't considering Rem's sleeping anymore.

She buried herself under the blanket, hearing him ask, "I'm to take this as a yes?" She hadn't stomached much since the night that Paluna was incinerated, and even then, it wasn't much aside from herbs and fruits. Delicious, but she was well accustomed to the taste after fueling on health-quality meals at the academy for her body and spirit. That alone wasn't filling for two nights.

"Breakfast would be nice."

Solus went on his way, and Leilana remained in her spot, watching him climb from the height of the cavern's entrance, landing on the grass. He turned back to her after he tucked some loose strands of hair out of his face. "Try to stay out of sight. We wouldn't want to have our location revealed, correct?"

"Don't worry, I can handle a little turmoil," she proclaimed. "Find something good out there!" He held up his index finger and thumb to his forehead as a salute before disappearing into the trees.

After an assortment of berries and venison came about for a suitable breakfast, the three set off for Kalonia. Leilana's mouth was continuing to water, the scent of the freshly slaughtered deer still lodged into her nose, cooked to a superb texture by her own hands. Rem had cut through the entrails without so much as a flinch, blood splattering about the cavern walls. The sight was gruesome, but the result was enough to wipe the idea of a helpless animal suffering away, if only for a moment.

"Some virtuous circle of life," Rem dubbed it. His tone was so nonchalant she couldn't help but wonder if he was trying to sway her from her worries or if he was keeping her from talking too much. With him, it was unclear what he wanted from her anymore, and she was certain that if Solus wasn't a defining factor in Rem's sense, then she wouldn't have gotten a word out of him about some of the statements that he threw at her.

"Look at that!" Rem suddenly exclaimed, extending a finger forward. Beyond the trees, shades of white had blossomed through. Solus elongated his neck to observe the buildings peeking through, holding up an arm to shield his eyes from the blazing sun.

"Kalonia," Leilana observed. "That must be it."

Rem brushed past the bushes lining the trail, stumbling over loose branches. He was quick to dive back into the shrubs after hearing a yelp from an unsuspecting by-passer, lowering his hand towards Rem and Leilana to assure that they crouch as well, not wanting to frighten anyone else in their way. Solus couldn't help but glare at him, unsure of what the young Prince was planning or considering. Without warning, he grabbed Rem by the arm and dragged him out into the open despite his protests. Leilana sighed before following the two.

Their first steps on the new ground were met with genuine amazement, and Rem couldn't avert his attention from the sight. The bleached buildings in Kalonia stretched towards the clouds, reminiscent of the castle in Linmus he had come to know and reside in for years. There were citizens roaming the checkered streets, rushing for the marketplace and bartering for their goods. Thankfully, there seemed to be plenty of merchants minding their booths and a variety of food and drink to go around. The area wasn't too crowded from the chaos.

Rem was the first to go rushing through the city after regaining his momentum, his smile bright at the view of all the people, the soldiers that were guarding the streets to keep people in line, and the shrines that rivaled palaces off in the distance. Kalonia was elegant to observe from a distance and a wonder from within. He hadn't gotten to visit Paluna, but now he knew that there were far more prosperous places that he was meant to explore. This was just the beginning.

Solus's expression softened as he watched the young Prince dash through the area, his mind away from the knowledge of Linmus. It was refreshing to witness, even if it was temporary. A brief respite was better than an endless spew of agony.

"Solus," Leilana began, watching over Rem as well. Solus smiled, peering at her in the corner of his eye. She folded her arms behind her back, clearing her throat. "I wish you both the best."

"You're awfully forward. Taking your leave?"

"Rem did seem pretty clear that he wanted us to part ways once we reached Kalonia. I'm planning to stay for the night and do a little research."

"I wanted to ask—what does your pilgrimage revolve around?" Leilana wondered if the students could discuss the manner of their pilgrimage with the others. She supposed that Hinju wasn't against it. Otherwise, many of those chosen to claim a totem would be outright confused and maybe a little upset if they went through the ordeal with no knowledge.

"I'm gathering totems," she began, "We're supposed to be discovering them in the hearts of other people from what I read in my journal. But I'm not entirely sure how to find them. There are so many different interpretations of what to look for that it's hard to pinpoint a single trait. Most people that I've encountered don't seem to have a single dominant trait about themselves."

"Well, that adds to the fun if you ask me," Solus told her, "It presents a challenge in choosing what quality is more domineering for someone. And it allows you to gain a new perspective on what that person is like." He sighed. "Are you sure that you want to endure that trial on your own? You might not be able to find Lancett out there, and even if you do, he might be caught up in trying to find Amiria."

"I'll handle it." Solus was about to interject, not sure how to address her decision before she took a step back, her right hand wrapped around her left wrist, unable to turn from him. "Don't worry about me. I should be fine on my own for a little while."

Solus crossed his arms. "I don't have doubt in your abilities. You have a multitude of colors in your soul like us all, fervently drifting through any trial presented to you. They reflect like a prism. It's peculiar to consider, but I think it's befitting of you."

His wording seemed a bit strange. He was speaking highly of her despite the little knowledge of one another that they held. From what she was processing, he seemed to be implementing that she has a lot of prowess and potential and that what strength she did possess would carry her through her pilgrimage. Or, so it seemed. Maybe not? Wait. Was he flirting with her? Was this what it felt like?

Solus grinned, amused by her clear confusion. Maybe she didn't understand his thought process. She was still naïve after all, and even taking that into consideration, there was much she needed to learn. "Did you want to say anything to Rem before you leave?"

Leilana glanced over at Rem. He was further ahead, starting up a conversation with one of the merchants, looking over pieces of armor and weapons, currently holding a freshly polished blade in his hands. She wasn't sure of the context, but she couldn't deny he was in better spirits. He was laughing and seemed to be confident. He swung the sword in his hands and showed off his skills, all while remaining subtle about who he was. No one caught on.

He probably wasn't going to remain that way if she was burdening him, sad as it was.

"No. It's all right," she told him.

As she spoke, she was stepping back, clenching her small hand into a tight fist, hidden behind her back to keep from worrying Solus. Their time together had been so scarce—only a day or two since they first met, but the truth was illuminating in her sight faster than she could process it. She hadn't wanted to leave. She wanted to know them both better, and to be strong enough to fight at their side. She wanted to voice her opinions to them, and to help them on their journey, somehow.

"Just tell him that I said it was nice to meet him." Without another word, Leilana turned on her back heel and ran off into the crowds of people, slightly shoving through them to keep from looking back. Solus extended a hand towards Leilana as she ran, wanting to find a way to convince her otherwise, but she was just out of his reach.

She forced herself not to heed Solus's calls to her. If she had acknowledged him, even for a split second turned to look up at him, she felt as though she wouldn't be able to uphold Rem's wishes. Solus would want her there. And she'd find a way to stay, to convince Rem that she could be of use. And the last thing that she desired was to burden him by practically pleading for a chance because it meant that she would be far from considerate about his feelings.

Solus dropped his hand, watching Leilana vanish into the crowd. He had to admit, he was almost unhappy to see her go. They had barely gotten to know each other, and though he was certain that she would be safe in this city, he couldn't help being concerned. Kalonia was vast, and she knew little of the environment. He and Rem were at least used to big cities or buildings after their life spent in Linmus, but she had been condemned to her school, training herself endlessly. There was so much for her to explore during this pilgrimage, and now he felt a little disheartened that he wouldn't be at her side.

He tugged on one of his front bangs, staring at the loose strands that fell to the ground from the gesture. "I suppose even a day spending time with someone holds more meaning than one would expect."

"Took you long enough to get here," Rem proclaimed after Solus returned to him, setting down the sword he was still debating on purchasing from the merchant.

Solus eyed the man at the booth, who was disappointed that Rem wasn't spending money yet. Sensing his distress, Solus decided to toss him some of the Nyte coins in his pocket, counting out the amount of ninety, just enough for the sword. The merchant grinned ear-to-ear, rubbing his grubby hands on the coins before gesturing to the sword. Solus almost shook his head at the essence of greed while grabbing the sword. He supposed it would suffice to have a worthy souvenir and still manage find a place to rest their heads for the night.

"Where's your little buddy?"

"She already left," Solus told him, gaze locked on the blade in his grasp, examining the polished metal. It was a bit dull, but it was in better condition than Rem's sword was. Changes could be made. "Oh, and she says that it was nice to meet you."

Rem blinked a few times. "Did she really? Oh, uh... I didn't think that she would."

"I would have felt it better that she didn't, but she insisted that she continue on her own."

"Oh, I get it. She didn't want to break a vow." Solus frowned at the conclusion. "Oh, come on, it's not like she's incapable of taking care of herself. Besides, we don't know anything about her aside from the fact that she's an Arcana. No reason to get attached."

"Your mother was an Arcana, isn't that enough reason for you to-?"

"That doesn't mean that every one of them is the same."

Rem traveled ahead of Solus, who hurriedly followed, not wanting to lose him in the chaos of the city, asking after him on where he was going. "I'm tired and I'm ready to call it a day. It'll be nice to be able to rest in a real bed after being in caves and forests for days on end."

Solus sighed. There he goes again with the Prince complex.

TEN

Leilana took a seat inside of what appeared to be a café, the scent of cocoa beans and freshly brewed tea enclosing the tiny space. She rested on the table and blocked out the sunlight by wrapping her arms around her exposed head. She didn't acknowledge the waiter that approached her table and asked if there was anything that she needed. She wasn't hungry or thirsty; she just wanted to think and be left alone, to try and forget that she had met Solus and Rem.

Like that was possible. They had saved her life. How do you forget something like that?

"How childish," she mumbled to herself before searching through her bag, pulling out one of her vast assortment of notebooks, jotting down some words among the dotted lines.

Breach the path of understanding.

She stared at the words for what felt like an eternity, the time elapsing so quickly that upon being asked by the waiter again if she needed assistance, the sun was setting. How many hours had gone by since she arrived in Kalonia? Were Solus and Rem safe?

...Wait, she wasn't supposed to be thinking about them.

The waiter looked anxious, so Leilana finally gave him an answer after looking over the menu, "I'll just take some chamomile tea." The waiter gave her a grin before scampering off. Leilana playfully rolled her eyes. Ah, ambition.

Analyzing the passages in her notebook, she recalled the

aura spiraling around Rem's body while they were in the forest and the afflicted tone that surged through her fragile mind. The spirits of the Warlords were crying, bestowing her with the opportunity to seize a totem. She didn't have to guess where those desires stemmed from, but now there was more to consider.

Was Rem a key in her pilgrimage?

"Your tea, ma'am," the waiter chimed, offering up a steaming mug. "It's a little hot, but I hope it's to your liking." Leilana gave a nod of approval before the man took his leave again. She continued her work, occasionally taking sips of the tea.

She needed to 'understand' Rem if his morality was going to be restored and she could claim the totem he possessed, whatever it was. He was a person that carried magical prowess, evident by his healing abilities. In hindsight, he was suffering further by using his magic to help others above himself. But that was nothing more than an assumption. She didn't know much about him, and now that they were on uneven terms, she couldn't get closer.

"Oh, this is hopeless," she scoffed, flipping to the next page in the notebook.

She paused, noticing thin edges of the open page. She ran her fingers along the torn fragments, her eyes narrowing in confusion. Strange. Someone ripped out one of the sheets, and it hadn't been her—she always kept her notes intact. She didn't hesitate to reach for the Lasette, thrusting out a hand forward in a swift motion, the book snapping open and the pages rushing along before stopping on a slightly crumbled and folded page.

She slammed her hands on the table, rattling the lukewarm teacup. Someone had been pilfering for information. Her spontaneous bout of irritation earned her misperception and astonishment, and she sneered at the onlookers. This was far from anyone else's business. They turned away faster than she could process. Only certain people, usually those susceptible to Minsuran blood could open and transcribe the pages of the Lasette. And she knew no others that were alive and kicking.

She read over the marked passage. The Orb of Concord, forged by Warlords of Old, a weapon that was near unascertainable. It remained undiscovered since the early civilization after the Warlords became a group chosen by others of their kind directly. No one was worthy of their power, and those that were had no idea where to search. And so, the Orb of Concord was hidden away. She knew well of the winded tale passed into her hands. The words were empty, the language lifeless.

Scanning the pages of the grimoire, Leilana was realizing that there were two people that, in theory, gained access.

Rem and Solus. How could they have unlocked the book and translated the text?

What they were planning to do with the information was obvious: they were going to look for the Orb of Concord. They had good intentions, a solid aspect of manipulating the Orb's power. But there was more they had yet to understand about the Orb of Concord's purpose, and how its power affected those chosen to wield it.

"Good grief," she mumbled, gathering her paperwork and stuffing it into her bag.

How much had they read? And how much did they truly comprehend their findings? If this was their new goal, then she was going to have to put her foot down.

Around dusk, Rem was people-watching from a local inn's rooftop, his expression contemplative as the wind brushed hair into his face. He didn't bother to move the loose strands. The guards securing the rooftop to monitor suspicious activity left him alone while he gathered his thoughts. Maybe he didn't seem the type to jump—apparently, a lot of people were doing that recently. He thought of Solus sleeping a few floors down, unaware of where he was. Then again, even he needed space. The two of them were going through the ringer, and the worst had yet to come.

Sudden shuffling reached him, and he drew his sword, stepping from the edge when a slight yelp pierced his hearing. A bulky green stalk emerged centimeters from the rooftop. A girl leaped off, hitting the ground knees first. His lips parted, his eyebrows furrowing, the entire ordeal baffling. He wasn't even sure if he was supposed to help the girl. Once the plant shrunk, he considered that the plant was born of magic and could be contained.

He faced the girl, her long violet hair tied into a ponytail with a thin red ribbon, her blue eyes glistening under the light of the fading sun. Her lips curved into a shy smile when she met his gaze. Rem stepped closer, raising an eyebrow. "Are you an Arcana?"

"I am," she replied, jumping to a stand, dusting off her ruffled black skirt, adjusting the hem of her long-sleeved navy-blue dress shirt. She folded her hands in front of her, feeling herself beginning to break into a sweat. "I'm sorry to disturb you. I just needed a place to rest. I've run out of money, and since no one else seemed to be around, I thought..." Her voice softened, and he leaned in more to grasp her words. "W-Well, I thought I could try sneaking in. I guess that didn't work out, huh? I'm sorry."

Rem grabbed her arm as she tried to leave. "I have a question for you." She didn't face him a second time, lowering her arm, but refusing to fight out of his grasp. "Is your name Amiria?" Silence. Rem's eyes narrowed. "I didn't see you, but I remember hearing about you."

"You were with that boy in Paluna," she concluded. "The one with the long hair."

"Why did you destroy Paluna?"

She swallowed, slipping her arm free from him only to rest her hand on her left wrist. "I don't think I should explain myself to a stranger."

"I'm not asking for myself," Rem began, "I'm asking for a friend of yours."

"Friend?" she repeated. "Which friend?"

Rem paused. He recalled that Leilana was still on bad terms with the girl, and the last thing that he needed was for Amiria to know that they were connected in any shape or form. He couldn't allow her to be put in danger again. He needed to be cautious. "Someone who really wants to speak to you." The two never broke their nearly identical, incriminating gazes. "I never imagined that I would find you first."

"Who are you?" Amiria asked, brushing away some of the wind-swept strands of her violet hair. "How can you sit back and chat up some girl you've never met?"

"My name is Rem. I'm, well..." He carefully thought over his words, and Amiria continued to stare at him with a raised eyebrow, unsure of how to react to his sudden bout of silence. He forced a grin. "I suppose you can call me a wayward warrior."

"A wayward warrior," she repeated. "Sounds charming. Much more entertaining in hindsight than acting as an Arcana."

"I wouldn't say that," he replied, "There are many mages that seem to be in high spirits because they get to travel. I thought that you were one too."

Amiria sighed. "I used to be. But not anymore. A lot has happened. But I'm sure that your friend has mentioned more than enough to you."

Rem's eyes met the sky, the tangerine shade overpowering the clouds, blanketing the city in a settling warmth. He rested a hand on the stone edge, overlooking the people below. They all seemed to be rushing home, and despite the scenery, they looked the opposite of tranquil underneath the sunset. "There's a lot that I've heard, but I only have one question."

"What is it?"

"Did you kill him?"

"I don't know," she stammered. "I started the fire in the shrine. Kindall pushed me out and then went to help Leilana and Lancett, and then he..." Her voice trailed off.

"Amiria." She jumped, gripping to the hem of her shirt. "What *really* happened in Paluna? I've spent a few minutes with you, and from what I see, you're quiet, and you're curious." He crossed his arms, keeping his back to the younger girl while concentrating on his turn of phrase. "I don't get the sense that you're a bad person. What caused you to snap?"

She was taken aback by the near interrogating tone. This was the second time that he had tried to force the information out of her, but it didn't seem to be borderline incriminating like before. Unlike his ally and Leilana, she was putting herself in a better position to be heard and truly understood, if she allowed it. She could sense his pain. Rem wasn't one to develop the drive to speak about his feelings openly, at least not with just anyone that he encountered. That wasn't how trust worked, and they both knew it. He had taken a realistic approach, a sporadic, distorted trait under the instincts of optimism, pessimism, and misunderstanding. Leilana was the same; she could see the two of them getting along in a strange manner due to how similar their logic was.

"I learned information about the Warlords," she started, stepping towards the edge of the rooftop to stand at his side. "I saw the pillar of Anise Kinsley carved by the people of Paluna—they detailed her right down to the tears streaking the copper stone, holding her axe in preparation for battle. I'm certain that there is something that traumatized her and made her not want to fight anymore. But as a Warlord, protection, and valor are traits that cannot be ignored."

"I never heard many stories about Anise Kinsley," Rem admitted, "But it was said that she sought a way out and perished for it. Some say that she was cursed, others that she took her own life to free her blood from the world."

"That's what I've heard too. Those that carry their will are condemned to eternal suffrage. That is what I've come to realize after reading over documents from Paluna's former Warlord."

Rem thought of his mother. He knew little about her history as an Arcana, her subjects hardly speaking on the manner. Arcana and Maesters were descendants of Warlords, and direct descendants of the original lineage were infrequent. Every Warlord held a different purpose, but what remained was their determination to live and learn. To hear Amiria state evidence on their suffrage from another Warlord was almost unfathomable.

Maybe becoming an Arcana or Maester meant becoming stagnant. And the ability to wield magic was the trade-off for self-loss.

"Magic comes with a hell of a price, doesn't it?" he mumbled.

"I've told you what you needed to know," Amiria stated, pushing herself from the edge. Rem returned his gaze to her, raising an eyebrow. She addressed his confusion, stating, "I'm still looking to find a place to lay my head, and I'd like to do so before it gets too late."

"O-Oh. I guess that's true."

Amiria giggled, folding her arms behind her back. It seemed like a typical response, but that was far from a bad thing. "It was a pleasure speaking with you. This is the first time that I felt like someone was absorbing my words. Maybe one day, we'll be able to meet again on better terms." Rem watched silently as she left, unsure of what to make of this strange girl.

Was Amiria really an enemy? Did she still seem the type to work against them? Sure, she had a breaking point after discovering that everything she worked for was destined to unravel, but what person wouldn't feel a little afraid?

This was all so confusing.

Rem groaned, gripping his hair. "I can't believe I'm sympathizing with her."

No. He couldn't. It was wrong to bask her in light; it was insane to even consider it. No matter what she felt, her actions were inexcusable. She burned down a town because of the information they carried. She indirectly caused the death of a friend. She left so much mystery behind her relationship with Leilana. Nobody was angry. That was a fact, but facts didn't adjust the overwhelming truth that her overreaction had cost innocent people their lives.

Solus would be disappointed in him if he was admitting her judgments were correct. He rested his hand on his forehead, turning to meet with the crowds of people lingering below. They seemed to be getting more frantic each passing second, and it was off-putting.

"Maybe I should just go to bed." He slapped the edge with his palm before leaving the rooftop, climbing down the three flights of stairs back to his room.

Leilana popped a squat at one of the three local inns, sinking in front of the table. She had half a mind to put her feet up and enjoy the moment, but it was considered rude. She had already chewed out the bellboy and the host while asking if they could lead her to the room where Rem and Solus were. Of course, they didn't provide personal information, rooms included. Of course, they 'couldn't due to hotel rules and regulations,' those savage fools. Didn't they understand how important this situation was?

Wait, no, how could they? They were too caught up in their own work to even consider anyone else's problems, but that was adulthood at its finest. Survival of the damn fittest.

Maybe they didn't want her around because of her torn clothes. But she wasn't going to explain to them why she was walking around as a homeless girl striving to be an Arcana, not when she was already further along than most. She figured that once she came into some money, she'd have to invest in a change of wardrobe.

After catching her breath in the lobby and fighting against management, she set off for the next one in her path, watching the sunset over Kalonia. People were shoving past, and a pair of broad shoulders colliding against her backside in a haste was enough to send her to the ground, dropping her grimoire in front of her. She sighed, wincing at the sight of her scraped knee before grabbing her treasured weapon, not wanting it out of her sight again.

What was up with everyone? Was it some night rush, and now they were getting antsy?

She rose to a stand, blood gushing down her ripped tights, under siege of completely tearing. She broke through the crowd, her lungs beginning to tighten under the pressure of bodies condensing together while speedily rushing through the tiny streets. As she propelled forward, her shoulder brushed along the miniscule build of another, violet hair coming into view. Her eyes widened and both girls whirled around to face each other.

The silence was impending, and their expressions mirrored one another. Shock. Confusion. And then a sense of heightened strain swiftly followed by lingering annoyance. There wasn't an ounce of movement out of place in the elapsing seconds; it was as if the people encircling them no longer existed.

"Amiria," Leilana's voice cut through the tension. "I hoped that I would see you again."

"I was actually thinking the same thing. We ended our last meeting on bad terms. I was hoping that we could try and talk it over."

"There isn't much to discuss unless you're willing to comprehend your mistakes."

"I have no regrets about what I have done," Amiria retorted. "Master Kosmin enforced the path to madness by giving us a reading, nonchalant while watching us writhe over new knowledge, unfeeling and unsympathetic." Leilana opened her mouth to retort, but Amiria kept talking, "Master Hinju sent us packing, and he did it with a smile, claiming that he was giving us the chance to travel and learn about other people, but he didn't think that we would be learning about our ancestors in the process."

"Amiria," she hissed. "Stop it. You're sounding delusional." Amiria rested a hand over her tote, her fingers lacing around her flute. She knew it. She knew that talking to Leilana would do nothing for her. She never understood anything or anyone, and she didn't try to. How was she to grasp her words?

"How can I be deluded by something right in front of me?! I held the words of the dead in my hands, of your own brother, a Warlord! I could taste their suffrage! How am I supposed to feel about it all?! Hell, what do you even know about his fate?" Leilana was surprised. Amiria didn't seem the type to curse, even under extreme pressure. "What do you believe anymore?"

"My opinion hasn't changed," Leilana replied. "I believe that there is more to the Warlords than shielding their thoughts. Ennis made mistakes. He knew the risks."

The sunset shifted to night.

"We can be different!" Amiria stared at Leilana as she continued speaking. "We can defy the odds, and we don't have to fear losing ourselves just because we're on a journey to discover others!" Amiria was shaking her head, unable to believe a single word, but the girl pressed on with her attempts of persuasion. "Master Hinju did, and I'm certain that Master Kosmin would have done the same!"

A low growl surfaced from the shadows, taking both girls by surprise. They hadn't noticed it, but the streets were almost absent of people now. Those that remained were scrambling to buildings, locking up their doors and shops. Leilana grasped the Lasette in her arms, her eyes darting in every direction. Amiria glanced at her flute, her own eyes tracing over the empty streets.

Where had that come from? What even made the sound?

ELEVEN

"Don't you think it's weird that everyone suddenly started crowding the inn?" Solus asked. "It seems like a hassle, trying to pin people into rooms, and it's relatively noisy downstairs."

Rem rolled over in his bed, yawning. It wasn't uncommon that Solus started talking aloud when he felt concerned. "If anyone is being noisy right now, it's you."

"I'm sorry. I'm just worried."

After a few minutes of listening to Solus's rambling, Rem sat up, rubbing his eyes. There was no way he was going to be able to relax. "Why are you even awake?"

"Commotion downstairs, didn't you hear it?"

"No," Rem groaned. "I was dead asleep."

Solus gazed out of the window. The streets were desolate, a far cry from how bustling and energetic they were only a few hours ago. It was as if ghosts had plagued the city and thrust everyone into a panic. They weren't from Kalonia; there were a few people in the city that weren't used to the customs. One of them was Leilana. What if she was still on the streets somewhere?

It couldn't hurt to check... could it?

"I'm going outside."

"W-Wait, what?" Rem shot to his feet as Solus exited the room, grabbing his room key from the nightstand and rushing after his companion. "Sol! Wait up!" He sped up his steps and grabbed Solus by the arm. "Hey! Where are you even planning to go?"

"I want to know why everyone seems to be hiding from the nightfall. It seems too strange that no one is outside. And if there's peril, I want to make sure that Leilana is safe."

"But she isn't even your problem anymore."

"I know. But that doesn't mean that I don't value her friendship." He grinned. "Don't you feel a little worried about her? She seemed very concerned about your well-being."

Rem could feel sweat dripping down the back of his neck. Oh, great. He was pulling this card from his stack again. Every time that Solus tried to guilt-trip him, he achieved it with a big smile on his face, which only added to the effects of the ordeal. It almost never failed; how could it when he had such a charming expression to tie in with his persuasive words? He couldn't go against it no matter how much he willed himself, and it pained him. How the hell was he supposed to lie to his face and say that he didn't care about Leilana, knowing full well that he did?

Rem was bouncing in his spot, groaning. "Fine, we'll go find her. But that doesn't mean that I want her around. I still don't trust her. And I'm not sure how you trust her. But you know what? Maybe she'll prove worthy. I mean, she's the only one with the knowledge we-" Solus was already walking ahead, and Rem jumped back a step. "H-Hey! You're already leaving?!"

"No time to talk anymore, Remiel, we must make haste."

"Solus!" Rem hissed. "At least let me finish my sentences before you go running off!"

A fierce roar shattered the silence, the ground vibrating under their feet. Leilana and Amiria were both trembling, even grasping one another's hands to ease the tension building around them, though neither of them was willing to admit it. Amiria swallowed, and Leilana stroked the girl's index finger with her thumb to coax her out of her stupor. Now they understood why everyone ran away before the shade hit. Leilana channeled her magic, the Lasette lifting into the air. Amiria put the flute up to her lips, a shrill note ringing from the instrument out of fear alone. The noise was enough to rouse the beast further, its sharp fangs bulging forward as it snarled and stepped further into view.

The street lights did little to mask the ethereal creature. When it emerged, it was standing upright on its hind legs, carrying a spiked club in its left hand. The horns atop its head stretched down the middle of its back, black fur coating its broad shoulders and legs. Leilana chewed on her bottom lip, rushing through the pages of the Lasette, tracing over the words hovering in her sight. Many times, she had jumped through these pages, studied the lore of the mystical creatures lurking through Adrylis. But never had she imagined that she could encounter a Dirionus type.

Dirionus, beings of high stature and spiritual energy fabled to harness powers recognized by the Warlords themselves, acting as familiars. But they were supposed to be peaceful martyrs to their designated lands. If that were the case, why was this one cloaked in shadow?

"What are we supposed to do?" Amiria whispered to Leilana, taking a step towards her.

"Fight," Leilana said simply. "Otherwise we'll be obliterated, and this city is going to keep being threatened."

"We can't take it down by ourselves," Amiria retorted. "We aren't experienced enough!"

"We have to do this *because* we're Arcana!" Leilana hissed, "This is the fate that we have been given! We are born to protect others! Who are we to abandon it?" She turned to the Dirionus-bred creature again and thrust out a hand, a gust of wind propelling forward. The Dirionus thrust the club into the ground and gripped to the handle, keeping itself secure in its place. "Even if you don't believe in the Warlords, we must think of the people! They run and hide because of this monster terrorizing them! Who are we to turn our backs on them?"

Amiria's eyes were darting between Leilana and the Dirionus. With a sigh, she stood at the girl's side, playing a few notes on her flute. A sudden void veil of protection cast over Leilana. Leilana followed the wind strike with several bursts of electricity raining from the sky, which seemed to do little damage towards their opponent. It seemed to almost absorb the power, its club nulling the effects. Maybe it had channeled its energy long ago. Leilana switched to ice, but the Dirionus timed her movements, dodging the attack. Once Leilana's spell had worn out, it propelled forward, thrusting its club into the ground, kicking up some of the pavement, throwing Leilana off balance and knocking Amiria out of the line of fire altogether. The Dirionus hovered over Leilana, club grasped in both hands.

Leilana let out a sharp gasp, planting her feet on the wrecked pavement, jumping out of the way of the strike, the wind rushing past her ears. She had barely heard the club slam into the ground, cratering the path.

Amiria seized the opportunity to stun the beast,

inhaling deeply before unleashing a sonic wave from the bottom of her throat. The Dirionus roared in retaliation, covering its ears, dropping the spiked club in the process. Leilana held up a hand, the Lasette thrusting the ephemeral limbs from within its pages, grabbing the weapon from the ground. She mimicked the stance that the beast had taken before swinging it, the hands effectively hitting the Dirionus, knocking it into one of the nearby buildings.

Amiria stumbled forward, her vision hazing, but she shook her head to clear any signs of vulnerability and stood her ground as the Dirionus regained itself. It locked its gaze on Leilana, who seemed to be recharging her power into the Lasette. It sped towards her, cutting through the spectral hands she had conjured. Amiria belted out another sonic wave, channeling more force into the action, the pavement beginning to thrust upward, knocking the Dirionus off its feet. Leilana flexed her fingers and sent a whirlwind of flames spiraling towards the beast. The combined tactic opened a crater under the beast, and it fell.

Amiria and Leilana approached the crater and peered down before looking at one another, Amiria sheepishly grinning while Leilana retained a confident expression. Their hopes were dashed when a snarl beset their ears and the Dirionus leaped from the crater, striking them simultaneously with the club and knocking them across the battlefield. The Lasette hit the ground with a thud, and the flute clanked against one of the buildings, remaining intact. Amiria gaped at the blood covering her chest, emerging from her ripped dress; she could barely lift her head, already winded from the excess magic usage. She clenched her fist and slammed it against the concrete. Leilana pressed her hands to the ground and pushed herself to a sit, the side of her face caked with the sticky substance. She scoffed, trying to wipe some to clear her right eye.

The Dirionus drifted over the two, holding up the club above them, prepared to strike them down swiftly and as painlessly as possible. Leilana swallowed, never taking her gaze from the beast, a certain quality opening her mind further. Now that she could look it in the face, she saw that its eyes were full of remorse, even if its actions spoke otherwise. Dirionus weren't meant to be malicious, only helpful. And that resided deep within. Which meant that this wasn't its doing, not fully.

"Stop," she whispered with as much energy as she could manage, though she knew that the words were futile for it to comprehend. "You can still make a change..."

Amiria shot to a sit, panting as she looked over at the girl, unsure of what her plans were. Was she trying to talk it down? It was too far gone already. Why put in the extra effort?

The Dirionus thrust down its club.

Leilana shut down and forced herself not to look up at the beast when she listened to the wind move at the swift motion. She felt a tug, but no impact came. She slowly opened her eyes, looking to her left and spotted Solus holding Amiria in his arms, both looking just past her. Leilana followed their line of sight, appalled by what she saw next.

Rem was holding up his sword, blocking the club with one hand, the other emanating a crimson glow. Basked within the aura, she noticed the remnants of a manifested claw. Rem's expression was fierce and easily rivaled the Dirionus.

"R-Rem... you came back..."

"Go," he told her, his voice almost guttural as he gave

the order. Leilana didn't hesitate to obey him, uncertain of what he was planning to do. Somehow, he seemed far different from the Rem that she had come to know. She almost collapsed while making her way to Solus but held steady. Solus stood, carrying Amiria, the girl fighting consciousness as she glanced over at Rem.

"Are you going to be okay?" Solus called, taking a step forward.

"Don't come!" Rem roared, pushing the Dirionus out of the way with his sword, taking Solus by surprise. "Keep them safe—that is your duty!"

Solus gave a small nod, looking to Leilana. "Let's go." Leilana stole a glance at Rem, watching as he held up his left hand and pushed back the club a second time, keeping a steady grip on his sword. "Leilana!" She snapped out of it before following Solus.

"What's the matter with him?" she asked, coughing afterward to clear her dry throat.

"I'm not certain," Solus told her, "I've never seen him behave this way. We saw what was going on from inside, and when Rem noticed the danger, he just... snapped."

"We'll have to put faith in him."

Rem smirked, holding out his glorified hand in a taunting manner. "Come on, you. Tell me about yourself." He kept striking the club with his hand, listening to the wood splinter, ignoring the timber shards lodging into his fingers. The blood was rushing to his head. The idea of killing this beast, one who had sent Kalonia into a panic, who harmed someone that his best friend valued, amused him. No matter how much he attacked, he couldn't leap into the mind of this Dirionus.

Maybe it *was* too lost in the darkness to regain itself. How disappointing.

Rem thrust back his left hand before slinging it into the Dirionus's chest, ripping out its heart and crushing it, letting it crumble away. The beast let out a piercing cry, its body disintegrating into dust over the course of a few seconds, drifting away with the wind. Its club fell to the ground. Rem sighed, dissipating the aura over his hand by clenching his fist before dropping to his knees.

He overlooked the destroyed roads. All of this broken rubble storming the once crowded streets. The people of Kalonia were in terror, and a grim outlook on the future of Adrylis was rising to fruition because of one creature's rampage. If one Dirionus could be corrupted by some unknown force, how many more could have met the same fate?

The ice of a blade reached his throat, and Rem's breath hitched. "Ah, young Prince. I never expected to run into you here."

Before Rem could manage any form of retaliation, a crimson aura spiraled about his body, clasping around his throat, lifting him off the ground. His lungs were caving, and he couldn't help kicking his legs to pry himself from the spell's siege to no avail. As the seconds elapsed, he found himself slipping into unconsciousness. No concern left in his opponent to eliminate him on the spot, he was dropped to the ground. Rem sharply inhaled and grasped his neck, coughing before facing his attacker.

His long silver hair was tied into a ponytail that reached the middle of his back, his face concealed by a white and russet-shaded mask that resembled the beak of an eagle. Rem shook his head, perplexed. Was this person sent here to kill him?

The three had taken refuge inside of a barely-filled corner store. Solus laid a hand on Amiria's cheek. The girl was breathing deeply and damped in sweat, unable to keep her focus. She ended up shutting her eyes to keep her head from spinning, resting against his shoulder as he lowered her to the ground.

"It seems to be the same as what happened to you before, Leilana," Solus concluded. Leilana stared down at the girl, silent. Solus cleared his throat, taken aback by her lack of emotion. "I didn't consider it before, but I've read that when Maesters and Arcana overwork themselves, their magic is put into a stasis. I suppose that the effects are like a cold for you."

"Just let me leave," Amiria proclaimed, absent of strength to place behind her words. "I don't know why you saved me. I'm not going to burden you."

"Don't act high and mighty now," Solus warned while pressing his hand to hers, forcing her to lower it. "You may have done inexcusable things, but that doesn't mean we will leave you to fend for yourself. Now be silent." Amiria sighed in defeat.

Leilana put a bottle of water up to her lips, tuning in to the citizens of Kalonia talking amongst themselves, though she could barely make out their words, not wanting to involve herself with the people of this town. None of them acknowledged more than their own well-being, and none seemed to carry a dominant trait found in any of the totems. It was a good idea that she kept to herself.

"I'm worried about Rem," Solus piped up.

Leilana decided to humor herself and people-watch. Maybe they could be of use somehow. They were crowding over one another to look out of the large window. They uttered about someone taking out the Dirionus. Not one of them had seen the assailant's face, but they spoke of a boy with the power of the spirits embedded in his left hand. She couldn't pinpoint the intensity of their emotions.

"Don't be yet," Leilana told Solus, "It sounds like everything stopped."

"The chaos may have slowed down," Solus continued, "But Rem is still out there."

"If you're going to search for Rem, then I'm going with you," Amiria proclaimed. Solus was prepared to interject, unsure of how she knew him and why she was concerned about him, but by then, she was already out of the door. He and Leilana looked to one another before making haste.

"Amiria, don't push yourself," Leilana began.

"Your focus should be on Rem," she responded. "He is your friend, after all. I just support him."

Solus rolled his eyes. "Well, if you're going to be 'support,' don't get into more trouble."

"No promises."

Solus sighed; that was never a good sign.

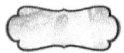

Rem was appalled by how hastily he was subdued,

unsure what this man's intentions were. One glance told Rem enough; the man confirmed his own identity without hesitation. The man stood stalwart and tall, much like the trees in the forest. He wasn't going to be easy to take down like the Dirionus. He kept a hand around his throat, still sore from the prior strangulation. He rose to a stand, gripping to his sword, extending his aura-driven claw outward to keep at bay.

"Who are you?" he almost snarled. "What do you want with me?"

"Isn't it obvious, Highness? Everyone wants your blood on their blade. You are the crown of Adrylis. Your death would ensure that this country could usher in a more refined magical era."

So, that was it. They wanted him dead out of desperation, not even considering how much was in jeopardy by taking manners into their own hands. But why? It didn't make any sense. What did his life have to do with the magic budding in Adrylis? And even if his death was necessary for such trivial reasons, corrupted magic would dig Adrylis deeper into a pitfall.

"I'm not gonna go down easy, you know," he proclaimed, clenching his left hand, the claws digging into his already torn flesh. "This is my kingdom. I will take it back with my own hands. And there's nothing that will change that fact, nothing!"

Rem took a grasp on the hilt of his weapon and charged forward like a raging bull, prepared to strike the masked man, but right as he was about to connect the attack, the man slipped through his fingers. His body vanished before the sword could cut him, and a blade plunged into Rem's back. He let out a gasp as he was kicked to the ground, blood seeping from his wound after the blade was removed.

His power was siphoned away, his hand reverting to normal.

The world spun. His body walked through pins and needles, the miniscule pricks of his wound striving to mend themselves in full bloom. Rem could barely make out the ethereal voice spiraling around him, guiding him forward. The voice of his guardian angel, seizing his time to return to a place which bore no name for him, though many called it a paradise. No. It was far too soon to consider dying.

"Remiel!"

The sudden cry of his name snapped his mind back into place for only a few seconds before he closed his eyes, collapsing into the masked man's arms.

Solus was panting, his throat scorching from calling out to his friend after seeing his current state but didn't hesitate to take up his sword in retaliation. How? How had his friend been defeated so quickly? True, his power manifested into this form recently, but Rem was still capable of more. Amiria and Leilana stood in the background, wanting to find a way around the situation and help Rem without having to expend too much energy. Amiria was still in a fragile state and sickly swaying to the point where she had even taken a grip to Leilana to steady herself.

"Who are you?" Solus exclaimed, "What do you want?"

"You both certainly like to repeat yourselves," the man specified, glancing down at Rem, who remained unconscious as he lifted him over his shoulder.

"Release him!" Solus shouted.

"You lack the knowledge on the Prince's true importance in this little game."

"'Prince?'" Leilana repeated, the words hitching in her throat. Was Rem Adrylis's Prince? The same Prince caught in the crossfire of Linmus's fall?

"You carry such a basic understanding of magic." He extended a hand towards Solus and clasped it into a closed fist. "But I can feel *your* soul stirring, wracked with agony over your burdens, cleansed by an incomprehensible acceptance."

"You don't know me," Solus said coldly. "Don't pretend to."

"Are you a Maester yourself?" Leilana asked, taking a step forward. If anything, all that they could serve is buying time. "There are few that can read auras as proficiently as you seem to be able to." Amiria was drawing in measured breaths, snagging wind of Leilana's plans. Solus took the method of work in stride, his fingers still lingering on his sword, unsure if he should strike. "There has to be some reason why you need Rem alive."

"You have no place to speak, girl."

"I am unworthy," Leilana replied, lightly bowing as a gesture of submission. "But I am an Arcana nonetheless. I only seek the truth." The man watched her eyes slant in a confident haze. "And this is one opportunity where the truth will prevail. Amiria."

Before the man could retort, Amiria unleashed a shrill note, which gradually became a sonic wave. Solus was quick to shield his ears, sword at his feet, gritting his teeth at the sharp pitch. Leilana had covered her own as well but could still make out traces of the sonic wave. The mask covering the man's face shattered to pieces, and his ears nearly split open. They studied his branded, scarred face, watching him writhe. His tanned complexion was splintering over time, corrupted by the resonance of Amiria's voice. His piercing crimson eyes were blinded by hatred, and though he fought to regain himself, he couldn't drop Rem or allow this chance of rebellion to slip from his fingers.

Leilana snarled. He wasn't giving up without a fight, it seemed. Amiria was growing tired, her muscles failing to keep her standing. Still, she kept up relinquishing her vocals until she felt her lungs caving in. Solus waited for Amiria to cease fire for even a second before he grabbed his blade from the ground and thrust it into the man's chest, avoiding hitting Rem. The man inhaled shakily, blood pouring from his ears and between his cracked lips. His eyes went void as he dropped to the pavement, Rem's body landing next to him. Solus rushed to his friend, lifting him slightly.

"Remiel!" he called, "Remiel, wake up!" He rested a hand on the young Prince's back but felt no open wound. No blood was seeping out onto his hand. Good. It was already mending shut.

"Is he going to be all right?" Amiria croaked, resting a hand on her throat.

Solus was taken aback by her genuine concerns. "I think so."

"Good. I'm glad..." With a smile plastered on her face, Amiria slipped into unconsciousness. Leilana interlocked her arms around the girl's waist as she fell, Amiria's long hair tickling her fingers.

"You did good, kid," she whispered, resting a hand on her head.

Rem's eyes snapped open, and he shot to a sit. "Where's the bastard?!" He clutched his head seconds later, collapsing back into Solus's arms.

"Easy there," Solus told him, "You're moving too fast." Rem groaned his response, rubbing his temples. Solus supported Rem on his shoulders as he stood, glancing at the corpse resting on the ground. "We'll go back to the hotel and gather ourselves. We will be safer if we blend in."

Leilana nodded in agreement. "You're right."

Rem stared at his open hand while Solus carried him away, unsure of what to make of what had occurred in his absence. It was all such a blur now, and he couldn't fathom what had come over him. All that he knew now was that he had the overwhelming urge to attack, maybe even beat the corpse, but his mind fought back and forced him to a standstill.

Maybe that was the drawback of being born as a Bloodlinch.

TWELVE

The voices circulating around the hotel lobby were over-bearing. The incessant chatter continued to grow as the bodies littered the open area.

"Mitholus has fallen."

"There is no hope for peace in Kalonia anymore.

"Our only protection is gone."

"Can we even stay here?"

Solus folded his hands and sat in silence to process what the gossip pertained to, and it hadn't taken him long to grow agitated. Of the four, he wanted to take the initiative after the crowds began forming outside of the hotel. They didn't know their faces, their names, or why they were here, but they knew the Dirionus slayers were hiding. The people of Kalonia were out for blood in an open pit, and all that the four teenagers could do was wait.

It was unbelievable how fickle people could be. But through the blurred lines, he supposed that he wasn't much better. He didn't know how to accept their words. How could a man seeking the death of a single person be a thing that's considered justifiable?

"Mitholus was the only one keeping our town safe," a woman whispered to another. "He was keeping the Dirionus at bay, and now they have both gone away."

"I heard some idiot kid interfered and killed them both."

"If I could see his face, I'd give him what for."

Solus shook his head. If only they could have known. If

only he could tell them that they were talking down the crown of Adrylis. Rem's name was being tarnished and for the first time, there was nothing he could say to end it. All that he could do was sit back and think.

The man that had attacked his Prince had a face and a name, just like him. Mitholus cared for this city enough to guide the Dirionus wayward without resorting to killing it. Contrary to its legion, the Dirionus's mind was plagued by dark magic. There was no saving a lost soul. Mitholus may have known that and continued to work against it. Or maybe he was the one controlling it, acting as a deceitful shield to those that admired him. There were too many pieces of the puzzle to fit together.

Still, this man defeated his best friend swiftly. The way that he spoke, he sought the power of the Royal Bloodlinch. He knew who Rem was and didn't hesitate to seize him after seeing the execution with his own eyes. This man was deceptive and lusted for magical energy. And if one person knew, how many more would retaliate in the same fashion?

Rem was in danger, and that in turn put Amiria and Leilana in the line of fire. Rem wouldn't allow innocent people to be thrust into their turmoil, at least not without a way to resolve things. They were still sleeping upstairs to regain their strength, Leilana keeping the mantle of protection over them. She was in no better condition, but she insisted after his thirst for more knowledge beseeched him. One false move and everything would disentangle. He didn't need to wait anymore. He had what he needed. It was nearly time to leave Kalonia and make due in another direction. More like Mitholus would be arriving sooner than later.

Leilana clutched the Lasette to her chest with all of her being as the clamoring of muffled speech drew closer. She kept her legs crossed and leaned against the wall behind the door to make sure that any intruders wouldn't see her, but she could barely keep control over her rising anxiety, rocking back and forth and bumping the wall in the process, drawing in a sharp inhale every couple of minutes to ease herself. She observed Rem and Amiria from afar; Rem was tossing in his sleep due to fervent dreams stunting a genuine rest, but he seemed to be recovering well on his own. Amiria was sound asleep and didn't so much as sniffle for the last hour.

She hoped that Solus would be able to return to the room without getting ripped apart for information by the people of Kalonia. He was still a stranger to this colony, and soon enough they were bound to catch on that he was connected to the fall of the Dirionus.

Still, now that she was in solitude again, there was so much that she couldn't comprehend. The first thought to come rushing was learning that Rem was born as Prince Remiel Vesarus, heir to the throne of Linmus. For years, she had listened to the stories that uttered his name beyond the skies, and never once did she consider the mere coincidences that Rem dragged through the mud. At least he wasn't completely obvious about his true identity.

Rem was the boy that unknowingly drew her to the idea of visiting Adrylis and learning magic several years ago. And only now did she remember that fact. Minsura, her own home, was resilient but resented the idea of spells forging their colony.

She heard tapping, which made her jump and nearly fling the Lasette. Solus stood on the balcony on the opposite side of the glass, waving to her and pointing down to the latch on the door. She stood up, setting aside her grimoire, the white skirt she wore over her bloomers falling to her knees again. She adjusted the collar of her blouse as she approached the window to make sure that the oversized shirt wouldn't slip down. It wasn't much, but it was all that she could find to replace her tattered clothes in the launders. She undid the latch and allowed him inside.

"Thank you. It was getting a bit chilly." He closed the door behind him, allowing his fingers to linger over the cold metal for a few seconds before turning to her. "How are they?"

"Still asleep. And nobody has come by."

"I couldn't tell," he admitted. "The area was so condensed that I couldn't walk straight. I had to climb around from the outside just to get back here. That was why I took so long."

"Did you find out anything?"

"The man that attacked Rem was named Mitholus." He clenched his fist, holding it behind his back to keep the girl from seeing his frustrations. "Everyone here knew him. He was guarding this city against the Dirionus, but the way that he came off seemed quite the opposite."

"That may be true," Leilana began, "but we have to consider the possibility of a hidden agenda. There had to be a reason why he could pick Rem out of the crowd. He was able to read his aura, but he couldn't do the same for us."

Solus loosened the grip on his hand and flexed his

fingers. "We should leave Kalonia as soon as we're able. He may be part of a clan."

"A clan? And here I thought that students were the only ones working in that fashion."

"You truly believe he was a Maester?"

Leilana folded her hands behind her back. "Each denizen carrying the will of a Warlord holds a talent unique to them. Ennis could speak to the Warlords of old and provide premonitions of the future. Paluna's Warlord, Kosmin, used tarot cards to accurately spin the ordeals in one's life and determine their set path, even if it should change down the road. This man Mitholus can read auras and use them to scout out his prey."

"That's quite observant," Solus pointed out. "But why would Mitholus seek Rem? Why guide the Dirionus down a corruptible path as well, when they are meant to be gentle giants?"

"It is easy for a Warlord's powers to become corrupt if they lose their bond to humanity. That is why we have been sent on this pilgrimage—to understand the people that we encounter. That way, when we become Warlords, we remain true to ourselves and others."

"You two sure are noisy," Rem called as he sat upright with the blanket he was provided covering his knees. Though he spoke in an aggravated tone, the hint of a smile was undeniable. "You know, if we're planning on leaving, we *all* need to be well-rested. You've been working your asses off, drop a load off your shoulders."

"And what are you planning to do in the meantime?" Solus asked. "Shouldn't you be resting?"

"Nope. I'm fine." Solus didn't look amused. "Okay, okay, look. I'll show you! Watch this!" Rem rubbed his palms together.

"N-No, Rem, you don't need to-" Before Solus could let out another word of protest, Rem was upright in a hand-stand, his hands supporting his weight. Solus closed his slack jaw at the sight of Rem's bright smile. "...And he's off..." Leilana was covering her mouth with both hands to hide her laughter, failing miserably. Solus couldn't help feeling amused and comforted by the gesture, and Rem bounded himself onto his feet, brushing some hair out of his face.

"See? Fine enough to do that and rip nothing out of place. That said, you guys rest. Let me hold down the fort for a little while." Solus and Leilana met one another's gaze before Solus gave a shrug. Leilana decided to agree. It had been a while since she'd gotten proper sleep.

The hotel was unnervingly silent. Rem kept his sword planted at his side in case someone tried to barge in, but he knew that his concerns on the matter had quelled.

"Never let your guard down," he mumbled to himself, drumming his fingers along the sheath of his blade. "At any cost. There is always danger around."

"Is that your mantra, Remiel?" He flinched at Amiria's call. She was sitting up in bed, her hair flowing down her back and caressing the sheets.

"Remiel," he scoffed. "I told you before, weren't you listening? My name is Rem."

"You don't have to hide it anymore. I know that you are the Prince of Adrylis. Leilana does too." Rem sighed, folding his legs, setting his sword down on his lap. It seemed like the more that people wormed their way through his secret, the calmer he became. How foreboding.

"Are you doing anything with the information?"

"Do you ask this to everyone that finds out your secret?"

"Not many people to tell."

Amiria gave a small shake of the head before stating firmly, "No, I'm not going to rat you out to the authorities or have you captured by the terrorists that overseer your kingdom."

"Okay, now that we've gotten past that, Solus and Leilana are asleep, and Solus and I have decided that we're leaving Kalonia. We don't want to take any more chances after what happened on the streets. Would you like to come with us?"

Amiria considered his words. Was it right to travel alongside them, knowing that she had still been a rival to Leilana? Fighting at her side once more did little to change her perspective, and neither of them felt comfortable around one another. Solus didn't seem to have any trust towards her, even when she desired to help Rem, which was his duty. There was no winning with her. Rem was the only one that seemed to acknowledge her as more than a murderer.

"No," she began, "I wouldn't feel right being here. Leilana and Solus are good allies to you, but I would do nothing but slow you all down. Leilana is skilled, and you can use her skills far better than you could utilize my voice. She can guide you back to Linmus."

"That wasn't what I was-"

"I think that you should be with people that trust you and earn that respect in return. I burned down a village. Do you really feel that I can be called a member of your team, knowing that?"

"Everyone makes mistakes, Amiria. That's part of maturity. You shouldn't burden yourself with the what ifs." As he approached her bedside, Amiria couldn't tear away from her gaze, taken by the warmth of his smile illuminating the room. "You seek knowledge." He took her hand, grasping her petite fingers in his own. Her heart was daring to jump from her chest, the gesture unexpected, yet it granted her a sense of comfort. "I can help you find what you crave not only as a Prince but as a Maester."

Amiria pried her hand free and rose from the bed. They remained in silence for some time before she spoke up. "I don't feel like it will work out. I can't travel with you." Rem bore his eyes into hers but found no traces of hesitation. He inhaled deeply, shutting his eyes.

"All right." He held up a hand and gestured towards the door. She tied her hair back into a ponytail with a thin ribbon that was wrapped around her wrist, gathering her tote from the floor. "You, um... I hope that you find what you're looking for and that you're safe."

"Don't worry, I can handle myself." She reached up a hand and tapped his nose with her index finger before slowly pulling back. "I trust that you'll secure your throne, Prince Remiel." Rem opened his mouth to reply, but by then, she had stepped out onto the balcony.

She cradled the tote at her side as she climbed up the railing, planting her feet on the metal bars to steady herself. She glanced back at Rem in the corner of her eye; he stood in the doorway as an observer, not daring to stop her. Many sought her head or some aspect of truth, and yet he would allow her to freely move about Adrylis and let her discover more for herself.

Somehow, she felt grateful for him.

She folded her arms behind her back and basked in the

guise of the moon intertwined with the midnight sky. He cleared his throat as a means of acknowledgment, the gesture making her heart soar. Amiria wasn't sure what to feel about his presence anymore. It seemed too surreal. "Thank you for believing in me."

"There's still a lot that I want to learn," he admitted, "So, you better not die on me." Amiria gave a nod before she held out both hands, a large vine spawning from the ground. Once it had grown to a considerable size, she climbed down. Rem watched her from above until the plant shrunk into a simple lily. Her powers seemed to carry more range than any other Arcana that he had come across. There was more to Amiria than she shared—more than he could ever understand. But at least he still had the time to uproot it all. What was left of her stepped further out of his sight over the course of a few minutes, and then she disappeared into the night.

"You know," the sudden call behind Rem started him. He nearly jumped off the railing, gripping the bars binding him. He couldn't even face Solus, unsure if he was ready to explain so soon that Amiria had left them behind. "You could have just talked to me if you were bothered by something." Rem swallowed as he turned. Solus was leaning against the door, hands in his pockets, a confident grin overtaking his features. "What ails you, Highness?"

"I wouldn't say something's bothering me," he admitted, pressing his hands to the bars. "It's more like what's bothering everybody around me."

"Do tell," Solus gestured on.

"People are out for my blood, something that I can't control. And yet, there are people that believe my magic is the key to shaping Adrylis anew. I think about how the people of Kalonia are looking for us solely for information on why I killed the Dirionus that was destroying their town. You killed their apparent Savior, and all that you were trying to do was protect me." He rested his forehead against the icy bars, continuing, "I feel like a pawn pushing people forward, or away, or even around."

Solus tapped the back of his head with his closed fist, and Rem didn't flinch. "And who, per se, are you pushing around or away? Because the last that I checked, we were supporting one another. And not just me, Leilana and Amiria are here to help, and there are people like Olen that want to see you prevail and take back what is yours. You have allies in many fields. Not to mention Phiran."

Rem sighed, the handkerchief in his back pocket growing heavy at the mention of the man's name. "Amiria left, Sol. She didn't feel comfortable around you and Leilana."

"Then that is her decision. You can't put the blame on yourself for something that she wanted." Solus rested a hand on his shoulder. "Focus on the task at hand. Your connections will reach your heart again, all in good time."

"I'm not worried about her. She's skilled. She can handle herself." Rem cleared his throat, watching people file out of the hotel. Dawn was steadily approaching. If there was the time to act, it was now. "So, what's the plan from here? Are we going to just sneak out?"

"We may have to settle with blending in. I have an idea."

"Oh no," Rem whined, "Not a Solace versus Soulless idea..."

Leilana woke thinking about Amiria's departure early in the morning after Rem explained his decision to allow her to leave. It wasn't unheard of for someone to run from their discomfort, but she seemed to bask in his light, even before learning his identity. Maybe knowing him would be enough to guide her wayward. It was dangerous to work alone, especially with new threats rising, but Leilana was left to hope she would manage until they met again.

"Okay, so this is what we're going for," Solus began, "Morning will be soon, and that means that people will want to have breakfast. It won't be as crowded in the halls, because the staff will either be serving or people will be heading down to the buffet area. We can use that opportunity to sneak away from the hotel and dodge the citizens of Kalonia."

"But what about the ones out on the streets?" Leilana asked, "What if they suspect us?"

"I have an arrangement," Solus continued, winking at her. "One of the merchants caught wind of Rem's arrival and shut his mouth after I bought a sword. Says he wants to help. He can get us out of Kalonia on his caravan and lead us to the east."

"I guess it pays to have allies in close places," Leilana replied.

"And how do you know that he won't bail on us?" Rem's voice wavered.

"There are supporters to Linmus—I happened to get lucky with the right one. And you know that even if we were caught up, we can get ourselves out of the situation." He held up his thumb to his neck and ran it from the left side over to the right. "Easy pickings."

"All right. I guess I'll trust you."

"Excellent. Now we just have to lay low and make sure that everyone starts filing out."

Chatter filled the halls, and the three listened carefully to the stampeding footsteps. They seemed to step right past their room. Maybe they had mellowed out more from the previous evening. It was a good sign.

"It's almost time," Solus concluded. "Are you both ready?"

"Always up for a good run." Rem's eyes suddenly lit up. "Or maybe I should say... climb." Solus turned his stern gaze on the young Prince. Rem let out a snarl, and the two became embroidered in a staring contest, coming to a silent standstill.

"I don't like where this is going," Leilana mumbled.

Leilana and Solus decided to remain together and maneuver the crowds, keeping on their toes. They both tried to be firm with their opinions, but Rem made it clear that he wasn't putting up with whatever social anxiety he developed. Leilana couldn't blame him. Crowds were, well, crowded. But a rooftop escapade was more dangerous.

"Do you think that he's okay? You both seemed pretty heated."

"I don't think it matters," Solus told her. "Rem's going to do whatever he wants no matter what. That's just how he is. He may be my best friend, but every now and again, we come to spats like this because of his arrogance. It's just how he was raised."

"I think it's fine to argue. It shows how close that the

two of you are to one another, and it shows your concerns. You can find your faults and resolve them. I envy that about you. I can't say that I've had a close-knit relationship like the two of you do."

Solus sighed in response, grinning. "Well, if it helps, Rem is the only friend I've ever known. At least until now."

"So, we're friends now," Leilana joked. "Is that what you're going on?"

"Only if that's what you want to call it. Friends, associates, allies, partners, spin it a thousand times, give it a thousand names." She couldn't help giggling. "I don't know what Rem is thinking when it comes to not trusting you, but you've yet to give me any off feelings, even as an Arcana. I think that you can be an asset to our group."

"I will stand at your side, and I will assist you as best as I can. No walls that Rem builds will ever tear me from that anymore. Especially now that you've read the Lasette."

Solus grew silent, and he could swear that he was sweating down the back of his neck. Finally, he spat out the words, "You knew?"

"Oh yes. I knew. I don't know how you managed to breach its pages, but now that you've seen something that was not meant for your eyes, I won't let you make any hapless mistakes. You're going to need someone to act as your personal guide into the unknown, and I doubt that Rem will be suitable enough." She tapped the tote at her side once. "This pilgrimage is valuable to my time, but I'm sure that I can balance if you'll let me join you." She rested her hands on her hips, smiling up at him. "I will see your journey's end with my own eyes. That is a promise."

Solus broke into laughter, which took her by surprise. "You are incredible. And here I thought that I was the only one capable of such speech." She rolled her eyes and shoved him in a playful manner.

Splitting off and sneaking down to the lobby to meet up with their secret informant seemed like a wholesome idea, but Rem was already cursing Solus's name for considering it. It was far from useful in a situation that involved three teenagers cheating death. Some strategist he was primed to be.

Rem settled with venturing to the top floor, where few would be able to notice him scaling the rooftops and keeping his balance with his aura-ranged claws, not wanting to run the risk of jumping through crowds on the interior and having someone look him directly in the face. Sure, this wasn't much of an alternative, but he'd have rather fallen and suffered a broken limb than be forced to run from one person evolving into thirty ratting him out as Prince of Adrylis.

"I don't understand the rumors." Rem's feet nearly skid across the splintered wood when the unfamiliar voice reached his ears. Crap, that's right; the guards were always on high alert to keep people from harming themselves or others. He planted his hands on the nearby window, taking care that no one was inside to try and expose him, relieved to find the room empty.

"What, about Mitholus's death? The circumstances are rather unique—they say that a boy from the outside elimi-nated the Dirionus, and Mitholus tried to retaliate but was brought down by another." People were catching on fast.

Maybe that was why Solus was so hell-bent on getting out of Kalonia.

Rem kept his steps paced, one toe up at a time while he trekked along the rooftops, peering out towards the balcony where the two men stood. They were a little further back, out of range for him to pursue them. Even if he could, he ran the risk of someone stepping out and finding him. He lowered himself onto one of the pedestals, stumbling over his feet. To regain himself, he broke into a run, grabbing hold of the nearby balcony where the men stood. Both let out near-simultaneous yells.

"How's it hanging, fellas?!" Rem called nervously. "Enjoying the morning?"

"What do you think you're doing?!" one of the guards exclaimed, still holding a hand over his chest to try and quell his nerves. Rem could feel his fingers slipping from the bars. He nearly smirked. Opportunity knocked far more than he let on.

"Dropping." He released the bars and fell the several feet below. The wind rushed past his ears and the morning glory above seemed to carry him further from any doubts. As the seconds elapsed, he recalled the power embedded in his left hand. He could use it to fend off the strike of a Diri-onus, a solitary and stalwart beast that carried the will of a Warlord. Such a feat was accomplishable, why was securing his life so different?

He channeled his remaining energy and thrust his left hand upward, his claw's aura spiraling around his body before clinging to the balcony where he fell. His barriers had evolved in full bloom when his true power came into play. Solus and Leilana were stepping out of the hotel when Leilana's essence gripped to the sensation engulfing Rem's body. Rem dispelled his magic once his feet touched solid ground, his hand remaining in the air a moment longer before he closed his fist. His fingers were pulsating, his heart pounding like a drum.

"Took you two long enough," he proclaimed when he caught sight of Solus and Leilana looking on. "I had a little spill and had to change my methods."

"We don't have time for your explanation-"

Before the three could make any sudden movements, a swarm of guards for the hotel was dashing out with rifles and swords in tow. Leilana almost shook upon seeing the guns—she had heard of them in passing and learned that the bullets were meant to kill, but this was the first time that she had seen them. Solus reached for his sword but faltered at the cocking of several of the weapons, his fingers lingering over the hilt before he ultimately lowered his hand.

"Were you the ones present last night before the Dirionus?" One of the guards hissed.

"Why, what gave you that idea?" Rem asked, extending his arms outwards. Solus shot him a glare, not wanting the situation to be turned on its rear because of any reckless temptations. As he spoke, the guards took to staring at Rem's exposed left hand, lined with scars and traces of the rooftop's debris on his nails, not a single glance out of place. Rem's confidence slipped away over the seconds of silence, but he didn't drop his arms.

"We came to Kalonia in peace," Leilana began, the Lasette snug against her chest. "And we intend to leave the same way at any cost." A shot rang out, and sooner than Leilana could process, her body was shielded from the attack, her face resting on someone's chest. It hadn't taken her long to realize that her savior at that moment was Rem. His shirt was slightly torn from the impact that grazed his shoulder, and his expression fierce, unnerved by the wound.

"I don't think that's how we'll be leaving," Rem mumbled, his voice reverberating through her.

Rem took the opportunity to swing forward his left hand, coated in darkness, his energy swelling about the guards. Every flick of his fingers ushered forth a new opportunity for guard-breaking. All that the guards managed to do in retaliation was keep firing, blindsided by the mystical power of the boy they were to seize, bullets piercing through Rem's skin. Still, he kept standing and willing himself to force them all away. He stood in the way of any bullets that could reach his two friends and took them in for himself. Leilana watched as the guards fell to the ground one by one, unsure of how to react to the situation. They didn't seem lifeless, their chests rising and falling every few seconds— Rem had merely subdued them.

For all the powers that he possessed between healing the innocent and outlandishly murdering his opposers, he still knew his place. He knew his limitations in where he morally stood. Remiel Vesarus was dangerous in that sense alone.

The guards littered the entrance, no longer of use in this fight. They didn't have a chance, and Solus knew it well after seeing his Prince's actions towards the Dirionus. Few could stand against one, but it was too much for Rem, easily overcome by Mitholus soon afterward. Still, even this was beyond the limits that he would seize for his own fortitude. Even in his moment of weakness, Rem never laid a hand on Mitholus. Mere humans differed greatly from the brutes that terrorized Adrylis, no matter their intentions.

Silence loomed over the region. The crowds dispersed. Solus grew fixated on how many laid quivering under the might of their spirited, hidden Prince. They wouldn't know, and they would not be saved today from harm. Leilana stepped forward and reached out a hand to Rem's turned back. His shoulders rose a few centimeters at her contact, and a trivial whimper tore through the silence.

In a swift motion, Rem collapsed onto the pavement, the aura engulfing his hand dissipating. His body fought to mend itself, the teal aura that formulated his healing prowess slipping through his system before spilling out, seizing those that he had dealt harm to. He flexed his fingers and rose to a sit, the bullets dropping from his body as if they never reached him in the first place. His hair sunk over his eyes as he folded his legs. He held up a hand, drawing his fingers closer together as if he were conjuring a fist. Leilana backpedaled, the grimoire slipping from her grasp, her body being lifted from the ground. She tried to call out to him, but each passing second stole her breath. She shakily gasped, clasping her hands around her neck to try and pry away the invisible force, to no avail.

"Rem!" Solus roared. "What are you doing?!" Rem held up his left hand as Solus was rushing to aide her, casting a barrier around the older boy. Solus's face smacked the wall, causing him to stumble back. He slammed his fists against the barrier repeatedly. "Remiel! Stop this! You don't know what you're doing! Listen to me!"

Rem stood, keeping his hands in the air to maintain both sources of power. Leilana managed to glimpse his current state. His vibrant brown eyes were shrouded in an amber haze, his body emanating a shadowy disposition that rivaled the brutes they faced in the past. It was as if he no longer existed.

"You possess knowledge," he spoke in a gravelly tone, the wave of his words rushing down her spine like chilled water. "I can feel the essence of your grimoire, and the soul of Ennis Erovina teeming within its pages. Without it... you are nothing. Barely fit to be called an Arcana." He clenched his right hand into a fist before dropping it altogether, sending Leilana to the ground. She let out a few sharp gasps, coughing violently as she rested a hand on her throat.

"Don't hurt her!" Solus cried out, slumping onto the ground, exhausted from the consistent push towards the barrier. "Rem...!"

No matter how much he tried to fight against the energy binding him, he was no match for a Maester. Born magic-less, intertwined with a prodigious Bloodlinch that knew not the limits of his strength versus any form of morality. And now that power was consuming him bit by bit, and all that he could do was watch. He punched the ground under-neath his scraped knees, unable to watch anymore.

"What's your end goal?" Leilana coughed out, "Killing me because you don't trust me? Or because I'm in your way?"

Rem hovered over her, giving her the chance to speak. She swallowed, unsure of how to piece together her words knowing that his incriminating stare would tear her down in an instant if she worked at convincing him that he had no reason to distrust her. The aura that surrounded him in the forest spoke it so—they were meant to walk a fragile line together. She was gifted with the opportunity to understand him further, and any lost chances would not only affect her pilgrimage but both of their lives. Now that they had met and interacted, they were intertwined.

"No," he said simply. "I'm only keeping you around because my friend sees something in you, and you happen to carry information that can save my kingdom. Nothing more. If my intention was to kill you, I would have done it long ago."

Leilana's heart sank. She knew. She had always

suspected that Rem was just dealing with her, but to hear it spoken aloud was gut-wrenching. He would never come to see her as more than some burden that his closest companion had dragged from the ash and grime and taken under his wing.

Rem lowered his right hand and the barrier holding Solus dropped. Solus didn't hesitate to rush to Leilana's side, stumbling as he ran, resting his hands on her shoulders and asking after her. Leilana couldn't face him, her eyes averted towards her dusty hands. Her bottom lip quivered. If she chose to acknowledge him, she would have broken down then and there. She wasn't strong, or useful enough to warrant a place beside them. All that she was good for was translating the Minsuran text and giving them information on the Orb of Concord. She and Amiria should have traded places. Maybe she would have been able to talk some sense into Rem instead of antagonizing him by presence alone.

Solus looked to Rem, his eyes darkening as he stood from his spot before Leilana. "Remiel." The animosity hindering Solus's usually calm tone rose awareness in Rem. "I thought that you were above something like this." That was the last thing he wanted from Solus. He was the one supporting him throughout everything—without him, there was no chance of survival.

"W-What did I...?" Rem reached up both hands to touch his face, to make sure that his mind and body were still intact. "I... don't... what's...?" He tripped over his words, his mouth dry, his stomach twisting into knots. What was this? Where was he? What had he said? Why couldn't he remember? Solus had seen this expression before. Rem became distraught whenever he was mentally suffering, and over the last few days, he was nothing but such. "...Sol..."

Solus extended a hand towards Rem, his expression

unchanging. "We need to leave now, Rem. It isn't safe here anymore. I can get us someplace better. We just have to move forward." Rem reached out his hand, but before he could take a single step, his knees buckled under him and he once more collapsed, his energy depleted. Solus grabbed his arm before he impacted, holding him in place. He carefully wrapped the limb around his shoulders and pulled Rem to his feet, supporting him.

Leilana remained planted on the concrete a while longer, her mind working to gather herself and wrap her head around Rem's words. Had he really meant them? Or were they some farce conjured up from his rage-plagued mind meant to draw out her inner weakness? Was she reading too far into what had corrupted him?

"Leilana," Solus began, "I don't think he meant it. At least, I hope that he-"

"It's all right," she told him, jumping to her feet. "I've come to know how Rem can be." She started ahead. "The marketplace, right? That is where we're to meet your informant?"

"U-Uh, yes, that's correct. Wait a moment, I'll be right with you."

There were some things better left unsaid, even to those that allowed their thoughts to waver and wander under the pressures of newfound information. Solus could only hope that Leilana wasn't someone that carried on in the face of overwhelming statements like Rem seemed to. The words would carry on alongside her until they rose to the surface again no matter how much that she tried to hide them in the crevices of her mind.

How much pain could one face before they cracked?

PART TWO:
UNCHAINED HEIGHTS

THIRTEEN

Lancett hated Amiria. He wanted to believe that he did. He blamed her, but every time that he considered tossing the thought around the playing field, he felt guilty. The instant that he visualized her face, he didn't envision a mien of detestation; all that he thought of was the innocent and modest girl that Amiria Farone used to be. She was scared and timid, but she found reasons to smile. She was still residing inside of her tortured soul somewhere, wrought with the idea of destruction cornering her.

Destiny could always be defied. That was what Kosmin had wanted her to understand when he addressed his reading to her, but the effects of the Tower card were already well in play now that Amiria had played her role in this pilgrimage of totem collecting. She had ultimately taken herself out. The idealism that her predetermined fate was going to swallow her whole was swinging through the air like a pendulum and pounding against her frail body.

Lancett found himself in a sizeable farming town called Linarus to the far east of Paluna. It took him about twenty minutes to scan over the area, greeting some people as he walked, feigning his usual smile. No matter how grateful he was for the opportunity to travel, he was inclined to make the journey alone, and it was tedious to consider. From every corner the open fields, herbs were lining the paddies. The faint aroma of antiseptic overtook his senses, but it was soon overpowered by another scent: peppermint. It eased his conflict, if only for a moment.

"Come on, we have to at least *try* and collect some leaves!" Up ahead he spotted two young men, one with long red hair tied into a ponytail, the other with neck-length black hair, glasses, and what Lancett swore were horn nubs on his scalp. "I can make some peppermint tea from scratch this way!" The voice had stemmed from the redhead, who was carrying a peculiar accent. He had elongated the 'I' in his sentence and in his haste, had also stumbled a bit over some of the vowels.

"We don't have time for this," the boy with glasses pressed. "We don't even know where we are, and here you are worried about tea."

The redhead scoffed, shifting his weight to the left side of his body. "What, calling me a drug addict?" His friend smirked before walking ahead of him.

"Cannot say for sure, really. Hurry up now, the others are waiting for us." The redhead was quick to give chase, the two walking past Lancett, who gave them a passing look as the scarlet hair brushed past his face. The two young men locked gazes before the redhead smiled, continuing after his friend. Lancett couldn't help but grin. Those two seemed to have definitive character, that was certain.

He went on his way, the paddies and naturistic atmosphere evolving into wood-crafted homes and lanterns. The houses aligning the open space were all fair-sized, the citizens contagious in the art of simplistic merrymaking. The sun was setting off in the west; they shared this trait with Paluna, lighting tea lamps to illuminate their closed-off world to the public. Groups of three at a time emerging from a building composed of brick and stone, a complete contrast to Paluna's straw huts. At least this place could survive a torching session. Their laughter was hearty and flamboyant, their speech nonsensical, and he could practically taste the liquor in the air. Some emerging from the building didn't seem much older than he was, and they were all content with how they were spending their nights.

Maybe he could unwind.

He pressed his hand to the door as he entered. Upon arrival, the all-encompassing sound of lutes occupied the room in tandem with laughter and mindless chatter. There were several tables and barstools, kegs full of beer set off to the side of the shop. He couldn't make out what the citizens of this town were discussing amongst themselves, but it was far from his place to intrude. Glasses were clinking in every direction, each one filled with an array of colors and mixed fruits, some with straws to further blend the mixture, some taken straight from the cup. Brave souls, he thought.

He had never touched alcohol before, and he almost wasn't sure if he wanted to.

"Come on, take a load off!" Kindall's voice broke through the cracks of his weary mind. He could almost see him grasping a bottle of liquor with a careless grin. *"Take a risk! Have a drink with me!"* Lancett nearly broke down recalling it. He had always rejected him. Always. And he never knew why he had because there was no harm, no foul, and certainly no risk in a single drink.

Kindall would steal bottles of red wine used for cooking and chug it straight. When he grew tired of the mundane taste over the course of a few months, he experimented with a variety of liquors before he upgrading to vodka. All that it took him was a good four sips. It was powerful enough that before it was used in Hinju's meals and burned out to create a soft palette, one bottle of eighty-proof could knock them both out in half an hour.

By the Warlords, nothing was going to feel the same without hearing his stupid laugh...

"You look like you could use a stiff one," a medium-high pitch called out, causing him to jump.

At the counter stood a girl with red hair braided down the middle of her back, a few strands of her bangs hanging over her sky-shaded eyes. She was cleaning out a glass with the apron around her waist, droplets of sweat on her forehead visible under the reduced lighting. She smiled, and Lancett blushed. The gesture wasn't overly comforting, but it was clear that she wasn't just fetching for him.

"What's your fancy?" Like others in the tavern, she carried an accent, but hers was shrouded under the guise of a more professional atmosphere. "You a lightweight or a madman with your booze?"

"I don't drink," Lancett admitted, leaning over the counter to get a closer look at her. She was almost shocked, not by his behavior, rather his words. "What do you recommend for a newcomer?"

"Why, that depends how drunk you want to be," she replied, tapping his nose with her index finger once. "I'll set you up. You won't even be able to taste the alcohol. First one's free for weary travelers." He watched her return to the myriad of glasses, bottles, and fruits lining the back counter.

"You know I'm not from here?" he asked.

She glanced over her shoulder and shrugged, continuing to smile while mixing up the drink, refusing to let him see what she was adding no matter how much he turned his head. She always seemed to move the glass just out of his view and didn't even grab anything while he was watching. That made him a tad nervous.

"It's not a big town, and it's rare to see different faces. You stand out enough."

"That's it?" He almost laughed but withheld it by clearing his throat. "I thought you would give some grand speech about how travelers are always in and out, trying to mooch free drinks off you."

"Oh, trust me, that happens less than you think. Then again, those same travelers tend to stop messing around and work on what is more important: resting." She rubbed her middle finger and thumb together over the glass while staring at him. "And trying not to lose their money buying drinks, of course." She set the glass down in front of Lancett.

Lancett picked up the glass, examining its contents. He detected a faint hint of vodka masked under the teal color. "What *is* in this?"

The girl glanced up at the ceiling, not sure if she should surprise him. In the end, she told him, "Strawberry-flavored vodka, blueberries fresh from the trees, and in your honor, a spritz of gin." She rested a hand on her hip, gesturing for him to move along. "Have a taste, let me know what you think."

Lancett lifted his shoulders before exhaling, putting the glass up to his lips and chugging down a few sips. He coughed in surprise, but within seconds, he was drinking more until the concoction was half full. The girl rested her chin on her hand, leaning over the counter.

"So, now that you've had my free drink, what do you think of it?"

Lancett blinked a few times, his eyes darting around the room, his vision unsteady. Maybe he drunk too fast. "It's, uh... it's kind of strong." He wasn't slurring his words just yet, and he still felt like he could concentrate his thoughts.

He didn't draw his attention away from her, continuing to drink the concoction slowly. "It's good. Makes me feel a little weird. Is that supposed to happen?"

"What do you feel?"

"Um..." Some of the liquid dripped down his chin, and he held up a hand to catch it before it hit his shirt. "I forget."

"My name is Sien Kaiser," she told him. "What's your name?"

"Lancett Lune," he said reluctantly, lengthening the 'u' in Lune by a half-second longer than intended. "I'm a Maester. I like magic. I like to fight. And I like this drink a lot." He drank the rest of the mixture before setting down the empty glass, which clanked loudly against the table. "And you're really pretty." Sien giggled. Seeping in already.

"Lancett Lune," she repeated. "'Keeper of the Moon.' I like it. It suits you well." He pointed an index finger at her and closed his eyes, nodding. The gesture made his head spin, and he placed his hand on the table to steady himself, blinking a few times before grinning sheepishly.

"Thaz wha people say." His words were blending, but he didn't mind. "A lot of peoples out there call me Lance. My bud Kindall got 'em hooked on it." He slammed his hands on the table, but she didn't even flinch. "It's nuts! But then again, he was kinda nuts. But I like yer name better. Sien Kaiser. You sound like a palette of cataclysm on rye."

She tilted her head to the right, chuckling nervously before taking a step back from the counter. "I don't think comparing me to food is the right way to flirt. That didn't make any sense."

"I'm a shitty flirt!" he laughed. "I can't even get the girl I like to acknowledge me, she's always so serious and focused on herself! It's selfish, but it's attractive to see how passionate she is. Like a doll!" She was noting his actions and reactions to everything that she was saying, writing them down on a napkin, humming a bit. "Whatcha doin' there?"

"Lancett, tell me something about yourself that you haven't told anyone else," she said simply, not looking up from her notes.

"One time I brought a girl to play, and mom made goat's milk," he spoke without hesitation.

Sien glanced up at him. "Goat milk? Sounds like it'd be thicker."

"Yeah-yeah, but 'sa lil' sweeter when done right. I gave her what was in the barn without telling my folks since they made it fresh every day, and right after that, she started sweating and coughing and throwing up. She had to stay the night." He scratched the side of his face with his index finger, blushing a bit. "Turned out the milk wasn't fully churned. Girlie left me hanging."

"Wow," Sien mumbled, "You *are* a terrible flirt."

Lancett rested his head on the table. "I also like to write... I try to write poetry..."

"Oh? So, you're a poet? Is that what you would be doing if you weren't a Maester?"

"Not good 'nuff. Plus, got a pilgrimage to work on, too many people to meet, girl to find... totems to try and seek out..." He yawned, shutting his eyes, dozing off at his spot on the table. "Warlord to be..." A light snoring reached Sien's ears, and she watched as people began to file out of the tiny tavern until it had emptied, guided by a girl with dark brown hair.

She wasn't older than eleven years old, but she carried such fire that it was closing time that it would strike fear into the heart of any man in her path. "Cici!" the girl called over, pulling the pink ribbon from her hair, her curly locks falling to her shoulders. "All done for the night! Did you have any luck?"

Sien set her napkin on the table, sighing. "Well, the mixture worked wonders, but note to self and note to you, Luna, truth serums crafted from Passionflowers are best effective on test subjects that don't have a sense of idiocy behind clouded logic. All that he was doing was trying to flirt just like the other guys. But it wasn't as graphic."

"He didn't try to make any moves, did he?"

"No, he's too sensitive. I can tell he's troubled—he walked in here looking lost. I'm sure that he needed the drink." Then she paused. "Oh, wait a second... maybe next time I shouldn't put it in alcohol. The guy did say he wasn't a drinker." She grinned. "I can use tea!"

"Why didn't you do that in the first place?" Luna whined. "Now we have to leave him here!"

"I'm sure that he'll be fine." Sien stepped over to Lancett and carefully wrapped his arm around her shoulders, pulling him to his feet. Luna trekked over to the two and held him by his waist, too short in stature to manage further help. "Hopefully he can sleep well..."

Leilana marveled at storm-clouds filling the open air, her hands caressing a thick pile of hay in the refurbished carriage. Horseshoes trotted along the lengthy trail, the informant checking in on them every so often. Solus and

Leilana found themselves unable to speak, conflicted over their experiences with Rem, the young prince sleeping in the hay, wrapped around him like a blanket.

The jog to meet with the informant drew attention from the people of Kalonia but leaving immediately was a far easier feat. They now knew the faces that played a part in the assassination of their deity and their savior, gone in one fell swoop. They would never be allowed back in that city; they were wiser off never returning. Met with a blank stare that evolved into a glare upon seeing citizens ushering them out in a less than friendly matter, the man on his horse-drawn carriage wielded a sharp tongue the moment that they arrived past his scheduled time, his scraggly brown hair up on all ends, covered by a top hat. He dressed as though he were attending a dinner party in Linmus, his overall appearance condescending. And they were stuck with him for the next day.

"I can only take you so far," the informant, who earlier gave them the name Lunious, specified. "Up to the Teir region, no more. You get off my carriage at the first town we reach."

"We understand," Solus replied, leaning over the cart to face the man, resting his chin on his hands. "We appreciate your help nonetheless, Lunious. You didn't have to."

"Oh, I know," Lunious scoffed, whipping the reins a bit harder on his steed to speed up their pacing. "As much trouble as you got into back there? You're lucky that Prince Remiel made it out in one piece! You know how screwed we'd be with no king in Adrylis? How would I be able to sell my goods if they're all chewing their nails and biting their tongue about this war? They're supposed to be preparing for it by buying me out!"

Solus gripped to the cart to steady himself when the horse jerked forward and hit a bump on the road. Leilana winced when her head hit the back of the cart, rubbing the injury, glaring up at the man, but by the time that he started up another topic, they were well past their annoyance.

"Jumping the gun and screwing up that bad. Kid's not so bright, is he?"

"He's bright but reckless, so it pans out," Solus admitted.

"Lady Karma's gonna nip him in the ass if she hasn't already." Solus visibly flinched, and Leilana sighed, leaning against the cart. He wasn't very subtle when it came to dealing with people and his emotions, was he?

"This guy is sketchy, and he's a little rude," Leilana told Solus upon him taking a seat. "What made you pick him out of the crowds?"

"He spotted Rem, claimed that he knew his mom and wanted to help us. That was his shorthand explanation." Solus smiled at her, resting a hand on his knee as he straightened his back. "Contrary to his questionable behavior, he has a kind heart. That is hard to find in trying times."

"I still feel like he could be a little nicer."

"People aren't perfect, Leilana. There is always something more that we want or expect from others in hopes of glorifying our ideals."

Leilana wrapped her arms around her knees, resting her chin on them. "I don't expect people to be perfect, Solus. But humanity leaves you wondering about their unworldly actions. They prosper, but they're really only looking out for themselves."

Solus allowed her words to sink in before turning his gaze up to the sky, folding his hands. "Sometimes that's how it is. We spend our lives wondering what instrument we are to play in this symphony of life. We learn the notes, string together the tools needed to craft an efficient sound, and we play again and again, and we hope to become better. We share that gift we possess with others who see us at work, and we form an unbreakable connection. That is meaning."

A faint crimson aura surrounded Solus's body, and before Leilana could react, it had dissipated, much like Rem and Kindall before him. That made two. Leilana grinned, tucking a loose strand of hair behind her ear. "You know, you have a funny way of spooling an analogy."

"It is a talent of mine," he joked. "Do you like it?"

"I do. It's comforting to hear."

He could turn the tides of his soul with the drop of a hat. Solus was a perfect foil to Rem's personality. He was stoic, motivated, gentle and kind, more of Rem's shield rather than his servant. He didn't let Rem dominate him but knew his place. Still, Solus's newfound connection was suspicious. There wasn't a drop of magic in his bloodline—she would have sensed his prowess, and he certainly wasn't a Maester like Rem. That left her considering that he may have woken to his part in her pilgrimage, but any magic was a mystery. There was no guidance from the Warlords. She would have to uncover his totem on her own.

Rem was a mesh of misunderstanding to everyone but Solus, which eliminated that trait. Solus wasn't the type to embody laughter or merriment and allow it to dominate him. His desire for friendship was undeniable, but he didn't go out of his way to achieve it, evident by the way that he treated Amiria. Humbleness seemed akin to his personality, but like the rest, that was also reliant on the person he offered it to. That left passion and love. His actions were passionate, his friendship with Rem and the desire to protect her on unbreakable levels. Then there was love, a concept that she couldn't comprehend.

"Is something wrong?" Solus asked, cutting through the silence. Leilana opened her mouth to speak, but no words rose. She folded her hands and cleared her throat, averting her eyes from him. Solus stretched out his hand to her, his want to comfort increasing. She wasn't normally this closed off.

"Getting late," Lunious called while looking over his map, causing Solus to lower his hand. "You kids might want to sleep. We'll reach the closest spot in an hour or two."

"I don't need to sleep," Solus replied. Leilana was settling under one of the blankets Lunious had graciously provided... for a small fee that cost the last of her funds. It would be a miracle if they could find decent refuge in the next town, given that Solus was the only one left with Nyte coins.

"Whatever's your fancy, kid."

Lunious tugged on the reins, the horse letting out a whinny before continuing down the beaten path. Solus glanced over the cart at the empty streets. Nothing along the way but paddies that overflowed and killed the grass. The springtime air was so crisp that he could taste the atmosphere on his tongue. Whatever lined their path to the eastern continent was abound in something much different from his northern roots or the eastern borders.

"What's the closest town anyway?" Solus asked a few minutes into the unfavorable silence.

"Linarus. Pretty small place, lots of paddies and farm-land, not much to go around. Got a great tavern though. The booze is top notch, could almost rival the castle bars." Solus wasn't much of a drinker, so he didn't step into taverns often, but the lure of alcohol did sound tempting as a respite.

"Did someone mention a tavern?" Solus looked over at the young prince leaning over the carriage to keep his balance over the rickety road. "I wouldn't mind going for some drinks." Solus visibly cringed—they were low enough on funds as it was, and now the prince was dying for a stiff one since the knowledge of his last birthday was catching on fast.

"Are you even old enough to drink?" Lunious asked.

"He's newly sixteen," Solus piped up. "Barely the age limit."

Lunious ushered his horse onwards, the animal's hooves trotting against the dirt, pushing up some pebbles now and again. "Better tell that to the tavern mistress then. I don't argue the idea of needing a little pick-me-up just to get through the night."

Solus followed Rem's gaze after receiving silence over Lunious's statement. He was staring down at Leilana, who remained asleep, bundled under the blankets. Sometimes, Rem was too thick-headed for his own good. Solus crossed his arms, smirking at the younger man's back.

"You know," The gesture caused Rem to jump, the chill of his friend's stare rushing down his spine. "If you want to protect her, why not just tell Leilana how you really feel instead of pushing her away and lying by saying that you don't trust her?"

"What makes you think I trust her?" he asked.

"You're like an epic, Remiel. It's easy to flip through countless pages and choose your favorite parts once you get through the story enough times over." After taking a place next to his friend, propping up his legs and resting a hand under his chin, he chuckled as he continued, "Besides, I'm your best friend. You can tell me anything in that silly head of yours."

Rem rolled his eyes. "Yeah, you're right about that. Even if I held my tongue, you'd chew it off."

Solus was beaming. "I'm glad you see it my way. Back on subject. What do you think of her?"

Rem sighed, crossing his arms. "I think she's a lot like you, but not like you at the same time." Solus raised an eyebrow. That was rather contradictory. "She puts me in my place and tries to do the right thing. Can be kind of annoying at times, but I value it. And if you like her right off the bat, it has to speak leaps and bounds for how she must be."

"Then why do you test her?"

"Because this journey isn't meant to be easy. People are going to be hurt, and others will die. She's got enough on her plate, and this is her first time seeing Adrylis. Why the hell does she need to get involved in my pilgrimage when she's got her own?"

"Bear in mind, this is your first time outside of the walls as well, and I haven't gone very far myself. But that is beside the point. I think that you should at least try to talk to her. I know that you remember what you said to her in Kalonia."

"Wha-I-"

"Epic," Solus repeated, tapping his forehead. "Now, time for talking is over. If we are going to be arriving in the next town, we'd best be prepared. I think that we can stop there and make our way to the next city on foot. Leilana does have her own map. Now, back to bed with you." Rem kept a finger pointed in the air, his mouth hanging open before he closed it shut, rolling onto his side. "Good night."

"Night." Rem paused before stating, "I'll try and apologize to Leilana tomorrow. I don't want her to stay angry at me. Or to die if she explodes."

"A wise move, Highness."

Lunious rested a hand on the side of his face and sighed. Conversations between nobility were so damn boring. Couldn't go around talking about money or women, nope, they just had to stroll down the path of war, redemption, and drama, drama, drama. Well, at least they were keeping their spirits up.

FOURTEEN

Solus was the first to jump from the carriage when they arrived in Linmus late into the night, just before eleven. The moon was still high enough in the sky for Lunious to briefly explain the phases of time and space to the three teenagers. Rem, uninterested by the spiel, took off after a few minutes to look for the tavern and settle down for the night. Leilana watched from afar as the young prince trekked through the open fields, talking briefly to the townsfolk that passed him by. At one point, she saw him give a nod in response and take off further into the area. Solus was hesitant to follow him at first, but in the end, thanked Lunious for the lesson and went after the young prince to keep him from running into trouble.

"That Solus kid sure does know how to take on burdens," Lunious began, taking a long drag on his pipe to clear his own air, letting the smoke run free. "Must be nice to have a heart mended for pain."

Leilana took to gathering their belongings in silence while the man spoke, stopping short when her fingers grazed metal. She pulled out what appeared to be a pistol hidden in the haystack. The barrel was icy, bound and built-in gold. There were traces of a powder lingering on the weapon, which she wiped her bag. She tucked it back under the haystack, not wanting to deal with the manner.

"You're awfully quiet, Leilana." He kept his back turned. "What ails you?"

She had never heard him speak with such sincerity—it was unnerving. She gathered her bag and held it close to her. "It's nothing. I should catch up with Solus and Rem. I don't want to be left behind."

Lunious stepped towards her, towering over her diminutive height. She took a step back, and before she could question him, he tossed her a bag, which she nearly dropped out of surprise. The texture was rough, but a durable hide, able to properly carry whatever contents laid inside.

"You've got a long journey ahead of you. Wouldn't want you starving to death."

"Thank you." She didn't want to seem ungrateful. He brought them this far of his own free will, even if the circumstances were confusing. "I'm sure that we could use this effectively." She jumped off the carriage and continued into town.

"Oh, you will! Food doesn't last forever, ya know!"

Leilana listened to the horse's hooves trot against the ground in the opposite direction before ceasing altogether. She turned around to find the merchant gone, and relief embellished her. She set the bag of food on the ground and opened it, an herbal scent overflowing from the interior. Fruits and vegetables, no meats or grains that could spoil too fast. It seemed normal enough, but there was something unsettling about it, and she couldn't put her finger on what. Maybe she was paranoid because Lunious didn't seem trustworthy himself. A man that talked to the people he was trying to help while keeping on his toes about what he said and why concerned her more than it had Solus.

She tied the bag shut, tossing it over her shoulder. The weight was immense over her tiny body, but not unmanageable. It would still be time before strength could grow along with her like Rem told her before. What was adulthood even like? Solus and Rem were older, but they weren't adults yet themselves. Lancett was a bit older than her, but still nowhere near drinking age like her new allies. Ennis was only sixteen when he set off on his path to becoming a Warlord four years ago. He would have been twenty now, but he died just shy of eighteen, nowhere near the proper age of adulthood.

She spent time aimlessly walking, unsure of where Solus and Rem had gone off to. The people of this town were basking under the moonlight, some with tired faces and dark circles under their eyes, others filled with chortles and proclamations to those they walked alongside, hoes and wool-sewn bags over their shoulders. Though spacious and filled with more greenery than she had seen in any town thus far, Linarus was nowhere near as spacious as Kalonia.

Daybreak was a long way off, and yet several people were still out gathering herbs and planting more in their place. It seemed to be their specialty. It was quiet. Quaint, almost. She could see a prosperous life here somewhere down the line. Maybe not a life for her as a Warlord, but it was a life to hope for someday. She set the bag of food down near one of the open fields, figuring that the villagers could find more use for it than them—she couldn't bring herself to trust anything relating to Lunious. Sketchy merchants were the worst kinds of people according to Ennis.

She spent the next twenty minutes or so roaming Linarus, rubbing her tired eyes every so often. She almost missed her warm bed back at Magiten Academy. Sleeping in hotels wasn't bad either, nor was sleeping under the stars or in caves, but there was no comparison to your own pillow and blanket. It wasn't long before she stumbled upon Solus and Rem standing outside of a small building chatting up one of the locals that had a drink in hand and a big smile on his face.

That had to be the tavern.

"Leilana!" Solus waved to her. Upon her return to their side, she briefly turned to Rem, who refused to meet her stare, biting his bottom lip to keep his tongue. "Sorry for leaving so suddenly."

"It's all right," she told Solus. "I found you, after all. So, you and Rem are going drinking?"

"We're planning on it. Care to join us or something?" Rem asked, clearing his throat afterward.

Leilana shook her head slowly in response. "I'm not old enough. I don't even think that I'd like it. It has a strange odor."

"I'm sure that's not the case," Solus chuckled, laying a hand on her head. "You just need to find something that suits your palette, like with food. But that's a lot further down the road anyways. I'll see about finding a place to lay our heads for the night, and you can go ahead."

Leilana reached up her own hands to lay across his, grasping the warmth of his palm for a few seconds before moving it away from her head. "I may go right to sleep, just so you know."

Solus grinned, nodding in acknowledgment. "Rightfully, you should."

"In the meantime, I'm probably going to read while I'm waiting for you to figure things out. I'll sit out here under the light. It's too noisy inside." Solus and Rem watched Leilana plant herself on a nearby bench, pulling out the Lasette from her bag, promptly scanning the contents of a random page.

"She's weird, but it's almost admirable," Rem admitted. "Always has her nose in that book."

"It is a treasured possession of hers," Solus implied. "Of course she'll take pride in its use. Let's leave her to her work and get that drink you've so desired."

Rem and Solus entered the tavern to boundless chatter, clinking glasses and merriment along with occasional risen voices due to the influence of the drinks in hand and spirit burning their souls.

"Welcome to Midstream," the proclaimed tavern mistress minding the shop piped up.

Both Solus and Rem were shocked to find that the owner was a girl around their age, having a few sips of a grape-scented alcohol. Solus was quick to point out that it had to be Moscato. Her long red hair was pulled back into a sleek ponytail, the wine glass between her index finger and thumb a bit slippery. She wore a sly grin, leaning over the counter to meet with the two new faces in her haven, bright blue eyes peering into Rem.

She briefly eyed her glass, holding it up as a sign of good tidings. "Want some?" She may not have had professional mannerisms, but at least she wasn't some loony drunk or a crazed old woman.

"Actually, yes, I do," Rem replied, resting both hands on the counter while meeting the young woman face to face. "Give me your Moscato." Solus covered his face with his hand, unsure of how this situation was going to unfold.

"Feisty, aren't we? I can set you up real nice-like while you're waiting. The first one is always free for weary travelers, and you look old enough. You're both sixteen, right?"

"Just turned sixteen last week," Rem responded.

Solus held up his hand in lieu of a wave. "Seventeen, actually. I would rather not take with nothing to offer up in return."

"Oh, you're no fun. And it was free too." She tucked some loose strands behind her ear.

"I'll take his drink then." Rem slipped past the girl's fingertips and claimed her drink for his own, putting the icy liquid to his lips and pouring it down the hatch before setting the empty glass on the counter, pushing it towards her. She spent the next minute in complete shock at how bold he was.

Solus was just as surprised as her, but came to his senses much faster, grabbing the young man by the arm, holding up a finger towards the waitress before pulling him away. "Remiel, that was rude. You're supposed to be keeping a low profile."

"I am keeping a low profile," he retorted, which earned him a sharp glare. Rem outstretched his arms in retaliation. "Everyone here is having fun, knocking bottles back, why can't I?"

"You have to think about your actions before you make them."

"Because I have more to lose," Rem scoffed. "Like hell. You're as bad as my parents were." Solus folded his arms, withholding a snarl.

"I'm just trying to make sure that you're safe," Solus said lowly. "That is my duty not only as your servant but as your friend. I'm not going to let you get too reckless."

"Maybe you should try it. It'll knock some years off your lifespan." Without another word, Rem returned to the counter, taking a seat at the barstool. Solus shook his head before taking a place at a booth on the opposite side of the tavern, unable to cope with his emotions. "You mix drinks well, it seems. Any chance I could have another, miss?"

She crossed her arms, narrowing her eyes. "If you don't rob people again and pay the tab, you're welcome in my tavern. That's grounds to get you socked. You're lucky it was me."

He nodded to himself. "I understand. And might I know your name?"

"Sien Kaiser, Sien like the color cyan. Apparently, it was my mother's favorite, rest her soul," she introduced herself. "And you?"

"Call me Rem," he said simply.

"Rem, eh? It rolls off the tongue."

"Not as much as Sien," he responded, raising a curious eyebrow.

"Well, Rem, I have but one thing left to say to you." She slid a glass of Moscato over to him, and he caught it before it tipped over. "Bottoms up." Rem smirked, enjoying the way that the sentence danced off her lips, slow and structured, almost challenging. With a shrug, he took a few slow sips of the drink, smacking his lips once at the taste. Sien didn't avert her gaze.

"What's a pretty girl like you doing running a tavern anyways?"

"It was my father's," she said humbly while wiping down the counter. "My younger sister and I handle things around here in his absence though."

"Traveling?"

"Dead."

"Oh." Rem swallowed his words, regretting them immediately. He coughed in place of any hidden words before merely responding, "My apologies." She smiled at him before turning away to attend to other customers. Rem lowered his head, mumbling, "I lost my parents too, so I know how you feel."

"It's nothing to fret over," Sien told him, setting her rag

on the counter again. "Loss comes with time, as does the healing."

Rem wiped his lips clean of the dripping booze. "You're a lot more formal than I took you for."

She once again smiled at him. "I could say the same about you."

Solus stepped outside, tired of the rambunctious atmosphere. Leilana was fast asleep on the bench, her head propped up against an arm, the Lasette half-closed. Solus took one look around the area, grateful that no one was around to notice her. He took a seat on the bench next to her, shaking her shoulder.

"Leilana. It's dangerous to sleep in unknown territory." She mumbled in her sleep, brushing his hand away slightly, and with a sigh, he leaned in closer, whispering softly into her ear, "I will steal you away with the night." That roused her from her slumber, and she nearly smacked him with the grimoire before he swiftly dodged, leaning against the bench. "Good morning to you as well."

"Don't do that," she warned, pointing a finger at him while wiping the remnants of sleep from her barely open eyes. "What was that, some sort of mantra?"

Solus sat up straight, realizing he was out of danger. "It is something my father used to whisper whenever Rem or I fell asleep outside. He was prone to scaring us, acting like some sort of demon."

"It sounds like your father is a bit on the strange side."

Solus chuckled. He had spent the last four years of his life under Cyril's watchful eyes, and sure, the coot was strange, playful, yet stoic, but he was father of the year solely for taking him in and raising him to be dignified and caring of others.

"He was a good man. I'm grateful to have known him as long as I had."

"Was he not your birth father?"

Solus shook his head. "I was adopted by the Brenner family. I was alone in the streets when Rem found me, and I was without memories of my previous experiences. I guess it was fate that brought us together in the end."

Leilana pressed her back against the bench. "There's not much that I remember about when I was a child. But moving forward has always been the better thing. Why harp on things that are going to keep you down? The past is passed."

"I thought there was a reason why I felt so in sync with you," Solus joked. "We're not so different after all."

"Cut from similar cloths," Leilana responded. "It makes sense. You remind me of my brother."

"I'm no Warlord. I'm not even a Maester." He laid a hand over his own heart, smirking. "I shall always just be Solus, servant to the future King."

Shattering glass tore their attention away from one another, and reluctantly, they returned to the tavern. Upon throwing open the doors, they found Rem hovering above another attendee, wiping blood from his lips, his eyes glinting a shade of amber. His Bloodlinch powers were slipping in again. Rem pressed his foot against the man's chest, shoving him onto the ground. Solus was about to sprint over to ease the prince's budding rage, but Sien reacted first, grabbing Rem by the arm, shoving him against a nearby wall, pinning him by his throat. Leilana's mouth fell open.

"No trouble in my tavern," she sneered, causing Rem to snarl. "Doesn't matter who threw the first punch, the last one is mine."

Sien released her hold on Rem, shoving him in the process, and approached the drunken man lying on the ground. She exhaled slowly, holding up both hands, a teal aura spreading over his body, cleansing his wounds. Solus curiously raised an eyebrow; he knew that there was a variety of Maesters and Arcana roaming as freelancers, but healers were among the rare breed.

"Someone send him on his way," Sien told the onlookers after getting the man to his feet, to which a woman stepped up to the plate, her expression apologetic.

Rem was already back in a booth, staring blankly at a glass of water while tapping the table with his index finger, watching the liquid shift about the condensed space. He could still see his mother's cool eyes gazing back at him. He slapped the drink aside, the glass shattering on the floor. Slamming his hands against the table, he rose from the booth and stepped outside. Solus groaned, chasing after him. Sien sighed, laying her hands on the bar stool. Taverns were a common place for fights to occur, the alcohol fueling already tortured minds, and she was used to healing others before banishing them for the night.

"So, you're a healer," Leilana piped up. Sien hadn't even noticed the young girl that had come to her side, her azure eyes wide with wonder. "I haven't met a lot at Magiten Academy."

Sien mustered up a tired smile. "I take it you've got questions?"

"I can understand if you're busy," Leilana responded. "But I'm curious to know more about your skills. I'm sorry if it's a bit forward."

"There's not much I could tell you—you're either born with it or you're not." Sien winked at the young girl. "Still, you're welcome to take a load off. I'm not gonna offer you a drink though, you still look like such a sweetheart and there's no way I'm letting any of these unruly men take a bite out of you."

Leilana raised an eyebrow at the strange context. Then again, if the girl was implying something dastardly, at least Solus and Rem would be quick to come to her aide. Or, at least Solus would. She reluctantly took a seat at the barstool, not wanting to be too far out of range from the tavern mistress in case more drama went down.

"I'm Sien Kaiser, by the way," she told Leilana. "I own this place."

"Leilana Erovina," Leilana replied. "I'm a student training to become a Warlord. I'm here with my friends. I think they'll be back soon." She had to use the term loosely for Rem's relationship with her, but it seemed to fare well enough in her eyes.

"Ooh, a Warlord, how fancy," Sien beamed. "Well, feel free to relax, like I said. I'll just be here."

Glasses were continuing to slam against the tables, clinking against one another in merriment. It was as though the fight that broke out only minutes ago was no longer an issue. Leilana flipped through the pages of the Lasette, mumbling a few of the passages to herself. She noticed that Sien would occasionally look over at her before continuing her work, and soon enough, the tavern began to file out when a small girl with long brown hair tied into a braid stepped out, outright yelling at the drunkards to get on with their lives until the tavern reopened in the morning.

"Not her, Luna," Sien told the girl as she set to approaching Leilana. "She's waiting for her friends. She's got my blessing." Leilana met Luna's gaze and tried to smile, and Luna shrugged her off, obeying her older sister's words before taking off to the back rooms, letting her hair down.

Leilana's smile wiped away. "I don't think she likes me much."

"No, she just doesn't know you," Sien replied, wiping down the counters with a worn rag. "You'll have to excuse her. Luna is a bit antisocial; she's been that way since our father passed away a couple of years ago. It's been the two of us for a while."

The tavern entrance opened, and in stepped Solus with Rem in tow, the young prince appearing both irritable and apologetic; to Leilana, it was an awkward combination, but she supposed that Rem was unpredictable, to begin with.

"My friend would like to offer his apologies for causing trouble in your tavern, Sien," Solus stated. When no words were offered up in confirmation, Solus shoved Rem's arm with his elbow, glaring at the boy in the corner of his eye. Rem let out a small grunt of discomfort before stepping to the counter, laying a hand on his chest and bowing to the waitress.

"Please forgive me."

"What happened back there, Rem?" Leilana asked, which allowed Sien to put two and two together in her mind that these were the friends she spoke of. Seemed like a solid crowd.

Rem scoffed. "Some idiot thought I was hitting on Sien and tried to pick a fight with me. And he dumped his booze on my hair like some prickly preteen, so I punched him."

"My hero," Sien mumbled sarcastically, and Rem merely stared at her. She cleared her throat, taking hold of the keys around her neck, approaching the entrance. "Well,

I accept your apology. But if you'll excuse me, I need to close for the night, and you'll need to leave."

"Wait, there's something I wanted to ask," Solus exclaimed. "Do you know of any inns around the area? We needed a place to rest for the night before we're able to continue our journey."

"A journey, you say?" Sien pursed her lips for a few seconds. "Where are you headed?"

"Classified," Rem said quickly.

"An Arcana, a stalwart man, and a rowdy boy. It seems like a common cluster of personalities. But, you're no ordinary travelers," Sien concluded, keeping her back turned.

The lock snapping into place from the inside was audible, which made Leilana hesitant. Sien stepped past them to seal the entrance to the back rooms, another distinct lock rushing through their ears. Rem's eyebrows began furrowing at the swift change of pace, and Solus was already resting his hand on the sheath of his blade, the anxiety shared between his two companions too much for him to witness without putting an end to the conflict himself.

"I heard around the grapevine of a group coming north from Kalonia," Sien continued. "They say that the group eradicated the Dirionus guarding the town and left without being too inconspicuous. And it's no coincidence that three strange faces have shown up in my tavern. Tell me, was it you three?"

"We don't know what you're talking about," Rem began, resting a hand on the counter in front of her, bearing into her eyes. "So, stop with the lackluster accusations, because you don't even know if they're plausible without reason."

Sien reached out a hand to lay on Rem's arm, and pain shot up his right shoulder, causing him to flinch. His injury still hadn't properly healed from their endeavors in Kalonia, and now that a proper healer had seen to it, he was bound to be exposed. She grabbed him by his shirt collar and pulled him to her level, resting her forehead against his, her eyes fluttering closed. Solus was about to step into action when Rem held up a hand to sway him.

"Seems you're running a fever," she mumbled. "I thought that you looked pale when I first saw you. Your breathing is a little irregular. Your clothes are beginning to tatter. You're obviously injured and trying to hide it. You were in a fight long before arriving."

She opened her eyes to meet his gaze, her expression both calm and stern. Rem stepped back from her, baffled by the diagnosis before laying a hand on his own forehead. She was right; he was warmer, and not even he noticed the fact.

"Am I right then, Rem? Or perhaps I should say, Prince Remiel," Sien hissed. Rem and Solus looked to one another, feigning confusion before returning their attention to their captor.

"You don't know what you're talking about," Rem began.

"Am I accusing without reason?" Sien scoffed. "Why have you come here?"

"Who's Remiel?" Leilana chimed in. "Our friend is Rem, remember?"

"Don't think I'm stupid," Sien replied. "His mannerisms in the tavern were more than enough to tell me that he was dignified, spoiled, and reckless." She pointed a finger at Solus, her eyes questioning. "He's the wayward Prince of Adrylis, isn't he?"

Solus kept a straight face. "No. Just a stupid boy." Rem's head snapped over to Solus, scowling.

Sien's eyes were bearing on Solus's being, and he still didn't crack. "If you're worried I'll open a can of worms on his identity, there wouldn't be anything in it for me. Let's face it, you'll need me."

"And what makes you think we'll need you?" Solus retorted.

"Rem is feverish, an early onset of a virus. I can whip up medicine to lessen his symptoms before they've surfaced. I can be his caretaker until he recovers, but I won't have secrets, or you will all be on the streets. And I don't think you would want that. There are many cold fronts at this point, and without early treatment, I doubt he would last the night without becoming too ill to move forward."

Leilana looked perplexed. "Medicine? I thought that you ran the tavern."

"It all brews," Sien responded. "I'm a trained herbalist, a tavern owner to pay the mortgage, and I lease. Or, you know, I could sell you the medicines that you desire on Remiel's tab and send you on your way, but it's not going to be cheap." Solus's muscles hardened.

"You can't-" Leilana tried to reason.

"Oh, believe me, I can. I am designated leader of this village, and I have a say-so of who gets to step on my grounds. I don't have secrets. I would like to be treated the same."

"You're just full of surprises," Solus admitted. "Tavern mistress, apothecary, and chief to a budding village. There are no limitations to your skill."

"The truth," Sien pressed. Solus stepped to Rem, laying a hand on his shoulder, a telling look on his face. Rem sighed, nodding in approval. Maybe it would help to have proper allies in better places, and Sien didn't seem the type to go running her mouth too often.

"I am Prince Remiel Ankove Vesarus. Heir to the throne of Linmus. This is my attendant, Solus Brenner.

And the girl is Leilana Erovina, an Arcana training to become a Warlord." Rem laced his front bangs between his fingertips. Sien raised an eyebrow, becoming intrigued by the direction that the conversation was going in. "Solus and I are searching for a way to restore Linmus. Leilana might have a way to help us, so she chose to tag along."

"I figured it would be beneficial to my mission as well, as I'm supposed to gathering totems for my pilgrimage," Leilana cut in. Sien nodded to herself. That did explain a lot; someone like Leilana didn't seem the type to mesh with royalty despite the formalities.

"I can't say much else aside from that, because there isn't much to mention. I just want to help my people, but no one even knows that I'm alive, and that's for the best until I come closer to my goals," Rem finished. "Now can you unlock the door and answer Solus's question about where we can stay for the night? I'm starting to feel tired and want to lie down. We'll be out of here tomorrow."

Sien sighed, opening the door to the back rooms. "This is the inn," she responded, resting her hands on her hips after untying her ponytail, her crimson locks flowing down her back. "We allow people to rest here if they're too drunk or just in need of a place to stay. If you can afford to, you're welcome to our beds. And only with my seal of approval will you be leaving tomorrow."

"What?" Rem croaked out merely from astonishment, clearing his throat quickly. "Why is that?"

"From what I've heard, a lot happened at Linmus. The kingdom fell, and many are unable to return to the land without permission. Those that do enter never seem to return. You've got a lot of work cut out for you in the long run. Besides, even if you could return to the kingdom, you won't get far if you aren't properly treated. You'd likely die before you got to the northernmost point of the continent. And what kind of apothecary would I be if I were to turn away the ill-ridden crown prince? It's sheer idiocy to let you try anything that reckless."

Rem's cheeks flushed. This was the first time that he had seen genuine generosity with an edge that didn't tie into his title. She was being hard on him rather than reluctant. "Thank you, Sien. I really do appreciate it."

She playfully rolled her eyes. "Yeah, yeah, whatever. Hurry it up, we don't have all night. You can work around the room arrangements however you'd like. There's only one room that's been taken, and the guy using it when to bed way before the chaos started."

Solus watched Sien guide Leilana and Rem passage into the back rooms, the lengthy hallway dimly lit by some candles. He kept his arms folded, pondering over the sudden gesture that Rem offered up. He was so cautious about his desire to keep his identity hidden, and no amount of alcohol intake could have ripped that morality away. Why would he in good conscience allow his guard to drop around Sien, someone that he only met a few hours ago? He supposed there was no choice but to trust Rem's judgment and wait for him to recover before asking him directly.

Within minutes, Rem was bundled under a blanket, a rather aged brass-colored mercury thermometer in his mouth. After the stress of the winding day settled into her body, Sien was barely awake, keeping a close eye on any significant changes. Solus was standing next to the door, rubbing his temples to rouse himself out of his own draining stupor while Leilana stood at his side, curiously watching Sien's handiwork. Sien waited for the device to steady before reclaiming it from his lips.

"Five points for my accuracy," Sien joked, waving the thermometer around to drop the thermos level. Rem groaned, hiding under the covers. Sien laid a hand over the spot where his face was. "You know, usually when people stay at my tavern, it's with bar-flu, not influenza."

Rem smiled, shrugging his shoulders from under the sheets. "What can I say? I'm different."

The tavern mistress took hold of the dripping rag, ringing it out before laying it over Rem's forehead. "Well, Mr. Different, you're going to be spending the next few days right here. We can figure out how you'll be paying off this room once you've recovered."

Rem's smile faded away. "Pay?"

Sien rested her hands on her hips. "Surely you didn't think that getting sick on my watch meant that you'd be getting free living space?"

"No," Rem mumbled, sinking further under the covers.

"Don't worry, it's nothing serious. May be stress over-load. Have you been sleeping?"

"Neither of us truly have," Solus stated. "We've been moving from place to place rather frequently and have yet to properly settle without some sort of turmoil following."

"Well, luckily you ended up running into my tavern then. Now you can ease up, if only for one night." She moved the covers from Rem's face. "And as for you, we're going to work on eliminating the toxins from your body so that you aren't too susceptible to any viruses through Adrylis. You're going to need to be in top form when you reach Linmus."

"Yes, ma'am," he whimpered.

"We'll do the same for you, Leilana, Solus. That way you don't end up falling short yourselves." Leilana nodded, looking up at Solus, who grinned back at her in response, shrugging his right shoulder.

"I'm going to study my grimoire a little before bed," Leilana told the two before stepping back. "See you both in the morning." Without another word, she exited to a room across the hall and closed the door gently. Solus chuckled to himself. It seemed that her work was never done.

"Is there anything you need me to help with, Sien?" Solus asked, watching Rem slip into a rather fitful slumber, though the question came out more strained than he would have liked. It almost startled him. He hadn't been sleeping the best, but was he really that exhausted?

"You should get some rest," Sien explained. "You look worn out." Solus tried to smile to play off her concerns, but he couldn't find the energy to muster it up genuinely. "I know you've been acting as Rem and Leilana's caretaker, but you don't have to kill yourself. You're allowed to ask for help."

"I'll rest when I see fit, I promise," Solus told her. "Leilana doesn't need the added burden when she already has enough on her shoulders. And you're already doing more than enough between running the tavern, caring for your younger sister, and now caring for us." His breaths were running ragged, his exhaustion becoming more evident. "Guiding Rem is my responsibility. I was entrusted this duty by my late father, and by Rem's parents. If I sit back and do nothing, what use am I as his servant?"

"The way that the two of you interact, you're more than just his servant," Sien retorted. "I doubt that he would want anything to happen to you." She pointed down at the sleeping prince. "Don't be as stubborn as this one, Solus. The two of you need each other."

Solus sighed, leaning his head back against the wall. "I know that. I just want to protect him. Remiel has been through too much for him to face his problems alone."

"Things are different now," Sien urged. "Don't feel like you need to shoulder his problems all by yourself. You can talk to me, and you can certainly talk to Leilana. I know that we barely know each other, but it's best to have someone to lean on."

"Thank you," he responded, arching his back into a subtle bow. "I'm appreciative, truly. I'll try and get some sleep."

Leilana climbed into bed a few hours after the tavern had settled, the Lasette bundled in her arms. She heaved a sigh and allowed her head to rest upon the warmth of the pillow, her hair sprawling out in every direction. There was light snoring protruding the wall opposite hers, making it easy for her to assume that the walls were paper thin and that everyone else was a heavy sleeper singing like canaries to the poor unfortunate souls left to endure the melody. She wondered if Solus could sleep.

She flipped through the pages of the Lasette upon rising to a sit again, her hair tickling the back of her neck. Shivers ran down her spine when she settled on information regarding the Orb of Concord. The image always seemed so... daunting. Solus and Rem were adamant about knowing more on it, but they couldn't translate the text like her. She gathered a pen and sheet of paper, writing down the text in linguistics more akin to them. Solus had provided her with a brief lesson on their scriptures, a more modernized language called Sentience. The letters were like the ancient Minsuran text, twisted in a manner unique to those that spoke and wrote in Sentience; that was how she could understand their worded statements.

Each letter was a word of its own in the Minsuran text, bound to chains of the tongue. They lashed out when a spell was cast, heeding the call, shaped into something of use. And all that remained was she to carry the Minsuran name and conjuring prowess.

The door swung open, slamming against the wall. Leilana nearly jumped out of her skin, the grimoire flying out of her hands before she reached up to catch it, mumbling the lost words before realizing that there was no threat in her doorway. Before her stood Rem, absent of his shirt, dripping with sweat. She slowly pulled the Lasette to her face, shielding her eyes from the sight, her face beginning to heat up.

"Hey, don't hide!" Rem exclaimed, keeping his voice low. He reached out his hands after trotting up to her, pulling the grimoire from her face, his eyes practically blazing. "I'm not looking to cause trouble for you *all* the time, you know."

Leilana wanted to scream at him to go back to bed and continue to rest but found it hard to avert her attention from his bare chest, her eyes flickering up and down between the muscle and his eyes. Rem didn't look too amused by her gestures, grabbing the blanket covering her, wrapping it around his body, planting himself on the floor.

"*Hey*," she exclaimed. "I was using that!"

He shrugged. "Well, as an Arcana, you win some, you

lose some, and this way you can actually talk to me without being distracted."

"What are we even talking about?" Rem grew silent, and Leilana leaned over the bed to get a good look at him. His eyebrows were furrowing, harrowed with deep thought, biting his bottom lip. His right leg bounced from the anxiety of facing his words head-on. She almost laughed at his shift into meekness within seconds. She figured that he was bad at expressing himself, which is why people never came to truly understand him, but she didn't imagine that he could be so sweet-looking. "You're sick, you know. Go back to bed, Rem."

"Can't," he choked out. "Can't sleep. Nightmares."

"Nightmares? What about?"

"It's not a big deal. I just wanted to be around some-one." So, he runs to her in his time of need, but not Solus? She supposed it was a change, and maybe even an opportunity.

"Don't be afraid. You can tell me." Rem was startled by her voice emerging so close to his ear that he accidentally bumped the back of his head into hers upon jumping. Leilana whined in response, rubbing the aching spot while Rem sucked in air through his teeth, clutching some of his hair.

"Sorry..."

"That wasn't nice," she admitted.

"No, it really wasn't, I'm sorry, you just scared me." Rem drew in a breath and exhaled, a shrill whistle escaping his lips. "Look, I wanted to talk about what happened the other day in Kalonia. I, um... I'm sure I don't need to go into detail on it. Do I?"

She shook her head, not wanting to relive the splintered words. "Not at all."

"That was what my nightmare was about. I didn't remember anything I said, not until it seeped back into my memories. I was confused and becoming incapacitated only added to the mix. I don't understand why I snapped, or what led me to take it out on you." He wrapped his arms around his legs, resting his chin on his knees. "I wasn't myself, and I don't expect you to accept any apologies from me. I dealt a lot of damage to you."

Leilana was appalled. He was opening his emotions to her.

"Truth is," he continued, staring at his empty left palm. "I wasn't always that honest with you. I want to be your friend, maybe not now, but someday when we're both comfortable with one another. It's hard to connect with people when you've grown up with a shell. Because I'm a prince, I can make little mistakes in the path that I walk now—too many people see me as a leader, someone meant to usher in a new essence of prosperity now that my parents are gone."

He rose to a stand and wrapped the blanket around her shoulders. She traced her hands over the woven cotton, her fingers grazing his once he had pulled away.

"I don't know anything about carrying my own burdens just yet. I still have growing up to do myself, so, um..." He briefly averted his gaze, his cheeks reddening. "Maybe we can grow up together."

Her heart swelled at his words, and she couldn't stop her heart from wildly pounding against her chest. "I'd like that, Rem."

Come to terms with understanding.

Ascertain the growth and development of a new beginning.

Rem was taken aback by her smile. A faint glow engulfed his senses as if the stillness of the night drifted away. He looked at his hands to find that the illumination hadn't sparked from her, rather from himself. He tried to brush it away like dirt, to no avail. He could see it. The magic was resonating with him, someone that bypassed the first step towards the totem of understanding.

Leilana grabbed his hand, catching him off guard enough to ease his tension. "It's all right. Just understand that something better is coming. For both of us."

"You know something, don't you?"

Now she was holding both of his hands in hers, the young Prince's eyes darting between her firm grasp, her eyes, and then his shaky palms. His breath hitched in his throat when he tried to ask what she was doing, and his fingers tensed before calming her words, "I think that you and I were meant to cross paths. Solus thinks the same thing. You were always meant to be a piece of my pilgrimage. I know that now. I will do my best to understand more about you, Rem. And I hope that you bless me with the same respect someday."

His mouth went dry. In those few moments, she almost sounded regal. It was baffling to witness. "I-I-Okay then. Thank you, Leilana."

FIFTEEN

"Shoot, I'm out of verbena for Rem's medicine," Sien mumbled after throwing open every cabinet in the tavern. "And there's not enough time to go to the gardens for more."

Leilana was watching over her from the other side of the barstool, and at her side sat the bored-looking second-in-command to the tavern mistress, Luna Kaiser. Her chocolate-colored hair was pulled into a loose shoulder-length ponytail, and she was catching up on her daily routine of studying notes on different herbs to brew.

It was downtime in the early afternoon at Midstream, the customers barely filing in, and neither Solus nor Rem bothered to make an appearance. Luna decided to check on them in place of the older girls and found that Rem was still fast asleep while Solus was tossing and turning, his slumber restless.

"Did you need me to run and get some?" Luna asked, looking up from her journal. As she spoke, a group of six rather rowdy men stormed the tavern, and Sien was quick to jump back into business mode. Luna scoffed to herself as she set the book aside, watching the men fawn over her older sister's 'valuable assets.'

"Maybe I should go instead since you're about to have your hands full," Leilana suggested. "I'm sure I could figure out what's needed."

"The field-workers know my norms, just tell them that I

sent you," Sien called while blending together a few drinks. "They should be out already."

Leilana promptly stepped out of the tavern to leave the Kaiser siblings to their work. She remembered bypassing the paddies and fields when she first arrived in Linarus, but under the night sky, it was hard to see anything noteworthy. She trekked about the lively village for a decent amount of time before stumbling upon the familiar paddies.

"Put yer back into it, new guy!" One of the men called over the fields, laughing. Leilana didn't take notice of who spoke.

"Not gonna get anywhere with those stubby arms if ya don't push it!" Another joined in. She was taken aback by their carefree accents, even after becoming used to Luna and Sien's speech patterns. Though some words seemed a little broken at the seams, something about their phrasing was inviting in a way that rivaled Solus's humble and prim accent or Rem's brash yet courteous undertone.

"Stubby? I've been told I'm quite muscular." This voice was different—one that seemed primed, drenched with tenderness and trained in a wary manner. It reminded her of her own.

"Don't go gettin' cocky!" That belonged to the first voice, and now she could identify him by his long grey hair pulled into a slick ponytail.

Leilana was overlooking the paddies and rows of dirt being worked on by the farmers of the tiny town when her vision lined with a young man in the fields. He was clothed in a plain white shirt covered in dirt spots, holes in the bottom of his baggy pants; they were a bit oversized on him, but he managed. He could barely lift the hoe in his grasp to slam into the ground and dig up the weeds that were considerably growing, far off the mark due to his footing. He wiped sweat from his brow, brushing dark brown hair from his forehead in the process and exhaled, which emerged as a whistle.

"Lancett?" she called. The sudden address made Lancett jump, dropping the hoe to the ground before he scrambled to retrieve it, whirling around to face her. He blinked a few times, the sun blinding him for a moment.

"Leilana? What are you doing here?" Then his mind snapped back into place and he once again dropped his tool to the dirt. "Wait! You're alive! I can't believe you're alive!"

She rested a hand on her hip. "I thought that was you. It's been a while." Lancett gulped; she didn't look too pleased with him, even if her tone was quite the contrary.

"Whoa-ho! That Lance's girl?" The farmer furthest left piped up without bothering to whisper, brushing some of his wheat-colored hair out of his face.

"Nuts! He was just talkin' about her!"

Leilana cocked her head to the left, mostly oblivious to the context, her hair caressing her shoulder. "I think we need to talk."

Lancett flinched, her tone still icing his heart. Every word that she spoke chilled him to the core. "O-Oh, yes, of course. Um," He stepped out of the patches of dirt, fumbling over the tools lining the area. "everyone, a moment, if I may."

"Don't go too crazy," One of the men told him, waving a hand in dismissal.

Leilana took a glance at the bag that Lunious had given her and scoffed. As hungry as she felt, she knew that it wasn't wise to accept food from someone that she didn't have complete trust in. She left the bag near the fields. Maybe the other villagers could favor it more?

"Follow me," Lancett told her, starting down the beaten path in the opposite direction.

Leilana stared at his back and watched him dust off his clothes, fix his hair, generally try to make himself more appealing to her eyes. She wasn't sure what he was going for, but he supposed that every little gesture would improve his chances. He seemed the type to try and quell a situation before it became too unbearable, but she was uncertain of what came if he failed. There was one thing that she already knew though; he wanted to talk about why he left and how he ended up in this place fixing up a garden. He wanted to touch base.

"Where are you taking me anyway?"

"I made a friend here," he began, placing his hands in his pockets. "She showed me a place where she goes to speak in private with her younger sister. I can explain everything if you will allow me." Leilana decided it better to remain silent until that time came. It was easier to gather her thoughts rather than let them bubble to the surface like Amiria's.

The two came to a stop just outside of town, where several trees and vines lined their sight. Lancett approached some vines hanging low and brushed them aside with his hand, knocking them to the ground and revealing a field of flowers beyond the base of the area. No light shone to the outside—no one would be able to see them, the exchanged words lost to the wind. To Leilana, it was as if they had stepped into another world, shielded from Linarus.

"Here we are," Lancett told her, gesturing her towards the field.

Leilana should have been elated; she was back with Lancett again after having searched for him, but she couldn't help thinking of Solus and Rem. They had spent time together, merely a week, and she was already well connected to their plight. She was practically their prisoner, too willful to free herself from their unbuckled chains.

"I know there's a lot to explain," Lancett spoke up. "But I want to know your thoughts."

Leilana sighed and took a seat in the grass, folding her legs, setting the Lasette on her lap. "I'll be frank—I'm not happy. We were supposed to stick together. Weren't we?" Lancett's mouth went dry. "You went off on your own to look for Amiria. You didn't come back to see if I was alive."

"I believed in you," Lancett cut in. "I know you, and I know that you would never back down and allow life to be stripped from you. And you weren't alone, which I am thankful for."

"Solus and Rem are decent," Leilana stated. "I would be dead if not for them." Her eyes were filled with sincerity. Her heart had already stemmed from a new light, all without him at her side. Lancett withheld a frown. He couldn't allow himself to be jealous of people that he didn't even know.

"I know that what I did was reckless, and you're right to be upset at me. But I want to try and explain why I took off like that."

She flipped open the Lasette and skimmed through the pages. "You'd better make it good." Lancett wanted to retort that she could have at least pretended to acknowledge him, but decided it was better to avoid a worse outcome.

"I mean, um... you already know that I left to search for Amiria." She silently nodded. "I felt like I had a duty to Kindall to bring her back." Leilana had to admit, she was intrigued. A duty to a lost friend; it seemed like something that he would do, being as noble as he let on.

"Kindall risked his life to save us all from the blaze," he

continued, "but he was so infatuated with Amiria that he chose to let her go, knowing that it could potentially cost him. And she feels as though his death is completely on her-"

"That's because it was," Leilana cut in. "You need to stop sugarcoating things. Amiria broke down, and she took it out on us. She may have good intentions, but her execution is not that of a person with a gentle spirit. I've seen more of her than you have since we stepped out of the academy, Lancett. Whatever rested in her always existed—it just needed a reason to surface."

"Then, you've found her?"

"I did, for a time. She left before anyone could convince her of any wrongdoings."

"I think that you're wrong about her. She was probably overwhelmed. Master Kosmin said so himself; Amiria is set to walk down a path of disaster and sudden change, and it's unknown whether she'll experience it."

Leilana shook her head. "Even so, she should have taken his words in stride rather than following them directly. He said that if we take the right actions, we can transcend his predictions and that no form of agony is set in stone." She looked up at him. "You know, for someone so adamant about making amends, you sure didn't do a good job of convincing."

"It's not my fault that you always try to bite someone's head off when you aren't satisfied with an explanation," he countered. "You always try to push people away."

"I don't try to," she responded. "I just speak my mind. If you can't accept that, then perhaps this conversation should cease while we're ahead."

"You sound *just* like Ennis," he said sharply, pointing a finger at her. Leilana felt her body stiffen. "Always so prudent and careful of what you say, yet you act so cold. I don't understand you, and yet I..." He grew silent, inhaling slowly before sighing. "I care so much for you, Leilana. But there's a lot that we both need to understand about others around us. That's what this pilgrimage is for. And if anyone can become a Warlord someday, it's you."

She wasn't sure how to take his choice of words. "What are you saying?"

"Being out here has taught me about struggling. The people in Linarus are working class, so most of their citizens are herbalists. They grow their own food. They are the only country that has the capability to heal the fatally wounded. The war in Linmus has slowed their progression—they can't venture far outside of the region without shadowed beasts attacking them."

That explained why Sien seemed distraught about her need to collect herbs, and the urgency about reclaiming new ones from the garden. "What a coincidence we were able to find this place then. We can help them."

"It's not really your place to worry..."

"It's not yours either. But here you are, an acting force." Lancett laughed at her words. She was right. He wasn't from Linarus, and yet he was taking up the art of survival for their sakes. Meeting Sien allowed him the opportunity to try new things, which led him to farm.

"All right, I guess you've got me there. Maybe you *can* help." He took both of her hands in his own, grinning. "Leilana... I think that once this war has ended, I want to stay here. And, if possible, I'd like you to stay with me." A faint aura engulfed Lancett's body, but he hadn't seemed to pay it any mind.

Breech the path to overcoming hardships.

Bond yourself and shape a new form of friendship.

Her eyes went buck-wild, and he quickly broke away, dusting off his hands. "Y-You don't have to answer that, I-I was just voicing my thoughts, pay it no mind."

So, he was a totem carrier as well. That much was evident. That was three people she could mark off that she had encountered so far. Rem, Solus, and now Lancett. It didn't add up so far that she had only encountered men as a part of her journey. But so far, the connections she had with each of them differed in many aspects. And Solus's was the only one that remained a mystery. Fate had plans in store, and perhaps remaining in Linarus would uproot them.

"Anyways, um, I'll take you to look for your friends, if they're in this town," Lancett stated. "Sien should be waiting for me."

"You know Sien?" Leilana exclaimed.

Lancett raised an eyebrow. "Wait, you know who Sien is too?"

"We met yesterday after my friend decided to stir up a bit of mayhem."

"I did hear about a fight in the tavern." Lancett's nose was scrunching up as he spoke, "I didn't take you the type to associate with troublemakers."

"It's a long story. But it's something for later. I need to gather some verbena and then return to the tavern. I've been out long enough as is."

Lancett grinned. "Right, of course. I'll show you the ropes."

Leilana and Lancett returned to Midstream after gathering the necessary herbs, where they found Luna and Sien relaxing in a booth, chatting up Rem and Solus.

"Hey, Sien, I'm back for the afternoon," Lancett called.

"Ah, good morning, Lancett," Sien beamed. Solus and Rem stole a glance at one another before acknowledging the new face in the room in addition to their friend standing at his side. Rem gave a half-hearted shrug, the name ever familiar, and yet, the tension looming about his friend's aura was steadily growing. Solus returned to his breakfast, pushing his eggs about. "I was wondering where you'd scampered off to when you didn't clean the tables. Luna covered for you though, the good kid she is."

"Sorry about that, I decided to try doing some field work after I was commissioned to take out some of the monsters outside of town."

"Monsters?" Rem repeated. "We didn't pass by any monsters."

"You came from the west," Sien began. "Lancett cleared out that region with some of the men in our task force yesterday morning. Most of them are coming from the north now. Why they chose our town, I assume it's because of the herbal scents that attract them. But we need them to make a living, so we have to keep fending them off."

"I wanted to help out somehow," Leilana told Rem and Solus. "I think it's only right."

Solus chuckled at the proclamation, ruffling her hair. Lancett cleared his throat to mask a scoff. "It never hurts to lend a hand to those in need, and it may bring us closer to the information that we desire. We'll get a head start while we wait for Rem to finish recovering and start up in the morning."

"I don't think we can afford to wait," Rem proclaimed.

"We wouldn't want to linger around for too long and end up having more issues befall the land."

"Are you sure that you're up to it?" Sien asked. "Your fever just broke this morning. You wouldn't want to relapse."

"I'll be all right. Besides, I'll have Solus and Leilana with me. There will be no trouble if they're at my side. We'll leave at sundown."

Lancett listened attentively before addressing the two young men at the table, grinning. "By the way, I'm Lancett Lune. You must be Rem and Solus. Leilana was telling me about you on the way here. I wanted to thank you for keeping her safe."

Solus picked up the coffee container, filling his mug halfway with the steaming liquid, adding in a portion of milk. After stirring the concoction, he dropped in a cube of sugar, unpeeled the orange on his plate and squeezed out some drops from a slice. Once he'd taken a few satisfied sips of his coffee, he feigned a smile, his budding exhaustion continuing to play a round of catch-up. Rem snagged Solus's coffee cup right from his hands, carefully taking a drink for himself, smacking his lips once at the citric after-taste before offering up a so-so gesture in response.

"It's nice to meet you, Lancett. Leilana speaks highly of you," Solus responded. "We're glad that you've reunited."

Leilana's eyes darted between the two; they were both smiling, but neither of them seemed genuinely happy with each other's presence. Rem forced himself out of the situation by getting up from his spot to retrieve a mug for himself, pouring a fresh cup of coffee while sitting in another booth, dousing it with sugar and milk.

"If you're going to fight, you may as well get it over with instead of acting like teenage girls," Luna said simply, flipping through a brochure from Kingsley that was left the previous night. Lancett snapped out of his stupor.

"I'm going to get some vegetables to steam," he mumbled before taking off.

Sien sighed, shaking her head, mumbling to herself, "I don't get how guys can be so closed off sometimes."

With the tension weighing off his shoulders, Solus finished his meal. After cleaning up the tavern, Sien and Luna assisted a third shift of rowdy customers that were in and out of the door within a couple of hours. Rem continued to stare at his eggs and nurse his lukewarm cup of coffee. Solus and Leilana took to updating themselves on more information involving Linmus off in another part of the café area while Luna was fixing more food to fill the tavern. It wasn't going to be long before people would pour in again for their daily conversations over some booze. Leilana adjusted the dial a few times before a clear signal traveled throughout the tavern.

"-a statement from a guard that was inside of Linmus's grounds at the time of the attack."

The female reporter's voice was soon overshadowed by the brisk tone of a man. "It was horrifying. I can still recall the fire spreading throughout the kingdom. I got a glimpse of Queen Rira inside of the throne room. She was trying to dispel them with her magic, but right before she could succeed, she was grabbed by the back of her head and thrown into a wall. I think her neck snapped. I'm not sure what befell the king. I was assigned by him to flee with as many survivors as I could-"

Solus lowered his head, wondering how many people had managed to escape the castle grounds. Leilana watched his expression soften before turning down the radio. "I know it's probably a touchy subject, but what did you do to escape?"

Solus shrugged, folding his hands, resting his elbows on the table. "I was outside of the castle grounds with Rem when the chaos started."

"That's a relief, at least."

"For us, but not for others," Solus continued. "A close friend of ours was hiding us away in his pastry shop because he knew that Rem was their target. He was killed trying to keep us from being discovered. The assailants were a group called the Order of Helix. There isn't much that we know about them, or why they want Rem. But they are tailing us —Mitholus was a member as well. But unlike when he faced the Dirionus in Kalonia, Rem doesn't have an ounce of fear. That is just something he was taught to prepare for. He isn't scared of death, and that's something most people can only wish for. It's something that *I* wish for."

Silence passed between them for the next few seconds, Solus's expression shifting from stalwart and contemplative to almost serene. Leilana felt reminiscent of Lancett, recalling his words. He wanted her to remain with him after their pilgrimage came to a fruitful conclusion, likely to live together. Maybe it was a passing thought for him after uncovering the cracks in his reaction. She cleared her throat, turning the dial to increase the volume again. She didn't want to pry too far into Solus's thoughts and make him uncomfortable. He didn't seem to mind her trying to return to the topic at hand.

"-were given word recently that the assailant in Linmus is confirmed to be a Warlord, but we are unclear about his identity. He seems to have acquired followers that were against the royal family, which is how he could carry out his mission." Leilana almost sunk at the words that followed, "We don't know yet his true intentions."

The woman's voice held no ounce of hope. She wasn't sure of the circumstances herself, and she was the one being spoon-fed the information on a constant basis. The more that people seemed to learn, the further that the light of Adrylis was beginning to slip away. Their figures of peace and momentum were no more, slaughtered at the hands of an opposer. The last remaining figurehead was a teenage boy forced to run away from the only home that he had known to ensure his own safety, wallowing in what security he had left for himself. And no one high enough on a splitting chain knew that he was still alive and well, trying to find a way around the walls binding his home to misery.

"In other news, *'Remiel Vesarus, Traitor to the Throne?'* What fate has befallen the spirited away prince? Many have assumed him deceased, but there is some speculation that he has been spotted in cities such as Kalonia-"

"Turn it off," Rem called over the warbling radio signals. "They don't know what they're talking about." Solus and Leilana glanced over at him. They hadn't considered that he was listening, but Solus wasn't surprised; he wanted to know about Linmus more than anyone.

"He was rumored to have been traveling along the eastern border into the Teir region, but his current whereabouts are unknown-"

Rem slammed his fork on the table. "Turn it *off*, I said." Leilana didn't hesitate to flip the dial to another station, transmitting static in return, which made all three of them cringe. She fiddled with the dials a bit more before shutting off the radio completely.

"I don't get it," Sien began, taking Rem's half empty plate from him once he had pushed it out of his sight. "Why not try to request an audience with the person in charge of the arson?"

"It's not that simple," Rem protested. "Even if I wanted to waltz in and demand some explanation, I'd be executed on the spot. Those people killed my parents, my friends, and destroyed everything, all because they opposed my parents. I can't move forward alone."

"Life can't stop just because of missteps and mishaps."

"I know, I just…" He rested his head on the table, covering his face. "I don't understand this. I don't even know what they've done wrong. I never looked between the lines to see their suffering because I was too young and naïve to think about it. I never got to really appreciate them, and I hate that I didn't because now I'll never see them again."

Sien stole a glance at Solus. He held up a hand as a gesture of following through with whatever she was planning. She took a seat across from him, reaching out a hand to stroke his hair. He couldn't face her, his head too heavy to lift. His eyes were watering, and his chest was tight. The sensation wasn't new, but allowing things to sink in was rare for him.

"You haven't had time to grieve, Rem," she said softly. "I think it's time that you did. You should stop being so brave. It's been some time now since they've passed. Have you ever thought about them above the kingdom's needs?" She was met with silence. "They were more than King and Queen of Adrylis. They were your parents, and you need to come to terms with that. You're always going to be more than a prince to them, and to the rest of the world. There are still people that believe in you, but you have to believe in yourself too."

Solus was surprised to see Sien taking everything in

stride. Normally, he was the one providing wholesome advice and adding comfort to the mix, but now he was giving her the reins. Leilana watched on with amazement and took her words in just as much as Rem seemed to. She knew this world better than any of them had, and it was evident in her demeanor.

Luna stepped to the table, folding her hands in front of her. "Um, Cici, I'd hate to break things up here, but the messenger has come. He brings news of the creatures up in the mountains. It's time." Rem rose from the booth, his hair sinking over his eyes to conceal his tears.

"Thank you, Sien," he told her, smiling as he ruffled her hair. "I'd better get out there. We've got work to do." Sien held out a hand, wanting to stop him, but unsure of how to convince him otherwise. By the time she could reach him, he turned his back, stepping over to his travel companions. "Sol, Leilana. Let's move."

"Want to ask just one more time. Are you sure you're up to it?" Solus asked.

"I've got no choice but to be," Rem replied, resting a hand on his hip. "We're here to help, and who am I to turn down a promise to a friend?" Leilana looked to the Lasette on the chair next to her, laying a hand over the cover. Solus gathered his blade. Rem claimed his saber from under the booth where Solus sat, placing it over his shoulders. "Sien, you have any trouble down here, you and Luna go running, no hesitation. Got it?"

Luna held her folded hands up to her chest, her eyes sparkling at the noble words. "He's so regal." Sien almost laughed.

SIXTEEN

Never had the coolness of mid-winter air felt so tender. Leilana was the furthest behind when they began their perilous northern trek up to the mountains. Every step forward ushered forth a wheeze from her burning lungs, her freezing fingertips brushing against the Lasette. Solus and Rem were handling things far better, at least a few feet ahead without any struggle against the rising altitude. Solus continued to stop and ask after her, stating that he could always carry her up the trail, but the nuances of her female pride rejected the offer. Solus shrugged at her remarks every time, a soft grin on his face. She'd come around in time.

"So, what exactly are we searching for?" Rem asked Solus after some time, tapping the hilt of his blade with his finger. "All this walking around and getting nowhere is annoying. Sien tells us to go up to the mountain range and then what? No monsters, and no leads."

"Well, let's keep in mind that we're not actually climbing the mountains, only traversing the plains under-lining them. We're bound to run into something the further that we walk."

"You better be right."

"I usually am."

Leilana shut her eyes, listening to the whistling winds roaring above her companions, the loose strands from her ponytail whipping her cheeks every so often. She couldn't break her concentration. The sound was atmospheric, but it seemed to grow fierce with each passing moment as if something was guiding it along. She could taste the dust in the air, hear light whistles gradually form into howls. She slowed to a stop. Any further and the wind could very well have carried her off. A force grasped by the hands of a mage rather than natural stability.

It wasn't unheard of. There were plenty of creatures in Adrylis that had the ability to harness the elements. Arcana, Maester, Warlord, Dirionus... there were options. Was it limited to just humans and their chosen Familiars?

Rem stared back at the girl, wondering what was running through her mind. She was adamant about uncovering the truth about the monsters in the region, but to stop short just before they came across anything was suspicious. Solus was pulling his hair out of his face to keep it from attacking him under the sharp windstorm, holding it together with a couple of bobby pins.

"Leilana," Rem called, knocking the girl out of her apparent trance. She jumped at his voice, nearly dropping the grimoire, but kept her composure. He didn't avert his gaze from her, his eyes calming. "I know that you sense something too, bound to this unnerving wind. What do you feel?" Leilana's lips parted, astonished by his almost noble gesture towards her. So, it hadn't been just her; he felt it as well. As expected of a Maester of his stature.

"This wind... it isn't natural," she told them, holding up a hand, allowing the breeze to caress her fingertips. The air became still every half-second, hardly noticeable to the naked eye, but evident to those with the same energy spiraling in their soul. She was used to this; somehow, it felt reminiscent. "It feels as though it's been conjured rather than acting as a natural element from the climate change."

"Meaning..." Rem pressed on, waving his hand as a continuation.

Leilana lowered her hand once more to clutch the Lasette. "Someone in these plains may be expecting us." Solus looked between the two mages, raising an eyebrow. It wasn't the first time that he was pushed out of the loop when faced with commanding reactions to the world around them, but now it was an antiquated idealism to interfere rather than acquired.

Leilana opened the Lasette and tried to fight against the wind to keep the pages steady, but in the end, Solus had to grab one side of the book while she grasped the other. She ran her hand along the words, searching for some glimpse of an idea. "I can't think of any spells that can negate the effects of the wind, not without causing a brisk storm."

"Maybe it's time that I took the reins." Rem cracked his knuckles and spread his legs a few inches apart, raising his hands in a slow motion, signing rectangular shapes in the air. Sparks of lightning surged through the windy terrain in one set area—the same place where Rem started his work. He extended his hands outward, the streaks increasing in size and number before spreading in a large enough mass to shield him from the gusts.

Solus took a step back out of surprise. "You've improved."

Rem clicked his tongue once, placing a hand on the spot before him. "Yep, somehow I have. May have been the jolt of power back in Kalonia. I can feel this barrier at work. But it won't hold forever, so we'd better move fast." He pressed both hands to the barrier and stepped forward, grunting slightly. Leilana swore that the sound of the barrier shifting was comparable to gear switches being activated. "Gotta keep this thing moving too! Just... working on an instinct!

Take my advice, don't try to distract me or I'm gonna crash and burn. Just stay behind me."

"We'll do our best," Leilana replied. "Try not to push yourself too far." Rem took another step forward and continued to move at a steady pace with the barrier intact, hissing at the pressure building around his body between the forceful winds and the electricity fighting through the currents. One wrong step or thought and a storm would brew faster than a kettle at a high temperature. Oh, magic, how you live to piss off the worthy.

A thundering roar cut through the wind, causing all three of them to stop dead in their tracks. Rem nearly lost his footing but caught himself in time to press his hands to the barrier again. Solus lowered himself into a defensive stance and reached for his sword, hand on the hilt, his eyes darting in every direction. Leilana stiffened before opening the Lasette, allowing the grimoire to drift above her head, just out of reach of the wind to keep from flying away.

"I don't think that's a good sign," Rem proclaimed. "Someone wanna tell me otherwise?"

"Nope," Solus replied, straightening his back again when the sound ceased. "Just keep on your toes, like we agreed earlier. We could be stepping into dangerous territory."

Leilana was about to lower the Lasette back down to her level when a powerful gust of wind split through the barrier, propelling Rem to the ground back-first. The Lasette went soaring across the air despite its superior weight, landing in a tree sitting on a perched hill. Leilana sprinted after it, the wind pushing her forward, causing her to stumble every few steps. Solus helped Rem to his feet and dusted off his shirt before chasing after Leilana to assist her, stopping short when an enigmatic figure shrouded in ravenous lightning propelled past him faster than he could process. He barely had time to reclaim his sword and pick up his speed.

"Leilana! Incoming!" Solus's words had barely reached the girl, but just as she whirled around to see what was fueling his concerns, a creature twice her size slipped into her gaze. Its eyes were a piercing amber, its lengthy ears brushing across her face. Its fur was a smoky shade, and it seemed to be much thinner in stature than the Dirionus from Kalonia. She couldn't breathe, every ounce of momentum sucked out of her. This was the first time that a Dirionus was close enough for her to feel its coarse breaths streaming down the back of her neck.

Solus leaped into the air and tried to slice it from above by bringing the sword down upon its back, but the beast stepped aside, vanishing. He scoffed when it reemerged a few feet away with a spring in its step, its large feet causing slight tremors. Leilana stumbled and fell to the ground, struggling to catch her breath. Solus stood in front of her, blade extended. The beast was relatively still spare its bouncing fixation, but at its current speed, anything could occur.

Rem scowled, his hair flying upward under the wind's unruly course. "I took down one of you already, and now I've got a special vendetta against you." He thrust back his left hand, which became shrouded in dark energy. "You crushed my barrier!" He broke into a run, swinging his hand out, the anger-induced vigor spiraling just past the Dirionus, who now turned its attention on Rem. It retained a lax appearance, and it almost looked unsure of how to react.

Maybe it wasn't accustomed to someone as powerful as Rem being around.

Master...

Leilana's eyes widened at the meticulous-sounding

word emerging from the Dirionus's mind, taking form through a broken whimper brushing past its lips. She held up a hand towards the base of the tree, the wind rattling the branches. Solus faltered, the sorrowful gesture overwhelming. He had almost lowered his sword, but he retained the vigilance necessary to strike in case Rem required his assistance.

Master... why aren't you coming home...?

"All of you are one in the same now, aren't you?" Rem shouted at the beast, eyes blazing with determination. "All of you Dirionus have been corrupted out of spite, attacking innocent people, or sending your grunts to do the work for you!"

Leilana clasped her hand into a fist, her eyes narrowing. The more that she focused her efforts on the Lasette, the closer that the book seemed to embrace it. The tree jerked forward one good time, the grimoire dropping from its branches, landing on her lap. Bringing her knees to her chest to keep the book steady, she began skimming through pages.

Rem seized the Dirionus, and the beast snarled, whipping its puffed tail at him. Rem rolled out of the way, dispelling the energy embedded in his left hand, gripping to his sword as he spiraled out of the way of an oncoming attack, striking its side. Blood splattered onto his cheek, the crimson ooze landing on the trail-way. Solus was baffled; the Dirionus wasn't moving nearly as fast as before when wanting to pursue Leilana. Maybe Rem wasn't its target after all.

Leilana signed the Minsuran symbols in the air. The spirits would act as a guide, stringing her through the unkempt emotions swirling in the hearts of those she carried at her side. "Qin... un... en... lien..." She lowered her head, wind chimes piercing her hearing. She could smell lavender incense burning, filling the shrine that housed her in her memories.

Rem brought up his sword towards the beast, intending to cut it through the back. The Dirionus whimpered, its eyes falling shut. Solus's muscles were stiff, the ordeal reaching its climax. The Dirionus was corrupted without a doubt, the aura spiraling from its soul much like the beast in Kalonia. But somehow, he could still sense it clinging to life. Waiting. Was it seeking its end? Or was it seeking a new purpose somewhere along the way?

Leilana thrust her hand out, a crescent barrier engulfing the region as if shining a new essence over the rage plaguing the minds of the agonized. "*Curosoi Kisen* (Binding Blaze)!"

The chilly winds ceased, the trail becoming lined with greenery, the dark branches, and trees subjecting themselves to the light of the crescent sun hovering above. Rem stopped moving, lowering his weapon before it escaped his grasp. Solus stared up at the sky, watching the clouds disperse as if they had never come to be. So, this was the power she inherited. The power of creation, far unlike any other, accessible through abandoned words and splintered memories tucked away in a single book.

And Leilana had only reached the tip of the iceberg.

Leilana was panting, her face dripping with sweat, her hand still extended forward in case that the spell hadn't seeped in. After a few seconds, she rested it on the dirt, nearly gasping for air. Her chest was tight, and she felt nauseous, all energy lost to her. She rose to a stand once she felt that she could overcome the ordeal. Solus wrapped an arm around her shoulders, ruffling her hair in a congratulatory matter. She weakly smiled up at him.

The Dirionus shakily rose to a stand and made its way

towards Rem, resting its head under the palm of his hand. It gave a small whine, nuzzling against him. Rem swallowed, rubbing the beast behind its ears, a bit confused by its actions, but amused nonetheless. Its amber eyes were replaced by a gentle hazel, and the shadows that fueled its actions seemed nonexistent.

Rem glanced back at Solus and Leilana, giving them a thumbs-up, grinning sheepishly. Solus gave him a thumbs-up back in response, chuckling. Leilana watched over Rem a moment longer, her eyes softening at the tender turn of events.

In the blink of an eye, a pitched cry of pain turned the tides further. Solus and Leilana could barely comprehend what was occurring. Rem was frozen, watching the Dirionus double over into his arms, rapidly shrinking into a diminutive size, an arrow protruding from its back. Blood dripped down the arrowhead, coating the weakened creature's white fur. Its large rabbit-like ears sank against its sides and covered its face, the creature's face scrunched up as if to fight against the agonizing pain.

"Well, now. I never expected anyone to ascertain the power to heal the Dirionus."

Rem didn't bother to look up at the figure in view wielding a bow pointed at his chest, taking to breaking the arrowhead through the beast's back, carefully removing it and tossing the remains aside. His blood-stained hands were trembling as he held the creature, felt its feeble, fading breaths on his wrists. It was still alive, barely clinging to what time it had left. Leilana's eyes darkened at the new presence, his chiseled face concealed by a mask that resembled the scaly hide of a snake, the decal impeccable to those without a blind eye for detail. His brown hair was pulled upwards into a short ponytail, borderline scraggly as it bulged out of its rubber band.

"I have underestimated you, Arcana."

Leilana took a step forward, ignoring Solus's firm grip on her shoulder, his silent plea for her not to push herself. Her legs felt little more than a thin elastic, ready to snap at any given moment. She could barely keep herself standing as it was, but she couldn't allow any signs of weakness to emerge to keep from losing the advantage.

"I think you overestimated yourself."

The man smirked, chuckling behind his mask. "I should have expected no less from the younger sister of Ennis Erovina, spirited by the Lasette's devastating vigor." He observed her movements, and Leilana held her breath, releasing it in the form of a slight groan. "Not so light on our feet when we work with borrowed power, are we?"

"*Borrowed?*" she hissed. "My power has always been my own."

The man brushed his fingers along the mask. "You can believe whatever you wish. Using the spells in that grimoire take a toll on your body. You are merely adopting something presented to you and melding it into your own style. That grimoire is meant to act as a guide, not a source. If you are to believe that this energy is yours, then you are already doomed as an Arcana—you will never achieve the title of Warlord on a power that is not yours."

"That's enough," Solus exclaimed, placing both hands on Leilana's shoulders to keep her in place before she lunged at the man. "Were you the one that called the beasts here to terrorize Linarus?"

"I don't need to tell you anything." The man turned to walk away, waving his hand in dismissal. "All that I am is a pawn in this game called life. Same as you all."

"Hey!" Leilana roared. She took another step, her vision collapsing. "Don't you dare try to walk away! You... you and all the others like you, you're...!"

"Leilana!" Rem exclaimed suddenly. "That's enough!"

She was about to call out to the man again when she stumbled and fell, her strength depleted. She gasped, glancing at her bloody, scratched palms. She wasn't sure when they got injured. The pain was acquired since escaping the walls, but now the wounds were noticeable. Solus knelt beside her, trying to quell her concerns. Leilana coughed, unable to catch her breath, her eyes shut to dim the light of the fading emergence from the Lasette.

The man eyed the young girl from afar. "Such determination." He sighed, holding up a hand behind him to gesture to the lowly figures in the bushes.

A pack of wolves cloaked in shadow sped past the man as he walked in the opposite direction, growling and snarling at the three. What was most peculiar about the situation was that the wolves didn't bother with any of them —they seemed to be venturing down the trail, their noses turned up on the airflow circling around them.

Solus pulled Leilana close to him, glaring up at the man. "You won't get away with this!"

"Oh, but Solus..." His name escaping the man's lips was haunting. Daunting, even, when considering his tone. "I already have."

He reached up his hands to clasp around his mask before tugging it away by the two loose strings holding it over his face. Beyond the faces of the unknown stood Lunious, his hair falling past his shoulders, his expression confident, yet cocky. Solus was appalled, but Leilana didn't seem too amused or shocked by the reveal.

"I knew it," she whispered, her fingers grazing Solus's

hand merely out of comfort. He interlaced his fingers with hers, the boiling touch of her skin evident.

"I should have known better than to go trusting some asshole that tries to buy me off with a sword!" Rem hissed upon recognizing the man's voice, no longer muffled by the mask. He jumped to a stand, the Dirionus secure in his arms, his sword pointed in the man's direction.

"Thank you, Leilana, for your patronage. It is because of the fruits that you brought into town that the wolves can destroy everything that they touch!" Leilana's heart skipped a beat, and she stared at the ground. She hadn't considered that she was guiding Linarus into further turmoil.

"Rem, go back to town!" Solus exclaimed. "Warn Lancett and Sien and as many others as you can to get as far away from Linarus as possible!" Rem took a step back, unsure how to deal with the sudden weight on his shoulders. Solus's eyes darkened, and he slammed his fist on the dirt to jolt the young Prince's attention back. "*Remiel!* There is no time to think! Go now!"

"R-Right, all right!"

Rem held the small beast in his arms as he ran past the two, briefly allowing his gaze to linger on them before matching his speed to approach the bands of wolves. They snarled and snapped their jaws at him, one tearing into his arm and tossing him aside like a scrap of meat. Rem rolled over onto his back, his muscles aching, his flesh ripping, dirt staining his clothes. He spat out some grass and wiped his mouth clean of the grotesque aftertaste, watching the wolves progress down the beaten path.

Rem was running out of breath, the winding jog several miles from Linarus. The Dirionus was losing blood, its body too battered to ensure survival. Its eyes had fallen shut, and it wasn't whimpering in pain anymore, but he could still feel its heartbeat through his fingertips. He was used to pacing himself, but now his concern for Sien and Luna fueled that blazing determination to reach them. He knew that Sien could handle herself, and he assumed that Lancett was already assisting other villagers as best as he could. They were used to a few beasts, but a wild pack of corrupted, bloodthirsty wolves?

Time was of the essence.

The wolves' paw prints guided him to Linarus, each step fresher than the last. The scent of rotten fruit was making him nauseous, but true to Lunious's proclamation, it was drawing out the wolves. He hadn't noticed it during the initial walk; it was safe to assume that Lunious had prepared in advance and timed their departure. He had led them here to begin with, and it was no coincidence that he was returning north. He had even passed the hint to Solus that there was going to be a showdown.

He hoped that Solus and Leilana could handle themselves.

"What are you planning to do, Lunious?" Leilana choked out. Solus was holding her arms, not wanting her in harm's way. "You walk these plains in a mask. You deceived us, and for what?" She shook her head slowly. "Better yet, I don't think I want to know why. You're so adamant about harming Rem..."

"Actually, my goal was never Rem. I know all about that kid and what he is."

"If you aren't seeking Rem's Bloodlinch powers, what is your end plan?" Solus asked.

"Why, it's the two of you," Lunious implied, extending his finger, moving down the line between them. "One of you has the power to cleanse this world of its turmoil. And one of you has the power to unravel all that we have ever known." Solus bore his teeth, his eyes narrowed in contempt. This was twice now that someone wearing a mask mentioned untapped power. "I bet that you can't tell which one of you holds which piece of the puzzle."

"That's the end of it," she breathed out. "No more..." Leilana thrust her hand forward, the pages of the Lasette spiraling out of control. Her arm was shaking, her breaths rough. "No more...!" Solus grabbed her wrist, and before she could retort, her vision began spotting. She collapsed into his strong arms, and Solus cradled her, stroking her sweat-drenched hair. The Lasette closed shut, the lock clicking into place. She tiredly groaned, and he sighed, laying her gently on the ground.

Solus rose, broadsword in hand. "You're a Maester, correct?" He grasped the hilt with both hands, lifting the blade inches from his face, his fiery emerald eyes the only visible essence of him remaining in Lunious's sight. "Allow me to show you the power of humanity." Lunious shrugged his shoulders, flexing his fingers, miniscule gusts of wind sweeping through his hand.

He held up a hand, wind splitting through Solus's core. His rubber band snapped in half, the crimson ribbon holding it together getting caught on a branch. His long hair was freely streaming through the squalls, smacking his face. The young attendant didn't falter, his eyes trained on the man even as the wind shoved him. He pushed forward, tightening the grip on his sword before swinging, the energy of the wind connecting with the blade, propelling back at Lunious. The man gasped, shielding his face with his arms, grunting at the sudden change of pace.

Solus didn't step out of turn or change his stance in the slightest, prepared for any more changes in the atmosphere. He was certain that the wind was gliding down his back. Lunious eyed him closely. A clever mind trick, Lunious thought, but an ineffective execution. Lunious smirked, signing some words before him. Solus narrowed his eyes to conjure up the symbols in his mind. The letters were in Sentience, which made his study easier to comprehend. He mouthed the pronunciation of each symbol under his breath, just out of reach to Lunious's hearing. "Firen-sain-to." He swallowed his words.

Strike fear into one's heart. Lunious wasn't the first to cling to a mask, hiding behind his motivation. Like others, he was looking to shape the world anew by breaking down the royal family and seizing its sole heir, making him fear for his life. And now they were attempting to do the same to him, and to Leilana. Any ounce of fear would throw them into danger. As Lunious started up another windstorm, Solus lowered his weapon and carried it at his side, rushing through the gales. The chill was little more than pins and needles on his skin. Still, he ran. Lunious was caught off guard by his increased speed, allowing Solus the opportunity to slice the man's hand.

Solus held his broadsword centimeters from the man's neck, the tip of the blade piercing his throat, droplets seeping onto the weapon. Lunious was holding his breath, standing completely still. Any wrong move and the end would come.

"Leave," Solus snarled. "Never come here again. Never do harm to innocent people." He fell back and Lunious took a few seconds to comprehend what was occurring. It was as if time had stopped. And surely, for him, it would have.

"I will have your head, Solus Brenner," Lunious assured. "And I will have that girl's book. I'll stake my life on it." The man cloaked himself in the wind that he harnessed, vanishing without a trace.

Solus sighed, falling to the ground, stretching out his arms across the mounds of dirt. Holding focus for an extended period was strenuous. Pretending to be calm in a situation that required focus above all was painful. Somehow, he'd managed both without sullying his hands. Alongside his ribbon fell a sheet of paper, both landing on his chest. He rested a hand on the note before holding it up to his face. The words were beyond him, but after mentally comparing them to the symbols on Leilana's grimoire, he was certain that the text was in Minsuran. After pocketing his ribbon, he made his way over to Leilana, the young girl pushing herself to a sit.

"Don't even think about it," he told her softly. He grabbed her bag and set the Lasette and slip of paper inside, placing the tote around his shoulder. Once it was secure, he scooped the girl up in his arms. She gripped to his sleeve, gazing up at him, her eyes falling shut every few seconds before jolting open to keep her attention even. "It's all right. You're allowed to rest."

"You're bleeding," she began, reaching up a hand to caress his cheek. Solus glanced at the reddish substance between her fingers, and he grinned. He wasn't concerned with the pain at all, not when there were others that were worse off. In fact, it was impressive that Leilana carried the same trait. "What happened, Solus...?"

He rested a hand on hers. "It's nothing, I promise. We're going back to help Rem. I want you to rest until then. No excuses." She sighed in defeat, resting her head against his chest, wrapping her arms around his neck. The sound of his racing heartbeat sent her mind aflutter, and she couldn't comprehend why. Maybe it was the swirling heat dulling her senses. Or maybe it was her concern for him, unable to protect him when she needed him.

Solus's palms were sweating as he walked, his nerves jumping through more rings than he could pick up, but his determination to return to Linarus and find Rem was winning out.

Rem came to a halt atop the hills overlooking Linarus. Screams besieged his ears, the sight of the wolves mowing down people in the peaceful farming village one by one unnerving. Blood was splattered on the ground, broken limbs and organs littering the once fermented and luxurious soil. Each passing second fractured his crumbling mind further.

"Sien," he breathed, sliding down the mound before rushing into the village. He dodged several marauding wolves lining the streets, cutting through them with the saber in his dominant right hand, stumbling over loose branches. The Dirionus started up whimpering again, noticing the distress in his eyes. Rem ducked behind one of the buildings, cradling the Familiar.

Every glance forward thrust more ruin upon his soul. Each cry of pain sent shockwaves down his back, and it brought him to his knees. He buried his face in the Dirionus's fur to hide his tears.

"What am I supposed to do...?"

This was no different from the state that Linmus was in. He could still vividly picture the flames, the smoke rising into the air, ashen rain covering the sky and engulfing the clouds to emit a hazy grey. But now, there was no lack of opportunity, and people could fight back. *He* could fight back.

He covered the Dirionus with his hands, a teal shade surrounding the creature. Over the next few seconds, the torn flesh mended itself, the bleeding slowing to a stop. The Dirionus regained its energy in seconds, looking up at Rem when he set it on the ground, whimpering and pawing at his feet. It was preparing to evolve when Rem placed his hand atop its head and turned to walk off. It was quick to rush after him, grabbing his pants leg with its miniscule fangs.

"Don't come," Rem said sharply, brandishing his weapon, startling the Dirionus. "You need to recover. I only stopped the bleeding. I can't afford to waste energy, and I can't have any distractions."

The Dirionus didn't heed his warning, leaping onto his shoulder. Rem slumped slightly at the weight gain, feeling its silken fur nuzzle against the side of his face, chatting him up in its own language. Rem couldn't understand it fully, only some choice words here and there due to his lack of knowledge of the art of a Maester's 'chant,' but it was in protest. Clearly, it wasn't taking no for an answer, as expected from a Familiar that was hand-chosen and bound to a Warlord.

"Oh, fine," he scoffed. "We can be partners for a little while. Just don't go making a scene."

The Dirionus leaped from his shoulder, wrapped its puffy tail around its body and ascended into a larger size, though not nearly as formidable as the height it appeared in.

Its tail grew in length, its fur brushing outward, shaping itself into an almost regal stature when it stood on all fours. Rem was covering his racing heart with his left hand.

"Try not to go too crazy, yeah? Meet me back around here, I'm gonna try and find my friends." It looked to Rem, snorting a reply, watching as the boy ran off.

It sped off into the village, growling upon reaching a group of wolves hovering over three corpses, chowing down on their entrails. They were a lost cause, but they were far from its intended target; hidden in the fields behind rose bushes were a woman and her two young children, masked under the scent of the flowers and bloodshed. The youngest, an infant, was crying and being bounced as a means of calming, to no avail.

One of the wolves exhaled, looking to the bushes, causing its allies to follow suit. The Dirionus pounced on the wolves, knocking them away with its claws, biting down on one of their backs to sway it from the family. It threw one to the ground with its teeth, the blood seeping between the sharp fangs, its hazel eyes flaring. Its muscles shook, determination fueling its strength. This was the purpose of a Dirionus—to serve under the will of its master. And when without support, to protect at any cost.

The wolves didn't back down, circling the Dirionus, who remained vigilant, its claws kneading the soil, focused on the footsteps around it. They pounced, and the Dirionus roared, an array of squalls bursting from its body at a rapid acceleration, cutting the shadowy beasts in half, their corpses landing on the ground. The Dirionus whimpered, covering its eyes with its paws.

"You..." The Dirionus shot up, snarling before its eyes landed on a young man carrying a girl in his arms, his hair resting on his shoulders. This boy, he was one of his protectors from the mountains. The Dirionus ran uphill to meet him, kneeling. "I'm relieved that you're safe." Solus reached up a hand to lay on the creature's nose. "My friend that helped you. Do you know where he went?"

The Dirionus glanced back at the town. Solus's stomach dropped. Hours had passed since their departure; laughter and merriment were replaced with damning silence. The crops that filled the prosperous town were ripped from the ground. The buildings were crumbling, and the spectral wolves were scattered about the area, salvaging the corpses littering the town. Every inhabitant that spoke to him on his way to the tavern would no longer be there to greet him.

It was like they had stepped into another world.

"Linarus," Leilana choked out, gripping to Solus's sleeve. He couldn't even acknowledge her, trying to find the words to express the grief he felt. "Linarus is falling..."

"I don't understand," he admitted. "Rem was supposed to be here. He was-" He cut himself off, noticing a small figure at the bottom of the hill.

He set Leilana down. She stumbled, surprised by the sudden return to the ground. He placed his hands on her shoulders to steady her, and once she was stable enough, he pursued the person, his shoes slipping along the morning dew. At the foot of the hill was Luna, clutching her bleeding right arm, the left side of her face caked in blood. Her braid was loose, several strands out of place. He grunted as he lost his footing, catching himself before he came close to impacting. "Luna!"

"S-Sol... Solus," she began, her bottom lip quivering, her voice hoarse. "M-My sister, she..." Solus didn't hesitate to take her hand, leading her up the hill. Her hands were shaky, her mind shattering, but the gesture of protection was undeniable. "S-Sien stayed behind with Lancett.

They're still in the tavern, I-I don't know what's happening to her...!"

"Don't worry, Rem is looking for them. I know that he is. He'll make sure that they're safe." He removed Leilana's tote from around his shoulder to place around the young Arcana's. "Listen to me. You, Luna, and the Dirionus, you get out of here, you go as far away as you can."

Leilana shook her head, her eyes laced with anger. Was he just expecting her to run away when Rem, Sien, and Lancett were in danger? "Don't ask me to do that."

"There's a time to be noble and another to weigh your options, Leilana," he pressed. "You are the only chance we have at finding help." He glanced over at Luna, who had taken to observing the Familiar, reaching up to a hand to stroke its fur, stopping short to clutch her wounded arm. The Dirionus whimpered, resting its head on her hand to save her the trouble. "Sien would want you to keep Luna safe. *I* want you to keep her safe. She needs someone that can relate to her, especially if we are left to anticipate the worst." He placed his hands on her cheeks, his eyes saddening. "Please... just trust me."

She pulled away slightly. "Solus, I don't know where I'm supposed to go. I don't know this land, where would I even begin to find help? How would I get back here, how... how would I be able to find you again? I have nothing to guide me. Please don't make me go by myself."

"You won't be by yourself," he said quickly. "The Dirionus knows this land, it was assigned to rule here. It can bring you back here." He was growing anxious, the low growls of the wolves looming from behind. They had spotted them. "But right now, you need to go."

He grabbed her by the arm and led her to the Dirionus, helping Luna onto its back afterward. Leilana was baffled.

He was so adamant about saving them, was he even considering what would happen to himself and how he could escape to the eastern border? Linarus was already a lost cause. She knew it, as much as she hadn't wanted to believe it. Like Paluna and Linmus, this piece of the world was crumbling under the reign of terrorists.

This was what war felt like. It never ended, only enhanced.

"Solus, please!" Leilana cried. "Please don't go!" Solus gave the Dirionus a look of impatience as he drew his sword, and the beast stomped its foot on the ground, a small gust of wind thrusting Leilana upward, causing her to yelp as she landed on its back beside Luna.

Solus swung his sword out in front of the Dirionus as a means of fortification and lowered his body into a defensive stance, his back to the three. "We'll find you again, we will. I promise." Three wolves emerged, slowly stepping to Solus. His eyes narrowed as he bit some dead skin on his bottom lip. "Dirionus! It is your job to protect those in need! I beg of you, keep them safe!"

The Dirionus leaped from the hill and touched base on solid ground, its legs carrying it far beyond the enemy line, seeking the city limits. Leilana whirled around to catch a glimpse at Solus, Luna gripping to her wrist to keep her in place, knowing that she'd try to go against the words of her friend.

Solus was fending off the wolves, pushing the one gripping to his blade with its teeth off the hill, causing it to hit its head on a rock, falling unconscious. He plunged his sword into the chest of one that was pouncing at him, shaking it from his blade and allowing it to roll off casually. He drew back his blade one final time, a crimson aura spewing from the weapon, though he didn't seem to take any notice.

Leilana's eyes widened at the sight. The aura dissolved quickly when Solus cut through the last wolf.

"Solus!" The Dirionus didn't turn back, even for a moment, and Leilana couldn't force it to. She watched helplessly as what remained of Linarus faded from her sight.

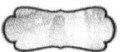

Rem burst open the tavern doors, where he was met with a group of masked figures enjoying their time and merriment. Bottles of booze were clinking and shattering in every direction and tied up in a booth with a gag in her mouth was Sien, her clothes ripped to shreds. At her feet was Lancett, recovering from a blow to the head, glass shards littering his vicinity. There were traces of blood on the shards, a touch on the back of his skull, his sword kicked several feet away.

"Now we've got a party going!" One of the masked men laughed, holding up a full glass of beer. "Prince Remiel's joined us! Let's toast to his life!" Sien whirled around at the sound of his name, calling out to him repeatedly through the gag while trying to pry herself out of the ropes holding her. Rem held up his sword, pointing them in multiple directions as the masked figures stood, stepping towards him.

"You did well keeping out of our sights for this long, Your Highness." A woman's voice this time, slithering and sneaking down his spine. "But now you've nowhere left to run."

Rem backpedaled, eyes darting every which way, but he didn't drop his guard. His palms were sweating, his words lodging in his throat as he asked, "Who are you people? Why are you after me?"

"Who we are is of no importance to you yet." One of the masked figures held up a hand, and Rem gasped when a stream of flames shot forward faster than he could process. He slid out of the way, the fire striking a nearby wall instead. He was tripping over his feet during the recovery, resting a hand over his chest to quell his racing heart a little more.

The moment didn't last, the air crackling when another blast of energy ignited in the room. Right as he was about to retaliate, a blade cut through and dispersed the flames. Solus emerged into his view, his normally tranquil emerald eyes reflecting an olive shade under the broken lights, a mental storm brewing in wake of his discovery. No. It wasn't just his eyes; he had transformed into a completely different person while this close. The aura spiraling through Solus's system, veering into Rem, was as tasteful as the salty air. He was running on empty, his body pressurized to move forward and assist those in need. It was bound to be his undoing.

"Did they tell you anything?" Solus asked lowly, his back turned, eyes locked on Rem.

"Not a word," Rem mumbled.

"I see." Solus extended his sword forward, watching the masked figures take up arms and set their magical vigor up for strife. "I suppose that we'll have to force the truth out. Are you prepared?" Rem stepped from behind him, taking up a defensive stance, gripping to his saber with both hands.

"Not like we have much choice. Always has to be the hard way..."

SEVENTEEN

It was all a blur. Leilana was unsure of how much time had bypassed them, but endless travel was going to catch up to them in time. Why hadn't they reached a town yet? The nights became winding and wistful—the stars above served as a reminder that life was continuing while it at a standstill for others, lost to time, trapped in the auroras that bound them to an unseen realm. Ennis was there, as were Rem's parents. Maybe Rem and Solus had already left to meet them, and she just didn't want to accept it. There was no trace of them anywhere beyond the cataclysmic fate of Linarus.

The Dirionus had done its job, spiriting them far from the destruction, growing weary from the excess movement. It buried its face in its paws and whimpered whenever they had down time to rest and gather food. Dirionus could only venture so far from their homeland without a sense of guilt left to follow. There was a chance that there was no land to return to, and Leilana couldn't understand why things had taken such a dramatic turn.

War was following them. War was following *Rem*.

"Linar-**kzzt**-destr-**kzzt**-" Leilana was fiddling with the radio dials and antenna to recover a better signal, but the damp cave and low voltage levels lent no helping hand. With a scoff, she gave the device one good smack, knocking it to the ground, the radio giving off a small whirring sound in response as if pleading with her to stop damaging it. Realizing her actions, she made way to retrieve it and held it close to her chest. This was her only means of learning about Adrylis's fate, and she couldn't afford to lose it.

She looked back at Luna, who was sleeping on the Dirionus's back, bundling in its fluffy fur. She hadn't spoken a word to Leilana since their departure from Linarus, and Leilana couldn't blame her. The girl was probably lonesome and missing her sister. Leilana could relate—she missed Ennis herself, even if she didn't get to become as close to him as Luna was to Sien. It was easy to miss someone that was no longer around and would never return, but Luna was left to hope that her sister was alive, and that was what scared her the most.

It was cruel, but sometimes it was just how life was meant to be. Or maybe it was just rotten luck that their tiny, isolated village was taken away to save one person. Now Leilana felt guilty for even thinking along those lines.

"-struggle to uncover any survivors from the once prosperous farming town. We are currently unsure of what caused the town's destruction, but we will be keeping up intel to uproot whatever tracks that we find. I'm Elina Karos, signing off."

Darn, just barely missed the segment.

"Looking for a romantic getaway? Visit the seaside ocean at Kinsley and receive up to half off your-" Leilana turned down the radio, no longer interested in the context.

Linarus was wiped off the eastern border, much like Paluna. That was confirmed, at least; they couldn't find survivors. That didn't write off the idea of Sien, Solus, Rem, and Lancett being dead. They could have escaped, but with Lunious and the other masked men running around, it wasn't likely that they were going to be unscathed. She groaned, burying her face in her knees. It wasn't a complicated process, so why did it ache her to think about it?

The Dirionus carefully rose and reached up its mouth to grab hold of Luna, laying her on the ground. Leilana reached for the Lasette, signing Minsuran letters with her hands and speaking as quietly as she could manage, "Bielien-an-ne-kir-en-te." From the Lasette's pages, a blue cotton blanket drifted onto Luna's body, covering her. The younger girl yawned, wrapping the new warmth tighter around her.

Upon Luna settling, the Dirionus shrunk to a miniscule size and jumped onto Leilana's lap, curling under her. Leilana leaned against a nearby wall to straighten her tender back, sighing. Her head was still swimming from the powerful spell she'd accessed, and now she was paying the price for leaving the manner to time rather than action. Her face felt hot, the area spinning despite her being planted on the ground. The Dirionus sat up, pressing its paws against her chest, whimpering a bit.

She rested a hand atop its head. "I'm all right," she said softly, grinning down at the beast. Her smile was insincere, plagued by the onset of exhaustion. "I guess it's easy to say that fighting takes a lot out of you, but it's even worse when you're an Arcana and you have to put a lot behind your magic." She ran her fingers along the open Lasette. "I wonder if Ennis knew any healing spells..." The Dirionus rested its forehead against hers, an amber aura flowing off the jewel on its skull.

"*Can you hear me?*" The voice was child-like and innocent. It was higher-pitched, much like Luna's voice, lacking experience and assurance.

Leilana blinked away the haze, her expression confused and conflicted on where the source lied. Her eyes were narrowing in thought, fixated on the miniscule creature. Its puffy tale was darting to each side, its eyes lit up at the sight of her as if receiving its desired acknowledgment. Wait. This wasn't making sense. Was a fever setting in more and making her delusional, or "Did you just talk...?"

"*So you **did** hear me!*" The Dirionus rested its paws on her lap once more. *"I thought that it would be easier to communicate this way! Now we'll be able to talk all the time!"*

"You're speaking in Minsura," she gaped.

"Oh, we Familiars know all the languages of the Warlords, bygones, and hereafters aside! I'm not limited to just Sentience or even Aluwus, the language of the people in the south! I can recite any language you ask me to a T!" The Dirionus seemed elated with the new development, but it was making Leilana's brain fry. She moaned, reaching up to her forehead, wiping away sweat. *"Um, I'm so sorry, this is probably all a lot to take in, especially if you're out of sorts..."*

"I'll be fine," she stated. "I need to get back to Linarus as soon as possible."

The Dirionus rested its paws on her chest again, as if to push her back down. *"No, you can't do that! I promised Solus that I would keep you both out of trouble!"*

"But what if *he's* in trouble?"

"Prince Remiel is strong!" The Dirionous pressed on, its words hindered with whimpers of protest on the surface. *"He's really, really strong, I know he's okay! He'll protect Solus!"*

"It doesn't matter how strong he is! It won't last him forever! I can't leave them out there by themselves!" she retorted, coughing afterward, raising her voice proving to be a hassle. The Dirionous flinched at the sound, its paw held up in front of its chest. The commotion led to Luna stirring, rising to a sit, rubbing the sleep from her eyes.

The Dirionus heard Luna yawn and went running to her, climbing into her lap and repeating the process of unlocking its inner voice to her. Luna raised an eyebrow, picking it up and holding it. One good look at the little creature after it began speaking to her told the young girl enough, it seemed. Luna stood up after setting the Dirionus on the ground, approaching Leilana with crossed arms, the blanket still in her hand.

"You know, if you were feeling sick, you could have said something instead of putting on a brave face." Leilana found the sudden emergence of her voice shocking, but she was more appalled at the scolding being turned on her. Somehow though, it seemed like a familiar twist. "Well, don't just stand there gawking. Rula says that you need to rest."

"Rula?" Leilana mumbled.

Luna smacked her forehead. "Oh, duh! The Dirionus there. He says his name is Rula. It's short for Rulakinja. It's a word in Aluwus that means..." She glanced back at Rula, who was ascending to his larger form for comfortability. "I think that he said 'sensible.' Right, Rula?"

"*Right!*" Rula beamed, puffy tail frantically wagging. "*My master Lorina gave me that name, and I treasure it dearly. But I prefer to be called Rula. It's easier that way.*"

Luna placed her hands on Leilana's shoulders, leaning forward to rest her forehead against hers. Leilana's face grew hot at the closeness, masked under her already rising fever. She coughed in surprise, her mouth closed to keep from hitting Luna. "So, time for talking is over now, Leilana," Luna stated. "Time for you to sleep." Rula trekked over to Leilana and tilted his nose, eager to help in any ways that he could. Maybe it was the first time that he was getting to really communicate with other humans.

Luna tossed her hair back into a ponytail, making way for the entrance. "I'll be right back."

"What are you planning to do?"

"I'm going to find herbs to make medicine. I don't know much about magic, but I do know how to treat illness." She folded her arms behind her back and gave Leilana a bright grin. "I've trained for an opportunity like this ever since I was little. So, let me help you."

"I can't allow you to go by yourself," Leilana explained. "And this illness shall pass, it's not like a cold or flu, only the effects are-"

Luna pointed a finger to silence her. "Don't try to convince me otherwise. Sick is sick. Remmy already told us about your case. He says that you're too stubborn to accept the right help, but I live with Sien—I don't back down." Was this kid *really* eleven? Quite precocious for her age, indeed.

"Are you sure that you can fight? Don't you want to take Rula with you so that you'll have protection? I'll have the Lasette with me. I can defend myself for a little while even if I'm incapacitated."

"I can help too, Luna!" Rula beamed. *"I know all kinds of berries that taste great! They help with strengthening immunity! Maybe we'll even get to make a super potion!"*

Luna found the proclamation thrilling. "Ooh, now that's an idea! We'll make the ultra-super-mega potion! And we will call it... Excelsior! That's perfect!"

"Perfect!" Rula agreed while Luna threw her arms up in the air. Rula let out a playful growl, and the two wound up butting heads, Luna giggling at the impact. Well, that confirmed her age.

"Come on, let's get going!" Luna then faced Leilana. "And you'd better be resting by the time that we come back. Don't leave the cave. We'll find our way around."

Luna seemed to resemble her older sister, slightly more mature and motherly despite her inferior age and experiences. It was appalling to witness, but somehow refreshing after being around the precocious Prince Remiel and the sweet yet serious Solus. These were the people of Adrylis, taking shape and growing into adults before her very eyes. And here she was, standing by their side. It was surreal—life was already changing.

Leilana reached for her bag, her fingers grazing over a slip of paper. Her heart was racing, unsure if a page had ripped from her notebook again or not. She found instead that the paper was a completely different color and texture from the one she possessed. She held up the paper before flipping it open, holding it up towards a crack in the cave to get a better lighting. When that failed, she laid back on the blanket, squinting at the barely visible letters written in a fine cursive.

I am one with harmony.

That was an interesting start, she had to admit. Tranquility was a vain subject, hard to achieve, difficult to maintain in an ever-changing world.

It is easy to be spirited away by the pleasures of magic, of conjuring something greater than yourself from an endless batch of pages.

I think of Leilana often, and I hear along the slanted gales that she is making herself known in the academy. She is the only one without any powers of her own to harness from her soul... but there are many reasons for it. Many words that I cannot give to her.

And so, I write, I craft, and I tuck away these words for

safekeeping. And I pray that they one day reach her. That **I** *will reach her again.*

Leilana's hands were trembling, daring to rip the flimsy sheet in two. This was all so confusing. It was obvious that this letter came from one of Ennis's lost documents, but how did it end up in her bag? Furthermore, what did he specify in his letter? What reasons did he have for her apparently lacking magical prowess? Sure, the Lasette was the source of her budding power, but it channeled a level of magic that existed inside of her already. Right?

There was something that someone was wanting her to see, and now that there were more pieces to the puzzle heightening in this discovery of self, she needed to know what. Her path was unclear from the start; that was what was laid down in front of her the moment that she stepped off the beaten path and found resolve in others more powerful than she was. Everything was spiraling out of control for a reason, and she had a place behind it.

She stuffed the paper back into her bag and gathered what was hers, climbing from the cave. She needed to get back to Linarus. Her friends needed her.

Life is fickle. It wasn't the first time he harbored such blunt thoughts while roaming the world with closed fists. Everything was meant to strengthen you—but with strength came burdens, and those burdens could tear the most cheerful person asunder right before the storm hit.

"Wake up, Your Highness."

The voice ushering him on was foggy; distant. But the

slap to his face was much more impactful in stirring him. He was preparing to retaliate when rattling chains and the binding force on his legs reaffirmed his decision. The world became vivid again, but the darkness of the room didn't do much for adjustment. The walls were grey, and only a candle set some light aglow. He was elevated; his legs were almost numb. He snarled, trying to pull his arm forward and snap the metal away, to no avail.

"Don't bother. Those chains are reinforced with the blood of Linmus's Guardian Dirionus—I'm certain you know stories of Yin."

Rem decided to acknowledge the voice now that he was coming to his senses. Some feet away stood a woman wearing a white cloak that draped down to her ankles, her face concealed by a mask resembling an eagle, the bird's wings on either side of where her eyes would be.

"You masked freaks seem to love messing around with other people's lives just to take a swing at me," he bellowed, leaning forward, the chains giving way slightly before jerking him, his back slamming against the brick wall. He exhaled, hissing down at the woman, "Why don't you let me down and I'll swing back?"

"Because then we'd have to kill your friends. And I doubt that you'd like that."

"You're bluffing, *hard*." He hoped that was the case. The masked warriors didn't take threats lightly. The woman sighed, digging into her cloak, revealing a silver orb. Rem sat back and watched as she manipulated the orb's properties, a projection appearing before them.

"Kirian. Prince Remiel needs some convincing. Show him his friends."

A plumper man with the mask of a bear on his face broke into laughter, his dark green hair standing up on all ends. "Man, he's not as silly as I was hoping, but that makes it more fun! All right, you three are gonna be my little play-mates! Who wants to play the first game?" Silence. Rem's heart was pounding against his chest. "No takers? Then I'll just have to pick for ya!" He was pointing a finger off to the left. "Eenie, meenie, miney, girlie, get over here!"

"Don't you dare!" Rem recognized the retaliating voice as Lancett's.

Now that Rem got a clear glimpse, there were signifi-cant differences in their situations; Lancett was bound in chains, whereas Solus was tied in rope, neither of them able to face one another due to being in chairs facing away. It almost seemed to show a power difference given that Solus wasn't in possession of any magic. It would be harder for him to escape from a rope than it would be for Lancett, who could ignite the thinner material.

The man sprang forward and grabbed hold of a girl with singed red hair, her face streaked with tears, which only aggravated the bruises on her cheeks. She cried out when he grabbed her arm and dragged her into view, holding her face up close to the crystalline orb in his possession.

"See the pretty girl?" Kirian mused. "If you don't comply, she's gonna die. Say bye-bye!"

Rem's heart stopped beating for a few seconds, his head swimming in confliction. "S-Sien..."

"Remiel!" Solus exclaimed. "Don't listen to them! You know they're trying to corrupt you!" Rem shook his head, gritting his teeth, staring at the concrete floors. "Don't take their bait! It is our duty to-"

"Oh, wanna rebel now, eh?" Kirian grasped Sien's arm, bending it against her back, causing her to scream. Rem's head shot up at the cry. "A healer is no good with a broken arm or a severed spine."

"Don't do this!" Lancett cried out. "Please!"

"Let her go!" Rem roared, fighting against the chains, the brick plastering beginning to give way against his weight and heightened rage. "I'll *kill* you! Leave her alone!" The woman behind the mask smirked, sensing the bloodlust burning through his frail body.

"You're a coward, hurting a woman!" Solus hissed, Rem's words ringing through him.

Kirian pinned Sien's arm further and she grunted in pain. "You shut your mouth, servant boy." Solus's eyes darkened, and he shut his mouth tight as ordered. Sien was still an innocent civilian through and through—he couldn't afford any unnecessary casualties. This was meant to be their fight.

"You'll be all right, Sien! Don't worry!" Lancett assured, trying to pry his hands free from the chains around his wrists. Solus was digging his nails into the rope, hoping that the durability wasn't as strong as he perceived.

"He's right, you know," Sien spat. "You are nothing but a coward, hiding behind a mask, thinking that you're doing Adrylis good. I've heard all about you from my father, ever since you emerged from the shadows." Solus's eyes widened by the words that followed, "You're an elite group of reject Maesters and Arcana that want magic to-" The man pushed her to the ground, slamming his foot onto her back, causing her to shriek.

"You're just a child," he snarled. "You don't know anything about what we've been through!"

"I know enough!" she pressed on, her nails clawing into the ground to compensate for her throbbing back—wiping out one pain by adding another. "I don't have to be an adult to know that this is wrong!" Solus could feel the ropes beginning to tear, and his fingernails continued to work furiously.

Rem's eyes were flashing amber, his sense of perception and reasoning dulling out the more that he was forced to endure this torture. "Stop," he growled, lowering his head to the woman. "I'll do what you want, just... just let them go."

"I'm glad that you see it my way."

"Prince Remiel!" Lancett retorted. "Hold on, that's reckless, you're-"

The woman looked at the orb, clenching it in her hand and causing it to dissolve, crumbling away like dust. Rem watched the shimmering particles fly past his face, silent. "You will relinquish your life to us, Highness. The fate of Adrylis has always been on your shoulders."

Leilana was certain that the world was spinning too fast. The sky looked green. Or were they supposed to be trees? Oh well, either way, she was making progress. She was skimming over her map, expanding the landscape every so often and peering over the landscape. She remembered bypassing a bunch of rice paddies on the ride to Linarus, and if memory served her correctly, they should be coming up soon. When she decided to stop for a spell again to see her progress, she noticed the rice paddies, and further east stood what was left of Linarus. She broke into a run, her muscles aching at the sudden change of pace. Her breaths were becoming labored, her vision spotting every so often.

Her first steps along the once tranquil pavement nearly made her double over. She could smell decomposition and taste the ash in the air. Bodies were littering the ground, not a soul left to whisper any pleas. The wolves were gone, some of the beasts fallen at the hands of defenders. She was stifling sobs as she progressed forward, her feet sloshing along the blood-stained trail. She reached up her arms to wrap around herself, trying to swallow down the tears.

Please, she thought. Please let her friends be safe. She couldn't bear losing anyone else.

Her first stop was Midstream. It was in tatters, glass everywhere, chairs overturned, booths ripped apart, but no one seemed to be around. She rested a hand on the counter. She could still hear Sien trying to offer them drinks, even wanting Leilana to rebel against the limits of age and have a sip. There were no corpses, which meant that her friends weren't around. She skimmed the halls, and still no trace of anyone. The beds were empty, the bathrooms clean as if people left without a trace. That was a sign, right? That meant that they were out of the crossfires for now. Maybe Rem and Solus had reached the tavern in time to get people out. But even so, where were they now?

She stepped outside, climbing the upward hills. If they weren't low on the spectrum to avoid the wolves and potentially Lunious, maybe they sought out shelter elsewhere. Upon reaching the top, she wasn't surprised to stumble upon a massive shrine-like building hidden beyond the trees.

"I feel a pull," she mumbled. They were here. They had to be.

"I want to know why your leader killed my parents and burned my kingdom to the ground. I know that it was him. I don't know anything about him. I've never even seen his face. But there had to be a reason why he wanted us dead. It couldn't have been my magic—my mother took care to make it known that my powers were untouched until I was ready."

"You've yet to see your real potential," she told him, removing the mask, brushing her pixie cut red hair out of her blue eyes. Rem slowly looked up at her, his mouth agape. "In the right hands, you could single-handedly end of the world."

This is going nowhere fast, Rem thought to himself, his fingers twitching in anticipation. He could hear the wall beginning to break apart. "You have given a request to have my life, the least that you can do start giving me these reasons. What is this guild?" She supposed that he had a point. He was primed to die, what was the harm in giving him the answers that he craved?

"We are known as the Order of Helix," she began. "We are a group comprised of Maesters and Arcana that failed their pilgrimage. But the choice was never ours; we seek revenge for our failure. And we seek the power that is comparable to Warlords."

They were mere apprentices hunting down someone that could be out of their league, but now his face had a touch of confusion. Somehow things weren't adding up the more that he listened. Someone had to be leading them.

"You say that you want to ascertain the power of Warlords, but what does it have to do with me? I'm not a Warlord. I was born a Maester, but I am not nearly prepared enough for such feats. If anything, you're flattering me."

"It's easy to see what lies on the surface..." The woman drew a dagger from her robe's sleeve.

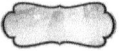

Leilana stepped inside of the shrine, encompassed in shades of grey, the lights dim. She was running her fingers along the wall to keep herself from tripping, fumbling around in the dark. She couldn't hold the Lasette in her hands to use any form of light; it was simply too heavy for her to hold in one hand.

She felt a hand on her shoulder, flinching at the coolness. Her vigilance heightened when she was pushed back into a brick wall, temporarily losing her breath at the contact. Standing before her was a masked man, greatly resembling Lunious and Mitholus. He was wielding an iron ball and chain, thrusting it at her. She narrowly dodged the attack, the ball slinging into the wall next to her. She couldn't help but stare at the indent before sliding out of the way of a second strike.

Well. This was a peculiar turn of events. So now these weirdoes were trying to pound her into ground beef. That made it easier to confirm that they were protecting something or some*one*. And that someone was likely a captive Rem.

She opened the Lasette, dashing away from an impending ball to wall contact, ducking away behind a stone statue. Now that she was crouching, her head was pounding, likely from the rapid movement to avoid the whole shebang of death by metal balls. She shakily inhaled, sweat rolling down the back of her neck, holding up a hand before slamming it on the ground, a burst of lightning striking from the heavens, cutting through the stone walls.

Leilana glanced up at the crumbling ceiling and watched as the bolt electrocuted the man's body, causing him to scream in agony. His mask split in half, blood was pouring from his mouth and eyes, his flesh beginning to melt away under the intense heat. Leilana watched the sight in horror, covering her mouth with both hands.

The man was human, just like her, and she was killing him.

The man let out a yell, hurling his ball and chain at her, knocking her to the floor. Leilana winced in pain at the contact, coughing harshly as she rose to a sit. No. It shouldn't have mattered if any of them were human, for their acts were still so inhumane. They wanted to kill Rem, slaughtered an entire village for the sake of reaching him and kidnapped her friends. They were stopping at nothing to try and achieve their goals, even at the cost of other lives.

She was clenching her hand into a fist as he set himself up to attack again. Not a word he spoke to her, and here they were as enemies. Two different moralities. Two different understandings in this fickle game of life, where only one could emerge and continue moving forward. She swung her hand out as he drew closer, the electrical surges still fluctuating off of his body.

"Interasan (bind)... kinzaiver (quell)..." His movements didn't still until she balled her hand up again slowly, his legs and arms binding together, constricting him. Her arm was quaking under the pressure, magic siphoning out of her body to keep him in place. Focus. The focus was impenetrable.

"Go on!" the man hissed.

Stop, she wanted to scream at him. She didn't want to

end up hurting him. She couldn't stand the idea of taking any human lives, even if it were necessary.

"If you're gonna hold me down, you may as well kill me!"

You know that you want to. Another voice chimed in, taking her by surprise, though her focus didn't wave. **Kill him. Kill him.** No, no, she wanted to beg. This wasn't the way. **You want to save your friends, don't you? Solus needs you... Rem wants to grow with you... let *them* be your guide...**

Her mind slipped through feeble cracks. Her eyes snapped open at the sound and she shakily exhaled, lowering her hand. His body became too bound to itself, his bones crunching together. His corpse slumped onto the floor, unmoving. His mouth was hanging open, the dried blood still fresh on his face, streaking down. Leilana dropped to her knees, clutching her stomach while vomiting on the floor.

"What's with the light show?!" Kirian hissed, looking back towards the door, slightly jerking Sien's hair along with him. "Always something around these parts, isn't there?" Solus was watching the man closely, his wrists finally unbound, the ropes around his chest loosening. He was holding them together with his hands to keep from drawing suspicion. His eyes were laced with anticipation, his foot bouncing.

"It sounded like electricity," Lancett began. "Maybe a mage got a little antsy?"

"No one around here gets that antsy!" Kirian retorted, stomping his foot on the ground. "A-At least *I'm* not antsy!"

"You're not going to go check it out?" Solus asked.

"Like I'm that stupid," Kirian scoffed, turning his back to answer a call on his own crystalline orb. "What?! What's going on, what's with the sounds?"

Solus gestured to Lancett, holding up one of his hands, wiggling his fingers to express his means of freedom. Lancett smirked. Sien was glaring up at Kirian, prying her hair free. Her limbs ached too much to move about the room, let alone heal herself—he'd made sure of that.

"What the hell do you mean there's an unknown Arcana in here?" Kirian said sharply, keeping his voice low to keep his captives from overhearing. "No one is supposed to get further than the front door. You guys screwed up big time, and I can't leave the premises."

Solus unwound the ropes and carefully rose from the chair, tiptoeing over to Kirian and tapping his shoulder. "Pardon." Kirian whirled around only to be met with a swift blow to the neck. The attack sent him tumbling to the ground, unconscious. Solus shook out his hand, grumbling, "Such meat on his bones..." Sien sighed of relief, clutching her bruised arm.

"Nice work there," Lancett told him. "How did you do it?"

Solus looked at his chipped nails, holding them towards Lancett with a half-hearted smile. "Compromise. I have been told to prepare for any situation. This was one of those times." He rested his hands on his side again. "We need to find Rem."

"Kirian said there's an Arcana in here," Lancett began.

"I think it may be Leilana." Solus didn't look too pleased, his nose scrunching in disappointment. It better *not* be Leilana. He was clear about telling her to stay with Luna and keep her safe, and yet she ran away to help them anyway. Sometimes she could be so stubborn, but that was a price to pay for youth.

"You're not helping her?" Lancett asked, noticing Solus's almost cold expression.

"His duty is to Rem," Sien answered, rising to a stand only to grip a nearby wall. "It was always to Rem. There isn't anything we can do about that. We'll support Leilana, and Solus can find Rem."

"You want to go after Leilana when you can't even help yourself right now?" Lancett retorted, grabbing the girl's arm. "At least take the time to heal yourself." Sien outstretched both of hers before holding up her hand to the ceiling, effectively freeing herself from Lancett, a crimson aura encircling her body. The wounds began to mend and close, the blood drying, shifting away from her body as if cleansing her. The physical pain had mostly dulled, but she was still stiff.

She smirked at Lancett after lowering her hand, flipping loose strands of hair out of her face. "You were saying?" Lancett rolled his eyes, and Solus was already set on his way.

"The two of you search for Leilana, make for the entrance and then leave Linmus. I imagine that Leilana's going to need support because her body is still undergoing a flux." Lancett raised an eyebrow at the remark. 'Flux?'

"And where are you going after you find Rem?" Sien asked.

"We'll meet you. It may take us some time, but try not to wait up too long." He left the room.

"Wait, Solus!" Sien called out, "You don't have your sword!" But by then, he was already long gone. Sien scoffed, resting her hands on her hips. "Just as reckless as the Prince..."

There has to be a way. There has to be some way out of this.

Rem was observing his captor's movements closely. The dagger would do little harm if it were a mere prick, even if the wrong place. He gave a small tug on the chains, listening to the metal rattle. The plastering cracked under the pressure. His eyes widened. That was it—one good tug could set him free.

"You haven't answered me," Rem pressed on. "What do you need me for? You all have enough magic to overthrow me. I'm nowhere near ready for these so-called plans to eradicate you. And even without that, you have possession of my country—*our* country. Why kill me?" The woman plunged the dagger into his stomach, causing him to gasp, gazing at the blood seeping down the weapon.

"The plan was never to kill you." She slowly dragged the weapon out of him, and he winced, panting. "Only to purge the darkness in you."

"You can't take away what exists in someone's soul, their being," he snarled, his fingers flexing before he thrust his arm forward, the chains and wall snapping apart, leaving him to hang. The woman stepped back, a bit surprised. "You are irrational and foolish to consider it." He swung his right arm forward, falling to the ground, landing in front of her. His eyes were hazy, fluctuating around his over-anxious emotions. "My friends. Where are they?"

"You won't save them!" she exclaimed, the polished metal on her dagger emanating a turquoise aura. "There is no stopping the war, Remiel Vesarus." He grabbed her by the neck, lifting her off the ground, his left hand engulfed in the ever-familiar shred of darkness.

She was gagging, choking on the last of her oxygen. The more that she struggled, the tighter his grasp became until the inevitable crunch from her neck snapping finally came. He dropped her corpse to the ground and stepped out of the room, closing the door behind him, slamming his hand against the knob to knock it off, kicking it aside. He dispelled the Bloodlinch ascension powers, clasping his hand shut and continuing down the winding halls of the grey line.

If he wasn't going to get any answers, then he'd have to take manners into his own hands.

EIGHTEEN

Leilana was stumbling down the halls, trying to avoid any unnecessary confrontation, but every corner brought a new opponent. Sneaking was becoming tedious rather than eventful, having to run the other way and risk returning to an old corridor, but it was better than overexerting what energy she had left. There was still no sign of Solus or Rem, but upon hearing around the grapevine, there were others besides them as captives—likely Sien and Lancett. There must have been consequences in agreeing to terms with these masked crusaders.

Still, each step forward led to two steps back knowing that one wrong move would cost her life.

She was turning down another corridor when two Arcana, identifiable by their build under the crimson cloaks, caught her gaze. Leilana went sprinting in the opposite direction to avoid any further issues. That didn't avert their attention enough to give chase. Of course, they weren't going to. She was no better than their captives, barging into the stronghold to try and save the day. She was ducking down from one of the wind spells only to propel forward, strong arms sweeping her off her feet.

Relief swallowed her when she connected with familiar green eyes. "S-Solus?"

"Leilana," he replied, nodding. "Fancy running into you here."

"I'm glad you're safe," she whispered before raising her voice to ask, "Is Rem all right?"

Solus averted his gaze up to the ceiling, fixated on how to answer. "I'm not sure yet. I'm trying to find him, but I haven't had any leads." He folded his arms. "But Rem aside, what are *you* doing here? I thought I told you to-"

"There!" One of the Arcana exclaimed from behind the muffled wall. Leilana heard a spark emerge from the swing of a staff and shoved Solus to the ground, covering his head with her arms to shield him from the obstructed rubble. She glanced up, noticing the wall to their left smoking, split apart by an inferno. The cinders were drifting, the plastering sizzling, no sign of their assailants.

"What on earth did you do?" Solus groaned, sitting up.

"I may have set them off to my presence," she admitted.

"Commendable work." She didn't like his sarcasm, but she knew that she deserved the cold shoulder—she had disobeyed his orders, after all.

"But I was only trying to help, Solus. I was worried about-"

"No time." Solus grabbed her hand, hoisting her to her feet. "They'll catch us if we linger for too long." Her eyes were darting back and forth between his hand and his collected expression. He must have been used to these forms of escapade.

He led her away from the rubble, ducking behind a corner. He put a finger to his lips, gesturing for her to crouch and lay low. She obeyed, watching him unravel the red ribbon around his wrist, snapping back the elastic to make sure that it was still intact. He no longer had a sword in his possession, taken away by his captors; he'd have to improvise.

"That's strange," one of the Arcana stated. She was

hunched over, her fingers grazing the still-sizzling plastering, causing her to flinch. "I thought for sure that spell
would draw her out."

"Don't drop your guard," the second said sharply. "It's
easy to state that they escaped, but even more convenient
if they-"

Before she could finish her sentence, Solus swung his
ribbon, wrapping it around her neck. Clasping the other
half of the ribbon's strand that returned to him, he tugged as
hard as he could manage before twisting it to the left, snapping the woman's neck. Leilana covered her mouth with
both hands to keep from vomiting, vividly reminded of her
own brush of annihilation moments before.

The younger Arcana was shaken by her ally's murder. It
didn't take long for a switch to go off in her mind, for she
began blasting several fireballs in Solus's direction, yelling
at him in a language that neither he nor Leilana could translate fast enough—possibly her home language rather than
Sentience. Solus side-stepped through the flames as they
fired at him one by one. It was peculiar; his expression was
dull, the situation taxing.

It was as though he were a different person.

Each nimble step made Leilana's heart twinge. His lack
of magical prowess dubbed him as the weakest link, but now
he acted with vigilance and concentration. He wasn't as
skilled as Rem, or even as her, for he was limited. Then
again, to her, Solus was always special. A hand was laid on
her shoulder, and she thrust her hand out to throw off her
assailant only for the strike to be grabbed.

"Easy there," Rem spoke, lowering her hand. "No need
to go pulling punches on the Prince."

"Hi, Rem," she managed, easing her racing heart. Rem
wasn't even looking at her anymore, his focus on his fateful

companion currently in the heat of battle. Solus whipped the ribbon around the girl's wrist, dragging her closer to him, a lustful haze in his eyes.

"Oh boy," Rem mumbled, causing Leilana to glance up at him in anticipation. "I know that look. He's in his 'soulless' mode."

"'Soulless?'" she repeated.

"Now then," Solus began, cupping the girl's chin in his free left hand. "What is a girl like you, burning with passion and such promise to the magical world, doing among these reckless criminals? There is something more to you..."

"My sister and I were training to become Warlords, but neither of us was qualified," she began, the words spilling from her soul, all from a single look. "We had nowhere to go."

"I see that you're prone to talking." Solus shoved the girl out of his grasp, knocking her to the floor. She was whimpering, trying to avoid his incriminating stare. Leilana was baffled. She was so persistent in ending his life, and now she was fearful. What about his expression sold her? Solus wrapped the scarlet ribbon around a decent chunk of hair to tie into a low ponytail. "I suggest that you find another trade. Magic is not for the weak of heart." She wordlessly scampered off.

"What was *that*?" Leilana asked, more to herself than anything.

"Serious Solus is 'soulless,' and Blissful Solus is 'solace.' Neutral Solus is Solus," Rem explained.

She was sputtering at the nonsensical declaration. "What? What does that even mean?"

"Oh, you'll see." Rem trekked up to Solus, tapping his shoulder. Solus nearly swiped his hand at the young Prince but instead laid it on his chest upon seeing the person that sought his attention, arching his back to lower into a bow. Leilana decided to leave them be, transfixed on Rem's words.

Soulless versus Solace. It wasn't the first time that she had heard the terms. 'Solace,' a word she vaguely knew the definition of—she could see Solus's sense of comfort towards others, and without a doubt, he was supportive of any sensible manner. But, what was 'Soulless' referring to, his bluntness?

Sudden darkness. Abrupt silence.

Rem's muscles tensed. Solus's heart fell through the floor. Leilana collapsed to the ground, blood spewing from her back. Hovering above her was an ever-familiar sword-wielding Maester gathering her into his arms.

"Lancett!" Rem roared, his left hand bound to shadow.

"Rem, hold on!" Solus exclaimed.

Rem dodged one of Lancett's swings, bringing up a hand to his face, knocking him into a nearby stone wall. Leilana was no longer in his grasp, sliding against the ground. Upon contact, Lancett's face shifted right before slipping straight, the damage erased. He cracked his neck once, shaking out his hands. Rem had to do a double take. Did that man literally just snap his face back into place? That wasn't humanly possible, was it?

"A shifter," Solus concluded. "Keep on your toes, we don't know Lancett's skills!"

At his words, the shifter slammed his foot against Leilana's back, eliciting a scream. Solus flinched, his eyes fixated on Leilana, his lips parting more. Rem snarled, interlocking his hand around the man's throat to toss him back, to no avail. He seemed to keep getting right back up and readjust himself before Rem could so much as land another attack on him. Solus could hear blood sloshing about his crumbling mind. He couldn't stop looking at Leilana no matter how much he willed himself not to overthink the situation. Still, the pained expression on her face spoke leaps and bounds. She needed him, and there was little that he could accomplish with no weapon to cut away their opponent.

He wasn't like Rem. There was little room to evolve when the greatest assets were morality and humanity. No magic shielded him, and every window of opportunity to become a suitable protector was shut away. Rem was capable of fending for himself just fine now that he woke to his birthright.

He wasn't like Leilana either. She continued to stand against Lunious, even when her body was breaking down right in front of them, even as life was slipping away. When they reunited, her eyelids had dark circles under them, and her arms were boiling to the touch. She was still fighting, all to reunite with them. Now she was weakened by the power drawn from the Lasette, injured by opposers to the throne, all because he wasn't strong enough to protect her.

The sword scraping the stone pathway was screeching in his ears, blindsiding his focus. Rem's grunts of disapproval were sealing the deal. He couldn't protect his Prince, nor could he protect the girl that stepped into his world and beckoned a new form of living in him. She could become anything, and she didn't know it just yet.

His hands were sweating, his knees heavy, chaining him down to reality again. He stepped past Rem as the young Prince was thrown to the floor, his eyes void of all essence. He pushed the shifter's hand away as he swung, the slight throb in his palm barely a threat. He reached up his index and middle finger, plunging them into the shifter's eyes, his nails becoming soaked in a murky shade of grey. Ah, the tears of a sullied mage. He swiftly dug out the limbs, causing the Maester to shriek and try to reclaim his lost vision. The sound was nearly demonic, reminiscent of a vulture's cry.

Rem was frozen, off-put by the sensation. This wasn't the first time he'd witnessed such a painful means to an end, but it was the first time he had seen his best friend's eyes so cold.

Solus forcefully slammed the shifter's head into the stone wall, his skull cracking. Solus clenched the man's hand while unintentionally bending them, his fingers snapping. The screams were no more, but the soul remained intact. Solus could still detect a heartbeat, faint but beating like a drum. Good. This person knew fear. Most shifters carried no emotional weight. No different from husks created by the very test that shoved them from the world.

Solus wrapped his right hand around the man's rather boney neck, the ribbon on his wrist slapping against his face at the swift movement. His nails were digging into tearing flesh, his teeth grinding the more that he shifted his weight forward. He continued to choke the shifter even long after the soul had left the body.

"Sol," Rem said softly, resting two fingers on the ripped flesh. Solus's mind tugged away from the situation at hand. "Come on, stop it, he's dead. It's over."

Solus tore his shaky hand from the man's neck, reaching out to graze the man's face. Upon contact, the shifter's power dispelled, revealing a young girl with braided blonde hair, her irises bloodshot. The shifter was a female the entire time, someone that no longer knew their own face and became mentally unstable. At least peace came easier.

"I'm so sorry," Solus whispered. He was struggling to stand, pacing himself towards Leilana.

"I stopped the bleeding," Rem told him. "But her physical health is significantly deteriorated." Solus gathered the girl in his arms, his left hand supporting her head while his right was locked under her legs.

"We need to find Lancett and Sien." Solus started ahead, and the young prince groaned before giving chase.

"What's taking them so long?" Sien mumbled, drumming her fingers on a stone pillar. Their captors had become so preoccupied with other manners that they didn't bother returning to the entrance. It was practically their great escape, and in minutes, it could fall apart. "Solus said to meet him here, and it's been forever!"

"No need to be impatient," Lancett replied, wiping the blood from his blade with a rag, keeping a firm grip on the broadsword and saber previously locked away. There were few places to hide weapons inside of an extensive shrine but scavenging them wasn't particularly difficult. "They'll be here. What I wonder is how we haven't run into Leilana. The guards were speaking a lot about an Arcana gone rogue, sneaking around the shrine."

"Are we even sure it's her? Solus said that she was safe, why would she come back?"

"Why else?" Lancett retorted, though he hadn't intended to be harsh. "She came looking for her friends." He sighed. "I don't understand what she's thinking. We barely have time as mages to live, yet she's so devoted to two people she just met. She doesn't give a damn about-"

A slap to the face slit through his words like a knife. The

right side of his face was throbbing, his teeth jabbing into his gums. It didn't take him more than a few seconds to process what had happened, but the realization that he was ranting so much that he deserved to be slapped so hard disturbed him.

"Hey now," Sien hissed, her hand still in the air to take another shot at him. "No one is safe from hurt. Don't go thinking that she doesn't forgive you. You did what you thought was right. You were troubled—your best friend died, the girl that he loved ran away blaming herself, and you couldn't shoulder that stress. You made a choice, and it led you back together. Accept your mistakes."

Lancett's fingertips brushed along his wounds. He wasn't sure what ached more, his face or his heart. It was so easy to leave her. It was easier for Sien to say that he was in love with her when he knew damn well that someone in love would never *abandon* their love. These feelings, they were drowning in sorrow, slipping through mud, rung out to dry and left behind. Sien was wrong. He loved her, and he couldn't embrace it. Now that she could look upon others with devotion, she didn't need him anymore. He was just an onlooker between four walls that could never speak up until the opportunity presented itself. He knew it; he just didn't want to believe it.

He inhaled deeply, his nails clawing into the thin fabric of his pants. "I think there are better things to seek than one girl's heart. I'll leave it behind if that is what it takes to erase my hurt." Sien was taken aback by his words, lowering her hand. He didn't stop staring at her, his lips upturned into a broken smile—hindered by the very pain that he shielded away when life took its toll.

"All right," Sien replied, resting her hands on her hips. "You want to start over, you've always got a place. Making plans is easy. Following through with them is tricky, especially when you're new to living. What do you want to do after this?"

"I don't know," he admitted. "I've still got time to think it over. Right now, I guess it's best to keep moving forward-" Footsteps went scurrying through his ears, and he snapped his head back to uncover the source, sword in hand, pausing upon noticing Solus emerge from the shadows.

"There you are!" Sien beamed, running over to the two young men before frowning at the girl in Solus's arms. Her arms wrapped around his neck to keep herself steady, her head resting against his shoulder. Lancett's palms were sweating, his breathing quickening at the sight. "Is she all right?"

"Let's just leave," Solus said softly, stepping out of the shrine without another word.

"What's his problem?" Sien asked Rem, who instead went after Solus rather than acknowledging her question. "What the-What's *his* problem?" She threw her arms up in disdain, scoffing. "What's everyone's problem here, and why aren't they talking to me about them?!" Lancett wrapped his arm around her shoulders and led her out, deciding that they couldn't afford to waste time.

The group of four were guided to the cliff-side caverns on the eastern border on Leilana's instructions, as much as she could manage before slipping into unconsciousness every few minutes. A downpour started up down the line, which left Rem to sacrifice his jacket to lay over her. Upon reaching the caverns, they were met with the harsh stare of the younger Kaiser child.

"I told her not to leave the cave, and what does she end up doing?!" Luna was fuming, throwing her hands up at the end of every sentence. "Not listening to the one with sense!"

Solus was ringing out his hair while Rem and Lancett both sat with shirts off, tossed aside to dry. Lancett was keeping his focus on other things despite staring directly at her, whereas Rem had given up on cooling her down altogether. The girl's ranting was comparable to the booming thunder only meters away from their current barracks, but even a storm wasn't as frightening or lethal to brave. Rula's tail was swishing back and forth, amused by Luna's scolding session. Sien was resting on his back while Leilana was fast asleep between his two large paws, bundled in several blankets. Rula didn't mind it; he was just happy to be around other people.

"Luna," Solus began. "Don't you think that you should calm down?"

"Don't you tell me to calm down," Luna snapped, pointing a finger at the older boy. Solus didn't even flinch, far used to confrontation. "You're just as responsible."

"How?" he responded evenly.

"She wasn't feeling well, and she was being reckless! You should have stopped her!"

"Don't be childish," he retorted. "You know that I had nothing to do with it. I can't control when her feet decide to correspond with her heart."

Solus stood up and walked to the entrance, marveling at the summer storm. Rem's barrier usage was increasing steadily; the lightning could barely reach it. The rain was striking the ground fiercely and didn't show signs of stopping, but that ensured that the Order of Helix wouldn't be running after them anytime soon. Lancett sighed, unfazed by the turn of events. Tensions were high ever since they'd left the shrine, so it was only natural that someone was bound to crack. Luna took a seat, crossing her arms with a scoff, turning up her nose.

"You know, if you were a little more considerate instead of throwing a tantrum, you would've thought about how they're feeling." Rem jabbed his thumb over at Leilana and Sien. "They've had a long day too. That's all he was getting at."

Luna's face reddened, flustered by the twist on her behavior. She crossed her legs, shifting her weight onto her hands. "I'm sorry."

Solus lowered his head, taking in the girl's words as he listened from afar. Loneliness, solitude, isolation... they manifested in many forms, and they shaped someone for better or worse. All the people in this cave shared that trait —one way or another, they lived without watchful eyes to guide them, bound together by circumstance.

"We should leave before morning," Solus told them. "That's when the storm will be letting up."

"Leilana won't be better by morning," Rem stated, his tone calming with each word passing through his lips. "Can we afford to put her in more danger?"

"Leilana can handle herself," Lancett responded, propping himself up to a more comfortable position. "If she could move around the shrine the way she did, then exhaustion won't stop her."

"Confident," Luna replied. "That's not like you at all."

"Every now and again, I like to see myself as an optimist."

"Then it's settled. All of you rest. The barrier should

hold for the night and mask our presence." Solus nodded in acknowledgment to Rem, who grinned in response. "By dawn, we head due north. Any questions, comments, concerns, or retaliation?" Silence from the peanut gallery awarded him a firm 'no,' and Solus sighed of relief.

"Are you going to sleep, Sol?" Rem asked while Lancett and Luna were settling into slumber a few minutes later. Solus continued to sit in front of the barrier, his back turned to the group.

"I need to think."

"You don't want to talk?"

"No. Not right now." Rem pulled away from the subject at hand upon hearing the slight irritation in his best friend's tone. He was accustomed to it when there was something bothering him, but Solus could be an enigma to open eyes. Once he became this way, it was hard to make him change his mind about discussing his problems with someone else.

"Night, Sol," he whispered. "Try not to be afraid of the dark…"

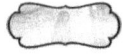

"Aren't you going to sleep?"

Solus was trying his best to ignore the constant question, but now that Leilana was addressing him, he felt guilty for remaining awake several hours past everyone else. Dawn was setting in, and though his muscles were stiff and his mind hazy, he sat still. She crawled forward to sit next to him. He knew that she meant no harm, but right now, he was too deep in thought to consider sleeping. That shifter's face ached him. Harming an ill-intended man was one story, but seeing placing a woman in the same position was gut-wrenching. The woman he murdered in cold blood had intertwined herself with the wrong crowd. He felt nothing initially, but now it was building like impenetrable stone walls; no pickaxe could tear them down fast enough.

"Solus, what are you thinking about?"

It took time to acknowledge her words. A blanket was snugly wrapped around her shoulders for warmth. Seeing her bright blue eyes laced with concern wounded him more than he could comprehend. She didn't know the lengths he had gone to protect her, to protect Rem. He wasn't sure how he could ever tell her what plagued his mind.

Where could he begin? Saying that it wasn't the first time he had isolated himself after a strenuous mishap? Did he just ignore her altogether, tell her to go back to sleep, focus on recovering, and hope that she would leave things at that? He folded his hands to contemplate his words. He didn't want to sleep. He knew that the nightmares would begin if he had.

"You know," she began, laying the blanket around his shoulders. "I hurt someone. It was a man. He was larger than any of us. He was trying to pound me into mush with a ball and chain. I don't remember a lot of what happened in between, but I remember hearing a voice telling me to kill him." Solus listened without a word of response, his hand gripping to the blanket around his shoulders. He had half a mind to rip it away and return it.

"I'm not sure where it came from, or why. I was so scared because mages aren't supposed to destroy our sense of morality. Killing people is exponentially high on that list. Amiria lost her way because of something that she uprooted along the way. She's alone, scared, and I don't know how to help her. None of us know where she is, what she's doing, or how to help her without setting her off." She wrapped her arms around her stomach, staring at the ground, her hair sinking over her eyes. "I don't want to end up like her. War changes people, doesn't it...?"

Solus sighed. "Leilana Erovina, you are not going to end up war-torn and alone."

"That's not guaranteed, and you know it," she retorted. "I can't cast powerful spells without running myself ragged. You've seen it happen since we've begun, why aren't you-?"

"Because you have us to guard your life," Solus responded. Leilana grew silent, resting her hands on the murky ground. Solus continued to stare at her, his expression a mixture of agony and stalwartness. "We are always going to keep you safe. That is what friends do for one another, is it not? I'm not going to keep repeating this."

"You seem so different lately," she said softly. "What's going through your head?"

"I'm not sure that I want to talk about it."

"It's all right if you don't. I understand completely. Just... whenever you do want to talk, and you feel like you can't go to Rem, you can always come to me." Solus watched her rise to a stand to return to Rula's furry solace before lowering his head to be alone with his thoughts once more. "Oh, and Solus?"

Good, she hadn't given up on him just yet. That was relieving. "Yes?"

Leilana was resting her hand on Rula's side, gently stroking his fur. "I remember something else Ennis told me. 'Make friends, ones that will last you a lifetime.' Sometimes adjusting to hurt can make you stronger. It becomes easier to mend your heart and face more of it rather than hiding and allowing it to consume you."

"Ennis was a wise man," Solus agreed. "He had to take

in a lot of hurt to become a Warlord. It is how they can divide themselves from omniscience. Magic is a touchy subject for a reason. There's much that we couldn't begin to comprehend. You're well on your way. You've already gathered together the strength that buds within you, and you are only going to grow stronger as you move forward." He rested a hand against the nearby wall, watching lightning streak the sky, the thunderclouds rolling west, away from the overpass of the cave. "You are an Arcana, bound by fate."

"What does that mean?"

Solus drew in a deep breath before continuing, "I want to ask something. Do you really wish to continue with us, even if there's a possibility that you'll lose your morality?"

Leilana stared at him from afar before averting her eyes to the ground, considering his words. Was it the best option to stay? "Why are you bringing this up?"

"You desire to become a Warlord, and staying by our side, continuing your pilgrimage alongside us, will test that morality. You could become corrupted. Do you want to take that risk?"

Things were adding up now; something happened to him inside of the shrine that made him begin to question his own morals. Maybe it was something that involved her, and that was why he didn't want her to lose herself in midst of the chaos. Why was he so fond of her anyways? He seemed to take pride in knowing her in a manner that differed greatly from Rem. It was almost as if he were...

No. It wasn't possible. He wasn't in love with her. They were friends, nothing more. Maybe she was the first female friend he'd had, and he sought to keep her safe for that reason. They didn't know nearly enough about one another to consider that option.

It was true, she could be corrupted. Lunious wanted her grimoire for himself, likely because of its connection to Ennis. But if the words of his note rang true, without the Lasette, her journey was pointless. She could never become a Warlord.

"No," she said without hesitation. "I want to stay by your side. You seek the Orb of Concord to end this war. Starting tomorrow, let's get serious about finding it. We'll find leads." Solus started to approach her, finding her heightened sense of determination charming. "We'll learn about why they created it. I'll do everything that I can to help you both bring Linmus back to prosperity. Just give me a chance."

Solus cupped her cheeks in his hands, his expression calm. Leilana's muscles went stiff, her legs shaking at the sudden contact. Many times, they had interacted this closely, but only now did she notice the hint of brown around his green irises, rivaling the forestry. The morning light was breaking through the dark clouds, the storm coming to pass.

He was leaning closer to her, and the warmth of his drawing breath was welcoming. Maybe he did love her after all, and she was scared to admit it. They were nothing more than comrades fighting for a similar cause. They both wanted to protect Rem, to protect Adrylis, and to better their land. Kissing him would be wrong. Being in love with him was wrong and tore against her pilgrimage. Love was forbidden between a human and a magical denizen. Everything about this seemed so wrong.

Even so, why was she pulling herself closer? Was she in love with him too? How could she allow him to be wrapped in this silly game if they couldn't stay together?

Before she could utter a retort, his tender lips pressed

against hers. She closed her eyes, snaking her arms around his neck to pull him closer. He rested his hands on her hips, then retracted, pulling away with parted lips. Leilana couldn't stop staring at him, unsure of how to respond, reaching up to touch her lips, the salt on his tongue a fresh taste. He had pulled back too soon, and now she was left with confusion.

Why did she want more? Why did she *need* more?

"I-I'm sorry," he whispered, taking a step back not only from the situation but from his racing mind. "I don't know what I was thinking-"

Leilana grabbed his hand as he tried to retreat, leaning up to kiss his lips once more. Soon after, she wrapped her arms around his waist, burying her face in his chest. Solus couldn't recall the last time he'd been in someone's arms like this, even if it made him hesitant, fearful. Not of her, rather of what he felt *for* her. Why her? Why did it have to be her?

"The love between an Arcana and a human is forbidden, Solus." Solus knew. He had always known. That was what made this so complicated. "Even so, I won't leave. I promise to stay. I will see this mission to the end. We'll finish this together. Everything will work out."

He wanted to believe it just as much as she did; she could tell by the forced tone he took on. There was an unmistakable hint of sorrow behind his words. There was always a consequence of war.

And it would come to tear them apart.

NINETEEN

Rem was the first to take notice of the silence between his two closest companions. Leilana and Solus were walking side by side, Solus with his hands in his pockets while looking off at the trees to keep his attention from whatever plagued his mind, Leilana with her nose in her grimoire. Every now and again, Solus would make sure that she didn't go bumping into anything, and once or twice he wasn't fast enough to keep that from happening. She didn't mind the aches, and he didn't mind pulling a little legwork to keep her out of trouble.

"So, we're supposed to be going north, but where do we go beyond that?" Sien asked, juggling a few peaches from a collection of bushes they bypassed on the way. Sure, it was technically stealing, but survival of the fittest goes a long way. Luna was reaching up to snag one from her, but Sien's superior height won out, the older girl snickering before handing it down to her. Lancett couldn't help sighing, and Rula couldn't stop his tail from moving at the excitement.

"I'm thinking that we should aim for Kinsley. It's en route to Linmus, after all," Rem concluded.

"Hey now, we're not nearly ready enough for that!" Sien exclaimed, tossing one of the peaches at him. Rem flinched, catching the delicate fruit before it hit his fore-head. His palms were stinging at the contact, but he supposed it wouldn't have compared to a possible headache.

"We're supposed to be getting leads to find this Orb of Concede-"

"*Concord*," Leilana corrected, eyes still on the Lasette.

"Yeah, that. Getting leads on the Orb of Concord to try and stop the crisis going down in Linmus, not charge right in and expect them not to kill us."

"I wasn't suggesting that we go right to Linmus. People in Kinsley talk and I mean *talk*. If we start in a place that's full of gossip, we're bound to hear some secrets. And what if one of those secrets happens to revolve around the Orb of Concord?"

"But if the Order of Helix is on our tail, we won't be able to shake them," Luna stated, juice from the mouth-watering peach still dribbling down her chin. Sien cleared her throat and Luna set to wiping her face. "Uh, sorry. At least not that easily. Guys like that can be a pain to deal with in the long run-"

"Like skirt-chasers!" Sien finished, resting her hands on her hips, proudly nodding. Lancett and Rem didn't look amused. It didn't seem to make sense in the context.

"I think that we should stop before nightfall," Solus proclaimed, thumbing over the map. "There should be a town up ahead called Erican."

"Oh! I have a friend that lives there!" Sien beamed. "I'm sure that he'd take us in for the night!"

"All of us?" Lancett mumbled. "Don't you think we should branch off a little, keep them off our trail?" Sien's smile was fading at his words, but the more that he spoke, the further that the hurt seemed to spread. She approached him, wrapping an arm around his neck, dragging him down to her level, causing him to stumble.

"No one is going anywhere. They can only follow us for so long with their numbers dropping." She slapped him on the back and he grunted at the dull ache. "Now then! We'll stay with my friend! I'll run on ahead when we get there! I still remember his house!"

"Cici, now that I think about it, didn't you mention that Gale is-?"

"No, no, Gale is never angry about my mishaps! Don't joke around, Lulu!" She placed her hands on the younger girl's shoulders and pushed her ahead. "Off you go now!" Lancett rolled his eyes, continuing down the abundant trail.

"That took a turn," Rem stated.

"I think it's refreshing," Solus replied. "She's quite optimistic despite her mischievous nature. I think it would be good for us all to have her around for a little while."

"As long as it's not a hassle."

Erican's close-knit landscape offered less natural elements such as paddies or trees when compared to Linarus. Bushels of roses were nestled under the afternoon sun, planted in front of each individual townhouse, the scent of fresh baked bread and sweets consuming the tiny town.

Upon arrival, the six split off to keep from drawing suspicion. Luna and Sien started for the man known as Gale's home while Rem and Solus took to guarding the town against any potential intruders from the Order of Helix. That left Leilana and Lancett alone. Lancett didn't mind; he was thrilled to explore the countryside. Even so, this opportunity alone with her allowed him more time to think of Sien's statements. Making plans to start over was easy. Following through was difficult. And now that Leilana was settled with Rem and Solus, there was no starting over with her.

Leilana's face lit up as she started towards one of the bakery booths, sniffing the air. The aroma was fascinating, almost intoxicating to the senses. Bread wasn't uncommon to find, of course, but fresh out of the oven? There was no finer scent that could rivet the stomach.

The shopkeeper chuckled at her growling stomach before handing off the loaf to her. "Would you like to try some?" She nodded frantically.

Leilana tore into the steaming bread. It was as if she had broken through a piece of heaven, the fragrance hinting of milk and butter. She bit into the fluffy grain, licking her lips before scarfing it down. After ordering a second, she handed off some Nyte coins that Solus had provided her with, hoping that it was enough before trekking over to Lancett, holding up the bread to him. Lancett couldn't help smiling at her as he broke the bread in half, returning the rest to her.

They didn't need to utter a word to one another for their friendship to kindle. Knowing that she was still fighting for her goals was admirable—she was determined to keep Adrylis safe in her own way, all while continuing her journey to becoming a Warlord.

"Leilana, there's something that I want to talk to you about. Do you want to take a walk with me? I'll buy you more bread for the trip." Leilana was continuing to beam at the mention of bread, and she nodded. Lancett returned to the booth.

She was calm. Hopefully, it stayed that way.

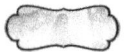

Lancett's fingers were clamming up. Leilana was at his side looking around the town. Why was it that every time these topics arose, his nerves were overpowering? The atmosphere did nothing to ease him. Lining each pathway, beaten down the stone walkway, were lifeless and empty buildings. Bakeries and convenience shops were packed with customers, but the homes were desolate. He was adjusting to smaller regions, but he couldn't deny the lack of calamity compared to the academy or any of the larger cities he had bypassed on his way to Linarus.

Leilana bit into a piece of bread. "What'd you want to talk about?"

"I was thinking about our last conversation, and I realized it was selfish to ask you to stay in Linarus after the war. You want to help others, and I'm not prepared to spend my life fighting." He laid a hand over the crystal charm on Kindall's pendant. "Traveling has changed me. I can't surrender my time to others to become a Warlord. I'm going to return to Linarus and rebuild it, no matter what it takes. Amiria was right. I don't need to be a Warlord to help others."

Leilana was appalled by his sudden, admirable decision. In such a short time, he had taken to the cozy little village that accepted him and taught him the value of hard work without having to resort to magic. "I'm proud of you, Lancett."

"I'd also like to ask a favor. I want you to find Amiria for us." She knew that 'us' was referring to Kindall as well.

"Tell her that we'll always support her and that we forgive her."

This was his gift, the essence granted to him from Kindall's totem—the connection to him that existed long after his passing. His soul remained. Lancett removed the pendant from around his neck and set it in Leilana's hands. A pale light engulfed the totem, spreading through their joined hands. Lancett and Leilana were facing each other the entire time, both a bit confused by the turn of events.

"What is this...?" she asked.

"I've seen this process before. I had something similar happen right before Kindall died. He gave me his pendant, and it sealed our connection. This is our totem."

"Do you know what it represents?"

Lancett smiled. "I've always known since we began. Our time together was short, but we will always be friends."

Friendship. *That* was his strongest attribute, something he shared with Kindall through thick and thin. Their friendship could transcend time, and now they were bound together.

"You sound like you're saying goodbye," she began.

He rested his forehead against hers, chuckling. "Never will we say goodbye. Only 'see you later.' I wish the best for you. This world will be yours." He released his hands, stepping back from her. "Tell everyone that I said thank you and good luck."

Before Leilana could respond, he was gone. There he went, off to continue his journey of self-discovery. Like Amiria, he had chosen to renounce his pilgrimage. She wondered how many more like them were in Adrylis, lost and confused, maybe even a part of the Order of Helix seeking a proper path to success.

Rejected Warlords. There were many like Amiria,

wandering with no motivation, trapped behind closed walls. She hoped that Lancett was better and remained true to himself.

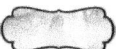

It was just after sunset when Sien dragged her companions back to the home of her friend Gale, who resided in a rather luxurious building just outside of the marketplace.

"Come on, Gale, you've got to forgive and forget some of those old pranks!" Sien whined, her gaze locked on the silver-haired man across the table. He was at least a few years older than the unexpected guests sprung on him by this spontaneously obnoxious girl, but by her standards, age didn't determine more than bitterness levels.

"It's not the pranks that I must forgive." Gale's voice was dripping with anguish, his face hidden away behind his long bangs. His eyebrows were furrowing, pushing past the sight.

The door opened not long thereafter, Rem rushing inside ahead of Solus. "All right, we finished our sweep of the area, and not a trace of the Order of Helix. Didn't even feel any magical presences outside of anyone here."

"No sign of Lancett anywhere either," Solus stated. "True to his word, he likely did end up leaving." Leilana was continuing to gaze at the pendant.

"That boy seemed adamant on returning to Linarus," Gale stated. Sien raised an eyebrow. "Yes, I met him. He wanted advice from an experienced Maester, and he happened to pick me from a crowd."

"If that's the case, Lancett must be able to read auras,"

Rem began. "I hear it's a common trait among other mages. Hopefully, he makes the journey okay, what with the enemies we've made."

"Never underestimate the power of a proper Maester, Highness," Gale proclaimed. "Now, I gave you the opportunity to lay your heads in my home for the time being. I suggest that you each get some rest. You have to become information brokers by morning, after all."

"Right, the Orb of Concord," Sien mumbled, rising from her seat. "I guess I'll turn in early then."

"No dinner?" Solus asked. "I was going to prepare something."

"Nah, not hungry."

After stepping into the hall, Sien was met with Luna's disapproving stare. The younger girl had a blanket wrapped around her shoulders. "Thought you'd gone to sleep already."

"I was, but there was a lot of discussions. I think we need to talk too." Luna took Sien's hand, leading her into the room that she was given for the night.

"I think that I'm going to turn in early too, actually," Leilana proclaimed. Solus frowned. "I'll have your cooking when I'm awake, I promise."

"You better," Rem responded. "The guy's got skills."

"Try to sleep well," Solus told her, smirking. "We've got a lot to do from here on, so any means of rest could become scarce. No more all-nighters with your studies."

Leilana giggled, waving her hand in dismissal. "Fine, fine, I can put it off for a night."

Leilana stepped into the hall to find Luna and Sien's conversation cutting through the thin wood of their bedroom door. Luna was raising her voice, and it seemed like Sien wasn't looking to back down. She stepped closer, resting her hand on the doorknob, pressing her ear against the wood.

"You should go with them to Linmus."

Sien laughed nervously. "Whoa, wait, what? I wanted to go back to Linarus though…"

"There's no life there, and you know it," Luna stated. "You used to love seeing other countries when daddy was still around. You think working at the tavern will bring him back, but it's making you delusional. It's been two years, Cici. You have to start accepting it."

"This isn't about dad," Sien tried to reason. "Linarus is our home, Luna, who are we to turn our backs on it? It's nuts to just leave!"

"I wouldn't turn my back on my home," Luna countered. "But there are more pressing manners. You're trying to deceive yourself by saying that Linarus is your haven, but ever since Rem showed up, you've been happier."

"That's not true!"

"Cici, listen to yourself!" Luna hissed. "You never get defensive! Don't let life pass you by before you get the chance to really experience it. You need to take more chances."

"What am I even chancing? Jumping into a war that doesn't bear my name, possibly getting killed? I can't fight as well as the others. I don't have enough time to learn."

Leilana heard footsteps rush against the floor followed by a thud. Someone must have fallen. "'You can't, you can't,' is that all that you're going to use to defend yourself? You can learn as you go. You always have. You were born to heal. Now is your opportunity to become a better person yourself. But you can't do that sitting back in Linarus hoping for change. What do you wish for, Cici? What do you want to become?"

Leilana stepped away from the door when it suddenly thrust open, Sien staring down at her for a few passing seconds before storming off. Luna was sitting on her bed, looking at Leilana from the doorway, her expression void.

"It's not nice to eavesdrop."

"I apologize. The noise was concerning."

Luna sighed, folding her hands. "Sien has always been a scatterbrain. She's tried to act like an adult since our mother died from an illness four years ago, but our father always told her to remain as she was. Then one day, our father went to deliver medicine in another village, and his body was found in a river. Losing him destroyed Sien, and she filled that void by trying to make others happy but couldn't keep herself happy. She doesn't like to admit that she can be a bit hypocritical."

"I don't think that sounds hypocritical," Leilana admitted. "I think she fears loneliness, so she laughs." Wait. Sien 'laughs.' She stole a glance at Lancett's pendant. "Pardon me, I have another manner that I need to attend to."

"But you-" But by then, Leilana was long gone. Luna sighed. "It's just as rude to leave a conversation unfinished, you know..."

Leilana went through several rooms before stumbling upon Sien's open door. She reached up a hand to knock out of courtesy before Sien stated, "You don't have to do that when it's open. I'm not hiding." She lowered her hand again. "And you don't have to just stand there."

Leilana stepped into the room, closing the door behind her. "I'm sorry for eavesdropping."

Sien crossed her right leg over her left, resting her hands on the bed to support her weight. "She sent you here to talk? She does that a lot."

"No, she didn't. I just wanted to ask you something."

"Shoot." Leilana was considering her words carefully; there was so much that she didn't know about Sien, and any wrong move could break any potential chance of earning a totem. She was a mage herself, and she may have carried the virtue of laughter if what Luna spoke was true.

"What *do* you dream of becoming?"

Sien was silent and furrowing her scarlet eyebrows, unsure of how to address the question. Leilana swallowed—maybe Sien really hadn't given it much thought despite having a sister like Luna addressing it more than once?

"All that I've wanted was to make people happy," she began, sitting upright again. "Life wasn't that charming. I worked in my father's tavern, and every day I would see new faces. They'd drink themselves into a frenzy. Some would laugh. Some would get angry. And others would just wallow in their pain and use booze to cool their jets. And then we started letting people that got too drunk stay in the tavern overnight, and I'd start pulling pranks to ease the tension. If I can make someone laugh, forget their troubles and cares, then that's enough for me."

"You want to be a jester?" Leilana concluded.

"*That's* what you took from all that?!"

"Am I not allowed to make jokes?"

Sien was taken aback, giggling before bursting into full-on laughter. "You're ridiculous for thinking you can't! Were you living under a rock all these years?"

Leilana shifted uncomfortably. "N-No, in an academy..."

"Well, don't worry about that. You've got people like me and Solus around now, and we'll break you out of that condensed little shell faster than I can plan a hootenanny."

"What is a 'hootenanny?'"

Sien laughed, slapping Leilana on the back. "Party, girl, a party!" Leilana found it relieving that she was back to more of a jokester persona rather than a hopeless sap sitting back waiting for change. Not that she was much better. "Know what, when you do become a Warlord, I'm throwing you the biggest one I can. It'd rival any party that Kinsley could come up with!"

"Not sure I'd want to go to any of their parties. They're too formal."

"Ugh, that's true, formal is so boring. But whatever! We'll go nuts, Lei... Leilana can be kind of rough on the tongue. Mind if I call you Leidibug?"

Leilana's mouth fell open at the quick change of pace. "Wha-*Leidibug*, what kind of name is that?! I'm not a bug!"

"But it's adorable, and you are a little bug-a-boo!" She twisted Leilana's nose for good measure, causing the younger girl to whine.

"Sien, Leilana! It is time for bed!" Gale shouted, startling the two. Leilana and Sien broke into laughter, the pace once more shifting. Leilana noticed a dim amber glow around Sien's body as she giggled her time away, covering her mouth to try and conceal her teeth. The happiness overflowing through her was genuine.

Breech the path to uncovering the truth behind laughter.

Where the dreams truly lie.

"You're the one that's adorable, Sien," Leilana stated,

taking a seat next to her. "Why hide behind your laughter? You can feel sadness when you're having fun, and the world would never know."

"There's always something in this world to cry about. And for every tear that drops, there is always a smile that follows. There is still good in this world, and no matter what, I intend to find what is destined for me. So even when I am sad, I'll keep smiling and helping others to smile too. That's the best thing I can do as some tavern-working apothecary."

"That's admirable," Leilana breathed. "I could never be strong enough to admit something like that."

"Don't worry. You're bound to have a happy life someday too, after all of this. We'll have peace in some way or another. No one is meant to laugh alone."

They talked throughout the night about the journey thus far, about the boys on their team, and even about the impending war. Leilana herself was just glad to communicate with a girl close to her age. She didn't spend much time with Amiria, the only other girl in that range, and Luna was in a league of her own. Talking with another girl was relieving after spending time with primarily young men.

But it was a world that she was happy to step into if it meant having a new friend and bringing herself one step closer to unlocking the secret to laughter. Sien was the perfect candidate.

"Leilana." Being woken up earlier than humanly necessary was one thing. "Are you having trouble keeping up?" Being woken up to travel was another.

Leilana yawned, stretching her arms towards the dusty light of the sun. "No, Gale, I'm fine..."

Either way, the day was set to drag on as it always had. She rubbed some lingering grime from her tired eyes. Rula bounded onto Leilana's shoulder, weighing her down for a few seconds before she adjusted to the new presence. Rula's tail flicked to-and-fro, clearly excited to be taking a new adventure.

"You still haven't told me where we were going."

Gale came to a halt at her words, the hefty stick in his hands used to support his already flawless balance plunging into the dirt. Leilana nearly walked into him, stopping just short of his feet. "I don't suppose you've heard of Lunare?"

"Lunare? No. Why? Is that where we're going?"

"*I've heard about that place!*" Rula told Leilana. "*Master said that it was once prosperous! Many people used to visit!*" Leilana almost laughed, patting the young Diri-onus's head, causing him to nearly roll off from the sheer bliss. Instead, he rested over her shoulder before jumping off to stand at her side.

"Lunare is the realm that Ennis Erovina ruled after ascending to his Warlord status." Leilana's body stiffened. "There is something that I would like you to see. There are aspects of the title that we Maesters and Arcana undermine when we first begin our pilgrimage. I gave this speech to Lancett as well. You two were among three in a total of your class to reach this point."

"Three?" she repeated.

"Yes. There was another girl that came here seeking knowledge on the first Warlords and their past, and once she had ascertained enough information, she left without a word."

"What did she look like?"

"She had the most peculiar shade of lavender hair."

"Amiria," Leilana breathed. "So, she's still on her own separate pilgrimage." Shame on that; Rem would have wanted to see her before she took off again.

"Her powers have wavered—it is the result of her decline from the ties to magic. Those that were bound to the pilgrimage's order have ample strength blessed upon them." Leilana thought of Lancett, newly torn from the pilgrimage. Soon, he would be losing his powers too. There was no way to forewarn him of the ordeal.

Gale looked to the skies. "The empty moon will be arriving again, and by then, every mage will be reaching their core strength. If Prince Remiel is to gain the power he craves, there's no finer night."

The Night of Emptiness. A single night that fell once a month where the skies were clear, absent of even stars and any form of light. A night where the spirits of the Warlords carried their soul-driven pupils to the next day with prosperity. A night where bloodshed was inevitable.

"How many days are left?"

"Ten. Linmus fell exactly twenty days ago. And there will be more nations to fall behind it if this ruin is not brought to order." The days were passing by so swiftly that Leilana couldn't even keep up. Thirteen full days slipped by since her pilgrimage began. At least twelve now since Solus and Rem came into her life. And there were to be more that would pass.

"What happens if we aren't fast enough?"

"There is no telling. That is why I am guiding you to your brother." Leilana couldn't believe what she was hearing. "It was his last wish to see you. I'm sure that he could provide you with the answers you need to bring this war to an end."

She was going to be able to visit Ennis again. Even if he wasn't there to greet her back, he would be there. Something of him remained.

Scorched trees, the wood splintered and charcoaled; buildings crumbling to the ground, the desecrated stones lining the mounds of soil kicked up. There was no chattering, not even the wind had reached the open area yet. Deathly silence, a near contrast to Paluna and Linarus.

"This place is creepy," Rula whimpered, burying his face behind his tail. Leilana was gazing forward rather than directly at the town, fixated on the utter silence.

"You don't look surprised."

It was nothing new to stumble upon a desolate place. There were plenty like Lunare, but there was one trait that glared at her. Every time that she saw lands that succumbed to war and ruin, she thought of the people left to watch it tumble. Some of those victims were long gone. For those that didn't, their suffering had barely begun. Those that survived the ordeal were left with nowhere to turn, or at the very least had to settle away from the homes they had known.

And she was safeguarded inside of Magiten Academy the entire time. She couldn't step out into the open world to save them, despite that being the role she was assigned to play as an Arcana. It seemed that each second spent in bliss would be ripped away like a bandage meant to hold every-thing together. The Arcana and Maesters were those bandages, condemned to having to reshape the world anew rather than fixing what cannot be changed. That was how the Order of Helix came about.

"Where can I find Ennis's grave?"

Gale started walking again, expecting Leilana to follow. She upheld the instruction, folding her hands in front of her to clench them together. They silently stepped through the ashes, Leilana's mind relaying the town's potential fate.

"Was my brother murdered?" she piped up suddenly. Rula was surprised by her grim undertone.

Gale straightened himself, tossing away the scuffed stick. "Is that what you believe?"

"You were there, weren't you? That's how you know where to find his grave. You knew him." Gale sighed, tugging on loose strands of the hair over his eyes. "Tell me the truth, Gale."

"I bore witness. But I wasn't quick enough to save your brother. His attacker ignited the town to draw him out. You know well of their predictable methods, but back then, they were barely known."

"The Order of Helix..."

"He came to this town, seeking my totem, and instead, he left with my friendship. He was young, naïve, but he left his mark. There was nothing I could provide him with in return. Sien leading you here was a glorious coincidence. It is as though time is repeating itself. I see so much of him in you."

"*Leilana,*" Rula began, overhearing static rising from the radio at her side. Leilana had barely noticed the sound, grabbing the device to turn it off before a voice emerged.

"Those-kzzt-to-" Leilana fiddled with the dials,

regaining a clear signal. Rula sat down, cocking his head to the side, unsure of the radio mechanics, but keeping patience. "-Arcana and Maesters of Magiten Academy have been dispatched to handle the situation. The remaining students that were left wandering Adrylis have yet to be tracked down to return to safety. There were at least four confirmed dead in the region-"

Leilana's lips parted. "Four of *us*, dead? There were fourteen to start with, and now..." She sat down next to Rula, holding the radio with both hands. "Where are they getting this information? What's going on?"

"We have no time to worry, Leilana," Gale stated. "We must move forward."

"But the students-"

"There will be more lives taken if you do not seek the necessary guidance," he pressed on. Rula rested a paw on Leilana's lap, whimpering slightly before gesturing to Gale. Leilana sighed and turned off the radio, returning to Gale's side.

Lunare's charred buildings disappeared when they stepped out of range. Hidden beneath branchless, ashen trees sat a cream-colored urn adorned with red drapes sitting atop a pillar, shielded behind an impenetrable barrier. At the foot of the pillar sat a folded black trench-coat, attire that the young Warlord was known for—walking amongst shadows, cleansing them with knowledge and fore-warning. Gale reached up a hand to rest upon the barrier, lowering it before gesturing to Leilana. Rula remained in his spot as Gale took her hand, pulling her closer to the urn.

Leilana laid her hands on the urn, her eyes watering. The texture was smooth and frigid, reminiscent of stone. It was beautiful to observe, but surreal to touch, to feel a spirit rather than the warmth of a body. So, this was Ennis now.

No short dark hair, kissed by the wind. No stormy eyes that rivaled the tenacious skies. No magic left to carry Lunare to prosperity or rebirth. Only ashes and dust kept intact by a friend that wanted him to have a proper memorial site.

Her lips were quivering. There were no words that she could bring to the surface. This was her first time seeing the urn—seeing *him* since his departure—and she couldn't give him a proper greeting. How could she have failed at even this?

"Say anything that comes to mind," Gale suggested. "He was waiting to see you, and he'll hear."

But that was what made it hard, trying to figure out where to begin. Sure, he could listen in a metaphorical sense, but he wouldn't be able to talk back.

"I..." She was sniffling, wiping her eyes. "Hi, Ennis. I finally became a proper Arcana, and I got some of your letters. I keep them in my bag. Your words are envying. I wish that I was more eloquent."

Gale stepped back, resting against one of the trees. Leilana lowered her hands from the urn, sitting on the ground, pressing them instead to the pillar, trying to keep her nerves steady. She didn't want to leave prints on the brass metal. She wanted to plead for ideas on what to say, but it was bound to be a lost cause. Now she was wishing that she had woken up the others to come along. Maybe it would've felt more natural that way.

"*Don't stop,*" a medium-pitched voice emerged from the shadows. Her head shot up, and before her eyes was a silhouette of a young man dressed in the very trench-coat that he sat on top of. Every button was in place, his jet-black hair resting just above his shoulders, grey eyes glowing as if the world was brightening anew. "*Tell me more. Where'd you find my letters? Did you like reading what I wrote?*"

Leilana straightened her back, his presence beholding. It wasn't real. It couldn't have been. He was dead, long dead. At the same time, he was basking himself in the Minsuran tongue. Nobody else alive knew it. Clearing her throat, she decided to mince the Sentience away in favor of what she was born with. "They sort of found me." She didn't know why she was trying to humor herself with the idea that he was speaking to her, but it was more comforting this way. At least it would be able to ease her mind and she wouldn't be left talking to thin air.

"That's different," he replied. How was he so carefree when she was on the verge of crumbling? *"But I guess there's always surprises. How's school? Did you manage to make any new friends?"*

"A few," she settled with. Amiria wasn't much of a friend, and Kindall was dead. That ruled out some friend-ship titles. "But I made other friends in Adrylis. One of them is a prince-"

"Remiel Vesarus?" Leilana faltered at his hasty response. Ennis raised an eyebrow, shifting his weight onto his left leg as he leaned forward, meeting her eye to eye. *"Princess Leilana Erovina, falling head over hills for the kingdom's prince."*

She held up both hands in retaliation. "I-I'm not in love with him, we're just traveling together, as friends. Honest."

Ennis chuckled. *"I was hoping not. I was going to haunt him."*

Leilana rested her hands on her lap again. "Ennis. I need your help."

Ennis smirked, leaning against the pillar, hands behind his head. *"So, you keep quiet for years, and the moment that you see me, you're on your knees begging for my assistance.*

How disappointing." Leilana shot him a glare. *"I'm just kidding. How may I help?"*

"We're in the middle of a war-"

He waved his hand in dismissal, his eyes closed. *"Know that part already, Lei, skip to the juicy bits."* Leilana scoffed. She may have missed him, but she didn't miss his obnoxious behavior.

"I need information on the Orb of Concord."

He opened one eye to face her. *"Ah, so that's it. You've been catching up on your reading. How much free time do you have?"*

"Not enough."

Now it was his turn to scoff. *"Way to kill the mood."* Crossing his legs and straightening his back, he pressed his hands to his knees. The carefree stature quickly evolved into one of prestige, signifying the growth of a Maester into a high-class Warlord. The sight was beholding; he seemed more mature, just a little. *"All right, listen closely."* He held up his right index finger, winking at her. *"I'll give you just one hint about how to find the Orb of Concord."*

Right as the words shaped on his lips, Gale's scream cut through the air. Chills were racing down Leilana's spine, which soon manifested into an icy wind slamming against her back, dispelling Ennis's silhouette. The winds howled, not a sound breaking the silence. No. This wind was different. It wasn't natural. She didn't have time to turn around and face the source head-on before Rula came running into her arms, nearly knocking her into the pillar.

"It's all right," she whispered to Rula, resting a hand on his head.

"I thought that you would come here, Leilana." She kept her eyes trained on Rula, trying to ease him out of his stupor despite the familiar voice chomping down on her tranquility. The young Dirionus was trembling, whimpering into her shirt. "My thanks to you, Gale, for guiding me to the place where Ennis Erovina rests. Not many are able to uncover his remains."

"L-Lunious." Gale was grunting in pain, clutching his bleeding stomach, dagger plunged into the open wound. He was careful in ripping it out, tossing it aside. "You died several years ago, in this fire!"

Lunious laughed. "Died? I set the flames." Leilana's heart skipped a few beats, and the blood fueling her heart instead rushed through her arms, repeatedly prickling the nerve endings. "You chose a formidable hiding place. No one would suspect secrets in a ghost town."

"It's really not that uncommon," Gale scoffed. "You just don't understand predictability." Lunious's response was a swift blow to the face, knocking Gale onto his back. Leilana wrapped her arms around Rula, her lips moving closer to his ear.

"Take Gale and run."

Rula glanced up at her, pressing his paws to her chest. *"I promised Rem that I'd protect you, always! I can't let you stay back here all by yourself!"*

"This is a time where you need to protect someone else. Take him and get back to Sien. Don't let anyone follow you or see you, and if they do... kill them. Do you understand?" Rula was appalled. She was normally calm, but this time she meant business, and that could have come at a dastardly price. "Go now." Rula ascended into his Dirionus form, licking her forehead once before taking off towards Lunious.

Lunious drew a dagger, preparing to cut down the mighty beast. Leilana held up a hand, the pages of the Lasette spiraling in the splintered wind. An inferno split from the open page, Lunious slicing through the blaze with his blade. Leilana was on her feet now, the Lasette in her right hand while her left hand was still extended forward. The weight of the grimoire was hefty, and she had to force her left hand to stop shaking to remain calm.

"Your fight is with me, Lunious." Rula slammed his paw on the ground, Gale's body drifting upwards just enough for the young Dirionus to lower him onto his back as he took off for the town.

"I never imagined that I could be claiming your grimoire so soon," Lunious proclaimed, the miniscule blade's hilt twirling between his chubby fingers.

Leilana was observing his movements closely, keeping on her toes about any tricks that he could pull. Solus had already dueled him once and settled things, but he wasn't here to act as a guide. Her heart was pounding, and her mind was racing, but no fear overtook her. It wasn't the first time that she had been alone in a fight against a formidable foe, and this was her chance to show Ennis what she had learned in the time they were separated.

"I take it that you have yet to accept your fate, that your heart is bound to a book."

Leilana thrust her hand forward, a stream of lightning radiating from the Lasette, rushing toward Lunious in a straight vice. The attack caught Lunious off guard, the sparks brushing off his skin as he swiftly stepped out of the way. Simultaneously, the two were signing symbols into the air marking the opposition of Minsuran and Sentience. Leilana's hands moved at a hastier pace and she grasped the open book with both hands, a blazing tornado emerging from the Lasette, lifting Lunious into the air, the flames igniting his cloak.

Lunious's already budding smirk was growing wide, his sharp, glowing teeth visible under the light of the fire.

Extending both of his hands outward, he brought them together into a firm clap, the winds at his beck and call dispersing the flames. Leilana exhaled, beginning to sign another spell in the air when Lunious grabbed her arm with the scarf around his neck as he was landing. With one tug, he dragged her towards him, knocking the Lasette from her hands. Leilana scrambled for it after untangling herself, Lunious grabbing her wrist with his scarf.

With a yell, she continued forward, the restraint around her difficult to break from. Her feet were moving one step at a time, and Lunious's blank expression hindered her progress further. She stretched out her right hand to the Lasette lying on the ground. The book moved a few centimeters forward in response, but just as it was about to lift from its solitary spot, Lunious tugged her back, throwing her into the pillar where Ennis's ashes sat.

She struck the pillar headfirst, the throb in her skull barely registering in her mind compared to the urn shaking above her head. The world was spinning. Her eyes were going dark. But it didn't matter anymore knowing that something more important was in her path.

The urn dropped onto its side and the brass splintered into several large shards. The shatter against the pillar reminded her of a glass bottle in the tavern clanking against the table—sudden, swift, and barely made an impact. But now there was nothing tangible in either of these places. The ashes poured out of the broken urn, some dropping onto her as well as the cloak resting at her feet. The rest spirited away with the morning wind, viewed nevermore.

Leilana couldn't breathe, reaching up to touch her face, ashes seeping up her nose, down her body. She processed that she still was alive, but her body was crumbling, like dry clay exposed to the sun. There was nothing left of Ennis

Erovina. He was already dust, trapped behind a cylinder coating and a barrier. Now he was condemned to remain as an ashen wind, meant to fade from existence.

Lunious picked up the Lasette, the weight of the book in his hand barely an issue compared to the young girl. The book slammed close as soon as he made contact, and he snarled, trying to force it open, to no avail. Nonetheless, he *had* worked for this moment, so it would not be in vain.

Tears were rolling down Leilana's face, her mouth agape as her eyes blankly met the liberating blue sky. She once saw promise beyond the clouds; now all that she saw was a haunting prison on the ground, whereas those that had gone away could take them for all eternity. Ennis was there. Kindall was there too. She wondered if Amiria missed their friend as much as she was beginning to, or if she was too focused on the world to think of him.

"For an Arcana, you lack the proper training of a mage." Lunious reached down to close the girl's mouth shut. Leilana wasn't even looking at him; his presence was nothing but another walking entity that was living to die. The world was the furthest thing away from her mind right now, and it was evident that she was gone based on the metaphorical void teeming around her fragile body. "Maybe someday you'll be able to see the truth."

He left her leaning against the pillar, and she didn't move. She couldn't.

There was no need to put any effort into continuing with no energy, no magic, and no reason to consider becoming a Warlord. What good was it? What was the point in even trying anymore? Why live this life without the idea that Ennis was watching?

Who was she meant to be now?

Rain on a fresh morning was supposed to be comforting, but to Solus, it was foreboding to sit at the window and watch the world from the inside. People were scrambling for shelter due to the sudden downpour, but not one of them was the girl on his mind.

Leilana had been gone for three days, and no one heard a thing about her. Gale was the only one that possessed the knowledge due to Rula having moved so fast that he couldn't keep track of his surroundings, but consciousness slipped through the elder Maester as he recovered from a near-fatal injury. Sien and Rem both worked tirelessly to assist the man until the darkest hour had ended. All that was left was to wait for answers. Solus grew tired of having to sit back, but he didn't allow the selfish words to roll off his tongue.

Rem stepped into his room after knocking on the open door. "We're heading north to Lunare."

"Why there?" Solus asked, thunder rolling through the air as he finished his sentence.

"Rula said that's where Gale took Leilana. Gale woke up, and he's coherent now. He said that he'll take us as soon as he gets some more rest. I'm hoping that the storm has passed by then, but we're going." Rem was leaning against the wall when Solus finally did decide to face him. "You should be prepared for anything that we could come across. A battle, a situation... maybe even a casualty."

"I'm always prepared," Solus replied. "Have a little faith yourself, Highness."

"I do have hope. She's becoming strong. But we can't write off just her skill to ensure survival."

"We'll find her. That's the end of the matter." Solus stood up, closing the curtains. "I'm going to find breakfast. Would you like something?"

"I'm fine." Rem sighed. "Probably going to take a nap before the murky trek gets underway."

"Wise," Solus stated. "It is better not to push yourself."

"You better sleep too," Rem pointed out. "The last thing we need is inadequacy." Funny to process Rem trying to swap their roles, Solus thought. It was almost mature of him. He decided to humor the young Prince by sticking out his tongue in response, mimicking him in his younger days. "That's just sadistic-looking. Never do it again." Solus forced a chuckle; some laughter was better than none.

TWENTY

True to Rem's words, the rain didn't let up, and the streets and grassy plains were murky, swamping them in the mud. Gale was heading the front of the three-man squad while Rem was bringing up the rear, both hands up to maintain a barrier that would shield them from the storm. Solus couldn't help admiring the amount of work that the young prince was putting in since his days of solitude, all for someone else. His nobility was reaching its peak.

They bypassed Lunare without a glance, too focused on the mission at hand, but Rem found himself questioning what could have driven someone so far that they needed to stomp on anyone in their path to achieving their goal. The circumstances of misfortune wrought upon Lunare were reminiscent of Linmus, and per Gale, Lunious was the culprit. Lunious himself didn't appear powerful on the surface. What if he was holding back the entire time?

"Just past here," Gale told the two as they stepped through the forest of ashen trees. Rem dropped his barrier, his arms and body exhausted. The storm was continuing to brew strong atop the trees, coating them in the cold water, but it wasn't nearly as drenching. The rainwater did little to cleanse the trees, the soot practically ingrained into the soil and branches that kept the trees standing for longer than necessary.

Solus trained his hearing on the water splashing in the

puddles beneath his feet, Gale's words distant. Any steps unlike his own that didn't fall in line with his comrades were bound to be a sign that there was someone waiting in the shadows. Lunious wasn't a fierce opponent, but one encounter was enough to warrant a warning signal in his mind—he was going to come back stronger someday.

Gale suddenly stopped walking, taking a step back when the sight in front of him became clear. "No..." The single word had barely brushed past his lips before Rem shoved him aside. Solus wasn't far behind, and both boys simultaneously grew quiet.

Seated under a pillar was a girl clutching a folded black coat for dear life, her dark hair sinking over her lifeless eyes. Further above were an array of shards, the color washed away from the metal. Her shoes were tossed aside, the elastics torn apart under the pressures of the rainstorm. Her body was soaked to the bone, shivers rushing down her spine. The noticeable quivers were enough to send Solus running to her side, resting his hands on her shoulders.

"Leilana, I'm here." She didn't look up, and the lack of acknowledgment made his heart sink. "It's me, Solus," he continued, his tone almost pleading for her to hear him. "Rem and Gale are here too, we... we were worried about you. We hadn't heard from you in days, and Gale said that you were attacked. We wanted to come sooner, but we didn't know where to find you, and I just-"

Stop, he told himself. Just stop.

He lowered his head, biting his bottom lip. No amount of words seemed to rouse her. He had failed her, and now there was no bringing her back.

Cold fingertips grazing his wrist told him otherwise. She was reaching out to him, grasping his sleeve despite the rest of her body language remaining unchanged. The folded cloak went slack, resting at her side rather than in her arms. A single touch reminded him that she wasn't going anywhere. A faint aura was beginning to surround his body, noticeable to himself, but barely striking his thoughts.

Rem stepped over to Solus and Leilana. "She's gonna be okay, right?"

"Yeah," Solus said softly, eyes still on Leilana. She lacked energy, the weight of the rainwater on her shoulders as hefty as the thoughts on her mind. They weren't aware of every detail, but something was plaguing her deeply, and there was nothing more to ease her. "We'll do everything to help."

"The two of you, go back the way that you came," Gale stated. "There's something that I must finish here. Have Sien draw a hot bath and dry off as soon as you arrive. We have a long night ahead."

"Thank you." Solus gathered Leilana into his arms, and the extra weight of her wet clothes became noticeable. Her arms were limp against him, her dripping hair sliding over his left wrist while his right arm was carefully supporting her weight. For the first time, he caught her staring at him. Her eyes were half-lidded, her rosy cheeks a cozy shade. Rem carried the folded cloak over his right shoulder.

"Where do you think that her book went?" Rem asked after the two exited the forest, cracking his knuckles before conjuring up yet another barrier to keep the two from getting too wet.

"I don't think now is the right time to talk about it," Solus said softly. "It's been an emotional time for Leilana. We'd best keep quiet on the subject." Rem nodded in agreement.

Solus looked at the forest. It wasn't difficult to piece

together the sequence of events since Lunious's departure, just as it was easy to comprehend his companion's over-abundant emotions. Her support system was wavering between the war, an array of crises, and even the lack of proper communication, which is likely why she didn't consider coming back to them, letting everyone know that she was all right. Maybe she wasn't as open with them as Solus wanted to believe.

"It isn't your fault, you know," Rem said, continuing to push forward with his barrier intact. "The way she feels, it has nothing to do with any of us. Not really. Sure, we could have done more to help, but all that we can do now for her is make sure that she can push past this."

"Rem…" Solus sighed, a grin overlapping his pursed lips. "You've grown up."

Rem raised an eyebrow, his focus nearly shattering. "Wouldn't say that. I just know how it feels to lose someone important. But enough talk, gotta keep my attention on one thing at a time."

"Right, my apologies."

Gale's house was silent when the two boys stepped inside, drenched from the downpour, mud-stained spots left behind at the entrance. Rem's barrier dropped only minutes before, and they ended up having to break into a sprint. Solus draped his jacket over Leilana's body in advance, shielding most of her body from the cold rain, tossing the wet fabric aside after reaching dry territory.

"Rem!" Sien called, racing to the entrance where the

boys stood, reclaiming their breaths and setting to removing wet articles of clothing bit by bit.

"Leilana!" Rula exclaimed, leaping from Sien's shoulder to approach Solus. The young Dirionus whimpered at the younger girl's condition, burying his face beneath his paws.

Sien was baffled by the change of pace, resting her hands on her hips. "I just—what happened out there? Why's Leidibug out of commission?" Rem was confused by the nickname, but instead of addressing it, he brushed it off.

"Sien," Rem began, slowly holding up a finger before leaning his head against the nearby wall, tossing his soaked shirt aside. The words came out almost scraggly, "Gale says to run a hot bath. We have a hell of a night ahead."

Sien turned her back to the two, covering her burning cheeks. "Hey, prince or not, don't just go around stripping whenever you feel like it!" She looked down at Rula, whispering, "H-Hey, don't mope, make yourself useful, go tell Luna to run a bath!" Rula silently left, tail between his legs.

"Can we avoid mishaps when we're not on the verge of catching our death?" Solus suggested.

"I'll watch Leilana for a while and see if I can get her to snap out of it," Rem stated. Solus carefully placed the girl on his back, and Rem tucked his arms under her knees, allowing the girl to rest her head on his shoulder, nuzzling her face against his. Rem's face reddened at the close contact before he groaned, disappearing into one of the guest rooms.

Solus's hand lingered over the buttons of his dress shirt. His ribbon was soaked to the brim, tied around his wrist, and his hair was becoming stringy and unmanageable. Of all the things to potentially relieve him of thought, mundane chores were all that he could use to avoid Rem's blunt words. It hadn't been his fault, seeing Leilana fragmented over spilled ashes, but in the weeks they had come to know one another, he'd hoped for something better.

At the same time, she saw the chemistry she shared with Rem. She desired to become closer to him but didn't pull away from Solus's intimacy either. Maybe he was moving too fast after all. Or maybe he was just fooling himself, thinking that a girl could fall in love with a servant, especially when their relationship altogether was taboo. She possessed magic as an Arcana, and he was a mere human. His feelings were conflicting with his ambitions, and with her pilgrimage.

"Hey." Sien was staring at him, laced with concern, but far was he from startled. "Leidibug's not the only person that looks under the weather. Are you going to be all right?"

Solus opened his mouth to address her, but the words wouldn't form. *Was* he going to be okay sitting back and letting things continue to unfold as they have?

"I'm fine," he settled with. "I just need some time to think." He started gathering the wet clothes left on the floor. "I'm going to dry these off if that's all right."

Sien wanted to interject and convince him otherwise, but by then, he departed. With a sigh, she leaned against the door, drumming her fingers on the wood. There were so many jokes stirring in her mind that she wanted to bring up, returning the cool smile to his face in the process, but now it seemed that laughter was going to be lost to the wind. The tiny home latched onto utter silence in a matter of minutes, and no amount of fun could restore it.

What a shame. This adventure seemed promising, and it was gliding on rocky territory.

Time drifted by before she decided to check up on Rem

and Leilana, finding that Rem was already gone. Luna must have finished running his bath sooner than anticipated. Leilana was seated upright on the bed with a blanket halfway covering her, clothed in a long-sleeved white night-gown, her short hair tied into two braids that reached her shoulders, still dripping wet. She was blankly staring at the teal sheets; she didn't even appear to be 'all there' due to the void expression on her face. Her thoughts must have been trapping her in a state of disarray.

"Leidibug." Sien stepped to the bed and reached out a hand to her. One wave and no reaction received. Sien knelt at her bedside, placing her hands on hers. There were no words that could convey Sien's thoughts but leaving Leilana alone in this state was far more dangerous.

The pain was inevitable, but suffering needed to be shared amongst many.

The night was uncomfortably still, not a creak out of place in the household. Gale returned hours after Solus and Rem, pieces of the broken urn wrapped securely in his rain-coat. Late into the evening, Sien would catch him trying to glue them together only to become emotional and stop to regain himself. The sound of his stifled sobs plagued her mind, and she ended up having to room with Luna just to manage decent sleep.

Rem took the first shift watching over Leilana to ensure that she didn't suffer a mental breakdown, but it was clear from her behavior that she wasn't acknowledging his pres-ence. Upon waking, she curled herself under the blankets further, hysterically sobbing. She refused to eat or drink, and any words spoken to her were lost. Rem couldn't stand seeing how miserable she was. He was so close, yet so far from her. In the air of the night, she lost control.

Tonight, she was more human than ever before.

Ennis Erovina was no more and hadn't been for years. Leilana knew. Word of the Warlords reached even the deafest ears. But what did remain of him was what tore her to pieces. The ashes that carried on his virtuous spirit, blown away. The urn that housed them, shattered.

The anguish went on for fifteen minutes before Rem gave up on letting her work things out herself. He crawled into bed next to her, pulling up the blankets slightly. She was curled up in a fetal position, her eyes bloodshot, her scarlet nose running. Rem cringed at how much of a mess she was but facing the vitality of misunderstanding was conceivable. If she wasn't going to notice him, at this point he was going to have to make her see that someone was there.

He inhaled deeply, wrapping his arms around her, pulling her close while stroking her hair, her head resting against his chest. She was hyperventilating when she reached his warmth, but as the seconds elapsed into minutes, she seemed to calm down. Her breathing slowed to a more manageable pace, and she was clinging to his sleeve as if wanting to keep some grip on this newfound reality.

"You know," he began, resting his forehead against hers. "When I was younger, my mother used to hold me when I couldn't sleep, just like this." He closed his eyes, recalling the woman's smile, her laugh. She was still here, mostly in spirit. "She was always gone, making sure that others were out of harm's way. My father was always in meetings or traveling, leading the other nations to prosperity while thinking of everyone, but I sometimes wondered if he just forgot about me."

Leilana knew the feeling. She was used to solitude herself, with Ennis running off acting as a sitting Warlord, and little friends inside of the Academy to guide her. She could still recall the days where she was awoken early, venture to the Commons Area of her school for breakfast and order the same meal. Life was mundane, empty after his departure. It was only after a few months that she first caught Lancett staring at her from across the tables, buried in a sea of people, Kindall laughing at his side. She could still remember his coy smile and his simple 'hello' before their parting.

Never did she imagine that she would walk such a fragile line with people that crossed her path only a select few times. Each meeting brought purpose, just as each parting would muster up memories and thoughts that would forevermore be left unsaid.

"I think about my parents all the time these days. I can still see the flames in Linmus while I watched from the outside. I don't know what became of their bodies. It's scary to think about things that you don't know, people that you miss..." Leilana coughed, and Rem rubbed her back, continuing, "I was used to being around others, but I never showed appreciation to them for taking care of me. I wish that I could thank them, but the only way that I can is by making things right. And I can only do that by becoming a better person, a better leader. This kingdom is mine, and it always will be."

Leilana's eyes were drooping, though her mind was still trained on his words. This was her chance at gaining more information on him, and she couldn't afford to lose it just because the room was a little toastier than she liked.

He pulled back his head, continuing to hold her close. "There's still a lot that I don't understand about myself, but now that I've breached my own security, I want to make sure that good people live on to see another day. Adrylis doesn't need to be rushed into a new era. There's so much life still breathing in this place that doesn't deserve to just... stop." He sighed. "I want to guide our people to a better future, and I guess what I'm getting at here is that, well, I need people like you and Solus, and even Sien and Lancett to help me because it's not possible to complete the task alone."

When silence was his response, Rem found her resting peacefully. Her mouth was closed, lax snores passing through her nose. Her grip on his shirt loosened. Slumber had come to her suddenly, but at least now she was at peace. It was appreciative, but now that he thought over it, he was pouring his heart out to her, and now she wasn't going to remember anything about it.

He sighed, resting his chin on her head. Her hair was woven, the texture like silk now that it was washed free of the rainwater scent. "There's no way that I'm ever getting that emotional again."

She was the first person that he had opened up about himself to since meeting Solus, always careful about who understood what, and where to place them, but that was a pessimistic nature of nobility—it was easy to be taken advantage of if you allowed just anyone inside of your head. Still, he supposed it was better this way, having someone else relatable to his side. They had both lost people that were important to them, walking this road as one. This was the girl that his best friend had come to cherish, just as he did.

Maybe it was fine to let her into his head just enough

for them to resonate if she was willing to do the same for him.

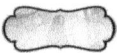

Leilana spent much of the following day sitting with a blank stare, shifting her focus between the window or the teal sheets covering her. No one really bothered her due to her acquired introverted nature, though she was never alone in her room for more than a few minutes throughout the day. It was like trying to talk to a blank wall, but they continued to work as they should to lighten the girl's mood.

Sien used her shift telling Leilana stories of customers in the tavern that she would prank or form some sort of bond with, and even explained how she and Gale grew up in Linarus before he awoke to his powers and became a self-trained Maester. Luna would provide her with light meals of broth, bread, and water to ease her stomach, though it seemed to go unnoticed as well, which led to the younger girl making pointless spats only to be led out of the room by Gale.

Rem and Solus divided their time caring for their ailing companion and watching out for the Order of Helix, but time and patience seemed to be catching up with them. They spent most of their nights fighting sleep already, but now the concerns were welling up. Rem settled late in the night on practicing his use of barriers; someday, he'd master the ability to conjure one large enough to shield a village from harm for years at a time. It would take practice and effort, but the challenge would be momentous.

The second day was a vast improvement after a wink of

sleep on all ends. The most significant difference lied with Leilana glancing at the open door every time someone walked past or came to check on her. Gale brought it up after gathering them, stating that it was a sign that she was coming to terms with what occurred. She needed more time, but everything would work out.

"Mental health is as viable to guard as physical health," he explained to the three teenagers seated at the kitchen table. "Be sure to keep your eyes open for any significant changes, for all of your sakes. It is easy to lose yourself in times of crisis, but never forget about those that stand at your side."

Sien observed Rem's ever-changing facial expressions throughout the explanation, knowing that his mental health was probably the most fragile among them due to the adversaries he'd come to face. Solus folded his hands, taking the statement to heart.

Rem placed both hands on the table and straightened his back before facing Gale head-on, smirking. "I will make sure that every one of us makes it out of this fine, and I stake my name on that. We will better this world with our own hands."

Gale chuckled, leaning back in his seat, crossing his arms. "I more than believe it. But now I am curious to see it in action, Prince Remiel."

Rem pressed a thumb to his own chest, smirk still present. "You will. I promise." When he heard frequent shifting about the back rooms, Rem's current stance faltered, and Solus rose from his chair to see to the matter.

Rem sighed. "I'm gonna go scout out the outskirts of town and make sure that Lunious or any of those other clowns didn't follow us back. Don't come looking for me." Sien was about to interject, but the door had already slammed. At least this time it wasn't in her face. Rem could be such an introvert.

Solus stepped into Leilana's room after knocking, used to the gesture despite Rem and Sien's obvious distaste for it. She was sitting on the bed looking over a scattered collection of papers from her bag, poking through entries and scriptures alike.

"What are you doing?" He was reaching to touch one of the sheets when Leilana slapped his hand away, though not with much force. He drew back his hand in surprise. "S-Sorry...?" She claimed the paper for herself, her eyes scanning over the context at a rapid pace before she set it aside. "Are you doing some more research for your pilgrimage?"

She paused mid-grab, holding up one of the half-written slips of paper—the same one that he had worked at translating from Minsuran to Sentience not long after they met. The Orb of Concord, a crystal crafted by the Warlords of old, said to bring about the end of the war; the start of a new era.

"Ennis." Her voice was strained by her lack of speaking. She rested a hand on her throat, clearing it enough to strengthen her levity before continuing, "He said that he knew where the Orb of Concord is, that he had a hint."

"We can worry about it some other time. Right now, you need to focus on resting."

"I can't," she countered. Solus folded his arms. "Lunious has my grimoire. I need to get it back if we want to have a chance at finding the Orb of Concord. We can't afford to waste time-"

"You're not going," he said sharply.

"Yes, I am," she retorted, slamming her hand on the bed. Solus had to grab her arms as she was trying to stand up and plant her back in her seat, effectively pinning her in place. She tried to wiggle free, but he leaned in closer, continuing to press his hands against hers. She glared at him, and his grip didn't falter. They were both mentally fighting to break the silence, but neither of them was sure how to tear through it without the sense of dominance and assertion coming into play.

"You're not going," he repeated, his statement firmer.

She broke one arm free. "It's my responsibility to help you, and I need the Lasette to do that."

Her shoulders were trembling, her eyes glistening. Solus knew right away that she was near tears; her body language always seemed to waver when her emotions were spiraling out of control. He couldn't forget the lifeless expression on her face when they found her in the rain—it haunted his dreams and reminded him that there was hope in this world that was beginning to fade, even in the most optimistic people. This world was crumbling at their feet, and there was little that he could do to quell it with his own hands. They weren't ready, not yet.

"Without it, without my magic, I'm... I'm useless! I need it!" As much as he wanted to keep the tears from falling from her eyes, this was one time where the ailing girl wasn't going to be contained. "Solus, please! I have to find my grimoire!"

"You're depending too much on your magic and over-working yourself," Solus interjected. "It's taking a toll on your health."

"No, it's not an issue!" she exclaimed. "I'm fine! I've improved so much! I just need a chance!"

"And that chance will come," he insisted, his tone becoming a bit forceful. "But you have to think about yourself too. You need to do more than depend on your magic to bail you out of every situation. Rem and I, we've been trained in swordplay since we were young, and Lancett was self-taught. Ennis even carried a weapon to mask his status."

"I don't need a weapon," she retorted. "I can't wield a sword, and there are few weapons that are within my reach. I'm not versed in anything more than magic."

"Then you need to learn something more to survive. This world does not run on the elements anymore—it runs on valor and vigor, and it takes many forms. Swords and sorcery, words and wisdom, chaos and cataclysm."

"What's your point?" she spat. Solus sighed heavily, moving his hands from her arms, instead of reaching up to slam his hands against her cheeks with mild force as if fighting to get the point across. She flinched at the contact.

"Don't pretend to be naïve now that I'm talking you down. Someone must, otherwise you're going to shoulder more than necessary. What makes you think that going off on your own to find your grimoire is smart when being by yourself is what got it taken away in the first place? Not only is it reckless, it is going to catch up to you no matter what you do."

His serious expression came coated with a genuine smile at the end, one that nearly made Leilana weak. His ivory skin was glistening under the morning light, but the dark circles under his eyes were reflecting signs of stress. It was becoming clear that he hadn't been sleeping well, and she was a direct cause of his frustrations.

He and Rem were working hard to set things right,

taking on so many burdens for the sake of their kingdom, and all that she seemed to do was get herself caught up in something outside of the main problem. It never failed. Every time that they were thrown into the crossfire, she got hurt or was left open to *be* hurt, which meant that she needed to be defended. Maybe that was the price of being trapped in the class of magic, whereas they were trained fighters.

"You've done so much to help us," he told her, his tone velvety. "And we still need you at our side, not only as an ally to our cause but as a friend. Don't put too much stress on yourself. We can handle a little more danger." He cupped her chin, gently stroking the flesh with his thumb. Chills were racing down the back of her spine. She bit some skin off the corner of her mouth and hid it away, trying to ignore the comfort of his breaths on her lips.

"Solus..."

"What are you doing, hiding from me...?" His tone was challenging, which only made her want to heed the call.

"Don't," she whispered, though she was still trying to lose herself in the sensation that stemmed from his lips. She could already taste the salt on his tongue, feel the heat of his breath on her neck. There was so much lust swirling through her mind that she wasn't sure how to keep track of it all. He was so much older than her, likely more experienced, and yet she couldn't control these emotions. Maybe it was because he was the first to show them to her.

"Why?" he whispered back, reaching out his free hand and grabbing her nightgown by the collar to pull her closer to him. The movement was slow-paced as if they were being tugged out of the reality that awaited them, but enough to snag her out of any lingering thoughts.

It was taboo. Being with him was forbidden because of

his humanity. They both had their own missions that happened to have a common end goal. He had to save his country from ruin, and she had to amass the proper strength to defend other countries. Yet, somehow it didn't matter. These similar end goals brought them together, and it allowed her the opportunity to meet Rem, to befriend Sien, to become more aware of what was going on in Adrylis. Why was she so drawn to him, of all people?

He ran his finger along her wet lips, his eyes softening. "Do you not want to...?"

"I can't get you in trouble, Solus." She nearly whimpered the words, which only amused him. "I don't want anything to happen to you..."

He chuckled. "Such a childish response."

"W-What do you mean?" she whined.

"Leilana, there's something you should know about me." He pressed his nose to hers, a boyish smirk curving onto his lips. "Servants are not allowed to take what they want from under their master's nose. It is a sign of disrespect, and the last thing that I would do is disrespect Remiel. But when there is something that they desire away from wandering eyes, they bound for it at all costs."

Was he implying that he wanted *her*?

She longed for his touch, lost in his sincerity. It was wrong, but it felt so right to be wrapped around his finger and let him sweet-talk her into just one kiss, one tender moment that could have led them so much further in a matter of minutes. Gone was her sense of morality, and far was the truth of any relationship that could have formed between them. Of all people in this world, she had chosen the servant to a wayward Prince with an insatiable hunger for bloodlust. There was blood on both of their hands, and now that trail had caught up with her as well.

"Why are you doing this?" she whimpered, lacing her fingers between the loose strands of his hair. He couldn't stop grinning, the light coat of pink on her cheeks fetching his attention.

"Because it's worth it to get you do my bidding," he joked, kissing her nose. She reached up both hands to cover her mouth and nose, eyes spreading like dinner plates. "Now, back to bed with you."

"What do you mean 'do your bidding?'" she called as he was exiting the room.

He gave her a wave from the bedroom door, his hand on the knob. "Good night, Leilana." He gently closed the door behind him, leaving the girl to her thoughts.

Their union was built on confusion. Their relationship, if taken too far, would affect her chances of becoming a Warlord. What if somewhere in the future after the war, if they got that far, they decided to get married, even have a child? Would that child become a Bloodlinch like Rem, condemned to a separate entity? Would their child be as broken and trapped as Rem was when his powers became too overbearing? What would happen to them then? What about her goals, and his dedication to Rem? They would conflict too often.

Leilana was reaching for a leather-bound notebook and a pen tucked away under the blankets, her mind over-flowing with ideas. There were so many mysteries behind her friends that she didn't know how to keep up. And then there was the lack of knowledge that she possessed her time before the Academy. They had been returning in bits and pieces, and she took to writing them down in a notebook she bought from Kalonia every chance that she got. The notes were her own, and she didn't allow anyone in her circle to see that she was crafting them.

They were clouded and scarce, but the Minsura clan remained deep within.

Spontaneously, she slapped the pages of information on the Orb of Concord out of her sight, knocking them all onto the floor. She listened to the sheets of paper rustle, the process sluggish and tedious. She rose from the bed, stumbling as she made for the door, smacking down the latch made to lock the door in place. Being cooped up in bed wasn't going to get her any further to her totems, to getting the Lasette back, or to being less of a burden on Rem and Solus.

Daylight was still burning strong. Leilana clutched the notebook to her chest, Ennis's oversized trench-coat draped over her shoulders while dragging across the dirt, making way for Lunare after stepping out of Erican's city limits. Her eyes were scanning the trees to keep out for Rem. As much as she didn't mind the idea of the company, the first thing that he was going to do was drag her back to Gale's house, and two days was more than enough to be trapped on bed rest from a mere ailment.

The trail-way leading to Lunare was still fresh in her mind, every rock and tree pulling her closer towards the scorched town. The sun was already beginning to set when she reached the town, and she knew that by now, the others would have realized that she was gone. Time was of the essence, and the light of the sun wouldn't be there to guide her anymore. She couldn't afford to walk back in the dark with the shadows looming about.

By the time that she'd reached the gravesite, she could barely make out the pillar, and her chest was tight. She sat on the ground in front of the monument, folding Ennis's trench-coat to the best of her ability, though it came out with a few wrinkles due to excess attempts. After a while, she gave up, setting it on top of the pillar, opening her note-book to the first fully written page before placing her hands on the monument.

"Ennis, I need you to help me reclaim something. It's been too long since I've thought of Minsura." Her fists were clutched so tightly together that her knuckles were begin-ning to turn white. "I'm straying from my set path. I want to help Rem and Solus. I want to complete this mission, I really do, but becoming a Warlord was the only way I knew to make things right. I need answers."

She shakily inhaled, her palms slipping from the pillar to lay on her lap. Somehow, this all felt pointless. She wasn't even speaking with him, rather his cloak. His ashes had dissipated. There was nothing left. So why did she drag herself here?

Plaguing her mind were hazy landscapes, absent silhou-ettes seated amongst one another, humming and singing in the Minsuran tongue. Bell chimes and windpipes were fresh in her mind, clattering under the wind's guided calamity. More words lost to time, moving past this unkempt reality beyond the trees. It seemed so far away, the days in Minsura. Separate from those basking in a budding culture yet providing the proper blessings to the people of Adrylis, helping to shape their world anew.

Ennis still remembered, didn't he? What their isolated home was like. He had always thought that shaping the culture that he was born into was important. She thought the same—adopted cultures should know of their origins, even as traditions are lost to new developments. That was why he continued to speak in his own tongue, and why she would read passages to herself in the dead language, passing it on to the friends she had made, those that learned variations transcribed from Minsuran. Sentience was a modernized form, the writing too broad and extended from simplistic words or symbols. Minor phrases were altered, and though they seemed easier to manage, there was no denying the changes that were made in the time that her clan had been eradicated.

There was so much that the world didn't know about Minsura, and times were still rapidly evolving. They would continue after the war's end, if they even managed to succeed in quelling it, and if she could continue her pilgrimage. If given the chance, who would want to know a departed language? Who would want to know anything more than necessary about her origins?

"I need to remember what happened." She sighed, lowering her body into an arch, pressing her forehead to her folded hands. There had to be something, anything he could provide her with. It couldn't be a lost cause with him gone. "Am I being lied to about my powers?"

Lunious's words were fresh; she was nothing but a pawn, bound to the past, trapped in the pages of a grimoire that was slowly stealing her life. Without it, she was powerless, and with every spell that she cast, she placed herself in fatal danger whether she won her battles or not.

"I don't know where I'm meant to go from here. What if I never get my grimoire back? Without that book, I'm useless." She lowered her head to press her forehead against the pillar where her brother's ashes were once beheld. "I can't do anything else to help. I didn't even get to finish my notes on the Orb of Concord, and we have no leads..." She rested her hand on the pendant around her neck, sighing. "I don't have a lot of information on my totems. Amiria's... probably a lot further along than I am right now. I just don't know what to do. Please, Ennis. Show me your true power. The power of a Maester unique only to you. Show me the Orb of Concord's whereabouts."

The indistinct echo of wind chimes guided her down the beaten path. She emerged inside of Magiten Academy, her eyes stinging from the burning lights. The classroom still looked the same; fifteen desks were lined up across from one another. The scent of freshly sharpened pencils was almost comforting, acquired over the years. She gathered some old textbooks, the scent of aged paper filling her nose. Jumbled red writing on the dark chalkboard drew her attention, but it didn't bring her closer to understanding what the concept of the day was.

Nothing had changed from the days she spent in the academy, but somehow it felt so... stiff. Normally, this would have catapulted her into a frenzy, and she would have thought more on trying to understand the lesson, but it seemed like empty thoughts were plaguing her mind. Maybe it was her experiences in the outside world that spoiled her or even trained her to look forward to better things than having a nose in a book. Maybe she was the one that had changed.

She traversed down the empty halls, her boots leaving audible remnants of each step she took. She wasn't particularly sure what time she resided in, or if the world was nothing more than a manifestation—a place where Ennis sought to provide his blessing.

"You sure did take your time."

She shrieked, the books in her arms hitting the ground all at once. She didn't bother to grab them, instead whirling around to face the man leaning against the wall staring at her with an almost conniving grin. He found this funny, somehow. He always found scaring people hilarious.

"Don't do that, Ennis!"

Ennis shrugged lightly. "Sorry, but it was necessary. You wanted me to be your guide, didn't you? I meant what I said about the hint."

"But how are you here?"

He tugged on the collar of the trench-coat covering him, the very one that sat at his grave. "There were ashes in my coat that didn't wash away in the rain." He stepped closer to her, poking her nose. "And there are some ashes within you as well." Leilana covered her nose for a moment. That's right, she had inhaled some of his ashes by mistake after they spilled. "A part of me is inside of you now, Leilana. How does that make you feel?"

She crossed her arms. "Like you're being snarky. I never liked that about you."

"I don't think you used that word right. I'm not criticizing you. At least, I wasn't before now." She blinked a few times. "But no time for a definition check. It's about time that I show you the way." He wrapped his arm around her shoulders, pointing towards the extended hallway. "Onward, dear sister!"

Silence could be maddening. As the two traversed the halls, the students seemed to file out of the school altogether. Even when classes had ended for the day, there was always something recreational after the fact, so the deafening quiet was off-putting. Ennis's steel-toed boots were clattering against the polished floors, his footsteps wide and purposeful as he walked ahead of her. Leilana couldn't help but marvel at his presence.

He was always so much taller; she distinctly remembered chasing after him in these empty halls. Back then, she would cling to his arm, lost in the crowds of older students. He never seemed to mind, even when faced by the other students, but deep down, he must have been troubled by her. He couldn't spend as much time as he liked with them, and he couldn't afford to slack on his goals. Maybe he was ready to leave her behind, so he kept working towards it.

But now that she was older, she could see the sincerity in his eyes when she scolded him. They never got to spend a moment like this together, and now they weren't even capable of much past this. It was all business and little love. Ennis still showed his affections, clear by his gestures, how he touched her, teased her, but he knew it too. This time together was fleeting.

"What would you have done differently if you knew what was going to happen in your future?"

Ennis didn't stop walking, but he was silently pondering how to address her question. The hallway seemed to spread further than either of them could have imagined, but perhaps it was for the best. "You mean dying, or becoming a Warlord and then dying?"

"Either one would work."

"There's nothing that I would change," he admitted. "Everyone has to go sometime, some way, and we have to make the most of that time limit. I left letters because I knew that I would probably never see you again, and they are reaching you in ways that I have never expected. Someone else has been collecting them, and they led you to me. It was my final wish to see how you've grown." He caressed her cheek, her eyes glimmering under the dim hallway lights. He remained still before pulling his hand away from her, sighing. "Even now, it doesn't feel tangible. But that's because I'm nothing but an entity with only a soul, not a body. You can feel my touch, hear my voice, but that doesn't make it real. It's easy to be deceived by the damned because we think about what to do with the living."

"But you aren't malevolent, Ennis. I called out to you, I sought your guidance to try and end the calamity in Adrylis. You know how it will end. You brought me here to help me, didn't you?"

"I did, but I'm hoping that it stays that way. By giving you the Lasette, I dragged you into my battle. You could have remained happy at the academy, and never learned magic, never struggled-"

"But that doesn't matter anymore, does it?" she cut in. Ennis closed his eyes, inhaling deeply. Clearly, he wasn't a fan of his words being pounced on before he finished speaking. "Right now, I'm traveling through Adrylis, and I'm on a pilgrimage to become a Warlord. If not for you giving me the Lasette, I never would have come this far."

"You would have been safer there!" he interjected.

Leilana's knuckles were white from how much she was clenching her fists together. Why didn't he understand? What was so hard about wanting to be in the open? "If I had stayed behind at the academy, I wouldn't have a bond with Lancett, Kindall, and Amiria. I would never have met Rem, Sien, and Solus. With them pushing me forward, I feel stronger than I did alone." Her eyes softened. "You wanted me to have friends, Ennis. You should understand how it feels to suffer in solitude. That's why you wanted me to meet others, isn't it? You never wanted me to end up like you."

Ennis kept his eyes shut, taking her words with a grain of salt and a heavy heart. "As your older brother, it was always my job to keep you safe. Neither of us knew what we were getting into. But you couldn't hang around me forever. That was no way for you to live, clinging to me. I'm proud that you stepped out of that box, but there's still more that you need to learn before you can become a proper Warlord. Something that not even I was able to achieve."

Ennis brushed his fingers along the brick wall in his reach, a crimson aura engulfing his palm as he swept his hand across. A substance comparable to a mound of dust flew off, rushing to his nose, though he didn't acknowledge the atmospheric energy. Signing the ever-familiar Minsuran symbols among the air, Leilana watched his face warp from one of leisure to unwavering concentration.

"Resujin mai wein (Reveal my way)."

Along the walls were miniscule Minsuran symbols coated in red markings, reminiscent of stained blood. Leilana stepped closer to the wall, placing her hand over it, squinting her eyes.

Power sleeps within the hidden passage, where ash rains from the heavens and bathes the fallen in cloaked shadow. It is there that reason and resonance reside as one.

"That doesn't make sense. Ash raining from the heavens... a place where ash falls? I can't think of any places like that, none that I've heard of. Not to mention that statement on reason and resonance." Leilana sighed. "And how did you know where to find this?"

"I rubbed against the wall by mistake and then started

to transcribe it for myself. Nobody in the school knew Minsuran or bothered to understand it. I didn't speak of it with anyone else. I had no idea what it meant until I stumbled upon the passage of the Orb of Concord in the Lasette. Then the dots connected in my head. And now that my time has come to an end, you're the only one left to carry this hint right to the source." He firmly placed his hands on her shoulders. "Someone wanted us to find it, Leilana, I truly do believe that. This is our last chance to carry on the Minsura clan and reform it."

"You want me to carry on our clan name," she repeated.

"Your life is your own. It has always been. Whatever path that you choose to walk will be the right one, make no mistake about that." He pressed his forehead to hers, and she shut her eyes, the coolness of his head unexpected, yet relieving. "I want you to carry on as the person that you are as you continue your pilgrimage. This world is full of mysteries, and you should explore them. Your friends as well. They seem to be reasonable people, and that is more than I can ask of those that care for you."

His voice was riddled with sorrow, then drew silence. Leilana allowed herself to look up at him and found that tears were rolling down his face, his lips pursed together as he chewed some skin from his bottom lip, trying to stop the incessant sobs from rising.

Leilana reached up to wipe his eyes with her thumbs. "Why are you crying? That's not like you."

He chuckled to mask his pain, though his voice was still choking up, "It's really stupid." Leilana did nothing but stare at him, unaccepting of his response. "It's just that they get to see you grow up, become someone important... that was supposed to be my job. I sit back and think to myself 'man, I really screwed up.' I didn't get to hold you enough when you cried or tease you when you made silly mistakes, or teach you how to cook, how to sew or take care of you while you were sick..." Now the tears wouldn't stop, and his grip on her shoulders was decreasing steadily. "I wasn't there for you at all when you needed me."

Wrapping her arms around him and knocking him so far off balance that he stumbled into the wall, she found herself crumbling at his words. Never did she imagine that he harbored such guilt about taking up such a powerful mantle. She knew that he was lonely, that he longed to see her, but this shed a new light on him.

"I did nothing but think of myself, and now it's too late to go back to change everything!" he shouted, the words echoing through the void hallways. He covered his face with both hands to keep from looking down at her, his skull connecting with the wall. His head was throbbing, but it didn't compare to his heart sinking further into the pits of depression than he could process. "I'm a shit for brains older brother! Why don't you hate me?! Why?!"

She buried her face in his chest, nuzzling against him. "Because you were just doing what you thought was right. How could I ever hate you for something like that? You thought that becoming a Warlord would keep me safe, but all that it did was invigorate something more in me. I will put an end to this war, and I will continue my path to becoming a Warlord, but I will not be bound to one place. I'll find a way to inspire others, somehow." She rested a hand on his head, stroking his hair. "I don't know what I can do to make a difference yet, but everyone will help me. They'll guide me to the ends of the world. I believe in them. And I believe in you."

"You'll make your way," he settled with, taking her hand in his own. "And you'll reach your goals. You'll pass with flying colors. You've got to." His breathing was becoming shallow, and his body like ice. "...Time is running out, Leilana. You need to return to your friends soon."

She unraveled his arms from around him. "Will I see you again?"

He smirked, kneeling before her. "I doubt it." He poked her forehead with his index finger. "But that doesn't mean that I won't always be watching how you do. Besides, you've got some interesting guys in your life now, and I'm sure as hell not about to sit back and let them hurt my little sister."

"Why does that not surprise me?" And yet, she couldn't help smiling. "It was good to see you, Ennis. I'm glad that we got to talk one more time."

"Yeah. it really was nice, Leilana. I hope you keep finding my letters out there. Should be five of them scattered around with the wind. They're bound to bring you into poetic justice."

Leilana kept that in mind. She only had uncovered two of them in total. Maybe she'd find some resolution for him if she could get the rest. He stood up, extending his hand forward, his fingers grazing her forehead.

"Good luck out there."

"I'll always love you, Ennis."

He almost faltered, feeling the tears starting up again, but shut his eyes and continued to focus on other manners at hand. Once his powers had reached an acceleration, an amber glow consumed her body and within seconds, she was gone. Ennis dropped to his knees. Once again trapped in the prison of his soul... but somehow, it seemed a little roomy.

Leilana opened her eyes to find that she had crash-landed on the dirt somewhere in between her rather ethereal traveling state, and she shot up, spitting some of the murky substance out of her mouth, wiping her tongue as clean as possible with her hands, slumping over out of aggravation. What a way to wake up indeed. She laid back on the grass, surveying her surroundings to find that night had once more fallen over Adrylis, only a few stars remaining to set the town aglow, the moon hovering further east. There weren't many nights remaining before the crater of the sky would vanish again, and more ruin would befall the land. She didn't know how many months would go by until she could bring Rem home, and even less how much time would go by until she could finish her pilgrimage.

Still, some miracles were possible. After all, she had already received one in the time she had made tracks down the grassy pavement.

"Leilana!" She glanced back at the familiar call of Rem's voice. How did he find her so quickly? She stole another glance at the pillar as she stood up, grinning as she took off to reunite with her friend. She swept her fingers along the trees and stumbled out of the bushes, coming face to face with the young prince, who blinked a few times at how close they were.

"Hey, there you are," he mused.

"*Leilana!*" Rula beamed, climbing onto her shoulder, nuzzling her cheek with his own. "*I was so worried about you!*"

Leilana was rubbing the Dirionus's fur as he spoke, grinning softly. "I'm fine now, Rula. Sorry for worrying you." Rula's eyes lit up at her words. "You too, Rem."

"You know, you really did worry us," Rem responded. "Gale ended up having to break down the door when it was locked, and when Solus found out you were gone, he nearly broke the dishes. I saved him the heart attack by coming to look for you. That means you're guaranteed a raincheck for an earful. What are you doing out here anyway?"

Leilana rested her right hand on her left arm to quell her budding anxiety. "I was speaking with Ennis. I was feeling really stuck since losing my grimoire, and I wasn't sure whether I would be able to complete my mission without it. There's not much point in helping you if I can't be a proper guide in helping you find the Orb of Concord."

"Wait, so you came here to ask him what you should do next because your book got stolen? That's what you're worried about?" Rem laughed, surprising Leilana.

"What's so funny?"

"I can't believe you're harping on something like that! I took you as someone that didn't worry about such mundane things, but I guess I've been wrong before."

"That's not true, Rem! I'm not, um... 'harping' on it, but I really-"

"Come on, you may have some of the answers, but you're not useless. Like Solus said, you're still growing too. We've all got things to figure out. You don't need to go depending on your book. With or without it, we're on the same side, and we'll fight until the end. That's just how we are."

He held up his hand to her, now curled into a fist. She was staring at his hand, mimicking the gesture with her own fist. Rem outstretched his hand, colliding his fist with hers.

Leilana glanced at her closed fist and smiled. "What was that about?"

"It's a little sign of our friendship." Her face was burning at his words, but she decided that it was smarter to brush it off as the heat of her rising temperature rather than any affectionate thoughts. Rem was changing his ways around her, and it was satisfying. As if reading her mind, Rem removed his jacket, laying it over her shoulders. "It's getting chilly out here, all things considered. I think it's way past time that we get back, or Solus is going to have both of our heads, especially if I end up catching a cold too. Rula, mind playing the carriage?"

"What?!" Rula whined. *"I am a Dirionus, hand-chosen by the Warlords, and you have reduced my likeness and strength to being used as a mere carriage?!"*

"I just want to make sure that Leilana doesn't go passing out on me," Rem said smoothly, folding his hands together in a pleading manner, his lips upturned into a smile. "O' mighty Dirionus, please forgive my callous words, for I meant no harm."

Rula's eyes narrowed and he let out a snarl before transforming into a more formidable size, allowing Leilana to climb on his back. *"Consider yourself lucky that you are Adrylis's Crown Prince, otherwise there is* **no** *way that I was going to let something like that slide!"*

By the time that Rem stepped up to Gale's front door late into the evening with a sleeping Leilana in tow atop Rula's back, Solus, Luna, and Sien were waiting patiently outside for them to return. Upon arrival, Solus and Luna took turns at chastising Rem for not returning sooner and neglecting his duties, while Sien rushed to hug Rem, explaining that she was worried when he didn't show up for dinner. Rem couldn't help but blush.

After settling in, Luna was the first asleep. Rem took to cleaning up after the dinner and dishes that became cold as it sat waiting for the two missing patrons, and Solus took a seat in Leilana's room while she slept to monitor her progress. Things were gradually returning to normal.

Leilana awoke in the middle of the night to Solus fast asleep in his chair, his chin resting under the palm of his hand. She quietly rose from her spot on the bed, wrapping a blanket around his shoulders to keep him warm, and stepped out into the hall. She stepped into Gale's office after hearing him mumbling and found him nourishing himself with a fresh cup of tea. Sitting firmly on his desk in a brass casing was a lavender-shaded crystalline orb, emanating a faint glow. His mind seemed to be rushing through the power of the device, for once his words ceased due to the new presence, it stopped glowing. She didn't connect the dots, but now she was certain that his skill had to rely on clairvoyance—peering into the wandering souls of Adrylis.

"I see that you're awake," he said softly. "How are you feeling?"

"Fine after real rest," she responded. "I wanted to ask you something."

"How may I help you, Princess?" Gale asked, taking a few sips of the drink.

"I want you to teach me how to use a weapon. I can't rely on my magic to help me anymore. I'll try to find a balance. I'll do anything that I can." Her eyes were spiraling with determination. "Now that I have an idea on where I can find the Orb of Concord, I'd like to retrieve my grimoire as soon as possible and end this oncoming war. I can't keep depending on Solus and Rem to protect me. There has to be more that I can do to support them."

"You've come to remember. I see your brother in you every time that we speak." Gale smirked, swirling the liquid in his cup. "There is much that we will need to study. For now, take everything in stride, as you will. Soon, we will begin anew."

ACKNOWLEDGMENTS

"There is magic in us all, and it takes shape in the
form of creation."

The Final Lesson began as a project for *National Novel Writing Month in November of 2016*, and since its birth, so many thoughts of morality, growth, and themes of friendship, love, loss, and good versus evil have emerged from the shadows. There was a lot of time and effort that got put into this winded saga, and I loved every minute of it. Seeing these characters evolve was a pleasure, and to see their future come to life was almost relieving. I guess they made the most of their tortures?

The inspiration for this story came from *Studio Ghibli's "Kiki's Delivery Service,"* a film that truly defined my childhood and framed my desire to fly higher than I ever could. I wanted to become a witch, but since that was unrealistic, why not just make my own? Shame that Leilana couldn't have a wise-cracking cat at her side, but it was great to have such fun characters like Solus, Rem, and Sien there instead.

As always, I would first love to thank *my parents*, bless their souls. *My mom* was always the one to teach me about the wonders of literature through her love of reading, and *my dad* always believed in my success as a creator. I love you both, and I miss you dearly.

My gratitude will always go to *my closest friends* and *fans*, for watching me evolve and carrying me closer to the end. I don't know where I would be without you all! You guys give me a lot of hope to push onward. I've come far since my first novel. I don't know how much I could ever put it into words.

This story's development helped me to grow so much as a person and see some new expressions through my characters, and since it first began, I've seen so many different styles, learned so many different tactics to improve, and I'm eternally grateful for each and every person that has set me forward just a little more, even if it's just some encouraging words or well wishes.

You guys... are truly the best.

Shakyra Dunn can't stray away from the impression that there is always an adventure around every corner! When she isn't playing the role of the Creator, she is marching through the worlds of her favorite video game characters or taking drives around her city to see the sights. Born in Chicago, Illinois, she currently resides in Cedar Rapids, Iowa, striving to experience more than the little town.

Other Books by Shakyra Dunn:
The One Left Behind: Magic (Book One)
First Words: Final Lesson